DEATH OFF CAMERA

Also by B.M. Allsopp

Death of a Hero - How it all began
Death on Paradise Island
Death by Tradition
Death Beyond the Limit
Death Sentence
Death Off Camera

B.M. ALLSOPP

DEATH
OFF CAMERA

FIJI ISLANDS MYSTERIES 5

Coconut Press

First published in Australia in 2023 by Coconut Press

Copyright © B.M. Allsopp 2023

www.bmallsopp.com

Contact the author by email at bernadette@bmallsopp.com

Print book ISBN 978-0-6488911-7-8

E-book ISBN 978-0-6488911-6-1

NATIONAL
LIBRARY
OF AUSTRALIA

A catalogue record for this work is available from the National Library of Australia

Exclusive to Fiji Fan Club members

One of the things I've learned about *Fiji Islands Mysteries* readers is that they are just as fascinated by the lovely islands of Fiji as I am. If you enjoy this book, I invite you to join our Fiji Fan Club. I'll welcome you with something new to read that you won't find in any book store. I'll tell you more after you've finished this mystery.

THE PRINCIPAL ISLANDS OF FIJI

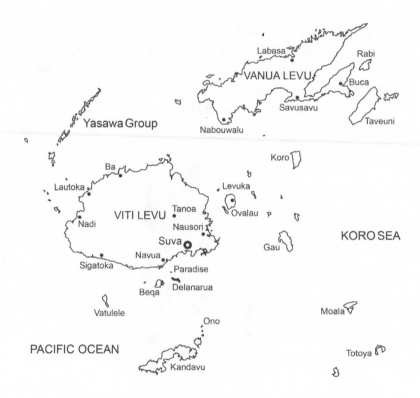

Labasa
Rabi
VANUA LEVU
Buca
Savusavu
Taveuni
Yasawa Group
Nabouwalu

Koro

Ba
Levuka
Lautoka
Tanoa
Ovalau
VITI LEVU
KORO SEA
Nadi
Nausori
Suva
Gau
Navua
Sigatoka
Paradise
Delanarua
Beqa
Vatulele
Moala
Ono
PACIFIC OCEAN
Totoya
Kandavu

AUTHOR'S NOTE: The village of Tanoa is fictitious, as are Paradise and Delanarua islands.
Other places on this map are real, but nearly 300 exquisite small islands
are omitted.

PROLOGUE

Ken Johnson paced down the path to the beach for the third time. Already the eastern horizon was lightening, and those darned seabirds were shrieking at each other. Seemed to him that they started the din a bit earlier every morning, when his exhausted body craved an extra hour's sleep. In his lowest moments, he envied the Champion players who hadn't made the finals. He trudged back through the tangled bushes to the spirit-house. When would his mysterious ally show?

The spirit-house wasn't genuine, of course. The last one vanished well over a century ago, left to decay when Fijians became Christians. But the three-metre high base had survived here on Motu Island. A fake temple of reed and thatch, built by Champion's Props department, now topped the ancient stones. He knew it was fake, but it still unnerved him. Maybe it was the long ridge pole protruding from its soaring roof like artillery. The whole thing reminded him of a prison watchtower. Mouldering ruins should be left to moulder, in Ken Johnson's opinion.

This time, as he got closer and looked up to the platform, he made out a dim figure. At last!

He waved. The figure beckoned. Used to the darkness, Ken ran up the familiar steep steps, striving to identify the person above him. He tripped, flailing through the blackness, heard the crunch of his head on stone. What a dumbass! What did the prize matter? Scrabbling at the air, he tumbled down the coral rocks to lie senseless at the bottom.

MONDAY

1

Detective Inspector Josefa Horseman whistled to Tina, who was fossicking among the debris at low tide. The mongrel looked in his direction, but just for a moment. A scuttling crab making for a heap of seaweed caught her attention. Tina bounded after the crab and pawed through the tangle, barking in excitement.

It was seven-thirty and time to get to work. Horseman whistled again, then called 'Tina!'

He got up from the seawall and walked away. In a flash, Tina was by his side. As he clipped on her lead, she shook herself, spraying him with sand and water infused with the briny scent of the beach, always overlaid with decay.

They passed the bowling club on their way to Victoria Parade. The white-haired keeper rolling the green waved. He was a retired cop who'd want to discuss the weekend rugby games, but Horseman waved back and pointed to his watch.

Horseman's mobile blared the Fiji national anthem as they were heading up the hill behind Albert Park. Tina's ears swivelled.

'*Yadra*, good morning, Matt. Just five minutes away from yours. Tina's ready for a snooze on your verandah.' Horseman's one regret about his new flat was that Tina had to lodge with Matt, his former landlord.

'I'm already at the hospital. I've got a death that will need a police investigation, so I thought I'd give you the heads-up before I notify your boss.'

'Appreciate it. What have you got?'

'Head injury. Patient was admitted unconscious yesterday and died an hour ago without regaining consciousness. I'll do the postmortem later today.'

'That's quick. What's suspicious?'

'Don't know yet. No, it's who the dead man is that's speeding up the process.'

'Come on! Spill the beans.'

'The poor guy is one of the Champion contestants.'

'You mean that American TV show? What do they call it—a reality show?'

Dr Young sighed heavily. 'Yeah, mate. Don't you know they're filming the next series out at the Bay of Islands? They've been there for weeks now.'

'Yep, I heard about it,' Horseman lied.

'Yeah? So you should, it's a money-spinner for Fiji. They've only been making Champion here for seven years.' Dr Young's voice was laced with irony.

'You know me. What little time I have for TV I don't waste on game shows. That time's reserved for watching rugby. Now that's a proper game.'

'Can't disagree there. But you're sounding defensive, mate!'

'You got me. Better tell me everything you know because the boss isn't likely to.'

'Righto. His name's Ken Johnson, aged twenty-two, American from Tennessee. The Champion set nurse who brought him in reported that he was found at the foot of some rock steps at sunup yesterday. It looked like he'd fallen in the dark, knocking himself out. She said he was quite an athlete, seemed perfectly healthy.'

Horseman imagined the scene. He shook his head at the unnecessary loss of a young life.

'Does his family know yet?'

'I'm not sure. Imagine how proud of him they'd be, being selected for the show. And now...'

'*Io*, yes, it's tragic.'

'Well, he'll arrive in my lab soon, so I'd better crack on. I'll call Superintendent Ratini next.'

'Okay. We're almost at your house now. I'll fill Tina's water bowl and leave her on the verandah.'

'Good, Joe. I'll call you when I have something.'

Horseman hoped that the young contestant's postmortem would suggest nothing other than a tragic accident. It would be easier for Ken Johnson's family.

It wasn't just concern for the Johnson family that made his heart sink, though. The success of his personal project demanded his presence in Suva. If he failed to meet commitments because he was working round the clock on a murder case, then the project could well fail, too. But what could he do?

Well, he wouldn't volunteer for anything. He'd recommend that another inspector lead the initial investigation. If the postmortem found cause for suspicion, he'd argue in favour of that same detective continuing as senior investigation officer. But how likely was Superintendent Ratini to follow Horseman's suggestions? Not very.

Still, it was Monday and Junior Shiners rugby training started at half past four. He'd be there whatever happened and could talk about the project with the team doctor.

***

Detective Superintendent Ratini entered the detectives' open-plan office and stopped at Horseman's desk. Even at nine in the morning, the boss looked dishevelled. His cotton trousers were unpressed and his shirt faded. He hadn't shaved and his grizzled black stubble mottled his face like a skin disease. Tidiness was not the most important characteristic for a detective, Horseman acknowledged. But what confidence would the public place in plain-clothes police who looked like they'd spent the night in a gutter? Especially a senior detective?

'*Yadra*, sir,' Horseman said.

Ratini nodded and handed him a paper. 'This could be a tricky one, Horseman. One of the Champion contestants admitted to hospital with a head injury just died. United States citizen. Most likely his family will want to repatriate his body quickly, so the PM's jumped the queue. As the deceased was young and healthy, protocol requires a thorough police investigation of the circumstances. I'm allocating the case to you. Try to avoid publicity, try to be quick, try not to irritate Fiji's distinguished foreign guests at the Champion location.'

'Sir, I don't want to irritate anyone. I'm happy for you to give the case to a more diplomatic detective.'

'Decision's made, Horseman! DI Vula's got the Forestry corruption case. You collared that serial rapist last week and your team's freed up. Your ongoing cases are minor. This takes priority.'

Ratini turned on his worn-down heel and walked away.

2

After crawling through the Suva wharf area clogged with traffic and salt-laden diesel fumes, Horseman accelerated along Marine Drive, heading west. Detective Sergeant Susila Singh sat beside him, peering out the window. Her disciplined ponytail hung over her crisp orange blouse. He was confident *she* would not irritate the foreign film crew.

Singh turned to him. 'I'm glad we've got this case, sir. I've often wondered how the Champion set works.' She sounded eager.

'Do you watch the show?' If someone as clever as Singh was a fan, maybe he should reserve his judgement.

'I wouldn't miss it. Though I sometimes do, of course. Work gets in the way.' She smiled.

'Don't you watch Champion, sir?' Detective Constable Tanielo Musudroka piped up from the back seat of the LandCruiser. He sounded incredulous.

'I caught an episode a few years ago. Couldn't see much reality, myself. But I'm interested to see how it all works if we can.'

'Do you think they'll let us look around, sir?' Musudroka asked.

'I don't know, Tani. Now the director knows about Ken Johnson's death, he might have cancelled today's filming.'

'You really should try to catch it. The challenges are way cool, and the contestants find their own food and build shelters. They're foreigners, so they don't know how. And no phones! They plot to bring their rivals down. Oh, this year there's a Fijian contestant—the singer, Mili. She'd be pretty useful to her team—she'd keep them from starving, at least.'

'I thought she'd been living in the States for years,' Singh said. 'She mightn't have learned village skills.'

Musudroka's enthusiasm was undaunted. 'But isn't it great Mili's in the show? Runner-up on The Voice? Just imagine if she wins! Ta-da! What a boost for Fiji! Why don't you like it, sir?'

Horseman hated to prick the young DC's balloon. 'I'm sceptical, that's all. Let's keep our minds open and sharpen our wits.'

As the road climbed, a wide bay came into view beyond the deep fringe of mangroves. The British had dubbed the protected waters the Bay of Islands. Even on a cloudy day, the scatter of coral islands was a special sight.

After another few minutes, Singh spoke up.

'Next turn on the left, sir. About five hundred metres.'

The side road through military land was sealed only as far as the old gun battery. Erected during World War II to protect Suva from Japanese warships, now the place was an official historic site. Horseman pulled up at a boom gate across a gravelled road. The guard, wearing a yellow Champion tee-shirt, came out of his tiny booth. Horseman held out his police ID.

'*Bula*, hello. Suva detectives here to see Mr Duke.'

The guard ignored the badge and stared at Horseman. He thrust out his hand. '*Bula, bula* sir. Wow, I didn't expect they'd send Josefa Horseman himself! It's an honour to meet you in person. I'm Simi.'

Horseman smiled and shook the guard's hand through the window. 'Were you on duty when Mr Johnson was taken to hospital?'

'*Io*, I was. The poor guy was lying on the back seat. Barbara the nurse was beside him.'

'What time was that?'

'Yesterday morning. Let me get the book for you.'

He dashed back to his booth and returned with a ring binder. He flipped it open, running his finger down the entries.

'Here,' Simi said, handing the file to Horseman. 'Ken and Barbara were driven by Charlie, Mr Duke's driver, in a company vehicle.'

'*Vinaka*, thank you, Simi. Do you log all traffic coming and going?'

'*Io*, sir. I'll radio to let Mr Duke know you've arrived.'

The boom rose and the detectives crossed Champion's threshold. The track wound down the scrub-covered slope to reveal a cluster of corrugated iron roofs.

'Looks like an army barracks, sir,' Musudroka said.

'I think it is,' Horseman replied. 'This whole peninsula's military land.'

'Is Champion leasing it, then?' Singh asked.

'Don't know. Let's focus on what happened to Ken Johnson.'

Another bend of the track and they were almost back at sea level. A wide fringe of coconut palms and hibiscus hid the barracks from the beach. The grey buildings lined up in straight rows, military fashion. Horseman pulled up in a bitumen car park beside a white utility with the Champion logo.

'Better back out and straighten up, sir. Don't you think? Don't want to sink the Police Force's reputation, do we?' Musudroka said.

Horseman chuckled. He enjoyed Musudroka's irreverent banter, but the young DC needed reining in sometimes. 'Enough, Tani. We're at work now. Remember, one of the Champion contestants has just died.'

About a dozen crew stood on the huts' verandahs, talking in twos and threes. At least, he supposed they were crew. Many wore the yellow Champion tee-shirt. Horseman approached the nearest huddle. 'I'm looking for Mr Duke. Can you tell me where he is, please?'

'Sure, he's on the challenge set. But he's shooting. You can't disturb him on set.'

Horseman smiled. 'We can wait till he's ready. Which way's the set?'

The young woman looked doubtful. Horseman showed her his ID. 'I'll take you there. Steve would be furious if you blundered into camera view. I'm Deepika, by the way.' Deepika was young and shared Singh's serious business-like manner.

Horseman smiled. 'We'll stay where you tell us, Deepika, I promise.'

'You'd better.' She flashed a smile.

They followed Deepika through the barracks huts, then an open area filled with shipping containers. The young woman waved her hand. 'Most of these are used for storing equipment and set props. They've converted a few to workshops.'

'They must be like ovens!' Singh said.

'Yes. Steve brought in portable air conditioners, but the guys prefer working where they used to, in the open-sided shelter sheds next to the car park.'

They followed Deepika through the container park, hedged by tall pines and a tangle of undergrowth.

She lowered her voice. 'The arena's on the other side. It's safe to come through this way. Follow me.'

A track led through the dark pines and brought them to what must be the barracks parade ground-cum-rugby field. Horseman stared, dumbfounded. Scores of people surrounded the field, wielding cameras and equipment he could not name. Some were up ladders, while others lay on their bellies. Scores more hovered or ran between positions.

At last Horseman spoke. '*Oi lei*! Wow! I had no idea.'

'How many crew do you have?' Singh asked.

'It varies. We only need some people occasionally. Today we have 210. I'm a staff clerk, so I know. There are ten of us in the personnel office alone.'

Singh's eyes widened.

Deepika clearly enjoyed astonishing the detectives. 'Champion's a medium-sized business for Fiji. Except it's temporary. But that only makes it more complicated on the organisational side and so we need extra staff. They have to set up everything, run it efficiently, then dismantle and close it down three months later. Then the army moves back.'

Musudroka's mouth hung open. 'Wow!' he finally uttered.

Deepika pointed. 'Steve's over there, up on the platform. Not a good time to disturb him,'

'What's happening?' Horseman asked.

'We're up to the finals—only five contestants left in the game. They're filming a challenge. Do you watch the show?'

'No, I'm sorry. Only time for rugby, I'm afraid.' She lifted her eyebrows in recognition. He was grateful she didn't want to talk about his current rugby status.

'Okay, there's a challenge in every episode. It's a physical competition, usually between teams, but only between pairs or individuals in the finals. Sporting skills count but also problem solving. Each challenge is unique, and the winning team gets something valuable, like food or equipment, to make life on the island camp easier.'

'Right, I don't have a clue what the island camp is. I think I should watch a few episodes for homework.'

Deepika grinned. 'Definitely, Inspector. You'll soon get the hang of how it works.'

'Don't worry, sir. Musudroka and I can fill you in.' Singh sounded amused.

Bamboo fenced off half the flat parade ground on three sides. The unfenced side faced the beach. A woman picked up breadfruit piled near the fence, tossed them into a wheelbarrow, then ran to the next pile, while her partner handled the wheelbarrow. Another pair of players sped along the opposite fence. When they'd got all the breadfruit, they raced to a bin and dumped them. Not bad, but a simple kids' game, wasn't it?

Next, each pair used instructions on a board to disassemble the wheelbarrow and transform it into a slingshot. They fired breadfruit at two large wooden masks painted on vertical targets like billboards. Clearly running out of puff, this stage challenged all players, who were wildly inaccurate. But some breadfruit hit the targets with a satisfying splat, leaving white pulp adorning the masks. One team scored five hits against the other's two. A clear winner.

'*Oi lei*, that was entertaining. Should be great on TV,' said Horseman.

'We'll make a fan of you yet, sir,' Musudroka said.

Deepika turned to them with shining eyes.

'There'll be a break now before they shoot the prize-giving. Now could be a good time to introduce yourselves to Mr Duke.'

'When does the day's filming end?'

'Well, I'm not involved, but probably after the prize-giving. It's often too windy in the afternoons for outdoor shooting. They could do indoor scenes, maybe.'

'*Vinaka*, Deepika,' Horseman replied. He'd like to find out more, but it was time to focus on his job.

They dodged among crew huddling over their equipment, pushing buttons and peering into monitors, oblivious to the detectives' presence. Steve Duke got down from his director's platform as they approached. He ignored his bustling assistants.

'Who are you?' Duke asked.

Horseman smiled and held out his hand. 'Good morning, Mr Duke. We're Fiji Police officers.' After a cursory handshake from Duke, he showed his ID. 'We've come to talk to you about what happened to Mr Johnson.'

Steve Duke's face shut down. 'I didn't call for you. The hospital got in touch to tell us Ken passed away. None of us can take it in. Just unbelievable—Ken was a powerful guy.' He paused, staring above their heads. 'May I ask what business this is of the Fiji Police?'

'I'll be straight, Mr Duke. You may not know that police clearance is needed for the disposal of all dead bodies here in Fiji. That applies to foreigners who die here, too. I don't know if Mr Johnson's family will want to repatriate his body to the States, but they'll need Fiji Police clearance to do so.'

Duke sighed. 'Okay, makes sense, I guess. Have you got some declaration form you need me to sign?'

'Well, yes, we'll need you to make a statement. But my duties extend beyond that. I'm leading an investigation into the causes of Mr Johnson's death.'

'I thought that's what the autopsy was for.' Duke was calm but defiant.

Horseman resolved to be genial. The director was in shock. 'That's right. The pathologist's report is vital evidence. We also need to inspect the scene of his accident and talk to you, the contestants and your crew.'

Duke frowned and waved his hand around the set. 'What? Look how many people are here! We can't stop the shoot!'

'I expected you may have stopped it already—as a mark of respect to your contestant's death.'

'We had a minute's silence soon after I got the news.' Duke broke eye contact, then glanced at his watch.

'I understand how difficult this is for you, sir. But we have procedures for going about our job efficiently. We've dealt with numerous potential witnesses many times. If you could take a break for an hour or so this afternoon and gather everyone together, we'll handle the rest. That will speed up the investigation.'

Duke shot him a belligerent look, then put his hands in his pockets and nodded. 'Okay, Guess I've no choice.'

'It's your choice to cooperate, Mr Duke. I thank you for that.'

Duke turned and spoke with a couple of hovering staff.

'Okay, my assistant says he'll set up a meeting for one o'clock in the canteen—that's back in the barracks.'

'Thanks, sir. We need everyone to attend. Could I have a staff list for the past three days?'

'Easy. Dave here can give you the daily call sheets. That's all employees.'

'And visitors? Would the boom gate log account for everyone?'

Duke lifted his eyebrows. 'Everyone who came by road. I can't account for anyone who walks in another way or arrives by boat.'

'I understand,' Horseman said. 'We can get to that later. First, I need to visit the scene of Ken Johnson's accident.'

'Oh, that was on Motu, the island where the contestants stay. You can only get there by boat.'

'Fine. I must see where Ken fell, wherever it is. We have police boats, but booking one will only delay us further. I'd be grateful if we could use one of yours.'

Duke stared as if he was mad. 'Right, Dave will get our boatman to take you across.'

'Thank you, sir. After I've looked around on Motu, I'd like to talk to you some more.'

'I'll see how I'm placed after the prize-giving scene's in the can, then.'

'Singh, I'd like you and Musudroka to organise what we need for the staff meeting. Can you work on that with Dave and Deepika? Staff lists, call sheets, whatever you can pick up.'

'Yes, sir.' She looked disappointed, but she'd see the scene later.

3

Zakaraia the boatman was stocky and strong. His sun-darkened skin was lined for his age, if his full head of jet-black hair was anything to go by. He greeted Horseman effusively and would have happily rehashed his rugby triumphs all day long. But Horseman was working at the brink of what might become a case. He needed to concentrate, miss nothing. Especially since Singh wasn't with him.

'You're a local, are you, Zak?' Horseman addressed him in Fijian.

'*Io*, Josefa, I am indeed. My village is not far away, just off the main road. As a child, I spent more time with my relatives fishing and gathering seafood around here than I did at school.'

Zak poled through muddy shallows until he could lower the outboard, then started the motor and accelerated. He turned hard to starboard, heading towards the mouth of the bay.

'Where's Motu Island?'

'Out further, closer to the heads. About a ten-minute run.'

'I can see three other islands nearer to the base, only a few minutes away with an outboard. Do you know why they chose Motu?'

'I do indeed. You see, Mr Duke hired me eight years ago, when he first came to Fiji scouting for locations. He and his Art Director. After the government offered him this military site for his base, he insisted they also needed a small island for the contestants' camp. Mr Duke wants the game to be real for the players. He refuses to fake scenes of them living on the island. So I took them to all the islands in this bay. No one lives here now. People only come here to gather seafood at low tide and have picnics.'

Zak slowed down and the motor quietened. 'I can't keep on shouting, Josefa. You'll soon see why Mr Duke chose Motu.'

After another five minutes Horseman could make out the palms and barringtonia trees fringing Motu Island, then a strip of white sand appeared. As the water shallowed, the sun emerged, and Zak put on his polaroids to help navigate through the reef. Then the coral shelved and gave way to seagrass, then sand, and the water took on the clear light green of Singh's eyes.

If Steve Duke had wanted the cliché of a coral island, then he'd chosen well. The land rose slightly from the half-moon beach, overhung by trees. You couldn't exactly call it a hill, but the soft undulation provided a better backdrop than a flat sand island.

'It's beautiful,' he said as he helped pull up the runabout on the beach. Zak thrust the anchor in the sand and lifted his eyebrows in agreement. '*Io*, it is, Josefa. Did God create anything more beautiful than a little Fijian coral island?'

Horseman gazed about and nodded slowly. 'It looks like a resort beach, only better than most.'

'Mr Duke and the Art Director wanted clear water and white sand. A natural beach littered with coral rubble, seaweed, leaves and sticks doesn't appeal to the viewers, apparently. Let alone rubbish that washes in too. We cleared up all the debris before filming started, and the contestants keep it pristine.'

'You've done a great job. The contestants, too.'

'*Vinaka*. This lee side of Motu also has a hill which protects the beach from the wind. They were pleased and said it didn't matter at all about the distance from their base. And there's one more thing Motu has that only the locals know about. And for Mr Duke, that was the icing on the cake.'

Horseman played along. 'And what could that be?'

'Come with me and I'll show you.'

Zak led the way along the curve of sand to where it tapered gradually to a rocky point. They clambered over the low ridge to another beach, this one less groomed and protected, bordered by a tough barrier of beach hibiscus and a scattering of coconut palms.

Above the scrub loomed a stone mound, or rather, a ruin of a pyramid. Seaside plants sprouted from the gaps between the stones. On top of the mound stood a small reed hut with a soaring thatched roof. Horseman stopped, astonished. This surely was no film set prop.

'*Oi lei*, now that's something! An old spirit-house. Am I right?'

'*Io*, you're right, Josefa. There aren't many left as tall as this one. Maybe they didn't build many so tall in the old days. How can we know? Most people don't know this is here. If they did, not so many of these shaped stones would remain, that's for certain. Mr Duke and the Art Director both wanted the mound in the show. They wanted its ancient presence—reckoned it was spooky.'

'Spooky?'

'*Io*, they like to create a bit of awe around old Fijian customs in the show. They say the Champion audience loves a hint of magic. Mr Duke went one better and put up this new spirit-house on top. He looked up old pictures and got someone from the Fiji Museum to supervise the building—it's just a façade of course. He even gave the spirit-house a role—it's where the contestants have to collect their instructions, which they call commandments.'

'You're joking!'

Zak laughed. 'No, I'm not, Josefa. They call it the spirit command post. There's a box fixed at the top with a plastic skull on the lid. The team leaders have to go up there when they hear the *lali* drum beat and bring down their commandments. But I'm rambling on. Man, you should have stopped me. This is what you've come to see. This is where Ken Johnson fell down yesterday. It's hard to accept that he never got up.'

4

Sergeant Ashwin Jayaraman, scene-of-crime officer, his three assistants and a photographer arrived on Motu within the hour. Horseman hurried from the contestants' self-built camp when he heard the police speedboat's powerful motor. The boat was now drawn up beside the Champion boat in the protected sandy cove. When the SOCOs had kitted up, Horseman led them to the ancient mound where their boss issued instructions and they began their systematic examination of the cleared area around the base.

The sergeant grinned and handed Horseman a set of blue overalls, a cap and overshoes.

'No entry if you're not properly dressed, sir,' he said while Horseman pulled them on.

'Quite right, Ash. Not sure how long these plastic overshoes will last, though. The coral stonework's sharp. Contestants have climbed up and down most days for the last three weeks. I'm surprised no one's fallen before. The steps are around the back.'

As the wall circled away from the beach it became damp and rough. Plants landscaped the surface, pushing stones aside as their roots dug deep and wide.

'Wow, hardly safe,' Ash said. 'But it would look great on TV.'

On a second look, the steps showed signs of recent work. 'Originally, the priest and chiefs would have got to the spirit-house by a notched plank propped against the wall. I think the set workmen must have removed stones at intervals to create these steps in the wall surface, which slopes inward as it gets higher. I had a good poke around, and you can see stones and risers have been set in concrete to make them more stable.'

'You what, sir? Did I hear right? Had a good poke around, did you?' Ash was only half in jest.

'Don't go apopleptic, I wore gloves, man! There's blood here near the foot of the steps, and probably plenty of it until last night's rain. You hardly need me to point it out to you SOCOs. But come up with me—I noticed smaller traces on two steps part-way. You'll find more, probably. Looks like the victim fell from quite high up. Maybe even the top.'

'Falling from that height onto sharp rocks could easily be fatal. No cause for suspicion in that. The poor guy probably smashed his temple, or another sensitive part of his skull.'

'Who's straying out of his field now?' Horseman shouted over his shoulder as he climbed the steep steps hand over foot. 'I left a pen beside those blood patches I noticed, by the way.'

'Don't fret, sir. I'll return your pens!' Ash joked, a little out of breath.

Horseman reached the top, glad to step onto the level platform. 'They're the property of the Fiji Police, so they're as much yours as mine.'

The platform overlooked everything but the mature coconut palms. The midday sun flooded it with light and heated it up too. After the cool dimness below, he screwed his eyes up against the glare and heat. He sat on the edge of the platform, his legs dangling so he didn't disturb any evidence adhering to the stone wall. Ash pinned a marker beside the second blood smear, labelled the bag with the scraping he'd taken and clambered up to join Horseman.

'Quite a climb,' Ash puffed. 'It's hot up here.'

'Young people these days! What you need is regular training, man.' They chuckled.

'I found something else I want you to see.' Horseman fished an evidence bag out of a pocket and passed it to Ash. 'I left a pencil stuck through the leaf it had caught on. Over there ...' He pointed with his chin, then pulled a ruler from his backpack. Reached down and stretched. The red pencil was less than a metre away from the third step from the top.

Ash sighed heavily, shaking his head. 'You detectives just don't get the concept of scene contamination, do you? It looks like an ordinary piece of fishing line. It could have blown here. Or someone dropped it.'

'Probably. But there's a chance it was part of a broken tripline, don't you think? Maybe tied between those two protruding stones—there and there.' He pointed with his ruler again.

'It's possible, sir. But I'll stick with the accident theory until there's more physical evidence.'

'Goes without saying, Ash. You might like to compare it with this piece. I cut it from a reel of line I found at the contestants' camp about twenty metres in from the beach. You'll see a path through the scrub at the opposite end of the beach where the boats are. That will need your thorough attention too. There was another camp that's abandoned now, occupied by the rival team of players. Would you believe they call them tribes? The boatman said it was on the other side of the hill. I don't know why they abandoned it.'

Ash's eyes lit up. 'Yeah, I do. They start off with two tribes, but as the eliminations go on, there's only a handful of finalists left, and they have to move in together. Stress upon stress, eh? This show's great at ramping up the pressure.'

'You're a fan too, Ash? I seem to be the only Fiji citizen who isn't.'

'So-so. But I can tell you anything you need to know. Just ask—I'm happy to fill you in, sir.'

'*Vinaka*. I'll do that. I've got an overview of the set layout now, I think. What I'd really like to do is spend time with you SOCOs. If this was sabotage or even murder, what could be easier than getting rid of evidence in the sea or this dense scrub? But you can't fingertip search the entire island, unfortunately.'

'We'll concentrate on the areas you've told us about first.'

'Great. I'll get Zak to run me back to the mainland camp now. The director has condescended to spare me some time. I'll send Zak back here to show you to the other camp. That's if you think you'll get to it today. Radio me and let me know.'

'Sure thing.'

'*Oi lei*, I nearly forgot. Don't tell anyone outside your team about the fishing line, Ash. I don't want any Champion staff or contestants knowing we found that. If one or maybe two know already, I want them to believe it's their guilty secret.'

***

'Come in, Inspector. Take a seat.' The director stood between two folding plastic tables. Coloured binders, index cards, and monitor screens covered the surface of one. He sat behind the other, where a single laptop was open. A notepad and a few pens lay beside it. A ceiling fan whirred.

'Mr Duke, this is Detective Sergeant Singh, who's been interviewing your staff while I've been out on Motu Island.'

'Welcome, Sergeant. Guess you're here to judge if my version contradicts anyone else's, huh?'

Singh favoured Duke with a disarming smile. 'Recollections vary, sir. We find that the more versions we hear, the more complete the picture we can build.'

Duke opened a small fridge and took out bottles of Fiji Water. 'No ceremony here, detectives,' Duke said as he passed around the bottles, beaded with condensation.

'I can see why you chose Motu as the contestants' camp site, sir. It's an idyllic coral island.'

'Isn't it? Picture perfect, and also video perfect. Glad you approve.'

'The old temple mound adds something special, too. Creates quite a mysterious atmosphere.'

'Sure does. That spooky pyramid decided me.'

'You've done some work on it—building those steps, for instance. I must say, I found them uneven and slippery, though. An accident waiting to happen there.' He turned to Singh, frowning. 'You'll agree when you see them, Detective Sergeant.'

'The Champion set is not an elementary school playground, you know. Our contestants compete in several areas: physical, mental, social. Ability to survive in a tough natural environment is crucial. They're eager to demonstrate that ability—it's what they've signed on for. And naturally, they've agreed to waive any rights to sue the company on the basis of conditions on the set during the contest.'

'Tell us about Ken Johnson, if you would, Mr Duke.'

'Please call me Steve. What can I say? Ken's the archetypal athlete—that's the role he filled on the show. His application was very strong. The selection panel had no hesitation calling him to audition in Los Angeles.'

'Who's on the selection panel?' Singh asked.

'The casting director and her assistant, a screenwriter, and my executive producer. They cull the applications and draw up an audition list. I don't know how they do it—we get mountains of applications every year from the moment we post a callout on our website.'

'Are you involved in choosing the cast at all?'

'Sure, I attend all the auditions—that's the next step. It goes the same way every year, but I'm always surprised how the successful guys stand out from the others. The selectors rarely disagree. And Ken Johnson stood out as a Champion contender more than most.'

'In what way?'

'Athletic, practical skills, could think on his feet. Leadership potential, although that's the least predictable of the abilities we're looking for. Handsome and a rare natural flair talking to camera. He had nil performance experience, but he shone in his screen test. I think that was because of his sincerity.' The director stared at his empty notepad. 'I'm sorry, it's still hard to accept he's dead.'

'Did you notice any weaknesses in him after production began?' Horseman asked.

'Not physically, not at all. But he was genuinely nice, a bit naïve. That can be a weakness on Champion, where we encourage secret cliques and shifting alliances. Plotting was totally foreign to Ken. He didn't understand it.'

'Neither do I. What do you mean by plotting?'

Duke looked astonished. 'You're serious?' He looked at Singh who smiled in encouragement.

'Well, I mean players sounding out others and agreeing to help each other. Specifically, agreeing not to vote each other out of the game. They also may agree to campaign against another player, to get him or her kicked out.'

'So it's not about the competition we saw you filming this morning?'

'Sure it is. But, er, diplomatic abilities are also essential.'

'You mean conspiracy and deception?'

Duke smiled. 'Sure, and betrayal too. The lot. You're getting the hang of it, Inspector Horseman. It's all about exciting the viewers, getting them to take sides, follow their heroes. The fans love it. But that side of the game wasn't Ken's strength at all.'

'He made it to the finals, though.'

'He did indeed.' Duke leaned forward. 'He was valuable to his tribe until now because he could reliably win the physical challenges and the prizes of food and tools for his team.'

'I can hear a but coming.'

Duke nodded. 'But I've observed through the seasons that players like Ken lose their popularity in the finals when the competition is between individuals. Their physical prowess becomes a threat to the survival of the weaker players who may conspire to vote them out. Unless the athletes are also skilled tacticians, of course.'

'Did that happen to Ken?'

'I don't know. We'll be filming some talking heads at Motu tomorrow. That's when we get players to voice their feelings and consider tactics to stay in the game. But no one will criticise Ken now.'

'I suppose not. Had anyone tried to vote him out already?'

'Sure, whenever there was a vote, players in the other tribe would try to get rid of Ken. But they weren't united, so it didn't happen. Ken often won immunity from the vote by scoring highest on challenges, too. That's one way we keep the strongest contestants in longer.'

'Did he have any particular enemies?'

'Again, I don't know.'

'Out of the finalists, who wasn't on Ken's team from the beginning?'

'Er...Desi and Bobby. I haven't noticed any particular antagonism to Ken from either of them.'

'Why would Ken have climbed to the top of the spirit-house steps while the others were still asleep?'

The director spread his hands. 'I doubt we'll ever know. An early morning walk to enjoy the sunrise?'

'Barbara Koroi, your nurse, tells me she got a call on the emergency radio around six o'clock.'

'Yep, the players may only use the radio link to Barbara when someone is seriously ill or injured. Emergency radio is a necessary precaution, but it's the first time it's been used this season.'

'Barbara reported that Desirée Lopez made the call. When she got to the island, she found out that Mili Kepa had found Ken at the foot of the temple mound. Can you add anything here?'

'No, I wasn't there. Barbara advised it would be risky for Ken to wait for an ambulance as he had a head injury. So she accompanied him to hospital in one of our vehicles. I never dreamed he could die but Barbara was aware his injury might be serious.'

No one spoke for a few moments.

'How long are your investigators going to be on Motu? The players need to get back to their camp.'

Horseman decided the director was still in shock and he would be sympathetic. 'Certainly not today, Mr Duke. Perhaps not tomorrow, either. The death of a fit young man demands a thorough investigation, don't you think?'

'Well yes, but Ken died of a freak head injury when he fell.'

'No one saw him fall, so until the pathologist completes his report, we'll keep an open mind about the cause of Ken's death.'

'Mr Duke, how is it possible to continue with Champion when one of the finalists has died?' Singh asked.

The director blinked several times. 'We went ahead with the challenge this morning before we got the news about Ken. It's tricky. I've got an internet meeting with the producers in LA this afternoon to thrash out a solution. I mean, most of the show's already in the can. What a waste!' He shook his head and stared at the detectives.

5

'Did he mean a waste of money, a waste of time or a waste of a young life?' Horseman asked as they walked around the verandah to the office Deepika had found for the police.

'Not sure, sir,' Singh replied.

Horseman sighed. 'No need to be so diplomatic with me, Susie. Now, let's see if we can talk to all four finalists this afternoon, before your meeting with the staff.'

'That should be feasible. They know we want to question them. They should be in the rec hall. I'm afraid there was no way to stop them talking to each other in the meantime.'

Singh radioed Musudroka and asked him to bring Mili Kepa to their office. Within a few minutes, the flustered detective constable was back. The young woman he ushered in was short and curvaceous, but she moved with considerable poise. Her cropped crinkly hair made her eyes huge. She initiated handshakes and introductions with the detectives. Star-struck Musudroka melted away.

'Take a seat, Ms Kepa.' Singh said, indicating one of the plastic chairs. 'I'm so sorry about the loss of your colleague. However, it's wonderful to meet you. You're the pride of the nation. Fiji's first Champion contestant!'

'Please call me Mili. I'm sure Inspector Horseman would easily beat me in any Fijian popularity vote.' Her voice was low, with a soft American accent.

'Did you get to know Ken Johnson well, Ms Kepa?' Horseman asked. He hoped Singh would tone down her enthusiasm.

Tears welled in Mili's eyes. 'Yes, quite well. We were in the same tribe from the beginning, so we both worked on our camp, getting food and cooking. The entire tribe lived together as well as competing in the challenges together.'

'That must be stressful at times,' Singh said.

'*Oi lei*! Extremely stressful! But we all knew we had to make a success of it, or we'd have no chance. Everyone had done their homework and watched all the previous Champion series.'

'As a Fijian you must have been quite an asset to your team,' Horseman said.

Mili looked down modestly. 'Maybe a bit. I've lived in the States since I was twelve, but I remembered how to forage for shellfish at low tide and how to fish. I taught the others. I couldn't build a shelter or beds, but I knew how and what trees to use. Ken was strong and good with his hands. I could tell him what to do. We made a good team.'

She looked up and her eyes welled with tears.

'What else can you tell us about Ken?'

'He was a nice guy, a southern gentleman. He was from Tennessee and spoke with such a southern drawl. I enjoyed listening to his accent—so musical. He liked looking after all of us in the team—being a provider. The look on his face when he'd caught a decent-sized fish—he was prouder of that than his athletic feats. Most of our wins on challenges were due to him.'

'What were his plans?'

'Of course, to win Champion and the million dollars! His parents weren't wealthy, and he wanted to help his little sisters. It seems he was on a football scholarship to his state university and wanted to go professional. But he was realistic about his chances for the national league. He thought if he won Champion, he might get a job as a television sports reporter or something like that.'

'Sounds like you knew him pretty well, then.'

Mili nodded. 'When our jobs are done, there's nothing else to do in camp but talk.' She smiled. 'But we're so tired we go to sleep very early. I do anyway.'

'Why did Ken go up to the spirit-house platform yesterday morning?'

Mili shook her head. 'I wish I knew. I wish I could help you. But I can't.' A tear overflowed and ran down her cheek.

'I suppose you go up there yourself, sometimes?' Singh asked.

'Only when the script calls for me to. I've got this hangover from childhood when my brothers and cousins spooked me with horror stories about the old times. There was a ruined mound in my grandmother's village. It was around a metre high—all the stones were recycled. But their nonsense about the priest drinking blood from sacrifices and so on terrified me.' She raised her hands, looking helpless.

'You mentioned a script, Mili. I thought Champion was a reality show.'

Mili smiled. 'It is, but the scene and shot sequences have to be planned out or the camera crew couldn't operate efficiently. When I say the script, it's really the storyboard. That specifies where each scene is, who's involved and so on. For example, it could be an early morning sequence of a player climbing up to the platform, opening the skull box to check for any special commands. If that player was me, I must do my job. I'm a trained performer, so I don't have a problem with that. But I don't go up there to enjoy the view in my free time.'

Horseman scribbled a note to check the storyboard with whoever was responsible.

'Did you ever go up the mound with Ken?'

Mili frowned. 'Yes, just once I think. The direction was to go up, open up the skull box, read out the command and discuss it between the two of us.'

'What was the command?' Singh asked.

'I can't really remember. It was at least two weeks ago.'

'Is it possible Ken was acting on direction?'

'No, not at all. Where was the camera crew? Anyway, they can't film on Motu after sunset. He must have gone up there on his own, maybe just taking a walk.' Mili replied.

'What do you think happened, Mili? Or might have happened?' Singh asked.

'If he was on his own, he may have slipped or tripped on the steps in the dark. If he wasn't alone, maybe the same thing. And who else could he have met but another player? We're alone on the island every night.'

'What's your morning routine on Motu, Mili?' Singh asked.

'The camp's in deep shade, but there's always someone who wakes with the light and feels hungry. The first up starts a fire and boils water for tea. If it's me, I eat some fruit--there're papaya trees not far away and we usually have a bunch of bananas in the camp. I make sure I leave fruit for the others and then go fishing. One way or another, we all wake up and have something to eat.'

'Is there filming every day? How does that work?'

'Most days, but every day's program is different. Sometimes the crew comes over early to do some takes on Motu, other times Zak brings us all back to the arena first thing for a challenge. At the end of the day's work, we get the program for the next day.'

'That sounds tough.'

'True. But it was fun until today.' She looked at the detectives, wide-eyed, as if surprised by a sudden thought. 'What will happen to the show now? What will happen to us?'

'We don't know, Mili. I understand Mr Duke will be talking with the producers in LA this afternoon,' Horseman replied.

Mili gazed at him, full of doubt, as if he knew the answer but was withholding it from her.

6

Desirée Lopez paused in the office doorway as if she'd stepped into a spotlight. She was the physical opposite of Mili Kepa: tall and thin, with full breasts which she thrust forward while she posed. She propped one elegant arm on a hip and pouted. The top of a hip bone jutted above the loose waistband of her artfully torn shorts. Horseman wondered how much weight she'd lost in a month of hunter-gatherer lifestyle. He also wondered about Botox and breast implants, but he didn't understand these things. He'd ask Singh later.

Horseman stood. 'Take a seat, Ms Lopez. Thanks for being punctual.'

'Desi, please, Inspector.' She glanced at the smiling Singh then returned her gaze to Horseman while folding her long legs beneath the table. She flicked her platinum blonde hair back over one shoulder. Her flawless olive skin surely had the help of make-up. He'd been told contestants were forbidden personal beauty products, except the company-provided 50-plus sunscreen lotion. It looked like Lopez had found a way around the ban.

'What can I do to help?' Her voice was soft and feminine like her skin.

'I'm told you've already helped a great deal, Desi. You used the emergency radio to alert the Champion nurse, didn't you?'

Desi bent her head modestly, exposing a centimetre of jet-black hair roots. 'I did, yes. Mili woke me up, yelling at me to come with her to help Ken. She was in a panic. She said he'd fallen onto the rocks below the old spirit-house. Unconscious, she said. I remembered our emergency briefing and decided to radio Barbara before going to Ken.'

'You did the right thing.'

'So Barbara said. When she arrived, we all helped get him on the stretcher and into the boat. He was breathing, but kinda ragged. How did he die? None of us understands.'

'No one understands that yet, Desi. The hospital in Suva has an excellent pathologist. He's examining Ken now, but we won't have an answer for you until he completes a range of tests and finalises his report.'

'I'm glad you have an excellent pathologist. But what Ken needed was doctors that could save his life. Don't you have that kind of doctor in Fiji? I mean, a competent one!'

Horseman ignored the barb.

'Were you on the same team as Ken from the beginning of the contest?'

'No, we were opponents. I only moved to the beach camp a few days ago when I became a finalist. You know, we expected the winner to be chosen on Thursday or Friday. Just a few more days to go—and now what's going to happen? Are you going to call it off?' Her beautiful brown eyes were hard.

'The show executives will decide that.'

Singh smiled in sympathy. 'Tell me, Desi, why did you want to be on Champion?'

'You're kidding! To win a million dollars! I've grown up with disadvantage all the way as Latino in California. My dad just wants to marry me off, my teachers never expected anything of me, so I didn't do great in school. My mom slaves as a maid and says I should be grateful. But they can't keep me down. I want a career in Hollywood and a win on Champion will be the launch I need.'

'How well did you know Ken?'

'Not well. Athletic, works hard at the challenges and in the camp. I don't wish to speak ill and all that, but he came across as pretty boring. You know, the classic blue-eyed all-American boy with nothing between the ears.' She smiled and lowered her voice. 'He's a racist, too.'

'Why do you think that?'

Desi brightened. 'Come on, you must know! He's a southern white boy—they're all racists. The way he treats—treated—Mili! He was so controlling. I could see that after my first day at the beach camp. He tried to be the big boss man, make all the decisions. That's racist.'

Desi's definition of *racist* was a new one for Horseman. Singh shot him a warning glance, so he let it go.

'Did you have a plan to win the contest?'

'I sure did, although it's none of your business. I picked Ken as just the sort of player the TV executives want to win, so I decided early on to forge alliances against him and vote against him in every elimination trial. And hey! I made the final, so it worked.'

'Ken made the final, too.'

'Yes, he did, but I don't think he'd have won. As well as boring and racist, he was kinda dumb. He didn't understand strategy.'

'Would you call yourself an enemy of Ken?'

'As far as Champion goes, yes. But—hang on, where are you going with this?' She straightened her back and glared at the detectives. 'You reckon I pushed him down the steps? You accusing me of murder?'

'Not at all, Desi. From what you said against Ken, I'm wondering how strong your dislike was.'

'We were opponents in the game. I wanted to defeat him. Nothing personal.'

'Okay. Do you know anyone who would qualify as Ken's enemy?'

'Well, all the other finalists. But as I said, nothing personal.'

Desi took a water bottle from the centre of the table, unscrewed it, and had a long drink.

'What do you think happened to him?'

'He went up the steps to the spirit-house, tripped and fell hard on his head. Musta cracked his skull. Maybe he died of medical neglect—I hope his parents pursue that. Senseless.'

'Is it likely he'd arrange to meet someone there? Maybe a secret plot?'

'No, Ken wasn't like that. But anything's possible I guess.'

She shrugged and heaved a sigh. Then she pushed her chair away from the table and got up, tossing her hair as she turned away.

7

After Desirée Lopez slammed the door behind her, Horseman finished his bottle of water, stood up and stretched his hamstrings, quads and back. A year ago, he wouldn't have done this in front of Singh, but now they were like old friends who no longer noticed each other's quirks. While he performed his prescribed exercises, Singh read through her notes and started on a new Fiji Water.

'Desi comes across a bit full-on, don't you think? Can we take her seriously?' Singh asked.

'Your guess is as good as mine. She could be just trying out a role she's devised for herself, practising her acting. But remember, she behaved in a level-headed way when she made that radio call to the nurse. I'm keeping an open mind on Ms Lopez. By the way, was she wearing make-up?'

'Yes, sir. Could be the work of a professional beautician.'

'For the hundredth time, Susie, I'd be grateful if you dropped the *sir* when we're alone.'

'I try, but it comes out before I know it. Sorry.' She grinned, her green eyes sparkling.

'As long as you try, I suppose it's okay. Am I right in wondering about Botox and breast implants?'

'No need to wonder. She's definitely got both those.'

'How can you tell?'

'She's obviously lost weight since the show began—her clothes were loose and Desi would not buy loose clothes, take my word for it. If those full, voluptuous breasts and lips were natural, they'd be thinner by now, too. They didn't match the rest of her body.'

'Makes sense, Sherlock. But why?'

Singh took a swig of water, then pressed the cold bottle to her face. 'For the camera. She thinks a perfect body will help her career.'

'Perfect? She looked, um, unnatural to me.' Singh might defend Desi if he uttered the word grotesque, so he didn't.

Three polite knocks on the door announced their next interviewee. Horseman opened it.

'Duane Marinos, Champion contestant. Are you expecting me?'

'Indeed we are, Mr Marinos. Come in.'

Duane Marinos was wiry, with greying hair. He looked strong but must have been in his late forties, surely too old for a contestant. He gave Horseman a bone-cruncher of a handshake, then sat. Sergeant Singh passed him a bottle of water.

'Why did you apply for Champion, Mr Marinos?' Horseman avoided placing stress on the word *you* but Marinos grinned and winked at him.

'Ha ha, you're curious about how an old guy like me got on the show? Well, lemme tell you, I'm fifty-three, the same age as Steve Duke. Steve's a man who prides himself on his fitness and he always includes an older player, often two. If you were a Champion fan, you'd know that, ha ha.' He wagged a reproving finger at Horseman.

'You're right, I know very little about the show. My colleague Detective Sergeant Singh is a keen follower, however.' Marinos bowed towards Singh, smiling.

'Then you'll understand the role of the elder contestant, Detective Sergeant. Officially, we're able to offer advice, share our skills and experience. Unofficially, we're another source of conflict, which is essential to the show. Oldies provide the generation gap conflict. We annoy the hell out of the young ones, just like in a family. It's a lot of fun.'

'Do you have a more personal motivation, Mr Marinos?'

'Sure, I line up with Steve. I want to show the world us older guys can give the young smartasses a run for their money. I'm a high school teacher, so I want my students to see that too. I've applied to be on the show every year for five years. I couldn't believe my luck when I got through this year. The whole school's right behind me.' His elation lit his face.

'Your students must have celebrated when you made it to the finals.'

'You bet!' His grin disappeared and he frowned. 'And now, this news about Ken this morning. None of us can take it in.'

'Tell us what happened yesterday morning, as you saw it.'

'I sleep like a log. One thing young'uns are better at is waking up quickly. Mili's screams woke me, but I couldn't respond right away. I just lay there, slow to come to while the others ran around. I heard Desi yell for quiet and heard her on the emergency radio. When I hauled myself to my feet I went after Mili to see if I could help Ken. I've got a first aid certificate. I knew he'd be in shock, so I took my sleeping bag and grabbed another one too.'

'How did you find him?'

'Mili's assessment was right. He was unconscious, but breathing. His pulse was irregular, skipping beats. I could see blood on his head and some cuts and grazes. I didn't want to move him, so we covered him in the sleeping bags. Desi came, told us Barbara was on her way and went down to the beach to watch for the boat. It was just getting light and quite cool. The warmth of the bags must have done him some good because his pulse was stronger just before Barbara arrived. I believed he'd be alright. I never dreamed he'd die.' He looked from Singh to Horseman, bewildered.

'We'll know more about how that happened when we get the pathologist's report,' said Singh.

'Did you know Ken well?' Horseman asked.

'You betcha. In the same tribe from Day One, literally and metaphorically. He was a great kid, a superb sportsman and helped everyone. Talk about team player! He was a hundred per cent for the tribe. Ken harnessed up and pulled the rest of us along with him.' Duane rubbed at his eyes.

'Ken was your competitor too.' Singh said.

'Only in name. I do my best, but if there's any fairness in this game, there's no way I could win against him. By the end of the first week, I decided Ken was the strongest player and my best chance was to support him every way I could.'

'Is there any fairness in the game, Mr Marinos?'

'I'll never know now, will I? Unless you guys uncover something.'

'Like what?'

'I dunno.'

'Did Ken have an enemy in the camp, Mr Marinos?'

'Desi. From the beginning, she tried to undermine him in the joint tribal councils. You know, sarky comments to his face and behind his back, palling up with players in Ken's tribe to get rid of him. Since she moved in to our beach camp, she's rubbished all his suggestions and his hard work to get food. Unbelievable! My God! She knew better than to try to get me to vote Ken out.'

'Why would Ken go up the spirit-house steps in the dark?'

Marinos shook his head. 'I've thought about this a lot, but all I can come up with is he couldn't sleep and went for a walk in the cool air. Or he heard something and went to check it out. Maybe he then noticed something up on the platform and climbed up to look. Have you found anything there?'

'The police search team are at the spirit-house now, Mr Marinos.' Horseman replied.

'Was he possibly meeting another player?' Singh asked.

'Possible, although out of character. Ken was guileless, naïve even.' He rubbed his eyes again and sniffed. 'But who could that be? Mili was up first, found him. When she got back, we were all asleep. She raised the alarm. So...'

They waited a few moments. 'Go on,' Singh encouraged.

'Nothing, I can't think of anything more to help you.'

'Often, when people experience a sudden death, they remember details after the initial shock wears off. Anything that Ken did or said that was even slightly unusual in the days leading up to his death could be important. If anything comes back to you, please get in touch with us direct.' Singh handed him a card.

'I will. Do his parents know?'

'The doctor treating him in hospital will have tried to telephone them. I'll be checking on that. Thanks for your concern.'

'A son like that—he'd be the apple of their eyes, for sure.'

8

When Marinos left, the last finalist was already waiting, leaning on the verandah rail looking out. Marinos clapped him on the back and spoke a few words to him. Encouraging, warning, or instructing?

Bobby O'Leary was short and stocky with red wavy hair. As Horseman shook hands and made the introductions, he hoped O'Leary used the company-supplied sunscreen according to directions. He probably did; he wasn't sunburnt and the skin between his dense freckles was white, almost translucent. Maybe mid-thirties unless his vulnerable skin was prematurely aged.

Singh fished a bottle of water out of the fridge and placed it in front of O'Leary. He smiled his thanks.

'How well did you know Ken Johnson?' Horseman asked.

'I only moved in to beach camp last week when I got through to the finals. But I certainly knew him from observation over the last three weeks. What a Champion! If the show was a simple sporting competition, he'd already have won. He seemed like a nice, straightforward kind of guy too. Since I joined his camp, I've seen nothing to contradict that impression.'

'Did you expect to reach the finals yourself, Mr O'Leary?' Singh asked.

O'Leary grinned. 'Not expect, no, but I harboured hopes. I was thrilled to make the final cut. You see, I've been a Champion fan forever, but I've never applied to be a player. I'm a college baseball coach and my colleagues and students have had enough of my obsession with Champion. They dared me to apply to the show this season, or forever hold my peace. They even went behind my back to my wife, who supported them.' He laughed. 'My two children, aged five and three, aren't old enough to understand, but Becky trained them to chant on her command: "Daddy, Daddy's the Champion". That was the final straw. Naturally I didn't expect to make it, but somehow, I did.'

'Out of the finalists, who was your pick for the winner?'

'Impossible to predict. Steve Duke likes to bring in a shocking twist or two at the end. But I guess this game's dead in the water now, so I'll be honest. I dreamed I might fit the bill of the unlikely winner.'

'How were you going to achieve that?'

'The only way would be to vote Ken out. And the best way to do that would be to vote Duane out first, because Duane's loyalty to Ken was rock solid.'

'What steps did you take in that direction?' Horseman immediately regretted his unintentional pun and prayed O'Leary wouldn't pick up on it.

'Well, Desi was on board. Mili resisted, told me she'd think about it. Desi intended to talk to her again yesterday, but after Ken went to hospital, all we could do was wait.'

'What was Ken doing near the spirit-house mound?' Singh asked.

'Look, I've no idea, what's the point in speculating? I've held nothing back from you so far. If I knew, I'd tell you.'

'Perhaps he was meeting another finalist secretly?'

O'Leary thought for a bit. 'Possible, I guess. But who? I can swear it wasn't me. I wasn't making any moves until after Desi had tried to persuade Mili to vote against Ken.'

Did Steve Duke think he was Machiavelli or what? Or running a stable of gladiators?

'There's water traffic in this bay at night, Bobby. Fishing, mostly. Do you get any visitors at night? Maybe locals who are curious about Champion, or people who don't know the contestants stay out here.'

'Well, once we did. We were worried when we heard them, but they were hungry fishermen who made a fire to cook some of their catch before they went out again. They invited us to join them. The fish was delicious. We didn't tell anyone.'

'I can picture that. What about Champion crew? You must get pally with some of the crew you work with? I imagine some of you enjoy meeting up after hours.'

'Visits to the contestants' camps are strictly forbidden, by order of the director himself.'

'Visits may be forbidden, but do they ever happen, Bobby?'

'Not that I know of. I don't think so, but I can't deny it's possible in theory. I bet if one of Zak's boats went missing it would mean instant dismissal for the security staff on watch.'

O'Leary was unlikely to disclose anything further today. Better to wait for the postmortem before pressing him again. 'I appreciate your candour, Mr O'Leary. We may need to talk to you again. Please get in touch direct if you recall anything odd that happened after all the finalists moved to the beach camp.' He handed over his card.

'I'll certainly do that. I want to help. Good luck!' O'Leary picked up his unfinished bottle of water, nodded to the detectives and walked out the door, closing it with care behind him.

'I'd love to chew that over with you Singh, but the boys will go on strike if I miss training this afternoon. Everything okay for the staff meeting here?'

'Absolutely fine, sir.' She picked up her phone and switched it on. 'Message from Apo Kau fifteen minutes ago. He and Lili Waqa are on their way to help with the meeting and the statements. Lili's customised the forms with the specific questions we decided on earlier.'

'Great, that'll work better than writing questions on a white board.'

'Should do. She's made two hundred copies too. Our new probationer's shaping up nicely, don't you think?'

9

Horseman would be late for training if he returned the police vehicle to the pool, so he drove straight to Albert Park, pulling into a space near the grandstand. He jogged over to the gaggle of boys gathered around the taps, and chatting to Constable Lemeki, his assistant coach from Traffic Division. The members of the Junior Shiners Training Squad cheered his arrival. Some frowned and checked their bare wrists, others gasped and pointed his way in mock-astonishment.

'Joe, Joe, you're on time!'

'What a miracle—the coach is here!'

'Joe, Joe, you'll get a free dinner tonight!'

Horseman laughed at their uproar, but fifty-year-old Lemeki's powerful bass cut through. 'Boys, show proper respect to your coach! When I was your age, the coach would punish such rudeness severely, probably expel you. Twice round the oval while Joe and I dream up your punishment!' But Lemeki grinned as he shook Horseman's hand.

'It means a lot to the boys when you can get here before we start, Joe. I didn't think you would today though. I heard you've been out to the Champion location. Is it true a contestant died?'

'*Io*, it's a sad business. We talked to the finalists and scoped out their setup while we wait for the postmortem results. SOCOs are still there. Man, what a big operation they've got out there.'

They watched the boys run, alert for signs of injury and illness. The ragtag collection of shoe-shine boys and street kids who lived by their wits would never admit to what they thought of as weakness. They valued their Shiners squad membership above all else in their deprived childhoods. However, they didn't see themselves as deprived, or even as children.

'Tevita's not here. That's not like him.' Horseman said.

'That boy's getting above himself, I reckon. He got cocky when Superintendent Navala got him his job washing police vehicles, but now Sergeant Walo makes him go to evening classes to learn to read and write, he's worse.'

How could Horseman get Lemeki to tolerate Tevita better? 'He's a lot happier now he can imagine a future. That's good, isn't it?'

'*Io*, but his crowing ruffles the other boys' feathers. Mine too.'

'I think this is him now, crossing Victoria Parade,' Horseman said, feeling vindicated. The barefoot boy carried his prized second-hand rugby boots dangling around his neck by their laces. When he got to the field boundary line he ditched his backpack, pulled on his boots, laced them quickly, waved to Horseman and Lemeki and joined the line of joggers.

The squad was more disciplined now. After splashing their heads at the taps, they lined up in front of their coaches, like puppies waiting for their ball to be thrown.

'Shiners, we're mid-way through the second round of the season. And what's your score?'

'Two wins, Joe!' Pita yelled. Cheers broke out.

'And three losses, boof-head,' called Livai.

'*Vinaka*, we know our numbers,' Horseman said. 'Not bad for our second year in the Juniors competition. What do you think, Constable Lemeki?'

Lemeki stared at the ground and rubbed his chin, considering carefully before looking up, straight at Horseman. 'I must disagree, Coach.'

The boys hushed. 'Our Shiners' results are great!' Lemeki clapped and the grinning boys joined in.'

'Lami High School, Marists and Suva Grammar are already through to the semi-finals. If we win against Samabula next Saturday, the Shiners will join them.'

The squad erupted with joyous noise again. Horseman held up his hand.

'Save the celebration for after you win, boys. Constable Lemeki, what can we do tonight to help the boys win against Samabula High School?'

'One, more accurate passes. Two, faster dodging.'

'That's the program for this afternoon, then!' Horseman said.

The two coaches demonstrated passing techniques in slow motion. The boys enjoyed their exaggerated displays. Soon they were practising in fours under the vigilant supervision of the coaches.

The two young detective constables, Musudroka and Kau, were keen Shiners volunteers but both were still at the Champion location, so Horseman found himself more hands-on with the Shiners this afternoon. The constant jogging, twisting, and dodging energised him. Six months ago, at his check-up in Portland, Oregon, his orthopaedic surgeon had told him he could never again play top-level rugby, or indeed any rugby. It was two years since he'd shattered his knee, after all. The surgeon believed a coaching role provided the right level of activity for him. An hour's training was testing him today. Maybe the surgeon was right. Just maybe, he should accept his has-been status.

Horseman blew his whistle for the break before the twenty-minute practice game that ended every training session. The boys made for the taps again and stretched out on the grass.

'That was a good hard session, Joe,' Lemeki said. 'Those young DCs of yours are coming on as coaches, but they like having fun too much. Not tough enough.'

'The boys like fun too, but you're right, Lemeki. They won't win unless they sharpen up their ball skills. Let's get them back on the field now.'

'*Io*. Is Dr Pillai coming with their dinner tonight?'

'Sure is. It'll be great to have him back after three months. Even though he got the training meals delivered while he was in New Zealand, I think the boys will be pleased to see him in person.'

'*Io*, the Shiners are the only junior team to have their own doctor—they're proud of that privilege.' Lemeki laughed. 'Grateful for the meals, too.'

Dr Pillai's car pulled up two minutes before the end of the practice game. The diminutive doctor ran to the centre line, from where he scrutinised the play with concentration. When Lemeki blew the final whistle, the boys noticed their team doctor and rushed over to him, shouting.

'*Bula* Doctor, Doctor, you came back!'

'Did you see me score the try, Dr Pillai?'

'What are we going to eat today?'

Dr Pillai clapped and laughed. A humble man, he always seemed surprised that the boys even recognised him.

'My goodness, boys, it's so nice to be back home. I need a few of you to carry our dinner from the car. Do we still have the trestle table?'

Dr Pillai had no shortage of helpers. The boys washed, then lined up at the old trestle from the grandstand. Dr Pillai presented each Shiner with a paper bag containing slices of *dalo*, the dense root crop they all loved, and some boiled chicken pieces. They sat on the grass and ate in contented silence, then returned to break bananas off the large bunch on the trestle and take a carton of milk from Dr Pillai's cool box.

'My goodness, it feels like I've never been away, Joe,' Dr Pillai said, a broad smile on his face as he watched the boys eating.

'They got fed while you were away, but they missed you, Raj. So many of these boys' families have let them down badly. You're here, week after week, just because you care about their welfare. Having you back means a lot to them.'

'They mean a lot to me, too, Joe. My word, yes. And I want to get cracking on our hostel project. Thanks for keeping me up to date by email while I was away. I'm not clear what you think of the charity model proposed by our Action for Children office. You were rather enigmatic if I may say so, Joe.'

'That's because I'm not sure if their procedure is right for us or not. I want to get a hostel for the boys up and running soon. I thought that a boarding house for teenage boys would be simpler than a home for young children, like the Sunshine Home. But every single aspect is so much more complicated than I imagined. I need your advice, Raj.'

'Our hostel could be a legal minefield, Joe. I think Action for Children's advice to set up a charity along the lines of the Sunshine Home is good. I also understand and share your frustration. If you agree, I'll brief a lawyer I know who can give us independent advice. Can we meet tomorrow to talk more fully?'

'Today I was called to a death out of Suva that may be suspicious. Would tomorrow night after dinner suit you? It's probably the only time I could get away.'

'Great, I'll be in touch and see if Shiv can join us. I know he'll help *pro bono*.'

Horseman pulled a fat document folder from his backpack. 'I copied everything I got from Action for Children for you. I'm relieved you want to speed things up too.'

Dr Pillai flipped through the documents while Horseman watched the boys drift away from training: some singly, others in twos or threes. Some had a mat on the floor in a relative's house, but many would sleep in their own secret nooks between alleys and buildings, under the museum verandah, in abandoned packing cases, beneath this very grandstand. They needed safe places to sleep urgently. But Horseman dared hope for more: a home.

10

Detective Sergeant Susila Singh closed her door with relief. She went through her usual routine on autopilot: opened the balcony door and the windows of her flat, put her backpack on a dining chair and unpacked all her work files onto the table. She'd go through the mass of statements from Champion staff while she ate. But what would she eat? She needed to go to the supermarket but not tonight. The day at the Champion set had exhausted her.

The landline phone rang as she opened the fridge door. It didn't ring often, but she'd kept it when she leased the flat, the extra cost well worth the better security it gave her. She reached for the handset on the kitchen wall.

'Susie, it's Joe. You're back home. Good. How'd it go?'

'Has something happened?'

'Not as far as I know. Have you eaten yet?'

'No, just looking in the fridge now.'

'I'd like to go through the Champion statements with you. If you're up for that. How about I get some take-away? You could bring the statements up here and we could eat while we read them.'

It was six months since they'd both moved into Seaview Apartments, but never before had Horseman asked her to work at home with him. There must be something more on his mind than the statements.

'Of course. sir—um—Joe. Great idea.'

'Pizza, curry, fish and chips...what would you like?'

'Um, I feel more like curry tonight.'

'Curry it is. I'll buzz you when I'm back home.'

Happy she had time to shower and put on fresh clothes, she was ready and sorting the statements when Horseman rang. The security system demanded she buzz his flat from the ground floor, so she squeezed everything she needed into her backpack and went down in the lift. Although there could be a better system, she felt thankful that it wasn't easy to get into the flats.

When she arrived, Horseman opened the plastic boxes on his table—far too many for two people. As he lifted each lid, a unique spicy aroma wafted up to blend with the others.

'Smells amazing. Who else is coming?' Singh asked.

'No one. Is that okay?' He looked puzzled.

'Fine, Joe. Just that it looks like a banquet for six! Is it from Hare Krishna's?'

'Yep, they're the best. Unless you wanted meat, of course.'

'Not at all. You know I love Hare Krishna's food. Why don't we eat first? The table's too full to spread the papers out.'

'Good idea.'

He passed her a Fiji Bitter, a plate and a bowl, put a spoon in each box and sat down. She was relieved he lost his awkwardness within moments of tucking in. They were both hungry and made a sizeable dent in all the dishes before pausing.

'Susie, look at this photo. I found some fishing line today near the steps to the spirit-house where Mili found Ken yesterday morning. I gave it to Ash, of course. I didn't get time to tell you about it. More important to interview all the finalists right away. What's your first reaction?'

She peered up close then zoomed in until the coil stood out from the dark stone, moss, and creepers.

'The mound's well in from the shore, so an odd place to be cutting fishing line. Maybe it blew from the beach and landed there. But I guess you've got another idea.'

'As soon as I spotted it, I saw it as part of a discarded tripline, I don't know why. Someone could have easily tied it across the steps. With malign intent.'

Singh was surprised. It wasn't like the boss to come up with far-fetched scenarios when simpler ones were obvious. She'd tell him straight; he wouldn't have asked if he didn't want her opinion.

'That's possible but a bit unlikely. Murder rather than an accident?'

'Possibly the culprit didn't intend that Ken die. Just put him out of action for a while. Even with a sprained ankle, he'd have to retire from the game. All four of the remaining finalists would benefit from that outcome.'

She couldn't disagree. 'No doubt about that. Even loyal pal Duane. So, let's get this straight. Another finalist arranges a dawn meeting with Ken at the spirit-house platform and sets up a tripline. Whether he or she turns up for the meeting doesn't really matter, does it? Ken goes up to wait or look around. Either on the way up or down, he trips and falls.'

He nodded. '*Io*, that'll do. Whoever set the booby trap, he or she was watching, removed the fishing line after Ken fell, leaving him unconscious and went back to bed. All this in the dark, so it would be hard to notice a small piece of line had dropped onto the stone wall. The booby-trapper stayed in bed until Mili got up, found Ken, and ran back to the shelter to get help. As everyone agrees about what happened next, we'll accept their version for now.'

'I wonder if two of them could have been in on it.' Singh was warming to the theory.

'Possible, but given the Champion ethos of plotting and betrayal, it would be a huge risk, wouldn't it?'

Singh tore a piece of naan bread and mopped up the dregs of various curries and condiments. For her, this was a highlight of an Indian meal, second only to the intoxicating fusion of aromas as the lids on the array of dishes were lifted.

Horseman helped himself from the half full containers. 'I hope I'm wrong, Susie. The last thing I need now is a murder case. I'm actually quite worried by the direction the Shiners' hostel project is taking, or not taking. The experts agree that the best way is to establish a charity. But it's getting all too complicated. I need time to get to grips with the legal documents.'

'I understand you're frustrated by the delays, Joe. But surely this project is too important to hurry. You and any other partners need legal protection.'

Horseman looked at her. 'Everyone agrees on that, but it's back to front, upside down or something. Those boys need protection, not me. All I want is to provide a roof over their heads.'

For the first time, she saw his sadness. She wondered about his trip to the States, six months ago now. He had said nothing about it at work. Had he suffered two blows while he was there: losing his rugby future and losing Melissa, his American girlfriend? That could explain his impatience with red tape on the Shiners' hostel.

'The statements can wait till the morning if you've got legal documents to read, sir.'

'No, I'd rather sort the statements. That way we can plan a timetable for tomorrow.' He stopped. 'Sorry Susie. If you'd rather call it a night that's fine. I'm happy to skim through them myself.'

'Not at all. I agree with you—let's get them done!'

Horseman quickly cleared the remnants of the meal away. Singh laid her laptop and folders out on the table, together with small notepads and a zippered bag of highlighters, coloured pens, pencils, and paper clips.

'We divided them roughly by status: those whose job took them to Motu Island, those who worked with the contestants at the barracks, and those who never worked with them directly but still may have observed them about the place.'

'Makes good sense, Susie. I guess your third group is the biggest.'

'By far.'

'Then I'll check those first. They're the least suspicious and possibly the frankest. I'll pull out any who saw Ken last Saturday for the timeline. Then we'll compare what we've got.'

'Okay, I've got a timeline template on my laptop. I'll add incidents directly there.'

'Sure, but let's lay it out physically too, until we get to the office whiteboard. My brain works better this way.' Looking a little guilty, he got a box of index cards from his desk and put them in the centre of the table.

'No excuse now! Let's get started.'

His handsome face cleared of worry lines as he skimmed each page before putting it either to the right or the left. Maybe he forgot his problems when he worked. She wouldn't be surprised as she was a bit like that herself. Or maybe his purposeful, business-like expression was a mask put on for colleagues.

When she'd reviewed the statements of staff whose work sometimes took them to Motu Island, made notes and added just two incidents to her computer timeline, she glanced at Horseman. His pile of statements was almost gone, and five index cards were lined up in the middle of the table.

'Looks more doable now, doesn't it? You can add these five to your computer timeline if you make index cards for your sightings.'

'Already made them. Only two of this lot saw Ken on Saturday.' She handed the cards to Horseman then turned to her laptop to enter his incidents.

'Would you like to call it a night?' Horseman asked.

She'd seen him exhausted by pain before, but he didn't look like that now. Rather, he looked energised.

'Not unless you do. I'd rather process all the statements if we can.'

He smiled. 'So would I. Let's divide the final lot—the ones who work with the contestants at the barracks. Then we can decide which staff to interview tomorrow. After what I've seen so far, I'm optimistic the number will be manageable.'

Singh enjoyed most aspects of her job but especially working alone with Horseman like this. He looked on her as an equal partner in a joint endeavour. That meant a lot. When she made inspector rank, she might never experience that again. Absolutely not with someone like Ratini, and there were plenty of senior officers like him. Was it possible she might regret that promotion which had been her goal since she joined the police?

She glanced at him and he held her gaze, intense and warm. If he made a move, what would she do? He put his hands on the table and pushed himself up.

'How about a cup of tea while we demolish the rest? I'll put the kettle on,' he suggested.

She wasn't sure if she was relieved or disappointed.

TUESDAY

11

At 8 o'clock next morning Horseman faced the eager junior detectives: Tanielo Musudroka, Apolosi Kau and probationer Lili Waqa.

'Sergeant Singh and I sorted the statements you gathered yesterday. Several Champion crew sometimes worked on Motu Island. We've got statements from a set decorator, props builder, and sound recordist as well as camera crew and production assistants. More than I was expecting. But I found out they shoot the swimming challenges on Motu because the water's clearer. There've been five so far, but none in this final round.'

'Sorta fake, isn't it? On TV it looks like the contestants are isolated at their camp. But they're not really,' Musudroka said.

'Tani, they can't be if you think about it. For every scene you see on the island, there's got to be a cameraman there pointing the camera! And others, too,' Kau explained.

'I kinda imagined they gave the contestants video cameras, and they shot those scenes themselves,' Musudroka said.

To save time, Horseman butted in. 'That sounds like a good idea, but maybe the quality of the do-it-yourself footage wouldn't be professional enough. The upshot is that this morning, while we're waiting for Dr Young's postmortem report, we'll interview all crew who worked on Motu. After that, we'll talk to some who worked with Ken Johnson at the arena or who saw him anywhere on Saturday.'

'When will the PM report come, sir?' Kau asked.

'Dr Young will ring me as soon as he can. I hope soon, but in the meantime, we've got potential witnesses to talk to. I've got two vehicles to give us some flexibility. Detective Sergeant Singh's waiting in the car park now. Apo and Lili, you go with her. The SOCOs should already be on Motu with the speedboat.'

The phone rang. Horseman grabbed the receiver.

'*Bula* mate, your friendly pathologist at your service.'

'About time too. Better make it quick, Matt. We're about to leave for the Champion location.'

'I've got something to show you first. Can you bring Susie along?'

'I'd like to, but the DCs can't manage the interviews we've got lined up by themselves. If what you've got for us really can't wait, Singh and the DCs will go on ahead and make a start.'

'Okay, see you soon.'

Horseman signed out the vehicle and drove up the hill to the Colonial War Memorial Hospital. Matt wasn't one for unnecessary secrecy; there must be a reason for him wanting Horseman to come to the hospital.

The pathology department was at the back, down a steep driveway. There was a roller-shutter with a discreet sign *Deliveries*. Horseman opened the narrow door beside it and went through to the reception desk. As usual, no one was in sight, so he rang the bell. Dr Young opened the door and smiled a welcome.

'That was quick. Come through.'

As his assistant folded back the sheet the pathologist's smile disappeared and his grey eyes clouded. 'Ken Johnson's the fittest, healthiest corpse I've ever examined. Such a waste. A reminder we're all vulnerable. See the head wound here? A hard blow on the right temple, or pterion to us doctors. Generally, the most susceptible part of the head because three bones come together here.' The scalp now covered the incision Dr Young had made in the skull. Horseman's stomach lurched at the puckered skin.

'Fatal?'

'Probably, but he survived for twenty-four hours. You should speak to his treating doctor, Manny Satush. Although it was a severe wound, Manny expected he would survive. I'll postpone my conclusions about the cause of death until I get the results of a full toxicology screen. I've put *top priority* on the samples, but you know that doesn't mean a lot to the lab.'

He switched on a large monitor and clicked on one of dozens of thumbnail images, zooming in until Ken Johnson's head wound filled the screen. Despite cleaning, the depression of the skull beneath the pulpy tissue was obvious.

'Is that injury consistent with falling down the steps of the temple mound? I emailed you a photo.'

'Probably. I found plenty of stone and coral particles embedded in the wound which I've sent to Ash at the SOCO lab. If they match their own samples from the scene then, yes. If they don't match—well, you've got a problem. So, there's another delay for you.'

'Don't I know it. Ash thinks they'll finish at the scene today, though. No case-busting evidence unearthed yet.' He swallowed and looked away.

Matt covered Ken Johnson's head again and stepped to the foot of the trolley. He folded the sheet back, exposing the feet and legs to the knees. Well-muscled legs that were bruised and cut. But one or two of the cuts didn't look like they were made by stone, even sharp stone. A fine straight scratch on the shin above the right ankle held his attention as he peered closer.

Horseman pointed to the cut. 'Could fishing line have done this?'

The pathologist's eyebrows lifted in surprise. 'I reckon it could have. I wondered about a tripline. That cut and another are completely clean. All the others had grains of rock in them. Joe, are you holding out on me?'

'I poked around the scene before the SOCOs arrived yesterday and found a bit of fishing line caught in the plants sprouting on the old stones of the mound. I handed it over to Ash. It probably just blew in from the beach, but it could have been part of a tripline too. I've only told Singh so far. If we're looking at malicious sabotage, one of the other four finalists is most probably responsible. So the fishing line scrap must be top secret for now.'

'Absolutely, Joe.' Dr Young pulled down his head magnifier and switched on its light, examining the fine incisions. 'The one on the right shin's cut through the skin. He was probably climbing quickly, maybe even running up the steps when it caught him first here. He stumbled and the line caught him again here, but he'd slowed so it's just a scratch. Then there's another shallow cut on the left leg.'

'I've tried to visualise how it happened, but I'm puzzled. I mean, wouldn't you fall forward if a tripline caught you? That could explain his wound on the temple but not how severe it is, could it? He wasn't falling from a height, was he?'

'I know what you mean, but you can fall with a lot of force by tripping against a single step if you don't see it. Did it myself a few years ago. My mind was miles away and I walked into a low kerb in the middle of a road in Sydney—some safety device. Huh, I went flying, put my hand down to break my fall, but the shock travelled up my arm and fractured my elbow. What an idiot! But I'll never forget the force of that fall. Scary. I was just lucky I didn't land on my head. And that the surface was asphalt.'

'So, you think it's possible. Do you agree he would have fallen forward?'

'Not necessarily. It depends on physical factors: the steps, his speed, the force of the fall and his instinctive actions to save himself. He could have tried to twist sideways, away from the steps, then caught his left leg on the line. He could have panicked and thrown himself back trying to recover his balance. Almost anything's possible.'

'How about this; the person he was planning to meet on the platform sees him stunned or unconscious near the tripline. Then he or she comes down to him and pushes him, so he falls to the bottom.'

'You surprise me Joe—you've really been pondering this, haven't you?'

'Of course. Where's the surprise?'

'No offence! I'll examine the body again in the light of your scenarios and get back to you. But I'm inclined to believe that if Ken was prone on the steps or beside them, someone pushing him down would have less force than if he tripped while upright, especially running. I could be wrong, though. I need to work this through, consult some references and most important, have another good look.'

'I appreciate it.'

'Not a problem. Terrible business. What's going on out there at the Champion site? I mean, bloody triplines!'

'I got the impression yesterday that the director encourages extreme competition among the contestants. Ganging up on team members and betraying them is expected. That's just a tactic you use to win.'

'You mean another finalist put him out of action! It's not rugby, mate!'

'Have you ever watched the show?'

'Not really, only when the kids had the last series on when I was visiting them in Sydney. They watch it because they like to see Fiji when they're homesick. That's what they said. My reminder that they're at university to study didn't go down too well.'

Horseman grinned. 'I can imagine. You've got two good kids there, you know. They impressed me when I spent time with them around Christmas. They'll come through for you.'

'I guess so. I know Talei would have been stricter with them. I often try to second-guess what she'd do in situations that come up.'

Horseman pictured the pathologist's vivacious Fijian wife, who died of cancer years before. 'You never know, maybe she would've trusted them to be sensible now they're older. Like their parents.'

Dr Young brightened. 'Maybe she would. Righto, I'll call you, Joe. Good luck!'

12

Horseman stepped onto the office verandah and heard Singh's voice inside, talking with a soft-spoken man. He went out into the quadrangle of army buildings and radioed Ash, who answered on Horseman's second attempt.

'Good morning, Inspector. We're back on Motu and alone. I approached from seaward as you suggested and landed there. I hope none of the Champion crew spotted us.'

'Great, try to keep a low profile but it can't be helped if someone discovers you. Any good news for us?'

'Maybe. We've found two more small pieces of fishing line: one at the base of a taller rock beside the steps. You'll remember you pointed out a pair of them as possible anchor points yesterday.'

'And the other?'

'At the foot of the steps, under the ledge. It must have been close to where Ken was found.'

'And your plan for today?'

'We've combed through the spirit-house clearing, the players' shelter, and front beach. But today's a new day. We've had another high and low tide, and it's breezy. We'll keep our eyes peeled but we can't keep on searching the foreshore on the off-chance. So today we'll search around the beach and the abandoned shelter on the other side of of the island and the rocky coves adjacent to the front beach. We'll finish today.'

'Great work, Ash.' Horseman lowered his voice. 'Any SOCOs within earshot?'

'I'll just walk away and call you back. Out.'

Horseman looked around the quadrangle while he waited. The frenetic energy of yesterday had died down. Of course, they weren't filming today. Had the executives reached a decision about the future of the series yet?

When the radio crackled to life, he told Ash briefly that Dr Young thought the use of a tripline was possible. 'Please don't tell anyone, even your own team. We don't want the contestants or anyone on the crew to know this yet. Radio me when you find anything interesting.'

'Sure, Inspector. Out.'

Horseman glanced up at the sound of a door closing. A young Fijian man came out of the interview room, saw Horseman, and beamed his recognition. After the customary handshake and best wishes, Horseman entered the office. He was surprised to see Singh had chosen Lili Waqa as her interview partner, then realised Singh would provide a more skilled model of interview technique for the probationer than would either Musudroka or Kau.

'How's it going?' he asked Singh.

'We've talked to three crew who've worked on Motu so far. Got them to explain their jobs in some detail. By the way, one's an intern, a Television Production student from the Fiji Institute of Technology. I understand a lot more about how Champion gets made, but none of them threw any extra light on the lead-up to Ken Johnson's death.'

She looked at Waqa with an encouraging smile. 'Early days yet!'

He needed to talk to Singh alone, right now.

'Have you checked how many staff didn't turn up to the meeting yesterday? If they're on set today, we need them to fill in the statement form.'

'No, we haven't yet, sir. We've ticked off the statements on the list of staff on deck yesterday. We need to follow up the others.'

'Lili can handle that. Lili, take the list and find Deepika in Personnel, please. I'll let her know you're coming. She can tell you which of yesterday's no-shows are working here today and give you contact details for those who aren't.'

'*Io*, sir.' Waqa shuffled through a folder for the list. She'd probably prefer to be interviewing with Singh, but her years of secretarial experience made her ideal for this meticulous task.

'There's another staff category I didn't think of yesterday, Lili. Any staff who worked on Saturday but not yesterday. They could have seen

Ken Johnson on his last day here. I'll ask Deepika if she could pull out those names too. You know what they say about no stone unturned ...'

'It gathers no moss, sir?' Lili smiled, her round cheeks creasing into dimples. Singh laughed out loud.

'Aha, we've got another joker in our ranks. You can challenge Tani. You know, I just meant we detectives turn every stone over.'

'And examine what's underneath,' Singh added.

'Isn't that a job for the SOCOs?' Waqa asked, all innocence.

'Go now, Probationary Detective Constable, before I pull rank,' Horseman replied, grinning.

After he rang Deepika, who promised to supply the information they needed, Lili hurried out. Horseman sat in the chair opposite Singh.

'You were a long time at the morgue, Joe. Is the PM report ready?'

'No, there are even more questions to be answered by tissue sample analysis and toxicology. But there are fine, smooth cuts on Ken's shins that are consistent with him running into a tripline. Matt's going to consult with Ash on the sample I picked up yesterday. Oh, I gave him a piece of the line I found in the shelter, too. We talked through different scenarios. He now agrees Ken's death is suspicious, even if it's malicious injury rather than murder.'

'Sure.' Singh frowned, a sign she was thinking through the ramifications.

'No one but Matt, Ash and you know about this evidence. I'll have to report to Ratini later today. In the meantime, it's likely no one on set, apart from the person who set up the tripline, knows about it. I want to lull the culprit into a false sense of security.'

'Yes, that makes sense.'

'But now I feel we need to throw that stone, with or without moss, into the sea and watch the ripples. Otherwise, everyone can just keep saying nothing forever.'

'Do you know you're always itching for action at the beginning of a case? It's only the second day, remember. What have you got in mind?'

'A visit to Steve Duke in the guise of reporting. He'll appreciate the courtesy. We'll drop our line and see if he takes the bait.'

'Joe, you complain about Tani's and Lili's jokes! It's a great idea! Let's do it.'

He smiled at her. 'I'll set it up with Duke for mid-afternoon. We should be finished with the staff interviews by then. And if we unearth a nugget from them that allows us to solve the case before then, we can easily cancel the appointment.'

13

'*Bula* Zakaraia, it's good to see you again.'

The boatman extended his hand to Horseman. It was hard, calloused, and strong.

'Please take a seat. This is my colleague, Detective Sergeant Singh.'

The boatman nodded.

'I want to concentrate on last Saturday, Zak. Did you see Ken Johnson at all then?'

'*Io*, Inspector. Several times. There was an arena challenge in the morning, so I ran over to Motu in the longboat at seven o'clock to pick up the contestants and ferried them back here to base.'

'Was anyone else with you?' Singh asked.

'No, Sergeant. Mr Duke wants as few as possible visiting Motu. "What's the point of an isolation island if anyone can go there?" he said. No need, anyway. The players always wait on the beach. I threw Ken the bow line and he held the boat steady while the others hopped in. My boys help when we land at the other end.'

'Oh, it must be nice having your sons working with you,' Singh said.

The boatman smiled. '*Vinaka*, Sergeant, but they're not my sons. My young assistants, I should say, but I just call them my boys. My own four sons have all pushed off into the world now and got good jobs, better jobs than boat crew. But I like being around boats and the sea.'

'You're essential to making Champion, Zakaraia.'

The boatman shook his head, dismissing the compliment, but he looked pleased.

'In your statement you wrote you saw Ken again at noon when you took all the finalists back to Motu. You didn't see him at all between seven and twelve?' Singh asked.

'No, I have nothing to do with the shooting. Sometimes it lasts all morning like it did on Saturday.'

'How was Ken on your run back?'

'Tired, but no different from the others. He didn't say much. Still jumped out and helped pull the boat up, then pushed it out again after the others had got out.'

'Did you see him again that day?'

'The next time I saw him, he was unconscious on a stretcher when I ferried him and Nurse Barbara back here the next morning.'

'How easy is it for someone to land on Motu though? One of the players told us some fishermen pulled up one night for a rest and a meal. The fishermen reckoned they didn't know Champion controlled the island for the duration of the shoot.'

'Well now, I heard about that and I'm sceptical. Maybe those fishermen just wanted a look at the players' camp. I suppose it's easy to land on Motu at night, but I think it's pretty uncommon these days. In the daytime it's also easy to go unnoticed if you come ashore out of sight of the beach we use. In the right type of craft, it's still possible to land on the rocky seaward side.'

'What's the right sort of craft?'

'A canoe or small inflatable, but you'd have to be careful.'

'Has anyone visited Motu at the invitation of one or more of the players?'

'You mean a romantic assignation?' Zekaraia asked.

Horseman smiled at the quaintness of his expression. '*Io*, that, and for other purposes too.'

'Perhaps to bring food—I hear the players get very hungry,' Singh added.

'Or simply to socialise, get to know the film crew better,' Horseman said.

'That's all possible but remember this. Last year a cameraman came to Motu at night to meet one of the women players who was waiting for him. Another player told the production manager the next day and both the player and cameraman were kicked out. While the contestants are all new each season, there's a very low crew turnover. This story's remembered and repeated. Not only that, but Mr Duke also made quite an issue of it in his orientation training for both contestants and crew.'

'Still, there'll be some who regard such an incident as a challenge,' Horseman said.

Zakaraia wagged his head, considering. 'True, true. You might not realise how competitive the players are. And they live at very close quarters—a situation guaranteed to spark conflict. It would be a miracle if a secret visitor remained a secret. And I couldn't trust any player to keep that secret. Every player would improve their own chances by reporting the rule-breaker. Arranging secret visits just doesn't make sense.'

Horseman spent all his working life around people who took absurd risks committing crimes that made no sense, so he wasn't ruling this possibility out. Not by any means.

'Have you heard any talk this season of any private visits to Motu, night or day?' Singh asked.

'None, apart from those so-called fishermen,' solemn-faced Zakaraia answered.

'You mentioned the fierce rivalry between the players. Has that rivalry escalated into arguments or fights this season?'

The boatman lifted his bushy eyebrows in agreement. 'Certainly arguments. Mr Duke sometimes sets them up himself. He says the television audience loves to see conflict. Nothing physical, of course. Not that I'd be surprised if players did come to blows sometimes. Again, they'd best think twice about it because one punch could get you the sack.'

He leaned forward, conspiratorial. 'I have heard of a few dirty tricks played this season, though. They're anonymous. Whoever's responsible has come up with a good way of upsetting players, putting them off their stride, as it were.' He winked.

'Dirty tricks?' Horseman hid his keen interest at this 'by the way' revelation and avoided glancing at Singh.

'Some would call them practical jokes. Like the giant millipede someone put in Desi's sleeping bag. She screamed so loud players in the other camp even heard her. Yet one of her teammates probably put it there.'

'Couldn't it have got in by itself?' Singh asked.

'There's a slight chance, I guess. But she hates what she calls *bugs* and always shook it out and rolled it tight when she got up. Then she put it in a zippered bag. She's convinced it was a personal attack.'

'I don't blame her. That happened when she was in the other camp, before the finals?'

'*Io*, I thought it could have been someone from the other team, but there's no way of telling.'

'What other dirty tricks have been played?'

'One player kept a secret food stash buried in a big tin, just for himself. A prankster planted a rotting octopus inside the tin. You've smelled a rotting octopus, I take it? Worst stink in the world. He got such a shock he yelled blue murder before he remembered his stash was top secret. He's since been eliminated. No surprise there.'

The boatman was getting such a wonderful reaction now he went on before being asked.

'Well now, I hear it all because I'm the first person from the outside world the players see every morning, so they've got to get it off their chests. I try to calm them down and tell them it's not such a big deal. None of these tricks or jokes was dangerous.'

'Have there been any others, to your knowledge?'

'Oh, there was another one. I think it was the first. The pit toilet's about 50 metres from the shelter for obvious reasons. The men don't bother going there when it's dark, but the ladies want privacy. Mili opened the door early one morning and a bucket of sea water tipped over her head. The trickster must have set it up during the night, but couldn't have known who'd be the first to open the door. The sudden shock scared her senseless but again, no harm done.'

'I'm interested to know about your boats' security, Zak.'

'There are always people about in daylight, so we just leave the small boats pulled up above the high-water mark after use. At night, we store them in the boatshed, which we always lock. We're lucky this is a military base because the boatshed's well equipped. The launch is kept in the shed on its trailer. When we need it, we launch it off the ramp and then leave it tied up at the jetty for the rest of the day. We winch it in before dark. There're floodlights on the shed that light up the ramp and the jetty.'

'*Vinaka vakalevu*. Zakaraia. You've been most helpful. If you do recall any more incidents or rumours of them, please get in touch straight away, either to Sergeant Singh or myself.' They both handed the boatman their cards, which he placed with care in a zip pocket.

14

'*Oi lei*, that was a bit of luck!'

'No, a bit of method, sir.' Her eyes shone.

'You asked him about contestants fighting and he revealed there's a prankster stalking Motu Island? I'm the first to call you a star interviewer, Susie, but if that wasn't lucky...' He stopped, realising he wouldn't have teased her like that six months ago, hoping she wouldn't mind.

Singh grinned. 'Could Steve Duke know about it?'

'I'd be surprised if he doesn't. But then, I've been surprised before.'

'Should we tell him?' Singh asked.

'Yes, let's see his response to what we've found. Any reason we shouldn't tell him?'

'Not really. Do you think there's only one prankster?'

'I don't know. I guess the first prank would provide a model and could easily provoke others. There're two kinds of incidents: those directed against a particular person and those that are random. The millipede was aimed at Desi, the rotting octopus at the food hoarder, whereas the bucket of water could have landed on anyone. We've been assuming the tripline targeted Ken, even that he was lured to the spirit-house. But what if it was random, what if he was there by chance?'

Singh frowned while she thought. 'It's an escalation of danger, though, isn't it? The culprit tried to remove all trace of the line.'

'Yes, the other pranks weren't hidden at all. And Zak wouldn't be the only one who took them rather lightly. Sort of schoolboy pranks, really. But a tripline strung across steep, uneven steps several metres high is criminally dangerous. Hard to believe that wasn't aimed at an individual. If it was random, the perpetrator is seriously unhinged.'

'Which may well be the case. On balance, I still think whoever set the tripline lured Ken to the steps.'

'Me too. But we'll keep our minds open, especially about whether there's one prankster or more among the five finalists. Both Mili and Desi have been victims of pranks. My mind boggles at the whole Champion setup.'

'Couldn't an outsider be responsible, sir? Like one of the crew who come to the island for their job, or at night in secret?'

'It's possible, Susie. But it would be much easier for a contestant to set up any of the pranks. There were only five left when Ken Johnson tripped and fell. We're investigating Ken's death, not the pranks, unless they provide us with leads. His four co-finalists all had means and opportunity to set that booby trap. All four share the motive of wanting to get rid of their strongest competitor. I'm horrified by such ruthless ambition. But Desi, Mili, Bobby and Duane must be our top suspects.'

'Agreed, sir. Let's hope—'

There was a knock on the door. DC Kau entered, his round, cheerful face a welcome sight. He closed the door behind him.

'Excuse me for interrupting, sir. I think you may be interested in talking to Eroni Nemi, from the Props Department. He claims there was an attempt to sabotage the set for one of the challenges.'

Horseman and Singh looked at each other. Singh's eyes were wide with surprise.

'*Vinaka*, Apo. We've just listened to another story of pranks played on contestants. We definitely want to talk with Mr Nemi now. Well done.'

Kau blushed. '*Vinaka*, Here's his statement. I'll bring him in sir.'

Eroni Nemi was lean and wiry, with a bony face and prominent nose. His hair hung in tight black ringlets to his shoulders. He may have worn it long to hide his large protruding ears which nevertheless were visible through the strands of hair. Visible but camouflaged, so the tactic was successful.

Introductions made, Kau left the room and Nemi sat at the table opposite Horseman and Singh.

'Tell us a bit about your job here, Mr Nemi,' Horseman said.

'Sir, I love my job. It's my first season on Champion, but I hope not my last. The Art Department took me on as standby props man. That means I'm on set during filming, moving props around and tweaking them if the director changes his mind about what he wants.'

'Does that happen often?' Singh asked.

Nemi clicked his tongue. 'Often, ma'am. The props master promoted me. After all, I'm a qualified carpenter. My boss gets plans from the art director for each challenge and we discuss them, sometimes decide on modifications before we start. It's a creative job too.'

'Do you ever work on Motu Island?' Singh asked.

'*Io*, several times. We set up the day before because Mr Duke likes the morning light.' His voice was high-pitched and pleasant when you got used to it.

'Tell us about the incident you suspect was sabotage, please.'

Again, Nemi clicked his tongue. Horseman guessed it must be a nervous habit.

'Not suspect, I know it was. It was a relay about ten days ago, maybe two weeks, the running sheets will tell you. Here at the base, in the arena. There were two sets of apparatus, side by side, one for each tribe. The players had to fetch slam balls, take them under a scramble net, run with them to a ladder, pass the balls to their partners, who climbed to the top, dropped the ball down a chute then descended by a zip-line. That player picked up the ball and ran back to the start, passed the ball to the next team player. Man, it was tough for most of them.'

Nemi was enjoying himself, glancing bright-eyed from one detective to the other. Horseman wished he'd get to the point, but knew it was better to allow a witness to tell his story in his own way.

Another tongue click. 'Man, what a good thing I checked everything again just before the shoot. A shackle on one zipline wasn't fastened properly. It would have given way as soon as the player stepped off the platform at the top of the ladder. He or she would have dropped to the ground and suffered a serious injury.'

'Are you sure the shackle was properly fixed on your first check?'

'*Io*, I'm sure. We not only examined all components, but two of us ran through the course ourselves. I actually descended on that zipline the afternoon before the challenge and landed safe and sound!'

'Who did you report your discovery to, Mr Nemi?' Singh asked,

'The props master, my immediate boss. That's Jack Owens. He's from the States. But I don't know if he took the matter any higher. It was like he hushed it up. He told me I'd done well, and we'd had a reminder to check, recheck and then check again, which is like his motto.'

'Do you know who tampered with the shackle?'

'No, but I've thought about it. Prayed about it too. But so far God hasn't revealed the scoundrel to me. But it can't have been a contestant.'

'Why not?'

'They hadn't left Motu Island for two days before that challenge.' There was a note of triumph in his voice.

'Have you heard talk of any other sabotage attempts, or pranks?'

'*Io*. I heard about Desi and the millipede.' He grinned and slapped his thigh. 'Man, that was funny. They're harmless creatures, as you know. And Mili and the bucket of water. Those two got frights, that's all. Not in the same league as the shackle.'

'I agree with you there, Mr Nemi.'

'Anyway, everyone thinks the contestants played those other pranks against each other. But as I said, a contestant couldn't have sabotaged the zip-line.'

'Who do you mean by *everyone*?'

Nemi shrugged. 'Who? The crew. Anyone I talk to, at least.'

'Including the contestants?'

'Mr Duke doesn't like crew and contestants mixing, so I don't. But I've overheard a few comments when I've been on Motu. Two of them wondering if it was one of the rival team or one of their own.'

'Do you know who perpetrated any of the pranks or sabotage.'

'No, only God knows.'

'And the perpetrators themselves,' Horseman said.

Eroni Nemi nodded slowly.

'Do you suspect anyone?'

'Everyone, sir.'

15

Steve Duke wore his fifty-three years well. His grey hair was cut fashionably short, like his designer-stubble beard. He stood tall and confident in his expensive casual clothes, holding his office door open wide.

'Good afternoon, detectives. I appreciate your courtesy in reporting to me first.' He didn't smile. He ushered them to the white plastic chairs.

'Good afternoon, Mr Duke.' Horseman did not encourage civilians he met on the job to use his first name, so preferred to use formal titles himself. Not only was it proper for the police to show respect to the public, but his official title and badge constituted the only authority he possessed, as Fiji Police detectives wore neither uniforms nor guns.

'Please call me Steve. Is the autopsy report completed yet?'

'Not yet. The pathologist briefed me this morning. The condition of Ken's body raised some questions that only a full analysis of tissue samples can answer. As it does everywhere, this analysis takes time and inevitably labs have a queue. However, Dr Young has classified the Johnson case as top priority and is following up with the lab manager.'

'Disappointing but not surprising. I had a tough call with Ken's dad, offered to make all the arrangements for Ken's repatriation back home. But Mr Johnson wants to see where Ken passed. Both he and Ken's Mom want to create their personal memories of the place where he pursued his dream. Mrs Johnson doesn't want to leave their two teenage girls at this time so Mr Johnson will come by himself. They're a family of modest means. The production company will pay any costs not covered by Champion's insurance policies. It's the least we can do. However, his visit is going to be very tough. How could it be any other way?'

'Yes, it will be difficult. We will also need to talk to Mr Johnson, so I'd be grateful if you could let me know his flight and accommodation details when you've made them. Probably email will be most convenient for you, but you're most welcome to phone as well.'

Horseman placed another card in front of the director. He may well have ripped the first one in half and flung it in the bin for all he knew. The director took the card and read it.

'Where does the name Horseman come from? Forgive me for getting personal, but you look Fijian.'

'Most of my ancestors are Fijian. Except for one, who was shipwrecked here in the early nineteenth century. He and a terrified horse were the only survivors. When the locals inspected their surprise bounty, the chief fell in love with the horse's beauty and desired the animal beyond all else. But Fijians had never seen an animal bigger than a pig, so were afraid to approach the creature. My ancestor soothed the horse and put on a riding display that convinced the chief to spare him from the cannibal ovens and give him a privileged position as his personal riding instructor, the *horse-man*. That title became his name, passed down to his descendants in the English style. Or perhaps he was American. We'll never know.'

The director was still, transfixed by the tale. After some moments, he thumped the table. 'Wow, what a story! Crying out to be on the screen!'

Singh smiled. 'It's quite a legend in Fiji.'

Their exchange seemed to have softened his attitude toward the police, so it didn't surprise Horseman when Duke offered to order hot or cold drinks. He glanced at Singh, before accepting with thanks.

'It's not my business, so don't feel obliged to answer, Mr Duke. But I'm curious about the future of the show. Of course, whatever happens will impact our investigation. Have you come to a decision yet?'

The director stiffened, then let this impertinence pass. 'The executives and I have thrashed out some alternatives, but all of them are distasteful. You will have noticed there's no shooting today, out of respect for Ken and to allow us all to process his sudden death. However, we need to decide on a plan for the show when we meet again this evening.'

An assistant wearing the Champion tee-shirt entered, with another close on her heels. They smiled and placed two trays on the table: one with a glass jug of tea tinkling with ice, lemon slices and tall glasses; the other with a plunger of aromatic hot coffee, mugs, sugar sachets and a jug of milk. Another mug held four red hibiscus flowers. They smiled again and left. Horseman and Singh eyed the trays.

'Why not have both?' Duke asked. 'That's what I'm going to do. A cold glass of lemon tea followed by hot coffee. You two up for that?'

'Yes, please,' Singh replied with a smile.

The director served them with a friendly smile and Horseman saw a hint of the charm that must be mandatory for a producer-director to solicit finance, organise staff and locations for the production including the myriad formalities and permissions he imagined the Fiji government required.

'Now it's my turn, Inspector. I have a question you may choose not to answer.'

'Fair enough. Go ahead.' He sipped the iced tea, which was the best he'd tasted.

'You mentioned the condition of Ken's body raised questions. Can you be specific?'

'Yes, I can. The most critical were fine incisions on his lower legs, most likely made by fishing line. They indicate Ken probably ran into a tripline stretched across the steps to the spirit-house. He fell onto rock and was knocked unconscious. This means both Dr Young and ourselves need to conduct a more detailed investigation.'

The director blanched beneath his tan. He carefully lowered his tea glass to the table, staring at them. 'I see,' he said, after a long silence.

Horseman looked at Singh.

'Mr Duke, we've discovered only this morning that there have been several incidents which some of your crew have called *pranks* or *dirty tricks*. All these so-called pranks could have been the work of one person or more. It's interesting that none of the staff mentioned them in their statements yesterday. We interviewed all four finalists yesterday and not one of them mentioned these incidents, even though two of them were victims. I find it strange that not a single person connected Ken's head injury with these pranks. What do you think is going on here?'

The director propped his elbows on the table and buried his head in his hands. Horseman signalled to Singh that they should wait. They both finished their tea and returned their glasses to the tray. Horseman took time and care over pouring three mugs of coffee, leaving plenty of space for milk. He placed one mug in front of each of them. He waited for half a minute, then spoke.

'Coffee, Mr Duke?'

The director dragged his head off his hands like it was a ball of lead. He gulped down the rest of his tea.

'Yes, thanks.' Duke helped himself to milk and stirred the coffee slowly.

'I knew about the pranks. I hoped we could keep that knowledge within the family, as it were. I asked the department managers to be vigilant but to ask their teams not to gossip. Most people believed the culprit was a contestant, especially as all the incidents occurred on Motu.'

'Except for the sabotage attempt on a zip-line apparatus here on base camp,' Singh said.

'What? I didn't hear about that!' Duke's annoyed surprise sounded genuine.

'Our informant claimed on the morning of a challenge he found a shackle which had been tampered with. He reported it to the props master and he fixed the problem. Naturally, we can't vouch for the truth of his statement.'

Duke wrote a note. 'I'll check. What was the date?'

'He estimated ten days to two weeks ago.'

'That's easily checked. We don't use zip-lines every day.'

'Getting back to the pranks, have you any suspects in mind?' Singh asked.

The director seemed to consider his answer while he drank his coffee. 'The executives have speculated, but there's not a shred of evidence against anyone. Not a single person has admitted seeing anything suspicious at the relevant times.'

'Why didn't you report these incidents to the police?' Singh asked, a puzzled look on her face.

'We didn't think they were serious enough and also we didn't want to feed our problems to the media machine.'

'I think Ken Johnson's death is probably linked to the pranks. Whoever set that tripline is guilty of sabotage, a serious crime. Steve, this is no time to be suppressing embarrassing information. I appeal to you to be open with us. Please share your suspicions and any rumours you hear so we can find out the truth about what happened to Ken Johnson. We'll stop now, but if we don't hear from you, we'll be back tomorrow.'

'I'll help any way I can, detectives.'

'It would be good to know the truth before Ken's father arrives, wouldn't it? The worst thing for a parent would be not knowing how their child died.'

16

Horseman met his team back at their office on the first floor of Suva Central Police Station. This was the first review of the Ken Johnson investigation, maybe a little early for a full-blown case review after only two days and the postmortem findings incomplete. Still, they'd hardly been in the office for those two days. It was time to stop running around and pull the complex threads of Ken's story together and make some sense of them. *Io*, time for some calm analysis.

Kau and Lili cleared the DC's table and set out the big aluminium teapot, milk, sugar, and cups with saucers. Singh prepared the whiteboard with publicity headshots supplied by Champion's ever-helpful Deepika. Horseman joined her, writing names under the photos.

'This makes a change, sir. I mean, such a glamorous lot of suspects!'

Singh's enthusiastic smile was infectious. She clearly relished the nitty-gritty detective methods of recording, categorising, noticing connections and patterns between disparate data items. Activities some investigators found tedious energised her.

As she taped the director's photo to the board, she said, 'I was a bit surprised you were so open with Steve Duke, sir.'

'I wanted to challenge his secretiveness. By letting him know how much we'd found out already, I thought we might provoke him to share more knowledge. And we can safely exclude him as a suspect. There's no way he can benefit from the death of a contestant; Ken's accident will probably put an end to this series and God only knows how much money he and other investors will lose. The whole Champion enterprise may fail. No, Ken's death is a disaster for Duke.'

'You're right, of course. I hadn't thought of it from the financial viewpoint. Do you believe he knew nothing about the zip-line incident?'

'I do. He acted like he'd been slapped in the face. He was annoyed that he didn't know about every single happening on the set. I guess it's no surprise that a director wants to be in control.'

Thumps on the stairs preceded Musudroka's arrival with a stack of pizza boxes. Kau brought five plates to the table. Horseman and Singh joined the juniors.

'Let's start right away. Pizzas and tea are best when hot. While you help yourselves, I want to say *vinaka* for your fine work yesterday and today. It's a strange new world we've entered out at the Bay of Islands, particularly for me. But I'm not too old to learn and I've learned more than I really want to know already.' Horseman paused until the general laughter and a jeer from Musudroka subsided.

'I'm going to summarise how much we've done so far. Quickly, because I can't trust Tani to leave me a slice of ham-and-pineapple. Yesterday we questioned all the finalists, the boatman and the nurse. You held a staff meeting and collected sixty-eight written statements which we've sorted and followed up with individual interviews. Lili and Deepika from Champion's Personnel office sleuthed out any staff who weren't on set yesterday or missed the meeting. Lili contacted all but one and interviewed them by phone. Have you got their statements, Lili?'

'*Io*, sir. They didn't report any extra information on Ken Johnson, but I'm satisfied all crew on set on Saturday have responded. Except one. I'll keep trying her.'

'Great work. You've been asking questions the entire day and found some nuggets. Our colleagues the SOCOs have also completed their search of Motu and the arena. Now I'm going to sit and eat your leavings while DS Singh provides you with food for thought.'

Smiles all around meant the team was happy. Was it the food or praise? Probably both and he was glad.

Singh wheeled the whiteboard closer to the table. 'The value of our statement forms dropped when Zakaraia the boatman told DI Horseman about a series of what he called pranks against contestants. Have all of you heard about these now?'

The junior detectives nodded and grinned. Singh went on. 'The crew and even the director tolerated them and assumed one or more of the players were responsible. But there was another sabotage incident of a zipline apparatus at the arena set. If the standby props guy hadn't picked this up and fixed it, a player may have been seriously injured. Mr Duke said no one reported this incident to him. His own order that contestants and crew shouldn't divulge the pranks to any outsider may be the reason for this. Fortunately, Zakaraia and two other crew interviewed today saw no need for secrecy. When we confronted Mr Duke with their reports, he caved in. I'll ask DI Horseman to tell you some news from the postmortem you haven't heard yet.'

'*Vinaka* for my first course. What I'm going to say is critical. On Monday I found a piece of nylon fishing line near the steps to the spirit-house mound on Motu. I suspected a tripline on the steps which caused Ken to fall. Of course, I handed it over to Ash. This morning, Dr Young called me to the morgue to show me fine cuts on Ken's lower legs, consistent with fishing line. I reported all this to Detective Superintendent Ratini an hour ago, and the upshot is that Ken's death is now classified as suspicious. However, this information is restricted to us five. I mean this. No sharing with other officers and certainly not with anyone on the Champion set or your own families and friends. Questions?'

His face earnest, Kau raised his hand. 'How can we know if the same troublemaker is responsible for all these incidents, sir?'

'We can't at the moment. But I'm convinced there are at least a few people on the large Champion staff who know what's going on. And not just the perpetrators. Always be sympathetic to potential witnesses who are probably in shock and scared. Appeal to their consciences. Expect them to do the right thing and they often will.'

'How, sir?' Worry lines deepened between Kau's eyebrows.

'Here's an example. DS Singh and I appealed to Mr Duke's better nature this afternoon, and he was more helpful afterwards. Talking with Ken's father has also influenced Mr Duke. Mr Johnson's anxious to see where his son worked and died and he'll travel here as soon as possible.'

'Now, our program for tomorrow. I'm hoping the postmortem blood and tissue analysis will come through, but there's no guarantee. Because we have no other leads, we'll proceed on the theory that the pranks, the set sabotage and the hypothetical tripline were the work of one person. The incidents were clearly escalating in the level of malice and risk to the victim. If I'm right, whoever set up the tripline on the spirit-house steps could be charged with manslaughter at least. Whether this was a prank gone wrong or something quite different is the question.'

'DS Singh, please make sure Apo and Lili know how to compile the case file correctly before you go home. That will be their job in the morning. The large number of statements make it a demanding task.'

'Yes, sir.'

'DS Singh, I want you to take Tani Musudroka to the Champion set. Top priority is in-depth interviews with all four finalists, none of whom mentioned the pranks yesterday. Why? Both Mili and Desirée were victims! Confront them with the pranks some of the crew described and see what you can get out of them. Follow up with any leads they may give you. I'll join you when I can, but I expect and hope both Dr Young and Ash will want to speak to me.'

'Yes, sir.'

'If we can make as much progress as we did today, we'll do well. Go home and get some rest after you update your notebooks and diaries. I'll be here for another hour if you have questions or if you happen to solve this case!'

17

With the junior detectives settled to their paperwork under Singh's active supervision, he got on with his own. He wanted to ring Matt and Ash, but rejected the idea. Where was the sense in interrupting either their work or well-earned leisure? They both knew he was hanging out for their results and would inform him right away.

After filling in his notebook and diary, he transferred his actions to the case running sheet. This was much easier now they used customised software. Superintendent Ratini insisted they printed the running sheet out every day and filed in an A3 binder. Horseman agreed with Ratini on this; the result was a more legible running sheet which sat on a small table, accessible to all officers, whether or not there was an available computer.

His mobile phone rang. 'Joe, if it's alright with you, I'd like to suggest we meet for dinner this evening, rather than after dinner. If you can make it, that is.' For a doctor, Kaviraj Pillai often came across as unusually tentative.

'Sure, Dr Pillai. Where?'

'I know you're a connoisseur of Indian cuisine, but I bet you don't know about this place.'

'Really? I thought I knew them all. Where is it?'

'Hibiscus Street in Raiwaqa. Second on the right.'

'Intriguing. I'm afraid I can't get there before seven-thirty and could be later. Will that be a problem?'

'Not at all, Joe. I'll be waiting for you. By the way, this place is very casual.'

He clicked Send after attaching his report for Ratini to an email. Why did everything take longer than he estimated?

Feeling refreshed after a shower and change of clothes, Horseman hailed a passing cab which deposited him outside what looked like an average modern suburban house, rendered in yellow stucco, and lit by external spotlights. There was no restaurant sign. He looked around, but the cab had driven away. Well, he'd better check before calling Dr Pillai. Colourful clipped crotons bordered the emerald front lawn. A concrete path curved around a young frangipani tree. He inhaled the sweet scent of its flowers with relish.

'Welcome Joe!' He looked up and saw Dr Pillai standing on the side porch, his face cut in two by a huge smile. 'Come in!'

Horseman didn't get it. 'Is this a new restaurant?'

'No, but as I said, it serves the best Indian cuisine in Suva.' He opened the door and called, 'Come, Shanti!'

A woman's voice yelled unintelligibly. 'Oh, she's too busy to leave the kitchen right now, so come in, come in. Welcome to my home, Joe. Here you will find the best curry in the city!'

Horseman couldn't utter a word for some moments. His mouth hung open as he went up the porch steps. As he grasped Dr Pillai's hand, he blurted out, 'You got me going there! I'm overwhelmed! *Vinaka vakalevu*, Raj!'

Actually, he was a bit ashamed—he'd known Dr Pillai for eighteen months but didn't know where he lived, whether he was married. Not a thing beyond the fact that he was a doctor. Yet somehow, they had become friends. There was a lesson for him there; maybe he'd work it out later.

'We'll just say a quick hello to Shanti. She hates being interrupted when she's cooking. She's got her sister working with her so anyone else is superfluous. Especially me.' He dipped his head in proud embarrassment. Horseman, much taller, again wondered at the density of the doctor's shock of coarse black hair which sprang upright from his scalp.

Horseman followed his host and the enticing aroma past a comfortable living room to the kitchen at the back of the house. The smell strengthened from enticing to mouth-watering. Two women worked amid pots on a gas stove and a clutter of electrical appliances. Their focus was intense, but they looked up, smiled, and nodded to Horseman when he stood in the doorway.

'Our chefs are Shanti, my wife and her sister, Vera. We'll go to the living room now. My brother-in-law's keeping an eye on the children.'

A man with gold-rimmed glasses was sitting cross-legged on a large Indian rug, playing a card game with three children. At least he tried to do so, while a toddler sat in his lap and grabbed at his cards. 'You three look after Sami now,' he said to the older ones, ignoring their protests as he sprang to his feet.

'This is my brother-in-law, Shiv Narayan. He's the lawyer I told you about.'

'It's an honour to meet you, Joe. Naturally, Raj has filled me in on your project. I've done some work with charities, so I'd be delighted to answer any questions you have about the legal pros and cons. After dinner of course.'

'That's very generous. *Vinaka*, Shiv.'

'And these scallywags here are our offspring. The two boys are mine and the two girls belong to Shanti and Raj. Don't worry, they've already eaten. They won't be joining us at the table for dinner.'

Four pairs of enormous black eyes glared at Shiv, who fell to the floor clutching at his heart. A gleeful toddler jumped on him and an older boy shouted something in Hindi. Shiv rolled around a bit, then hauled himself to his feet.

'Roughly translated, he said "Stupid Daddy".' Dr Pillai chuckled.

'What's this, encouraging the children to be rude, Shiv?' Shanti appeared and placed a brass platter of dainty savoury pastries on a low table. Vera followed with a tray of drinks. She pulled a small table away from the wall, placed four plastic bowls on top and, stern of face, directed the children to pull up cushions and sit. Each bowl held a variety of pastries and triangular sandwiches. Shanti came back with glasses of milk and placed one beside each bowl.

'Please show Mr Horseman that we have taught you table manners, children. You ate two hours ago so you should enjoy supper.'

The three older children murmured their thanks, briefly brought their hands together and tucked in.

'Come sit with us, at least for a bit, ladies. You deserve a break. What will Joe think of us?'

Shanti and Vera sat down with reluctance but relaxed a bit as guests passed drinks and food around the table. Horseman felt bad about delaying the meal; Shanti and Vera looked tired. They had probably been preparing food since early morning. It wasn't long before the savouries disappeared.

'Raj, please can you finish setting the dining table? We'll bring the food in five minutes.'

Shiv jumped up. 'Let me help carry the dishes, my dears.'

'Why don't you set up the DVD? They can watch *Happy Feet* while we eat. They'll probably fall asleep in half an hour.' Shanti yawned.

'Right away. It's a school day tomorrow, but occasionally we must break the routine.'

As Horseman expected, the meal was a feast for the eyes and nose as well as the taste buds. His instinct was to pig out, but he forced himself to resist the entreaties of his hosts and accept only a modest quantity of each dish. That still added up to a heavy meal: dosas, paneer, curries, sambals, chutneys, pickles and tandoori-baked chicken and bread. Shiv and Dr Pillai cleared away the remains. More than satisfied, all five relaxed over their bowls of thin dahl.

'I know you three have business to discuss, so don't go to sleep at the table, boys.' Shanti's voice was brisk. 'I'll bring your tea to the lounge room.'

She wanted them gone and who could blame her? Horseman wouldn't hold them up by trying to help. He knew they would refuse any offer.

'*Vinaka vakalevu*, Shanti and Vera. I've never had a better meal in my life. When Raj invited me to the best Indian restaurant in Suva, I had no idea I would be invading your home and putting you to so much trouble. But his assessment was correct. I'll be keeping the secret of the best restaurant to myself, however.'

'It's been an honour, Joe,' Shanti said. 'Cooking is a joy for Vera and me. Especially for such an appreciative guest. Please come again whenever you like. Raj tells me you're not far away.' The ladies bobbed a brief *namaste* and started stacking the remaining dishes on trays.

Horseman moved into the lounge room to find all four children asleep and looking angelic. Their fathers switched off the TV, picked them up and carried them out. At a knock on the door, Shanti rushed to let in four teenagers who disappeared with her.

'Some nieces and nephews who live down the street,' Dr Pillai explained. 'They've come to do the washing up and clean the kitchen. Joe, don't worry about Shanti and Vera, they've got enough help.'

Shiv produced a briefcase and pulled out documents. 'I've made copies for you, Joe.' He selected some and put them in front of Horseman. 'But first, tell me more about your idea to set up a hostel for your Shiners rugby team.'

'I want these boys to have a safe roof over their heads. Basic, but a home. Some are orphans. The majority are runaways or were kicked out of home or village for bad behaviour. Others live with relatives under sufferance in crowded conditions. None have ever gone to high school, and some have only a few years of primary school, so can barely read and write. Dr Pillai can tell you about the health of these boys.'

'Yes, he's filled me in.'

'One boy got bashed up last year and admitted to hospital. Father Francis took him in as an emergency on his discharge, got him into an adult literacy program and the change has been miraculous. In a way, the boy was lucky to be beaten up.'

'Is the Franciscan hostel a model you would like to follow?'

'In some ways. Father Francis only accepts boys who enrol in a formal training or education program and stick at it. He works hard at finding the right programs for individuals. I want to do that as well. Last November I discovered the Sunshine Home which I'm sure you know. The matron and other women on the staff created a more homey, maternal atmosphere which impressed me. Although the hostel Dr Pillai and I envisage would be only for boys, I'd like to have a live-in woman manager who would be more like a housemother.'

Dr Pillai nodded vigorously.

'Your hostel as you describe it would definitely qualify as a charity. I understand from Raj you're reluctant to get involved with red tape and lengthy legal processes. That's entirely your choice. However, I'll just summarise the pros and cons of making your hostel a legal non-profit entity. That should motivate you to read the documents I've given you in full.'

A teenager sidled in and awkwardly placed a tray of *chai* glasses on the low table. The subtle scent of the spiced tea was soothing.

'Go ahead, please Shiv.'

'It's not too hard to register as a charitable trust under Fijian law. I recommend you use a lawyer to guide you in the process and draw up a trust deed. This would specify the objectives and powers of the trust, the eligibility of trustees and how they are appointed. Not much more than that. If your documents are complete and correct, the process should take no longer than a month, or two at the most.'

'That's good to hear. But wouldn't it be even simpler if I paid the deposit for a suitable property myself, which I think I can afford? Raj here has also promised a generous contribution.'

'That's a terrible idea, Joe! You could easily be bankrupted before the hostel started operating. What if Raj loses his money overnight? What if you, God forbid, should die? Wouldn't you want the hostel to continue?'

That was a shock. The meetings with the advisors at Action for Children hadn't put it so bluntly. He looked at Dr Pillai.

'Once you've satisfied the requirements, your charitable trust would own any property and be liable for debts. The charity, not you, Joe. This is extremely important.'

'You're intimidating me now.'

'No need. Well-meaning individuals like yourself need protecting. The trust doesn't depend on individuals to continue. It has an existence of its own in law, and can employ people, hold bank accounts, insurance policies. Your charity would also qualify for exemption from tax.'

'You've persuaded me to take this idea further, Shiv. What are your thoughts, Joe?' Dr Pillai said.

'You mentioned cons, Shiv?' Horseman prompted.

'Sure, there's no avoiding the red tape, legal and government fees and so on. More than this, it takes time to select and appoint trustees and learn new ways of doing things. Your lawyer can help with all this. To me, these are nothing compared to the grave risks your registered charitable trust will protect Josefa Horseman from.'

'Yes, it makes sense. But I'd better read this pile you've given me, including the fine print.'

'Another pro is that a registered charity is much better able to solicit donations. People trust a charity more than an individual with their money. Even if you don't plan to do this now, your ambitions for the hostel may grow. You might want to establish another hostel in Lautoka, for example.' He looked up, embarrassed. 'Forgive me, Joe, for speculating about your means—none of my business. But a charity must file publicly available accounts annually with the Registrar of Titles. That adds a lot to the public's trust.'

Dr Pillai finished his chai. 'That's a relevant point, Shiv. We should look to the future, to an extent anyway.'

Horseman nodded. Why did his mind resist Shiv's good arguments? Perhaps it was because he hadn't thought of all this himself.

'I fear I'm expressing my opinions too frankly, Joe. Relaxing after a good meal in my in-laws' home will do that. I'd be more circumspect if you'd approached me as a client in the office.'

'Not at all, I appreciate your frankness.'

'However, I'm being objective. This hostel could be your legacy, Joe, just as much as your rugby achievements. If you take the time to set it up right at the start, that's much more likely.'

'I can't thank you enough, Shiv and Raj. The best food for body and mind! I think I'll walk home to aid my digestion of both. I'll say my goodbyes to Shanti and Vera and get going. I'll be in touch soon. Thursday training, Raj?'

'I'll be there, Joe.'

WEDNESDAY

18

The next morning at nine o'clock he was alone in the detectives' office. The others had left for the Champion base to interview the finalists again, this time in greater depth. He still didn't understand why they had all failed to mention the prank incidents on Monday afternoon. There had to be a stronger reason than Duke's order to keep quiet about them, surely.

His emails to Dr Young and Ash Jayaraman at the SOCO lab remained unanswered. Again, his fingers were itching to call them, but again he resisted. Phoning them couldn't hurry the analysis of physical evidence. He reviewed the running sheet binder. As he expected, the print-out was up-to-date and correct. He expected no less, with Singh supervising the DCs. The case file was last in line for his scrutiny and again, it was complete.

He went to the kitchenette to make a cup of tea, then stopped himself. Ridiculous to pace up and down like a caged animal when he was free to go where he chose. He chose the SOCO lab first, followed by the pathology lab. Taking a personal interest in his colleagues' work would not irritate them as much as a ringing phone. He'd buy fresh doughnuts from a street vendor to sweeten his welcome.

Ash laughed when Horseman handed him the large bulging paper bag, but it was a cheerful laugh. 'Blatant bribery,' he said. 'Always works, doesn't it?'

'Not at all, a reward for your hard work. There's enough for everyone, I think.'

Ash called a break. The lab had to be kept pristine, so the SO-COs took their breaks in a separate room or outside. A technician brought tea to Ash's cramped office.

'Not much for you yet, sir. And I can't promise there's going to be much more later. The fishing line sample you collected from the spirit-house mound exactly matches the one from the players' hut. But miles of this stuff is sold every day all over the country—we'd be wasting time attempting to trace the source of each sample. And what would it tell you if we did? Nothing.' Ash looked as frustrated as Horseman felt.

'*Io*, you're right.'

Ash continued. 'All the blood samples are from the victim. We haven't taken fingerprints. All the players and at least ten crew would have left their fingerprints all over the place.'

'True. All the eliminated contestants' prints could be there too. I understand they've left the country so we couldn't identify them. Oh, one thing. Dr Young sent over grit samples from Ken's wound. Do they match what you took at the scene?'

'Gosh, that's critical, isn't it? I overlooked it!' He glanced at the boxes of evidence bags on the bench. 'We'll pull them out and start examining them now, sir.'

'Vinaka, Ash. I'll leave you to it. I'm off to see if Matt's got anywhere chasing up the toxicology lab results. Call me about the grit, please.'

It would only take him ten more minutes to walk further up the hill to the hospital and he needed the exercise. The flowering rain trees interlaced over the middle of the road, shading walkers from the fierce sun. He enjoyed the stroll until his mobile vibrated in his pocket. It was the call he'd been waiting for.

'Matt, great to hear from you. Just heading your way. Got some news for me?'

'Yeah, you'll be interested in the tox screen results. The victim tested positive for MDMA.'

'What? That's ecstasy, isn't it?'

'Yeah, aka molly. So-called party drug, bloody dangerous. It's an amphetamine.'

'Unexpected. I thought the players were in total quarantine there. Anything else I should know?'

'Nothing significant. Pretty normal in fact.'

'Did the drug contribute to his death?'

'Hard to say. I found his organs in good health, so I'm inclined to say no. If he'd been a long-term user, I'd expect to see changes in his heart and maybe other organs.'

'Have you decided what you're going to put under cause of death yet?'

'Ha, ha. I'm going to look at the organs again, especially the brain.'

'You've just handed me a tool to prise open the secret world of Champion. If you can tell me whether he fell or was struck with a rock, I'll buy you a Fiji Bitter after work.'

'You owe me more than one! You'll know as soon as I do.'

19

After contacting Singh and Steve Duke, Horseman set off for the Champion site. When he turned onto the road to the historic gun emplacement, he pulled to the side and got out to stretch. The loveliness of the bay below and the dark sea beyond the reef hit him afresh. The emerald islands, fringed with white sand and black rocks, refracted the light like gems. For him, this was all the high he needed. Why would anyone seek more with lethal chemicals? But millions did, and he had to accept that fact.

Another motive for the MDMA popped into his head. The drug suppressed the appetite; could that be why a Champion player might swallow such a dangerous little pill? The Champion contestants were given only a small ration of rice, and the coconut palms, breadfruit trees, and gleanings from the shore at low tide would certainly prevent malnutrition. But probably not hunger.

He met Singh with DC Apo Kau at their interview room, now furnished with everything needed for making tea and coffee on an extra folding table.

Singh saw his approving look. 'I brought the kettle, the rest is courtesy of Champion, sir.'

'*Vinaka*, DS Singh. Very thoughtful of you.' He opened his backpack, extracted a file and a packet of Paradise coconut biscuits. 'Steve Duke is expecting us in half an hour, so let's have a cuppa while I fill you in on the latest from the lab.'

Kau filled the kettle with bottled water and took their orders while it heated. They sat in silence with their tea, all three digesting the MDMA bombshell that might blow apart Ken Johnson's death. Or not.

'Who have you talked to so far?'

'Duane. He admitted the pranks happened but denied knowing anything more and was adamant that he wasn't responsible. Said he suspected a contestant who's now been eliminated.'

'I got the impression he was fobbing us off there, sir,' Kau said. 'Just giving us something uncheckable.'

Kau was usually reluctant to chip in, so this show of growing confidence pleased Horseman. Maybe he just couldn't get a word in when Musudroka was around. 'Do the dates fit?'

'All except the last prank, sir. By then, the player Duane named was off the set.'

Singh put down her mug. 'Musudroka and Lili are questioning Bobby.'

'Check if they're finished, Apo. They can both join you here to interview Mili while DS Singh and I visit Steve Duke. But we've got ten minutes, so let's finish our tea while we plan how to present the director with our latest news.'

***

The director looked older than he had yesterday. He reached for his bottle of water, clutching it in his hands. For security? A physical object within his control? Or maybe just to cool himself down.

'MDMA? There must be some mistake! In the States, labs get samples mixed up all the time—that sort of thing's often on the news. I imagine your labs here would stuff up even more often—tropical climate, less control ... The Fiji way, hey! I insist on another test before I'll even consider this possibility. Drugs on the set! Champion has a zero-tolerance policy on drugs.'

'I agree we should eliminate any doubt, Mr Duke. I'll arrange a second test with Dr Young right now if you'll excuse me.' He pulled out his mobile phone and went out to the verandah.

He returned to hear Singh say in a sympathetic voice, 'It's a shock, isn't it? We didn't expect this result either.'

'Dr Young has a worldwide reputation, Mr Duke. He's undertaken to supervise the second toxicology screen personally.'

'Hmm, sure, thanks,' he muttered.

'Ken's parents would want no less, don't you think?' Singh asked.

Duke's brow furrowed with anxiety. 'Do they have to know?'

'Not at this stage. They have a legal right to the final postmortem report, but that's delayed again now.'

'If the MDMA result is true, it will make everything worse for them. For me, too. Ken was the least likely player to take drugs.'

'Who is more likely?'

'What? Anyone, but dammit, there are no drugs here. All contestants are screened on arrival and the rules are clear—instant dismissal if drugs are found. That applies to cast and crew. No exceptions.'

'Mr Duke, we know that's true. But drug takers, and indeed, drug suppliers, believe they will never be discovered. We know this from experience. Don't you?'

Singh was so encouraging Horseman wondered how anyone could resist confiding in her.

'Guess so. We kicked out three players from previous shoots. That's in an eight-year period. Not one in Fiji though.'

'And really, it wouldn't be hard to keep some little pills secret, would it?'

The director shrugged. 'We do everything we can to keep Champion free of drugs.'

'I'm sure you do. You're not to blame,' Singh assured him.

Horseman continued. 'Steve, there are three possibilities. One: Ken Johnson brought the MDMA pills to the island and took them for an unknown reason. You don't believe that, right?'

'No, that's not the Ken I knew.'

'Okay. Two: Ken got the pills on set, supplied by a cast or crew member. Again, for an unknown reason.'

Duke shook his head. 'I don't think so. But I guess it's possible.'

'Three: someone on Champion made Ken take a pill involuntarily, by crushing it up and mixing it into his food, for example.'

The director brightened a little at this. 'That theory fits better with the Ken we all knew. But there's a fourth scenario you haven't mentioned, Inspector. Your test results are false, due to a lab mistake.'

'We'll be able to rule that one in or out tomorrow.'

Now was the time for Horseman to make his pitch. 'Steve, you're dedicated to Champion. We need your help to resolve Ken's death for his family. If you're right, someone here supplied Ken with MDMA, with or without his consent. No one knows the contestants and crew better than you. Please think carefully. Who could have done this?'

'I don't know, dammit. Did the drug kill Ken?'

'The pathologist's doing more work today to settle that question. But at the least, the supplier committed a serious assault, and at worst, murder.'

'Take your time and think it through, sir,' Singh said with an encouraging smile. 'Maybe try a process of elimination. You'll most likely remember something a person did or said that didn't arouse suspicion at the time.'

Duke ran his hands over his short hair. 'And what do I do then?'

'Call us. Do nothing more.'

Duke looked from one to the other. 'You know, both of you would make great contestants.'

Horseman smiled at Singh. 'From what I've learned so far, I'm not sure that's praise,'

'Sure, it's high praise,' the director replied. 'I'll try to help but right now, my head's all over the place.'

'We're wondering how many others at Champion are taking drugs,' Singh said. 'Aren't you?'

'No, I've told you. The location is a drug-free zone. If Ken's second test is positive, which I doubt, then it was a one-off incident.'

'I hope so. Nevertheless, we need facts to understand Ken's death, not just opinions. Dr Young has kindly agreed to supply testing kits for Champion cast and crew, along with an assistant to help your nurse with the sample collection.'

The director's mouth widened in horror. 'You can't do that!'

'Sorry? You said you screen all players and employees for drugs before they start here.'

'And you said if anyone is found to be taking drugs, it's instant dismissal,' Singh added, with a puzzled frown.

'We've produced evidence of drug-taking here, possibly resulting in death. I assumed you would want to screen everyone again without delay.'

'We just want to help. We thought you did, too,' Singh added.

The director looked from one to the other, bewildered. 'Of course I do. But it's like you cops are taking over here. What's the justification? We wait until the results of the second screen on Ken. Champion is my show and I decide what happens on set!' He brought his water bottle down for emphasis but stopped himself before it thumped the table.

20

'For a minute I thought he was going to go along with us. Then he got spooked and I lost him.' Horseman said.

'Nice try, sir. The drug testing proposal made him shy away.' Singh was always diplomatic.

'You expertly softened him up and I blew it, you mean. And now everyone's got a minimum of one day's warning, maybe more.'

'Should we ask Desi about drug taking on set or are we keeping quiet about it?'

'We can ask her what she knows but we'll keep Ken's MDMA result to ourselves. That applies to all Champion interviews. Desirée strikes me as a gossip. I'm hopeful.'

His plan for the afternoon was for Musudroka and Kau to speak again with the crew who worked directly with the players on Motu Island or at the arena challenges back at base. They would also fish for any anecdotes about drug-taking. Lili Waqa would wrangle the selected crew and files. Once the interview with Desi was over, she would escort interviewees between the two offices so that no time was wasted. The plan should work.

***

Desirée Lopez was not amused. After taking her seat with grace, she frowned at Singh and pouted at Horseman. He tried not to laugh, reminding himself this strange woman may well have much more to tell him.

'It's good to see you again, Desi. How are you getting on after the shock of Ken's death?'

'Not well, Inspector. Now I'm post-trauma, just a jangle of nerves and a roller-coaster of emotions. I hadn't processed the news on Monday, but I told you everything I know. It was me who radioed Barbara to come help Ken. I'm here now under protest. Why have you hauled me back to grill me again?'

'I'm sorry, sudden deaths always hit the living hard. You just said it yourself. When you've witnessed such an event, you rarely recall all the details until later. I'm grateful for your previous help. Now we need to check some new information with all the finalists.'

Desi shrugged her strong-looking shoulders and pouted some more. Was Singh right about the Botox? 'Alright, I guess.'

'Yesterday we heard about a series of pranks played on contestants, including one on yourself. I'm sure you remember that now.'

'Oh yeah—holy moly, I clean forgot to mention the pranks. I nearly died of fright when that monster bug crawled onto me. Ugh-gross, gross, gross! But does that have anything to do with Ken's death?'

'We have no idea. We need your help.'

'Wait a minute! You—you're not saying that Ken did that?'

'We don't know. Do you think he could have been the prankster?'

To her credit, Desi gave this question some thought. 'Dunno, but nah, it's not him. He was too boring and unimaginative.'

'Do you know who played these pranks?'

'No. I wish I did.'

'You must have your suspicions though. If Ken was too unimaginative, who had the right personality?'

'I suspected a couple players, but they're eliminated now. I never assumed the same person played all the pranks, though. After the first one, the others could have been copy-cats.'

'Have you got any likely suspects for me now?'

'I did just wonder about the millipede ... well, Mili's Fijian, knows about them, knows they're harmless, may have played with them as a child. It would be a breeze for her to find my camp. With her natural stealth, she could pull it off. Mili may be soft-spoken, but she's su-per-competitive. She'd have to be, to be runner-up on The Voice. I'm a threat to her, but she's no threat to me. So, she'd have a motive to spook me. But I don't know whether she played any or all those pranks.'

'Could any of the crew have been the culprit?'

'I guess. Everyone assumed the perp was a contestant. But several crew knew Motu inside out. Now the bucket on top of the bathroom door—that one had to be set up at night, but it wouldn't be that hard to paddle across quietly in a canoe. As for motive, that's a bit trickier.'

Beneath the glamour-bimbo persona, Desi had a cool head on her shoulders.

'Did you hear about any pranks in the arena?'

'No ... oh, hang on, I heard talk of some apparatus failing in the stadium, a flying fox, I think. But the Props found it and fixed it. That's if I heard right. I paid little attention to that because they test the rig before each challenge. I trust the rigging crew. Hundred per cent.'

'What about drugs? Do you know of anyone indulging in drugs on the set?'

'No, no way. If Steve found out, you'd be dead!'

He couldn't believe his ears. 'Really, Desi. Do you think Steve killed Ken Johnson, then?'

For the first time, she lost control. She slapped her head, quite hard. 'N-no, no, no! Why did I say that? You gotta believe me. Just a stupid way of speaking. I mean, Steve's obsessed about drugs, he hates them. Of course, I don't mean literally dead—I just mean sacked from Champion, kicked out, dead as far as the show was concerned.'

'I understand, Desi. Please calm down. Why are you so flustered?'

Singh leaned towards Desi. 'Are you frightened of Steve, Desi?'

Tears rolled down Desi's cheeks and she sobbed, her face in her hands. Singh grabbed a box of tissues and passed them to her.

'It's alright, Desi. We'll wait until you're ready to talk to us again. Try to have a sip of water.' Singh moved Desi's water close to her. Horseman shifted his chair back. He wouldn't speak until Desi spoke to him.

Time ticked slowly until Desi's sobs subsided, she dried her eyes, sipped some water, and looked at Singh. 'No, I'm not frightened of Steve. I'm just overstressed by all this, Ken's death and everything—the end of my dreams. Just when the game was going so well for me, or that's what I thought. Sorry I broke down—where that came from I don't have a clue.'

'That's quite alright, Desi. We can continue talking if you want to or stop for now and you can come back when you feel ready.'

Desi sniffed, took another tissue, and blew her nose. 'I'm ready now.'

She turned to Horseman. Her affected bimbo mask was off, and she came across as a sensible young woman.

'You were asking about drugs on the set. It's hard to know—no one confides in other people here, even if they really like them. Obviously, they don't want to lose their place in the show or their job. No player would trust another with a secret of any kind, let alone an admission of drug-taking, or an offer of drugs or a request for drugs. You'd give that person the power over whether you stayed in the game or were chucked out, and much more. What I mean is no one has confided in me, but I guess it goes on, probably only in private. Not for me. What's the use of party drugs if you can't party?'

'Some contestants could try to enhance their performance in the challenges with drugs,' Horseman said. 'Do you think that would drive players? After all, illegal drug use pervades sport and efforts to stamp it out are only partly successful.'

'It's quite possible. But as I said, no one's said anything to me about it and I've seen no one taking or handling drugs. But if it's pills, they would be a cinch to hide.'

'I agree. Thank you for talking to us. I'm sorry you were upset.'

'Don't forget to contact one of us if you think of something else that happened, Desi,' Singh added.

Desi gave them a weak smile, took her water bottle, and left.

'Did you buy all that melodrama, Singh?'

'Dunno, sir. When she broke down, her distress seemed real. She convinced me anyway. But after she recovered, I remembered she was an actor. I wonder.'

'Me too. She broke down when you asked her if she was scared of Steve Duke. There might be something in that to follow—'

The door was flung wide, and a man strode in, hand outstretched. Like Horseman, he was medium height, but his bulk, his full bushy beard and expansive movements made him look much bigger. An anxious Lili Waqa scurried in his wake. She puffed.

'Sorry sir, I couldn't keep up. This is Lui Tuvoli, your next interview.'

'*Vinaka*, Lili. No problem.'

Horseman stood and shook the man's still outstretched hand. A
powerful grip but the skin was smooth and soft.

'*Bula vinaka*, Josefa Horseman. It's an honour, sir. Wow, I never
thought to meet my hero here on the Champion set! Or anywhere, in
fact. I can't believe my good luck!' He let Horseman's hand go, spread
his arms wide to embrace the spartan room and repeated, 'Wow!'

Clearly Desi Lopez did not have the monopoly on melodrama on
set. Horseman introduced Singh and asked, 'What's your job here, Mr
Tuvoli?'

'*Oi lei*, now that's an interesting question! And no simple answer.
I'm not here all the time—I come and go. I'm a go-between—*the*
go-between, actually. A fixer.' He grinned.

'What do you fix, Mr Tuvoli?' Singh asked.

'Please call me Lui—both of you.' He glanced at Horseman. 'I
source whatever the film crew need and get it for them. From Fiji if
possible, but sometimes from overseas if the crew's contacts can't supply. That's unusual because the Champion executives have excellent
networks, as you'd expect.'

'What sort of items?'

He spread his hands wide. 'Anything and everything. That includes
equipment, props items, tools, and materials like paint and hardware. I
also find tradesmen who can do repairs, emergency or otherwise. And
so on.'

'That sounds very interesting. How did you get the job?'

'Aha, I sort of grew into it, or rather it grew around me and I made
it my own.' At their blank stares, he added, 'Do you know that one of
our government's conditions for foreign companies filming in Fiji is
that they provide Fijian students with work experience and informal
training? Such a good idea, isn't it?'

He beamed so engagingly that Horseman couldn't help responding
with a broad smile and nod. Singh seemed unimpressed.

'What's this got to do with me? That's what you're thinking,
Sergeant? I better get to the point, eh? I teach film and television
production at our Fiji Institute of Technology here in Suva. My own

background's in news photography. I've been teaching full-time for six or seven years now. Love it! The courses are practical and so I've kept up my network of contacts, expanded them actually, into sound, cinematography and more.

'To cut a long story short, FIT gave me the extra duty of liaising with Champion and placing our students with their crew as interns. As you can imagine, we'd like all of them to work here, but Mr Duke only wants a few, so they don't slow things down. But we've got a good relationship, so he's taken on more students than he wants but I haven't got as many placed as I want. It's either a lose-lose or a win-win. I choose to look at the result as a win-win.'

'Well done, Mr Tuvoli. How do the students get on here?'

'They tend to be overwhelmed at first, but each one's assigned to a crew mentor who shows them what to do. They soon gain confidence and love their jobs.'

'Have you ever been to the players' camp on Motu Island?'

'*Io*, I've been lucky. I've been there to visit our interns. Several are assistants in the Camera, Sound, and Props departments.'

'Do you go out there often?'

'Not really. I've been several times as our interns aren't all working out there at the same time. I check how they're doing in different contexts and roles. All part of their assessment for their practical work, which I discuss with their Champion mentor.'

'I see. And your fixer role?'

'Because I'm back and forth, checking on the students, crew started asking me how to get this and that in Suva. I'm a hospitable guy, I want to help our international guests. So I'd offer to find what they needed and offer to get it for them if they gave me the money upfront. It's now more formalised, so I'm part of the official procurement and purchase order process, which is smoother.'

'Even though you're here part-time, I suppose you hear some of the rumours and gossip flying around the set?'

Tuvoli laughed and brought his hands together in a resonant hollow-palmed clap. '*Io, io*, you said it! I reckon I hear more than some, because my students are working in so many departments: Camera, Art, Editing, Production, Post-Production, Visual Effects.'

'What's the drum on the future of the series after the death of Ken Johnson?'

The fixer's smile vanished. 'Some think it's the end, others believe Mr Duke and his executives will come up with a way to save it. We're all waiting for an announcement. In the meantime, my students are working with their mentors on shooting continuity scenes and in post-production.'

'What's post-production exactly, Mr Tuvoli?'

'Aha! That's what turns the pig's ear into a silk purse! The magic of editing! Editors assemble all those little scenes into a complete ep, with the aid of visual effects department, sound, and music too. All these guys are called technicians, but they're really magicians.'

'Did you say *ep*?' Singh asked.

'*Io, ep* as we say in the trade, or *episode* to you.' He chuckled.

Horseman resented the cheap shot at Singh but admired the fixer's enthusiasm. He was probably a good teacher.

'What have you heard about the pranks against the players?' Singh asked.

Tuvoli's eyes became wary. '*Oi lei*, silly ploys to unnerve stressed contestants! I've heard plenty but nothing to convince me that any particular player is guilty. All speculation. How can anyone but the guilty know if they were all committed by the same person? Still, no serious harm done!'

'Ken Johnson died, Mr Tuvoli.'

'You're not suggesting he died because of a prank, are you? My God, you are!' He leaned forward, avid for more.

'We're keeping open minds at this stage. But foul play is a possibility we must consider,' Horseman replied.

'Have you heard any gossip that a crew member was committing the pranks against players?'

Tuvoli lifted his brows in surprise. 'No, no I haven't. All the talk I've heard is about which of the players is guilty. But it's possible, isn't it?'

'You tell us, Mr Tuvoli.'

'Hmm ... *io*, I'd say it's possible, especially for crew who work on Motu regularly. I haven't thought about it before.'

'Does anyone spring to mind now that you're thinking about it?'

The fixer shook his head. 'No, it's possible, but crazy.'

'You'd hear stories about drug use on set, I'm sure,' Singh suggested.

The fixer took this idea in his stride. '*Io*, but very few, actually. You know everyone's tested before they're taken on here? It seems to me players and crew are generally on board with management's zero-tolerance policy.'

'Which drugs have featured in the few rumours you've heard, Mr Tuvoli?'

The fixer shrugged. 'Oh, the gamut. I've heard mention of marijuana, cocaine, amphetamines. That's about it. That's more than enough, eh?'

'Do you mean people allege these drugs are in use on Champion?' Horseman asked.

'Not often. Someone might say, "Wouldn't it be cool to break for a joint now?" as a joke. No one admitted to me they'd taken drugs on set. Well, they wouldn't, would they?'

'Have any cast or crew asked you to get drugs for them?'

'No. Where's this going?'

'Have you ever sold or given drugs to anyone on Champion?'

'No, I haven't. *Oi lei*, who's saying this?' He half-rose from his chair, then slumped back again.

'We're asking everyone these questions, Mr Tuvoli. No need to worry.'

The fixer grinned and spread his hands again. 'Of course, Sergeant, what was I thinking?'

After Tuvoli departed, Singh said, 'Seems to me our fixer can come and go whenever he feels like it. Probably no one pays him much attention, just assumes he's visiting interns or fixing something.'

'I agree. We're due some evidence. Ken's MDMA hasn't helped us much at all. I have more confidence in our lab than Steve Duke does. When the second sample tests positive, we'll push for all players and crew who visit Motu Island to be screened.'

21

Detective Superintendent Ratini was a poor substitute for his predecessor, in Horseman's opinion. His former super, Navala, had a quiet authority that no subordinate dared challenge and Horseman wished he could emulate. At work Navala always dressed formally in long-sleeved white or blue shirt, jacket, tie and tailored *sulu*, the wraparound skirt worn by both sexes in Fiji. Only recently had Horseman understood how Navala's dress and old-fashioned courtesy had demonstrated his profound respect for the force and the citizens he served. Without any explicit instruction, this attitude rubbed off on all the young detectives who served under Navala. While they wouldn't copy his dress, or not until they were two decades older, their work clothes were fresh each day, clean, ironed, and in good repair.

This was one reason the whole CID floor at Suva Central Police Station was still in a state of culture shock at the appointment of Ratini. Few had adjusted well to a boss who looked like he'd slept in his work clothes, which were often frayed or missing a button. But this was not Ratini's worst failing. He was impatient, rude, and took pleasure in belittling subordinates with his sarcastic tongue. Especially Horseman.

He tapped on Ratini's door and waited for the impatient instruction to enter.

'*Bula*, sir. I'd like to brief you on today's work on the Ken Johnson suspicious death case before the team assembles for our review. When is a good time for you?'

'You've already interrupted me, Horseman, so you may as well stay and say your piece. Keep it short. If I want details, I'll ask.' Ratini took off his reading glasses and closed the departmental binder with a thump. 'Well, hurry up and sit down.'

This was as hospitable as Ratini ever got with Horseman, who immediately sat.

'The forensic finding of MDMA or ecstasy in Ken Johnson's body elevated his case from unexplained death to suspicious death. We had already decided to pursue Johnson's death as a prank gone wrong, as I reported yesterday. This morning we broke the news of Johnson's MDMA to the director, Steve Duke, who flatly denied any drug use by Champion cast or crew. He demanded Johnson's sample be tested again, to which I agreed.'

'*Oi lei*, the Fiji Police are not lackeys of some crackpot Hollywood director!'

'I agree, sir. However, a second test on request is within the guidelines and potentially strengthens the evidence.'

Ratini heaved his trademark sigh, ending in a smoker's cough.

'If the first result is confirmed, I think the director will permit us to screen all cast and crew. Dr Young can arrange test kits and liaise with the Champion resident nurse.'

'Hmm. Go on, go on, man,'

'After the director, we interviewed all four finalists again, together with all crew who worked with the contestants. We asked about drug use as well as pursuing the pranks on the set.'

'And?'

'Everyone agreed that despite Duke's zero-tolerance policy, drug use was possible. No one admitted to using drugs themselves or knowing of anyone else who did.'

'Anyone you suspect?'

'One guy stands out for opportunity. Lui Tuvoli, who comes and goes, supervising the interns from FIT's Film and Television courses on set. He's expanded his job informally to a fixer: finding whatever the production needs in Fiji. The motive for drugs is easy money. It's just possible he set up those pranks, but we're almost wasting resources checking on his movements for those times. A contestant's much more likely to be the prankster.'

'*Io*, I agree there. No reason the prankster and drug supplier are the same person.'

'No sir. As Ken Johnson was likely a victim of a prank and MDMA, it would be a neat solution if they were. But we'll keep on following every lead we get.'

'Better hurry up, then! Go in hard on this Tuvoli. Doesn't matter if he's got nothing to do with Johnson's death, if he's supplying drugs, we want him behind bars! Maybe you like hobnobbing with Hollywood, rubbing shoulders with celebrities. Suits you to spend days out there at the Champion place, eh? Maybe this Duke will get you to replace Ken Johnson!'

Horseman knew better, but he couldn't help himself. 'No sir, we must go there, because that's where Ken Johnson lived and died. He went nowhere else in Fiji.'

Ratini's mouth twisted in his one-sided smirk.

'Be quick about your meeting, man. I'll come in about half an hour. We'll celebrate an outstanding achievement. All the CID together.' His eyes held amusement and a hint of triumph.

***

Horseman did as Ratini asked him. The team had already shared their thoughts on the drive back to Suva. Their additional information was meagre, and their notes were consequently brief. Horseman and Singh drew up two plans for Thursday, one if the second drug test was positive, and another if it was negative. Everyone was working on updating the running sheet, the case file or their official diaries when Ratini walked in.

He'd changed the old khaki tee-shirt he'd been wearing earlier, thank God. The short-sleeved striped shirt was clean although crumpled. He tugged it down in an effort to straighten it but gave up when he saw he'd lost a button over his developing paunch.

'Let's move to Inspector Vula's end of the floor, detectives,' Ratini said, looking back towards the stairs. 'Ah, here's Detective Chief Superintendent Tauvaga, our special guest.'

Everyone murmured respectful greetings to DCS Tauvaga, who was old-school in dress and dignity. He exuded an avuncular benevolence, but Horseman had learned on a previous case that his sharp eyes missed nothing, and his sharper mind rapidly processed what he saw. No wonder Ratini had changed his shirt.

When they were all present, Ratini took centre stage. 'While some of us have been mixing with celebrities on film sets, and others mixing with Suva's villains in the gutters, DCS Tauvaga has revealed we have a celebrity here in our midst at Suva Central CID.'

Ratini must have rehearsed this speech for the benefit of Tauvaga. Despite resenting the personal dig, Horseman had to admit it was an effective hook. Detectives glanced at one another, all intrigued. What was coming?

'I'll now invite DCS Tauvaga to reveal the identity of our celebrity.'

'Officers, the Commissioner telephoned me yesterday with news that delighted me. The results of the recent round of officers' examinations are finalised and about to be published. I am proud indeed to announce that one of Suva Central's detectives has taken first place in the national Inspector's level list.' Everyone looked at Singh. After all, she was Suva Central's only candidate in the exam. Tauvaga's effort to draw out the suspense, like in a TV reality show, fell a bit flat. Still, respect demanded they wait for the announcement.

Tauvaga registered the direction of their looks. He smiled. 'I can see some of you have guessed. After all, you are detectives, aren't you? With no further ado, I ask you to congratulate Detective Sergeant Susila Singh. Step forward, DS Singh.'

Singh looked down in confusion but in a moment straightened her shoulders and shook the chief superintendent's hand. 'You have an excellent record in the field, in addition to this academic success, DS Singh. I have no doubt your appointment to the rank of Detective Inspector will be very soon, indeed almost immediate. Congratulations indeed!' Singh blushed as DCS Tauvaga presented her with a certificate and shook her hand again. Ratini followed suit. Everyone clapped heartily—even some men who thought Singh was treated favorably couldn't argue with her exam result.

The tea trolleys were wheeled in, loaded with the essentials of Fiji catering: an impressive tropical fruit platter, scones, curry puffs and cake. Horseman chatted to colleagues as he stood in line, waiting to congratulate Singh. He wasn't at all surprised she'd topped the exam. He knew how important this was for her. But a pit of fear opened inside him. There was no vacancy for a DI in Suva. What would he do without her? The others drifted away to the tea trolleys, and it was Horseman's turn to congratulate Singh. Her green eyes shone as he shook her hand, but words failed him. Finally, he said, 'Let me get you a cup of tea, this coffee will be terrible.'

THURSDAY

22

Dr Young rang the next morning. 'No surprise, mate. Ken Johnson's second test returned identical results to the first. I'm faxing the full screen details through as we speak. I'll send an email with just the conclusion and MDMA level for your file. Feel free to forward that to the boss out at Champion: if he feels he's in the official loop he might be more friendly. And don't say I don't do you any favours!'

'Never! *Vinaka vakalevu*, Matt. I reckon Duke will approve the drug testing. I told him I wanted everyone tested but that will drag out the process. I'm confident only the four players and a dozen crew are of interest to the Ken Johnson investigation.'

'I've got it in hand. Seru from the lab will liaise with Barbara at the camp. The screening kits are ready. We only need labelled urine samples produced and collected under hygienic conditions. Seru can help Barbara with that and get them back to the lab pronto.'

'I guess even sixteen samples is casting the net wide, given it's more than three days since Ken died.'

'Yeah, but MDMA lasts longer in the system than cocaine or cannabis. And if anyone ingested the drug more recently, the evidence may not be admissible in relation to Ken's death.'

'Agreed, but it's grounds for further questioning and leaning harder on them. That can produce relevant information. And the director will be grateful. Whether there'll be a production to sack anyone from is still up in the air.'

'Really? I thought it would be dead in the water.'

'Seems there are technical ways and means to continue. Duke wants to sound out Ken Johnson's father about what he wants. The poor man arrives today.'

'Yeah, I hadn't forgotten. His son is ready for his visit.'

'Mr Johnson refuses to fly in a small plane, so Duke and his driver went to Nadi airport to meet him and take him to his Suva hotel. The poor man will need a rest after his long flight and three hours on the road. He might even sleep right through until tomorrow morning. I've left a note with reception asking him to ring me when he's ready. If I don't hear from him by late afternoon, I'll call at the hotel. There's no need for him to come to the station—I'd rather meet him and give him the forms and certificate he'll need.'

'Okay. If all that happens this afternoon, maybe you could bring him up to the hospital afterwards. If you can't stay, I'll get him back to the hotel myself.'

'That'll work. I'll call him now and pray that wherever he is on the King's Road has mobile reception.'

Horseman called Steve Duke's mobile at ten-minute intervals. On the fourth call, Duke answered then pulled to the side of the road to keep the flukey connection. He accepted the positive result of Ken Johnson's second drugs test with equanimity and approved testing Horseman's proposed subjects that very day, if possible. Mr Johnson wanted to eat when he got to the hotel before he had a rest.

'Would it suit you to join us for lunch, Inspector? I'd like to talk to you again, but not on the phone. This would save both of us an extra trip.'

'Good idea. What time do you estimate?'

'See you in the restaurant around one o'clock. Better get back on the road now.'

***

Horseman stood as Jethro Johnson approached. He was around sixty, his body lean and hard, like he still did physical labour. His short brown hair was wet and neatly combed, his blue check shirt was ironed and tucked into the belt of his Bermuda shorts. Only the sunken, lined flesh of his face and his lifeless eyes told the truth: he had flown halfway around the world to visit his dead son.

Duke made the introductions, and they sat down. The waiter, fore-warned, greeted them with a subdued smile, handed them menus, then brought water.

'I'm very sorry that such a tragedy has brought you to our islands, Mr Johnson.' Horseman hated using the trite phrases and wished he could do better. 'As the leader of the investigation, I can assure you that your son's death has our full-time attention. I'll also do everything in my power to make the official procedure as smooth as possible.'

'My wife and two daughters are having a tough time dealing with this. When Mr Duke told me ... I mean to say, a tragic accident is one thing, but ... you suspect Ken's death wasn't natural?' The father's eyes implored him to say he'd made a mistake.

'We do. Some circumstances aren't clear, and the forensic results aren't complete. Our field investigations are thorough because we want to find the truth for the sake of your family.'

'Steve here thinks y'all could be dragging it out.'

Horseman glanced at Duke, whose focus remained on Mr Johnson.

'I promise you we're working as fast as we can to reach a conclusion. Lab analysis takes time, but getting people to tell us what they know can take even longer.'

The waiter approached them again and served bread rolls.

'However, you need to eat after your long journey, Mr Johnson. What would you like?'

'I don't think I can eat anything right now.' He picked up his bread and tore a small piece off it.

'Do you like fish, Jethro? It's usually good. Fried or grilled?' Duke suggested.

'Okay, better have something. Grilled, please.' Mr Johnson put the piece of bread in his mouth. A good sign, Horseman thought.

They all ordered fish and chips. The food looked and smelled invit-ing. Eating in silence allowed the trio to ignore painful reality and get used to the presence of their unchosen companions. Even Mr Johnson ate with appetite. But he must have been mulling things over because when he'd finished, he aligned his knife and fork neatly on his plate and looked at Horseman, his eyes now resolute.

'I know you have your duty, son. You must find the truth, whether or not I want to know it. I understand that. Ken understood duty, too. His ambition to win Champion was to get a million dollars, not the honour and glory. He'd won a college scholarship, but his little sisters probably won't. He wanted to put them through a top college, which is beyond our means. That goal was driven by love and good old-fashioned family duty.

'But he loved his sports and was very competitive—maybe too competitive. I don't know. I do know he was doing what he most wanted to do in the entire world, and he was excited to be in Fiji. It was his dream come true. His precious and wonderful life was cut short. But how many people pass away living their dream?'

It was an awkward silence, both Horseman and Duke nodding solemnly. Horseman guessed Duke, like him, didn't want to risk a well-meaning remark embarrassing or offending Ken's father.

'Steve here has kindly asked me my opinion about what should happen to all the episodes of the show he's shot with Ken. I have some ideas, but I'll sleep on that. It's never good to be hasty. Steve, I sure appreciate you inviting me to the set this afternoon, but I'll leave that until tomorrow. I'd like to see some of the footage with Ken, if y'all can arrange that.'

'We'll do that. I can talk to you more about that over dinner this evening.'

'I don't want to be rude, you're a generous host, Steve, but I need to be on my own tonight to sort things out in my head. Thanks for everything. I'm sorta disoriented here, so in the morning ...'

'I'll pick you up myself and take you to the set, Jethro. Don't worry about a thing. And I'll get some DVDs featuring Ken to you here later today.'

Mr Johnson nodded. 'As for the terrible necessities of your business, detective, the sooner that's done the better. However, I'll cope better after I have a nap. Two hours will do me.'

'Shall I call for you here at half-past three, sir?'

'Sure. Holy moly, it feels like midnight to me!' He looked around. 'Y'all are very kind. I'm grateful.'

23

Singh didn't know what she'd expected, but she was relieved. She hadn't encountered instant drug testing kits before. The patient technician from the forensic lab explained the protocols to her during the drive out to the Champion base. *Instant* turned out to be a little exaggerated, but only a little. You could get a positive or negative result in less than five minutes. Or rather, not positive, but non-negative, which sounded like a double negative to Singh.

Nurse Barbara Koroi tested the women discreetly in spaced private appointments. The lab technician managed the men. The whole process was complete inside two hours. Singh and DC Kau came along to follow up a few crew who had missed being interviewed so far. They worked in their office on the main quadrangle, not even within sight of the First Aid post where the drug screens were done.

She allowed herself a rerun of yesterday afternoon's formal announcement of her Inspector's exam result. Embarrassing that Ratini had forced the whole floor to attend, but the warmth of most of her colleagues had touched her. After eighteen months of minding her own business, and working for Horseman most of the time, she'd realised she belonged to the whole CID team.

But not for long. How did she feel about that? She'd been so focussed on the exam as the gateway to promotion she hadn't planned beyond it. Well, in a way she had: she'd taken a lease on her flat in Seaview Apartments knowing that as an inspector she'd no longer be eligible for Police department housing. She'd been looking for a temporary roof over her head but had never dreamed she would find a refuge and a home she loved. She would have to give her flat up since there were no current vacancies for an inspector in Suva. It was possible to turn down an offer of appointment but if she did it would count against her with the police hierarchy.

Then there was Joe Horseman. There were few of his calibre in the force. Anyway, did she want another boss of his calibre, or did she want him? She would have to think about that.

DC Kau stomped in, a frown on his usually genial face. A glowering Desirée Lopez was hard on his heels. 'Sarge, Ms Lopez insists on speaking to you, even though Nurse Koroi has explained—'

'You bet I do!' Desi shouted. 'I wanna protest to someone with authority, and it seems, Sergeant, that you're the most senior officer here today. Where's your cute boss? I'd prefer to talk to him.' Her voice had lost volume as she spoke. Maybe she just needed to throw her weight around a bit, *prima donna* style.

'Please sit down, Desi. DC Kau is right—you'll have to put up with me today.'

'Okay, you've been nice and reasonable. I need your help. The nurse tells me I tested positive on the drug screen. Impossible! She gave me aspirin herself yesterday. Surely that's what the test picked up.'

'Don't worry, Desi. First, they classify no one as positive on the result of these instant tests. Nurse Barbara explained that didn't she? They're reliable, but not quite as reliable as lab tests. Your test sample will be taken back to the lab in Suva this afternoon and analysed by gas chromatography which will give an accurate result. Your sample will only be classified as positive if a drug shows up in that test.'

'But I can't be positive! It's not possible!' Desi put her face in her hands and sobbed. Not sobs again! Singh felt her impatience rising but strove to fight it. How would she react if this happened to her? She moved the box of tissues close to Desi.

'Please calm down, Desi. Tell me what's worrying you.'

Kau retreated to the corner table and put the kettle on.

Desi mopped her face and took a deep, shuddering breath. 'Don't you get it? They're trying to get me out—thrown off the game!'

'Who's *they*? You must have your suspicions.'

'The prankster, of course. The drugs are just another prank, aren't they? That guy's tampering with the samples. He, or she I suppose, must have substituted a contaminated sample for mine.'

'Let's check the process you went through again. Nurse Koroi waited outside the toilet door while you urinated into the test cup, right?'

Desi nodded. 'Sure, and it's only a half-door. Embarrassing!'

'Did you give the cup direct to the nurse?'

'Sure, Barbara was right there, holding her hand out.'

'What did she do then?'

'She put a stick in it and chatted a bit while we waited. When the stick changed colour, Barbara told me she had to send the sample to Suva, to the lab, because it wasn't negative.'

'Desi, think about this. No one could have tampered with your sample, because only you and the nurse handled it, right?'

'I guess not.'

'And your test kit was sealed. You opened it yourself?' Desi looked down and nodded.

'And I understand the test is automatic. Was Nurse Koroi wearing gloves?'

'Yeah, she was. Okay, okay, there must be another way!'

'I can't see how, Desi. The best thing for you now is to relax. You'll get the results from the Suva lab analysis tomorrow.'

'Water's boiled. Would you like tea or coffee, Ms Lopez?' Kau asked.

Desi sniffed. 'Oh, white coffee will do.'

When Kau brought her coffee and tea for Singh and himself, Desi was more composed.

'Gee, thanks. That test was a real blow, a kick in the guts, after all I've been through. But I guess I overreacted.'

'That's alright. How are the other finalists coping?'

'Okay, I guess. Maybe they're not as sensitive as me. Since Monday when we moved on base here, we haven't spent a lot of time hanging out. We're pushed too, you know—quite busy, actually. Continuity and the story producer are getting us to do extra scenes where two of us have brief conversations. I've done two talking head scenes already.'

'What's the plan for the series?'

'Beats me. We're not in the loop. Maybe they're just keeping us busy. Who knows?'

'Are you shooting on Motu again?'

'Twice for me. It's weird when we're not staying there. It seemed so remote before. Now it's just a little picnic island ten minutes across the bay.'

'You mean you don't have to find your own food anymore?' Singh smiled.

'No! Our food's basic, but it's cooked for us, and we eat in the canteen with the crew. Mili and I share a room and Duane and Bobby have another. A proper toilet and shower. Not really any adventure now. Guess we're just waiting for Mr Johnson.' She looked rueful.

'Oh? I believe he was due to arrive today?'

'Yeah. People are saying Steve's gonna bring him here this afternoon.'

Singh looked at Kau. She'd better check if Horseman knew what was happening.

24

Steady drum beats roused Horseman as he strolled through the centre of Suva after lunch. He couldn't budge the image of Mr Johnson's face from his mind: controlled, dignified and entirely bereft. The clap of wood on wood got louder as he approached Jubilee Arcade. Then the volume decreased as the chanting rose. 'Suu-sine, Aunty, Suuu-sine Uncle, suuuu-siine!'

What was Tevita doing here? He should be at work, washing and polishing vehicles at the police garage. Shouldn't he? Disappointment flared in Horseman's chest at the thought that Tevita had once again thrown away a rare opportunity. He'd assumed that because the boy had been working at the garage for close to a year now, he was settled and content. Or had Tevita been another case for Horseman, a problem to solve, a loose end to be tied neatly with a bow?

Come on man, he scolded himself. *You're taking a step way too far. Why not ask the boy what he's doing back at the shoe-shine business?*

The rapping speeded up to a crescendo then slowed. 'Polis like a mirror, siine like a mirror, a mirror, suuuuu-siine!' Tevita's voice was deepening, more sonorous. Horseman wondered how old he was. Fifteen, maybe even sixteen now? The drumming and chanting suddenly ceased. Tevita must have scored a customer.

As Horseman wove through the bustling entrance to Victoria Parade, he saw Tevita wore the khaki work shorts and shirt of the police ancillary labour squad. While the boy rejuvenated his customer's worn black sandals with a thin smear of Kiwi polish and unsparing buffing with an old tee-shirt, Horseman observed him from a metre or so behind. Tevita was no longer skinny. Muscles in his neck, shoulders and back had developed thanks to his regular food, basic as the menu at the barracks was. When he finished the shine and accepted the dollar coin with a smile, Horseman stepped from behind and planted one foot firmly on Tevita's box.

'Joe! Joe! Joe! *Bula, bula, bula*!' A huge smile transformed the boy's face.

'*Bula vinaka*, Tevita. I'm pleased to see you being polite to your customer. How's business today?'

'Okay, Joe. I just come here now, you know. Sergeant, he let me stop work early today.'

'Why's that?'

Tevita cast a critical eye over Horseman's brown sandals. 'Getting old, Joe, eh.' He first brushed off dust and bits of dried mud, then carefully applied polish with a small rag before a brisk brushing and final polish with a cleanish rag.

'Sarge tell me to work later on the top bosses' cars—you know, Joe. Commissioner and Deputy Commissioners. Meeting at United States Embassy tomorrow. I say I got training, but Sarge says I can do it after training. Like a mirror, eh Joe? Cars all same shoes.' Tevita beamed as if he were the luckiest boy in the world. In his view he'd come pretty close.

A peremptory rap on the box and Horseman obediently switched feet. 'So I got a few hours off this afternoon. Better come down Jubilee Arcade and make some money to save up, eh Joe?'

'Excellent idea, Tevita. But you need some time off, too.'

The boy stopped applying Kiwi and laughed out loud. 'Oh, Joe, I'm working man now!'

'True, true, I guess you are. Are you saving up for something special?'

Tevita grinned again. 'Sure, sure, very special, Joe. Secret now, but you see later.' The boy was bursting to tell his secret.

'Come on, you can tell me, Tevita, can't you? I promise I won't tell your secret to anyone.'

'Oh, no way, Joe. No way.'

'Okay, you can save money and you can keep a secret. Full marks!'

Another rap with the brush back on the box signalled both sandals were done. Horseman removed his foot and gave Tevita five dollars. Much too much, but he intended to take up more of the boy's time with a few questions.

'Better buy new sandals soon, Joe. See here—this leather strap get very thin, nearly worn through, will snap soon. Heel too—look!' He twisted Horseman's foot around. 'Too worn down, Joe, you walk crooked, that no good.' He frowned. Horseman could picture Sergeant Walo assessing Tevita's work at the police garage with exactly the same expression.

'I've been talking about my idea for a Shiners' hostel, for the training squad players who don't have homes to go to at night. Something like Father Francis's hostel at Flagstaff. Have you and the other boys been talking about it?'

A broad smile lit Tevita's face again. 'Course, Joe, course! Can you do it?'

'I've been talking more with Dr Pillai and some other people and yes, we can make this happen, if we can raise the money. There will be a lot of forms to fill in—many, many forms. I want to know where you think would be a good place for the hostel. You see, a building near the centre of Suva would be much too expensive. A suburb in the hills or along the King's Road towards Nausori could be possible. Further away would be better—we'd get a better house for the same amount of money.'

The smile left Tevita's face. 'Remember when you send me to Father Francis' place at Tailevu? Like prison, Joe, like prison. And too far away. I city boy now, Joe. Gotta be Suva. Somewhere on edge is okay if bus stop is close. Now I got my job in police garage, and night school and training.'

'*Vinaka* for your thoughts, Tevita. But there will be rules wherever the hostel is. Like no fighting. Otherwise, it won't be a safe home for anyone. I'll also ask the others what they think after training this afternoon.'

'All think same, Joe. All think like me. True, true.'

'I believe you. But what you want will mean the hostel will take longer, maybe years. That's because we'll have to borrow more money from the bank to get a building in the suburbs.'

'No point of hostel if no boys want to live there, eh? Better find the right place.'

Maybe the real estate business would be a better fit for Tevita.

'Don't worry, Joe. Me and boys got a plan. Secret plan. You always say make a plan, eh Joe?'

25

The Champion police office door banged open, the inside handle chipping the wall.

'Help, *ovisa*, help! You've got to come now!'

Kau moved fast to block the agitated man's entry, grasping his shoulders.

Singh sprang from her chair.

'Calm down, please sir. Tell us—oh you're Mr Nemi, aren't you? Eroni Nemi, the from the Props department?'

Nemi shrugged off Kau's restraining hands.

'It's fine, DC Kau. I've met Mr Nemi before.'

'*Ovisa*, it's Mili Kepa. She's collapsed on the beach. Screaming, screaming. Then she fainted—'

'Did you call the set nurse?'

'Another bystander has gone to get her. I hope she's got there by now.'

'Did you see what happened?'

'Not really. I was sorting through some driftwood to use for props. She was there when I arrived, paddling at the edge.'

'Apo, fill the kettle and bring it to the beach when it boils. Quick!'

'Mr Nemi, you said another bystander. Was there anyone else around? Did you leave her alone?'

'One or two others, but not close by. I yelled at them to look after her. But I couldn't wait. I don't even know if they understood.'

'Mr Nemi, find a bucket and run back to Mili. Quick as you can! I won't be long.'

Singh dialled Barbara Koroi's mobile and let it ring while she grabbed her backpack and ran out the door. After eight rings, the nurse answered. 'Sergeant, have you heard Mili Kepa collapsed on the beach?'

'Yes, Mr Nemi just rushed in to tell us. I sent him back in case she was alone. Are you with her now?'

'On my way—nearly there.'

'It sounded like possibly she stepped on some kind of sea stinger. DC Kau put the kettle on and he'll race the hot water to the beach.'

'*Vinaka*, Susie. If that's the problem, speed is critical.'

'See you in a minute, Barbara.'

As she ran onto the beach, Singh heard screams of agony. Blood curdling: high-pitched, harsh like jagged coral, and loud as a flock of screeching gulls. Singh knew only basic first aid so thank God the nurse had made it first. But where was Mr Nemi? She ran up to Nurse Barbara and Mili, who had a shiny shock blanket around her. Her skin was ashen. She panted rapidly in between tortured screams.

'Look at her foot, Susie. She stepped on something, but whether a stone fish or blue-ringed octopus or something else, I don't know and I'm not about to waste time by looking in the shallows. Stone fish can bury themselves in the sand and stay alive on the beach for hours, anyway. Keep splashing alcohol on her foot while I take her blood pressure—if it's dangerously low, we need to get her to hospital immediately.'

Mili's right foot was twice the size of her left. Two puncture wounds stood out on raised areas of bluish skin. The rest was an angry red, dry, and flaking.

'Dribble the bottle over the wound. That's the way. What's keeping your constable and Eroni Nemi? I need to immerse her foot, but I haven't got a plastic box big enough. Oh, good, her blood pressure's low but not dangerously so—not yet, at least.'

It seemed to Singh that Mili's screams were subsiding, or perhaps she was just getting used to the horrible noise. The nurse knelt behind Mili and raised her to lie against her body, half upright. She gently coaxed Mili to swallow some water and pills.

'Pain relief and antibiotics for now. But she needs—ah, here come the boys.'

Eroni was first, with two buckets. Kau ten metres behind carrying the kettle outstretched. Singh hoped he hadn't scalded himself running with it.

'Good, this one's big enough. Take the smaller one, Eroni and get some sea water. Mili, that pain will ease very soon. You're doing so well, dear. Can you lean on Sergeant Singh for me now while I look after your foot?'

The nurse poured some sea water into the large bucket, directing Kau to add hot water.

'That's enough. Let me see.' Barbara swirled the water around. 'The hotter the better, but we don't want to scald you, Mili. Here, let's get your foot in this nice warm water.' She carefully bent Mili's right knee and put her foot in the bucket.

'There, now. That will feel much better soon. Could you stand the water a bit hotter?'

Mili nodded. She had stopped screaming, but her moans and whimpers distressed Singh just as much. Barbara swiftly elevated Mili's foot above the bucket while Kau added more hot water and mixed it around. With great care, Barbara placed the swollen foot back in the bucket.

'Mili, we'll get you into a car now. Your foot must stay in the hot water. We'll take you to hospital where you can get antivenom. Whether the toxin's stone fish or something else, that will help a lot.'

'Does Mr Duke or anyone else know about Mili's accident?' Singh hoped the nurse didn't interpret the question as implied criticism.

'Well, he should. Of course, I phoned him and left a message as soon as I heard and told the man Eroni sent to find him.'

'Okay, I'll check he received that, if you don't mind. You need to attend to your patient.' Barbara shot her a sharp glance, then nodded. She positioned the cuff on Mili's arm and focused on the scale as she pumped the rubber bulb.

Eroni Nemi hung back from the little group. He thrust his hands into his tangled hair to cover his ears. His eyes squeezed tight. Tears rolled down his cheeks. Singh raised her voice over Mili's renewed cries.

'Mr Nemi, have you any idea where Mr Duke or his deputies are?'

She repeated her question more loudly before Nemi's eyes opened and he lifted his hands from his ears.

'Sorry, no, Sergeant. If he's not in his office, maybe the editing studio, but—I don't know!' He glanced from one to the other, wild-eyed. 'May God help her,' he said softly, then bowed his head in prayer.

She had to decide. 'Barbara, you know better than me how critical speed is for Mili. If you don't want to wait longer, Kau and I could take you and Mili to hospital in the police LandCruiser. Kau can drive and I'll help you look after Mili if you need me.'

Barbara raised Mili's foot again as Kau added more hot water to the bucket. She frowned. 'Mili will recover but we can't let her endure this excruciating pain—the antivenom helps a lot with that. So many thanks, Susie. Let's get going.'

'Apo, bring the vehicle down to the beach. Mr Nemi, can you clear that driftwood out of the way?' It was distinctly odd giving orders with Mili sprawled against her, half unconscious, panting rapidly. At least the girl was breathing.

Barbara swirled the water and immersed Mili's swollen foot in it again.

Singh was relieved when Horseman picked up the phone. 'Susie. I'm with Matt and Ken Johnson's father at Pathology. I'll just step outside.'

'Sir, Kau and I are about to leave the Champion location with Barbara and Mili on board. Mili's suffering from what looks like a stonefish sting. Can't talk now, send me a text if you like. I'll see you at the hospital if you're still there.'

Could this be something more than an accident?

FRIDAY

26

The next morning, Horseman drove back to the Bay of Islands to catch up with the interviews Mili's crisis had interrupted.

Singh turned to make sure Musudroka and Lili Waqa in the back seat could hear her. 'I called Barbara Koroi before we left. She said Mili's no longer in danger but needs pain relief and monitoring for another twenty-four hours.'

'Thanks to you, Sergeant. Barbara told me your quick thinking and action saved Mili's life.'

'Team effort, sir. Apo was just as quick and kept a cool head.'

'Apo's had enough action for a day or two. He was quite happy to stay in the office this morning and write up the records.'

'I'm proud of you, Sarge. My boss, a hero—imagine that!' Musudroka called out from the back.

'Why are you surprised, Tani? I wasn't, not in the least,' Horseman said.

Musudroka ignored Horseman. 'How did you know about the boiling water? Apo said as soon as the man burst in saying Mili had collapsed on the beach screaming her head off, you told him to put the kettle on! He thought you wanted to make tea!'

They all laughed, even Singh. 'Whatever Apo thought of me, he obeyed my orders without question—a lesson for you, Detective Constable.' Singh sounded stern but Horseman saw her eyes dancing when he glanced at her.

She continued. 'Tani, you've done the same first aid course I have. If someone collapses on the beach in excruciating pain, it's pretty certain they've been stung or bitten by one of our deadly creatures—sting ray, jelly fish, sea snake, blue-ringed octopus, cone shell, and more. The stonefish is the most toxic and the pain's supposed to be the worst in the world. Even you'd scream, Tani.'

'Not me, Sarge,' Tani replied with a straight face. He frowned. 'I don't recall hot water treatment.'

'It eases the pain, not sure how. Seriously, you need to brush up, Tani. Maybe we should all do a refresher course.'

'Mili's doctor says she should be comfortable enough to be interviewed this afternoon. I want you to do that, Sergeant. You helped her yesterday, so she may open up to you. Shame we couldn't get two vehicles today, but we'll work something out.'

Lili laughed. 'Tani won't mind walking back. He's so tough,'

'Time to focus on the day ahead, constables. First, Dr Young will phone us with the lab test results on the three non-negatives, then we interview any confirmed as positive. Second, the lab will also let us know the identity of Mili's toxin. A stone fish is just a guess based on her symptoms and the fact she was paddling in the shallows on the beach.'

'Could this have been a prank, sir?' Lili Waqa asked.

'I don't think it's likely, but we've got to investigate it because of the history of pranks on set. I hope we can eliminate the possibility. At the moment we've only got Eroni Nemi's report of what happened. We've got to find whoever he sent to fetch Barbara.'

'I checked with Barbara, sir. She knows him as Nik from the Camera department. Lili asked Deepika. Looks like it's Nikhil Seth, a local assistant camera operator.'

'Good, he may be able to identify others who were there. It's important to talk to all of them.'

Horseman's phone pinged. He checked the message. 'It's Steve Duke, no less. He and Mr Johnson are going to address the entire cast and crew in the canteen at eleven and we're all invited. I'll accept and just hope that by then we know more than we do now. An interim deadline for us, detectives.'

'Reckon they've decided about Champion's future, sir?' Musudroka asked.

'Probably, Tani. When I took Mr Johnson to see Ken's body yesterday, he asked Dr Young when he could issue his final PM report. Matt promised he'd send it to him today. I'll check with Apo later.'

*****

Nikhil Seth looked young despite his wispy moustache and goatee. He tapped on the open office door and strolled in. He'd gathered most of his shoulder-length black hair into a messy ponytail.

'How is Mili?' he asked.

'Still suffering, but she'll recover. The doctor wants her in hospital a while longer.'

'That's good. Not that she's suffering, but that she'll recover, I mean.' He smiled, embarrassed.

'How do you like your job here, Mr Seth?' Horseman asked.

'Great, sir. What a wonderful opportunity for me.'

'In what way?'

'Well, I'm lucky to have a job covering sport for Fiji One, which I enjoy. But working on Champion with Hollywood professionals is another level, and a higher one. It's not just what I'm learning, but the people I'm working with might help me if they like my work.'

'Ken Johnson's death must have changed everything here?'

'Yes, of course. It's terrible. But we're still busy, mainly with editing the footage we already have, but also shooting continuity scenes with the four finalists left.'

'Why were you on the beach yesterday afternoon?'

'A late lunch, after working hard all morning, re-taking some scenes. Actually, I had lunch in the canteen then a short stroll on the beach to freshen me up.'

Horseman nodded at Lili Waqa, who asked, 'Were you alone, Mr Seth?'

Seth smiled at Lili. 'Nik, please, Constable. No, Filo came with me. She's one of the FIT camera interns. We worked together all morning and had lunch together too. A nice kid.'

'What's Filo's surname?'

'Lali, I think. Or Nilali—not quite sure.'

'Don't worry, we can check it against the staff list.' Waqa made a careful note.

'How many others were on the beach when you got there?'

'Not many. I noticed Mili, of course. Not only a finalist, but a Fijian—we're all hoping she'll win, aren't we?'

'Did you say *bula*?'

'Yeah, just in passing. We didn't want to intrude.'

'What was she doing?'

'Walking slowly at the water's edge, letting the waves wash over her feet. She was looking serious, talking to that funny props carpenter with the big ears. What's his name?'

'Eroni Nemi, was it?'

'I think so. Something like that.'

'Did you see anyone else on the beach?'

'Actually, a couple of boys were fossicking around the rocks with sticks. After crabs, I guess.'

'Do they work on Champion, too?'

'I don't know, they were way off near the point.'

'Anyone else?'

'Not that I saw. But we were walking away from the path coming from the arena. So we wouldn't have noticed anyone who came onto the beach behind us.'

'How far away were you when Mili started screaming?'

'How far from Mili? Probably around a hundred metres. Actually, I couldn't say if I heard her at first or not. There was a breeze, and we were walking away from her and Eroni. But when I heard someone scream and keep on screaming, we turned around. Eroni yelled out, beckoning us to come. So we ran back as quick as we could.'

'What did you suppose happened?'

'It was frightening—Mili screaming her head off, sort of pointing at her foot. I thought something must have bitten her: a sea snake, jellyfish? Eroni was in a panic and I don't blame him.'

'Did you think she could have been angry at Mr Nemi?'

'Angry? Oh, did he attack her, you mean? No, she was screaming in agony, physical agony, no mistaking that. Anyway, no one would attack Mili. And the props carpenter, Eroni, comes from the same island, I heard. He's her self-appointed protector.'

'He could be a nuisance to her, then?'

'Oh, no, I didn't mean that. I haven't heard any gossip like that. He's a funny guy, protective in a good way, well-meaning.'

'Tell us what happened when you caught up with them.'

'The props guy was literally pulling at his hair, looked like he'd gone mad. But then, up close, Mili's screams were disturbing, kinda inhuman actually. He pulled himself together a bit and yelled at me to go get Nurse Barbara, said he was going to get the police. He asked Filo to stay with Mili. Poor kid was scared stiff, but she did as he asked. Luckily, the nurse was in her aid post. She made a call, no answer, she left a message. Inside ten seconds, she grabbed her bag, told me to find Mr Duke and tell him what happened and Mili would need to go to hospital. Impressive.'

'Did you find the director?'

'No, nor the production manager or line producer. It looked to me like they were all in a meeting together, maybe off site. No surprise there.'

'You didn't go back to the beach?'

'After I'd run around asking everyone I could think of, I headed back there. I met the police LandCruiser taking Mili to hospital, on the way. The officer said he'd tell Barbara I hadn't been able to find an executive and thanked me for my trouble.'

'Where was Filo?'

'The officer said she was upset, and Barbara had told her to get herself some tea, that she and the police could manage. I caught up with Filo later and she'd calmed down.'

'Thank you, Mr Seth. You've been very helpful. Please give your mobile number to Constable Waqa so we can contact you again if we need to. And if you have Filo's number also?'

Horseman left the room and called DC Kau from the verandah. He was grateful it was so easy to confirm Nik Seth's account. If true, grateful too that Kau had exercised both caution and tact with Seth when he met him on the path to the beach.

He'd need to be discreet himself to check if Eroni Nemi and Mili were tied by the unbreakable Fijian thread of kinship and place. But he was reluctant to tug Nemi's thread; the man was on edge. If Mili was fit for interview this afternoon, he could safely delegate that task to Singh.

27

Horseman and Singh sat together in the canteen, where the tables were folded and stacked to the side and the benches set out like in an auditorium. Deepika had escorted them to the front row—a good spot to hear the principals at the front table, but terrible for observation. Under the circumstances, Horseman judged it best to comply, but he hoped Musudroka and Waqa were on full alert as they hovered at the back and sides.

The atmosphere was electric. The low buzz of conversation rose in volume as the minutes of waiting passed. Then a man from the front row stood, approached the microphone in front and switched it on.

'Ladies and gentlemen, Mr Duke and Mr Jethro Johnson, Ken's father, are approaching. Can everyone hear me?'

A few seconds later, three men entered. Duke escorted the grieving father to a seat at the table and the third man sat beside him. The audience rose to their feet with a low rumble. Mr Johnson stood up and patted the air. When everyone had sat down, the director spoke.

'Thanks to all of you for your spontaneous show of respect to Mr Johnson. He assures me he is well rested after his long journey. Earlier this morning the production manager and I showed Mr Johnson over Motu Island and our mainland location at his request. Since Ken passed away, the executives and I have been thinking hard and long about the future of this series of Champion. We devised several workable scenarios. However, we decided we would best respect Ken, an outstanding competitor, by involving his father in the decision, if he was willing. Not only was Mr Johnson willing, but he has been pivotal in our discussions today. He's asked questions which we in the industry have forgotten to ask and the answers led him to a logical choice. It's a choice all the executives support, including the executive producers and casting director back in LA.'

The tension was crackling now.

'Ken's dad will speak briefly a little later, but he wants me to announce the decision and explain what's going to happen.'

Horseman's phone vibrated in his pocket, but he was too exposed in the front row to check it. He glanced at Singh, but her attention was on the director. He would have to wait.

'I think you'll be pleased to know that Champion will continue.' The collective sigh of relief was audible, muffled applause broke out here and there amid shushes.

'Mr Johnson wants the series completed and screened as his son's tribute and legacy. And it will be a fine one. We will dedicate the series to Ken. His father has rejected technical post-production solutions where it would appear that Ken took part in the last episodes that remain to be filmed. The next episode to be shot will begin with the announcement of Ken's death, and the four finalists will continue with the challenges. The last episode, the crowning of the champion, will be low key and include a homage to Ken.'

Sober applause broke out again and this time no one shushed. Horseman discreetly consulted his phone. Duke raised his hand to end the clapping.

'Mr Johnson's honesty is inspiring. He told me Ken's motivation was to win a million dollars for his sisters' college education, and then some for himself. Mr Johnson knows how important the prize is to competitors. But what can we do? Some of us suggested giving the prize money to Ken's family since he was the most likely player to win. But now that the game will resume, we've looked at other ideas. An insurance policy is part of all contestants' contracts. Mr Johnson is quite satisfied this payment will cover Ken's sisters' college tuition and wants the full prize money to go to whoever wins the game. He wants to be transparent about this.'

Horseman exchanged a glance with Singh as they joined the less restrained clapping. There were even a few cheers.

'Before we stand for a minute of silence, remembering Ken Johnson, his father has something to say.'

Silence descended. Mr Johnson walked to the microphone. 'I'm mighty grateful to Mr Duke, the other executives and the police officers who have been so kind to me. This is a beautiful place where my son was so happy to be. Mr Duke gave me a wonderful DVD with lots of footage of Ken, here on location at Champion. I watched it last night. To pass away living your dream is somethin' fine, even if it is way before your time. Ken's life was cut short in Fiji. His mother and me, we wondered if we should let him rest here. But we're selfish, so we're bringing him home to Pigeon Forge, Tennessee. I'll be honoured if y'all will join me for a minute thinking on my boy.'

The entire audience stood and bowed their heads. Was Ken's killer among them? Very likely.

28

Singh found Mr Johnson's few words moving, and the solution for Champion rather impressed her. She hoped it could work. She joined Horseman outside the canteen. The Champion crew gathered in small groups, buzzing with excitement, albeit at a low volume.

'What d'you think, Joe?'

'I think Steve Duke handled it with respect and taste. A difficult occasion – not a funeral, not a service, more a business announcement. But I'm wondering what Duke will do when he hears our lab confirmed two of his finalists tested positive for MDMA. The text came through during the meeting—I've forwarded it to you.' He grinned his infectious grin.

'Who? Desi?'

Horseman nodded. 'Yep. Guess the other.'

'Mili?'

'Why Mili?'

'She's an entertainer, she's in a drugs milieu.'

Horseman held up a warning finger. 'It's Bobby O'Leary.'

'Really?'

'The sports milieu is also rife with drugs. A text came from the hospital too. Mili's doctor will allow you to interview her after two o'clock. You take the vehicle and Lili Waqa. I'm going in hard on the MDMA positives – there are two crew as well. One of them's got to spill the beans on the supplier, surely. I'll keep Musudroka to restrain me if necessary. I can't take this wall of silence much longer.'

'No, I feel the same way.'

'Mr Duke has invited us to a buffet lunch in Mr Johnson's honour. We should go as a courtesy, and we'll mix and talk. Watch and learn, too.'

'Great idea. Then I'll get on the road and be at the hospital by two.'

***

After a slow cruise along the streets surrounding the hospital, Susie gave up on a parking space. She approached the boom gate and told the guard she had an appointment with Dr Young at the mortuary, then drove down the steep slope and pulled up beside the single steel door. It bore the modest sign Pathology and an electric button. Singh checked she'd left enough room for an ambulance or truck to turn into the adjacent bay. This was now closed by a rusty roller shutter, but Singh knew how much Dr Young hated careless people blocking his Deliveries entrance. Quite right, too.

'We'll walk up the drive to the main entrance,' Singh said to DC Lili Waqa as she locked the LandCruiser. 'I know Matt would be fine with us coming in through Pathology but...'

'There he is. *Bula*, Dr Young.'

Singh turned and smiled with pleasure as Dr Young strode towards his door. The lanky, sandy-haired pathologist was one of her favourite people in Suva. He loved to teach, and she'd learned tons from him. She'd miss his friendship if she was promoted out of Suva. *When* she was promoted out of Suva, she corrected herself.

'*Bula*, Lili, *bula*, Susie. How nice to run into you two. But today's news hasn't been the best for you, has it?'

'No, the boss got your text as we listened to the Champion director announce that the show would go on,' she said.

'You don't say!'

'At the express request of Ken Johnson's father, who wants it to be a memorial to his son. Duke doesn't know about the positive test results yet—or maybe he does if the boss has told him. But better news is Mili is fit to interview. Lili and I are here to do that.'

'Ah, Joe's clever. How could Mili resist telling you two everything?'

Singh grinned again. 'Flattery is always welcome, Matt, but she could resist easily. I just hope the stone fish poison has some sort of truth drug effect.'

'Hmm, you never know. Come in this way. If you've got time, call in for a cuppa on your way out.'

'Thanks, Matt. We'll see how it goes.'

As they climbed the stairs, they glimpsed Lui Tuvoli, Champion fixer, crossing the landing above them and continuing along the corridor. Could he be here to visit Mili?

A minute or two later they found Dr Carroll, the worried-looking doctor treating Mili. Like Horseman, a European ancestor had bequeathed his surname, but his more numerous Fijian forbears were responsible for his appearance. He led them to a tiny staff tearoom.

'Oh, sorry, looks like someone's swiped the chairs. We'll just have to stand. Mili was quite acute when admitted but she's now doing very well, thanks to the nurse at the Champion camp. She immersed her foot in hot water right on the beach. Speed is the life-or-death factor with these bastard sea stingers.'

Lili piped up. 'It was actually Detective Sergeant Singh, you know, Doctor, who—'

'Team effort, Doctor,' said Singh, glaring at Lili. 'How does the hot water work?'

Dr Carroll's gaze was appraising. Was she worthy of an explanation? Possibly, because after a moment or two he replied.

'The toxin of the stonefish, and of many other venomous stingers has a protein base, which is denatured by heat. That means heat changes its venomous character. Simple as that. But hot water isn't often available where people get stung. As I said, our Mili was lucky and thank God you and Nurse Koroi were on hand. Oh yes,' he smiled, 'Barbara told me about the clever officers who turned up with a kettle of hot water before she'd even asked them. Well done!'

'Why is the antivenom necessary, then?'

'This fish's spinal barb injects a lot of venom in an instant. You saw how Mili's foot and leg swelled so quickly. The antivenom deals with what's already inside the body, the hot water takes care of what's in and around the wound site. I pulled a couple of barb fragments from Mili's foot. I thought they were stonefish, and the lab has since confirmed my guess. I'll discharge Mili tomorrow morning. Once she recovered from shock, and the pain subsided, she's improved hour by hour.'

'Are you in touch with the Champion director, Steve Duke?'

'No, just with Barbara, the nurse out there. I assume she communicates with him.'

'I suppose so. You may not know that Mr Duke announced just two hours ago that the filming will resume at the request of Ken Johnson's father. It's really not police business, but will Mili be fit to continue?'

Dr Carroll raised his bushy eyebrows. 'That depends on when and what she's required to resume. Her foot will be sore for a while. I don't think she could run without crippling pain, but people always surprise me. They're unpredictable.' He smiled, his eyes sad.

'Would it be possible to make someone step on a stonefish?'

'What? Do you think that's what happened to Mili?'

'No, just wondering if I can rule that hypothesis out, Doctor.'

Once more, his eyes were appraising. 'Let me think. I guess it's possible. If you saw a stonefish in the shallows or on the sand, you could call out to someone to join you and if the fish was in front of you, they could step on it, if they didn't notice it themselves. But unless you guided or pulled them onto it, the chances they'd step on it wouldn't be high, would they? Maybe if you were walking beside someone, talking, it would be easier to steer someone onto it. Even so, no guarantee—far from it. And if the other person noticed it—well, you'd be sprung, wouldn't you? Seriously, I don't recommend it, Detective Sergeant.'

She smiled. '*Vinaka vakalevu*, Dr Carroll.'

'A pleasure.' He lifted his white coat, rummaged in a trouser pocket, and fished out a dog-eared business card. 'You can give that to Mr Duke if you have the chance. He can ring me any time. I'll be in touch with Barbara, anyway. Let me take you to Mili now.'

Mili seemed to be dozing. Her right foot was elevated but didn't seem swollen to Singh's inexpert eye. Dr Carroll tapped her on the shoulder.

'Mili, can you wake up now? You've got visitors.'

The girl stirred. 'What, more visitors?' She struggled to open her eyes in the bright light streaming through the glass louvres.

'I'll leave you with her now.' Dr Carroll smiled and left.

Mili pulled herself up on her backrest of white pillows. DC Waqa plumped and adjusted them until she was comfortable. 'Can I move the pillow under your foot? Is it comfortable?' At Mili's nod, she gave that pillow a workout too. 'Better now?' she enquired.

'Oh yes, much, *vinaka*,' Mili answered, smiling. 'I didn't expect this treatment from the police! Nurses in disguise, are you?'

Mili looked well, although it must take the body much longer to get back to normal after an attack by the most venomous fish in the world. They would need to be gentle.

'We're all qualified in first aid, at least,' Singh smiled. 'I'm glad you've had visitors. We saw Lui Tuvoli downstairs. Did he come to see you?'

'Oh no, just Barbara Koroi, the nurse, but of course you know her from when the evil stonefish stung me.'

'How much do you remember about getting stung?'

'I've been trying to remember. It's all a bit blurry.'

'Did you go down to the beach with a friend?'

Mili frowned. 'Oh no, just the opposite. It's been so hard since Ken died and we moved to the barracks. It's like a city compared to Motu.' She gazed out the windows, in a dream. 'Everyone rushing around, a cramped little room with Desi. I wanted to be by myself in a natural place.'

'It was a good thing Eroni turned up then, wasn't it?'

'It certainly was. I hadn't been there long when he arrived. I was ambling along the sand at the water's edge, soaking in the peace and beauty. Eroni came up behind me and called out, so I stopped. He'd come to pick out bits of driftwood for set props. We walked along for a bit until he spotted some on the high-water line and went to look it over.'

'What did you do then?'

'You know, this is where my memory becomes hazy. Maybe the effect of the poison will wear off in time and I'll remember. But I must have continued along, lost in a daydream, not paying any attention to where I put my feet—that bit's obvious, isn't it?' She smiled a rueful smile. 'The next thing I remember is unbearable, unbearable pain, screaming my head off and Nurse Barbara holding me and telling me I'd be okay soon. Later you propped me up—I can never thank you enough—and Barbara and a man put my foot in a bucket of hot water. That was such a blessing. I was still in agony but not as bad as before. I must have been unconscious some of the time, I think.'

'You certainly gave us all a scare, Mili. Eroni looked terrified when he came to our police office shouting out for us to help.'

'Oh, did he?'

'Was anyone else on the beach?'

'Just a few people, but they were quite a way off. I should be grateful to Eroni then.'

'Yes indeed. Do you know him well?'

'Just a bit. He's a standby props, so we used to run into each other when we were shooting.' She looked down, suddenly shy. 'He's a bit of a fan, actually. Told me he saw all my appearances on The Voice.'

'Someone said you're from the same village.'

'Oh no, I don't think so. We are both from Taveuni Island, though. My parents would know. I migrated with my parents to the States when I was twelve. I've forgotten a lot about village life. I embraced my American school. I was heavily into choir and music and then got a music scholarship. That was my teenage life and my proud parents encouraged me all the way.'

Singh could remember life before she was eleven clearly. She must have been a child who harboured resentments, as the myriad taunts about her light green eyes remained vivid. Everyone else at her school, including her friends, had brown eyes, and it was probably only a few who teased her. But that wasn't what she remembered. Would she have forgotten her life in Fiji if her family had left for greener pastures overseas? Surely not.

DC Waqa piped up. 'I've seen The Voice too, Mili. You're a wonderful singer. What made you apply for Champion? Such a different sort of competition.'

'Oh well, the casting director approached my agent with an offer of a place. I was quite reluctant, but my parents urged me on. They said it would be great for my fans in Fiji and indeed for the entire country. The contestants are in isolation here, so I have no idea if people are even interested.'

'They are more than interested, Mili. The whole country is behind you.'

'But how can the show continue now?'

'Two hours ago, Mr Duke announced Champion will resume. Ken's father wants the series completed as a tribute to his son. How do you feel about that?'

Tears filled Mili's eyes and trickled down her cheeks. She mopped them with the edge of the sheet.

'That's—that's wonderful news. I wish I could meet Mr Johnson.'

'He's a very nice man, down to earth and honest. Inspector Horseman and I just had lunch with him, the contestants, and the executives. They all send you their best wishes. Mili, it's none of my business, but do you think you'll be fit enough?'

'Oh, I don't know. I'm sure Mr Duke will work out something with the doctor.'

'Do you want to go back?'

'Oh yes, if I can. I do like to finish whatever I start, even if I don't win. I've had that drummed into me for so long, I can't consider quitting. My parents would be so disappointed.'

'Do you know who's been supplying drugs on the set?'

'Oh no, I really have trouble believing that story. I tested negative, I think.'

'Yes, you did, but some other people were positive. It's double-checked and a definite fact.'

'Well, they kept it to themselves, that's all I can say.' Mili sounded quite resentful.

'Did anyone ever offer you pills on set?'

'Oh, no, never.'

'Did you ever ask any of the others for pills?'

Mili yawned. 'No. I'm getting sleepy again. Thank you both for coming to see me.'

Singh got up. 'Oh, I brought you some snacks for when you're feeling peckish.'

Mili brightened. 'Gee, thanks so much. Crystallised pineapple and pawpaw. I think I'm peckish already!' She tore open the packet of pawpaw eagerly.

29

After lunch, Horseman and DC Tanielo Musudroka tidied up their Champion office for the MDMA-positive interviews.

'How can we force these idiots to tell us the supplier, sir?' Musudroka asked.

'We can't, Tani. I wish we could. They probably won't give up any names. But we must give them the opportunity to do so. I've been trying to think of a carrot we could dangle instead of a stick.'

'Sounds good. What's your carrot?'

'Watch and learn, Tani. Watch and learn. Who's our first?'

'Bobby O'Leary, age 35, sports teacher and baseball coach.'

'If he's not waiting outside, find him and bring him in.'

Musudroka ushered O'Leary in six seconds later. His fair skin looked more pink than a few days ago. Had O'Leary stopped using the company-supplied sunscreen?

'Take a seat here, Mr O'Leary. Would you like a bottle of water?' Musudroka placed the bottle on the table beside the contestant.

'What's your feeling about Mr Duke's meeting this morning?' Horseman asked.

'Surprised, actually. I expected him to announce the shoot's cancellation.'

'Are you pleased it's going ahead?'

'Yeah, guess so. Just tough getting my head around it is all. And we were all so in the swing of it before. Since Ken died and we moved here, we've just been shooting bits and pieces for four days...I dunno. It's all gone flat. It'll be tough resuming, I reckon. More like acting maybe.'

'You tested positive for MDMA yesterday and an independent lab analysis has confirmed that result. What's your response to that?'

O'Leary ran his fingers through his short red hair. 'I don't know how that happened. It's a mistake because I've never taken any drugs, anyways.'

'Never ever, or never on the Champion set?'

'Never on the Champion set. Everyone tries out drugs when they're young and foolish.'

'And when was that for you?'

'In college. That's a long time ago now.'

'Has anyone here offered you MDMA in the form of ecstasy pills or mollies?'

'No, never.'

'Have you asked anyone at Champion to supply you with any kind of drug?'

'No.'

'Have you heard of anyone at Champion who supplies drugs for contestants or crew?'

'No.'

'What do you think Mr Duke will do when he learns of your positive test?'

'I don't know. His policy is to sack anyone caught taking drugs. But I'm not sure it's ever been tested. Not in this series anyway.'

'How would you feel if they sacked you from the show?'

'How would I feel? Like someone threw a bucket of cold water over me when I was dreaming the most wonderful dream of my life.'

'Mr O'Leary, there's a chance for you to avoid testing the director's policy as it applies to you. If you give us your supplier's name, Mr Duke won't hear of your positive test.'

'Really? You can really do that?'

'Mr Duke has no legal right to your medical information, Bobby. You may have agreed to provide it in your contract, but that's not the law of the land.'

O'Leary took a long swig of water.

'Would you prefer to write it down? Here's paper and pencil.'

'I would if I could, Inspector. But I don't know the supplier. If there is one.'

'I'm sorry you can't help, Bobby.'

Musudroka got up and opened the door for O'Leary. 'Good luck in the contest, then.'

The second interview, with cameraman Nikhil Seth and the third, with the junior boatman, Nete Kafoa, were just as unproductive.

'This is weird, sir. Can four lab tests possibly be all wrong? What's your take on these guys?' Musudroka sounded nearly as frustrated as Horseman felt.

'*Io*, it's possible all the lab tests were wrong, but that's extremely, and I mean extremely, unlikely. It's best to pursue the most probable hypothesis rather than such an unlikely one.'

'So we assume the tests are all correct, that all four took drugs and are bare-faced liars.'

'You've got it, Tani. Whether one of them is also the prankster, or the drug supplier, or both, we don't know.'

'Fifty-fifty, you reckon then?'

'*Io*, as far as we know now. I must say, I'm bracing myself for our next chat with Ms Desirée Lopez. With her, a sensible conversation can turn in an instant into sobs and floods of tears. Talk about melodrama.'

'I'm looking forward to meeting her sir. Shall I go and get her now?'

'*Vinaka*, Tani. How about you lead off the questions this time?'

Desi looked better after a few days at the Champion barracks. Her hair was lustrous, her face less drawn and she wore clean shorts and top. Musudroka couldn't take his eyes off her as he placed a fresh bottle of water and a pencil and paper on her right. His silence continued after he sat beside Horseman, who had to prompt him to begin the interview.

'Oh, um, let's begin, Ms Lopez. Were you surprised by Mr Duke's announcement that Champion would continue?'

With some ostentation, Desi repositioned her water and paper and pencil to her left side.

'It's a right-hand world, Detective Constable. All my life, I've suffered for being left-handed.'

'Sorry, Ms Lopez.'

'Never mind, but here's a tip. In future place things for interviewees' use in the centre of the table. That way, you won't make left-handers feel awkward when they have to move them.'

'Good idea, Ms Lopez. I'll do that.'

'And please call me Desi. Now, to answer your question, it's a yes and a no. Yes, I was surprised that a southern racist like Ken Johnson's dad would approve of the show continuing with a black and Hispanic among the finalists...' Desi paused.

Horseman admired her technique: first, putting Musudroka down and second, distracting him from his purpose.

'Oh, who's black?'

Now Desi looked disconcerted. 'Who? Mili, of course.'

'But Mili's Fijian.'

'Fijians are black.'

'Well, we think of ourselves as Fijians, not black.' He considered his bare forearm. 'Don't we?' Musudroka frowned in confusion.

'Yes, most of us do, I agree. But let's get back to the question, Detective Constable.' Horseman willed Musudroka not to get drawn into an exchange about why Ken's father was racist.

'Oh, yes. Desi, you've told us you were both surprised and not surprised by the decision about Champion. Why were you not surprised?'

Now it was Desi who frowned in confusion. 'Um, did I? Ah, yes. I wasn't surprised in the sense that Steve is so clever and capable, I expected he'd be able to work something out. Looks like he persuaded Ken's dad to his own point of view, too.'

'Is it the right decision, in your opinion?'

'Totally. To cancel the show just because Ken died is so unfair to the other finalists. We deserve our chance.'

'How do you rate your chance?' Musudroka asked eagerly.

Desi favoured him with a playful smile. 'I'd say I'm in the running. But nothing's certain. That's the nature of competition, isn't it?'

'Will your MDMA positive drug test affect your chances?'

'I'm trying to ignore that. As I told Inspector Horseman, this test is a mistake. I've never taken party pills on Champion, or any other drug for that matter. Please don't upset me.' She sniffed and tears overflowed her eyes.

Horseman quickly put the box of tissues in front of her, neither to the right nor the left. He imagined he was Singh and said gently, 'Please try to calm down, Desi. We value your help. Can you continue, do you think?'

She dried her eyes, sniffed again. 'Sure, I'll try.'

'The other positives didn't say where they got the drugs—'

'Other positives? Who?'

'We can't disclose personal medical information, I'm afraid.' Horseman nodded to Musudroka to continue.

'You're our last chance. Do you know who supplies drugs on Champion?'

'No.'

'Has anyone asked you for drugs, or asked you who to get them from?'

'No.'

'Desi, you must have wondered about this. Do you suspect anyone of supplying drugs on set?'

Desi's lowered her head. When she looked up at Musudroka, her eyes enormous under her thick eyelashes, she whispered, 'You understand, Detective. Yes, I have thought about this. In my opinion, the drug supplier must have been Ken Johnson.'

'Ken?'

'Makes sense, doesn't it? He brought the pills with him, hidden somewhere for his own use and to sell to others. Or share, as we don't have any money on Motu.'

'Why?'

'Maybe to improve the performance of his tribe. That's why he never offered them to me or my tribe.'

'That's a neat theory, Desi. How will Mr Duke react to your positive result, d'you think?'

'What? What happened to medical privacy? You were all for it a moment ago!'

Horseman spoke up. 'This is different, Desi. Mr Duke requested tests for selected employees after Ken's positive result. He was acting on evidence and it would have been irresponsible of him not to do so. I'll give him the results when we've finished our interviews here. I'm duty bound to do so.'

Desi was silent. Then she replied, 'My guess is that Steve will come up with a solution as he has before. You said I'm not the only positive. So if he sacked me and at least another, that leaves a final with two players, maybe only one. In effect, he'd be cancelling the show in a blaze of terrible publicity. Despite the results, he has very little choice but to ignore them. Don't you agree?'

'We'll soon know,' Horseman replied.

30

Horseman pondered the paradox that was Desi Lopez as he walked to the director's office. Did she suffer from some psychological disturbance or was she an actress auditioning for different roles? She could be intensely emotional, rational, melodramatic, and shrewd all within a minute or two. Could she be the prankster or drug dealer? He could picture her setting a tripline for Ken, but surely she hadn't meant Ken to die. He hoped her beauty hadn't prejudiced him. She was clever, but perhaps not as clever as she believed.

He cut through the canteen, making a diagonal to the wide door at the back corner. It was now restored to its usual dining configuration: two rows of long rectangular tables with benches and chairs. A few steps from the doorway, a glimmer in the corner stopped him. Something flashed in a shaft of low afternoon sunlight. Something he couldn't pass by.

On the floor near the wall sat a shiny metal box, probably aluminium. He picked it up and put it on the table and tried the catches. It opened easily. The inside was moulded to hold several components of an expensive-looking microphone. One of the audio technicians must have left it behind after the meeting. But there were other explanations, so he removed all the items and checked the box. No secret compartments, false panels or anything wedged behind the lining as far as he could tell. He'd find the head of the Sound department if he could do so before he met with Steve Duke.

A grass quadrangle separated the hall from the row of executive offices. Nikhil Seth stood talking to two other men in the shade of a breadfruit tree. Seth waved and Horseman strolled across.

'What do you think of the announcement, Inspector?' Nikhil asked.

Horseman smiled. 'My opinion's worth nothing. But it makes sense. What about you guys?'

'Pleased as punch. No one likes a cancel. Ken's dad was a hit with all of us!'

'A very decent man.'

Seth was eyeing the case Horseman was carrying. 'I just picked this microphone up. Someone must have left it behind in the canteen. D'you know where the sound crew hang out?'

'Well, Don's the sound recordist. He's working on a video of Ken's dad's visit here. Bit weird, though. The mike was set up on a stand at the front of the hall. Still, he could have packed it up and left it behind. I can return it to him.'

'No need, thanks. I'd like to have a word with him, anyway.'

Seth glanced at his companions. 'Well, he'll be glad to have it back.'

'We've had a few losses in the Camera department and not because crew have been careless. There could be a thief at work here,' another man added, shuffling his feet.

Seth looked embarrassed. 'We can't prove it, though. Could be those things got lost.'

'Come on, man. How likely is that? There're just too many of them.'

'Did anyone report the thefts to the police?' Horseman asked.

'Don't think so. The director wouldn't want the press to get hold of it and blow it up. Bad for Champion's reputation. And what could the police do?'

Horseman bridled, but tried to keep his voice friendly. 'We do have some success in recovering stolen property. But if you could help me locate Don, I'll check this item with him.'

'Sure, I've got time. I'll walk over to the sound studio with you. It's a bit tucked away. See you guys later.' He waved to his companions.

Seth led Horseman back around the canteen, skirting the main quadrangle.

'How many missing items have you had?'

'Around half a dozen. Smaller things, as you'd expect.'

They approached an addition sticking out from one corner of the quad. Seth pointed out two wooden steps up to a door. 'That's the sound studio. There's no way in from the quad verandah.'

'*Vinaka*. I doubt I would have found it without a guide.' Seth looked eager to walk with him, so he said, 'I'll let you get back to your work, Nik.' Seth took the hint, turned, and walked away.

Horseman knocked and waited. After some time, the door opened and a harassed-looking man said, 'Yes?'

'Excuse me for interrupting your work. I'm Detective Inspector Joe Horseman. Are you Don?'

'Yes.' Don was abrupt, eager to return to whatever he was doing.

Horseman held up the microphone case. 'I was passing through the canteen and noticed this lying on the floor. Is it yours?'

'Well, we use those but I'm sure ours are on our shelves. Come in. I'll check.'

The studio was windowless and carpeted. The ceiling and walls were lined with insulating material. On one side, a couple of cubicles were curtained off with quilted fabric.

Don turned to his assistant, a pudgy young Fijian. 'Vili, check the Sennheiser omnidirectionals, will you? We should have three.'

'Sure,' said Vili, staring at Horseman, before going over to a long wall of industrial shelving.

'Are they there?' Don asked, abrupt as before, his pale face creased with worry.

'Two where they should be. I'll just check all the shelves. The other one could be in the wrong place.'

Vili searched while Don tapped away at his laptop.

'Can I check the serial number on the mike you found? I've pulled up ours.'

Horseman handed over the case. Don unscrewed a component and pointed a screwdriver at an engraved serial number.

'See, it matches the highlighted number on my spreadsheet.' He indicated his laptop screen. Horseman checked. The numbers matched.

'My life would be easier if everyone kept such meticulous records. It's yours. Did you take it to the canteen this morning?'

'I took one as a backup for the main mike, yes. I don't log serial numbers for what we take in and out ourselves, only if another department requests a loan. I can't be sure this was the backup I took.'

'Have you lost any other items?'

'Well, as I've just demonstrated, you don't realise something's missing until the next time you want to use it. We seem to have lost a small sound recorder. Annoying, but if something small gets dropped in the scrub or rocks or water, it's hard to find.'

'Do you suspect theft?'

'It happens. Just opportunistic. The local hires are great, but there's the rare one who supplements his income by stealing. Sometimes the oddest things that would be impossible to sell—last year a very heavy lighting ballast that would be useless on its own went missing.'

Vili headed to the door, muttering something about the canteen.

Horseman got out his notebook. 'I'll just take down the details if you don't mind.'

Don gestured to his laptop. 'Sure, you returned our mike so go ahead.'

'Who do you report missing items to?'

Don shrugged, looking confused. 'It doesn't happen to us often. And we don't exactly 'report' something's missing, as far as I know. When we notice it's gone and we need to replace it, we go through Purchasing. To order, we have to explain why we need the item, and that's where we'd fill in *lost, stolen or strayed*, as it were.'

'I see. Thanks for the information.'

'No bother. Thanks for the service!'

As he retraced his steps towards the director's office, Horseman struggled with this new piece of the puzzle that was Champion. A prankster, a drug dealer and now a thief. One criminal or two or several? Organised or random? And who killed Ken Johnson? He hoped the set thefts might help identify the killer, but right now they just added to the confusion. His purpose in seeking out Steve Duke was to tell him the results of yesterday's drug screening. He expected he'd react in the way Desi Lopez had predicted. But how would Duke take the news of a thief on set?

31

'Desi? I don't believe it!' Duke shouted. His eyes darted around his office then with reluctance, focused on Horseman again.

'I'm afraid there's no doubt, Mr Duke. The forensic lab did a second analysis of Desi's sample with the same result as the instant test kit Barbara Koroi used. Positive for MDMA.'

The director deflated a little. 'Oh well, Barbara's rock solid. What does Desi have to say about it?'

'Quite a lot, actually. She's upset and flatly denies ever taking drugs or being given pills by anyone here. She nominated Ken Johnson as the most likely candidate for supplying drugs.'

'Ken? Nonsense. He was a genuine clean-living guy like his father. What did you think of his dad, by the way?'

'Very impressed. He was generous in refusing the prize-money and encouraging the contest to continue without Ken.'

'You bet. But back to my problem. Bobby's positive too. That doesn't amaze me, Bobby's always played his cards close to his chest. Still. I'm surprised. He seemed a straight-up-and-down kinda guy. So, what've we got here? Two out of four finalists took drugs, and we don't know yet if and when Mili can resume the competition. Ken's dad wants the show to go ahead, and the press release has gone out. My hands are tied, aren't they?'

'Can you cancel your zero-tolerance on drugs policy, just like that?'

'What? Aren't you getting far too nosey, not to mention judgemental? No, the policy still stands, sure it does. But our situation is desperate, so I'll have to ignore those test results to keep the commitment we've just made. You've gotta be pragmatic to survive in this game, Inspector.' He consulted the report again. 'And Nikhil Seth too? Can't do without him either. No, the only way is to shelve this report.'

'It's your choice, Mr Duke. The police won't be making it public.'

There was a knock at the door, followed by a young assistant bearing a tray. She set down a plunger of coffee, milk, sugar, and mugs and left.

'We don't have the finesse of you Fijians with the snacks, Inspector, but the coffee's strong and fresh.'

'Nothing's more important than that.' Horseman sniffed the aroma with appreciation as Duke poured.

'Another matter's just come to my attention, though. By chance. It seems there's been a spate of thefts of equipment from the set here. No one reported these incidents to us. A pity because we could help a lot with such a problem.'

'Thefts? No, we run a tight ship on Champion.'

A tight ship that was springing leaks one after the other.

'If you haven't heard about them, maybe you should set up a direct reporting system. I've just heard that unless a missing item is re-ordered through Purchasing, there's no formal way of reporting a theft. Is that correct?'

'I don't know. I don't deal with every little administrative detail.' The director was irritated now and with good cause.

'Have you heard about any missing items?' Horseman asked.

Duke ran a hand through his well-cut grey hair and shrugged. 'No point in holding out on you, Inspector. Yep, I've heard it goes on a little, here and there. Just opportunistic theft by the local hires, I believe. Better to cop the losses than to get a poor reputation.'

'How does your insurance company view your tolerant attitude?' Horseman smiled.

'I think that's my business, Inspector.'

'If you called us in, the thieves would get the message that maybe it's not a good idea to steal from the Champion location.'

'We're guests here. I prefer to be self-sufficient, not make demands on Fiji government services like the police.'

'We're always happy to help visitors to our country, Mr Duke. We're embarrassed when criminal elements target investors like you. How would Champion suffer if you sought police help? It's the thieves whose reputations would be damaged.'

Duke sipped his coffee, so Horseman did the same.

'Since I started investigating Ken Johnson's death five days ago, I've learned of a series of pranks against contestants, some of whom have taken illegal drugs. That means someone is supplying the drugs, whether obtained locally or imported by contestants or crew. Now up pops a thief on Champion, possibly more. There must be a connection between Ken's death and the recent surge of crime.'

'That may be so, Inspector. I have no way of finding the truth about that. I have just a few days to achieve my purpose in Fiji—that is to film an entertaining TV game show series. I've gotta focus on my goal.'

The director aged before Horseman's eyes as his brow furrowed in anxiety. Duke was right—how could he find out the truth? That was Horseman's job, and he would pursue it whether or not Steve Duke cared. What's more, if Duke intended finishing the shoot in just a few days, that had to be Horseman's deadline too.

32

Horseman was in the middle of updating the case running sheet back at the station when Dr Pillai called. Their appointment had slipped from Horseman's mind.

'Good afternoon, Joe. I'm hoping you don't mind me checking with you. Are you free to meet Shiv and the others a bit earlier, at half-past five?'

Dr Pillai was much too polite to admit his call was a reminder, but he'd witnessed Horseman's frequent late arrivals and occasional absences from Shiners' training and even games.

'*Io, vinaka* for reminding me, Raj. I got back from the Champion location a while ago. Is there something wrong?' He shuffled through the loose papers on his desk. He was sure he'd printed out the agenda.

'No, no. Are you ready to sign the application Shiv's prepared?'

'I think so. Shiv's documents make sense: all in order as far as I can judge.'

'I agree. My goodness, it's a big step though, isn't it? This meeting will be the time to raise the smallest question and slightest doubt. Unwise to rush in, Joe.'

'You're the angel, Raj. And I'll try not to play the fool.'

'Ha, ha, very funny but untrue. I'll be seeing you soon, then.'

The light dimmed and Horseman glanced at his watch. Much too early for twilight. He looked out the louvres. Black clouds were rolling in. Black and threatening. When he left the station, the heavy curtain of rain made it hard to see anything. Yet vehicles, horns blaring and wipers struggling, hurtled through it as if their lives were at stake. It was knock-off time and workers crowded the narrow footpaths, spilling on to the road, holding their umbrellas low. His early days as a traffic constable told him there would be accidents.

The office of Patel, Narayan and Smith, Solicitors was above a busy fabric shop in Victoria Parade. He deposited his umbrella in the plastic bucket outside the door and went in. The receptionist smiled, reached into a cupboard behind her and presented him with a dry towel.

Horseman glanced at her name badge. '*Vinaka*, Evi, how thoughtful.' When he'd mopped himself down, she ushered him into a conference room where Dr Pillai, the Action for Children adviser, Gloria Chung, and Shiv Narayan already sat enjoying a late afternoon tea.

'Come in, Joe. You'll remember my secretary, Rina, who'll take notes. But perhaps you haven't met Meri Street, the Save the Children publicist.'

Horseman shook hands and Rina poured him tea from the gold-edged china teapot. Evi placed the plate of biscuits in front of him then left, shutting the door.

'Joe, it's my greatest honour to help realise your vision of a hostel in Suva for the homeless boys in your Junior Shiners squad. You and Dr Pillai have wisely chosen to register the hostel as a charity. We'll check through the application documents and if you agree, sign them off this afternoon. However, there are one or two details that Gloria and Meri could give us some guidance on first.'

'Sure, I'm happy to consider any advice. What are these details?' Horseman said. Dr Pillai nodded.

Gloria Chung smiled brightly. Her Chinese forbear who had set up business in Fiji several generations ago had bestowed her straight hair, almond eyes, and prominent cheekbones. The rest of her striking beauty came from her Fijian great grandparents. Gloria had a formidable reputation in Suva for developing her family's simple café into three thriving restaurants, each targeting a different market. When she took up the reins of Action for Children five years ago, she surprised both the Suva business world and the not-for-profit sector. At previous meetings, Horseman had felt a bit intimidated by her brisk no-nonsense manner. But she meant well and knew a lot.

'Joe, I'm thrilled you're taking prudent legal steps to establish your project and that Mr Narayan is helping you. I notice on the registration forms the name of the proposed charity is Hostel for Homeless Boys. That strikes me as a classification rather than a name. Don't you agree?'

'*Io*, that's not what the sign on the front door will say. We haven't chosen the hostel's name yet. I understand this is just the legal entity's name for the forms.'

'Once that name's in the computer it will crop up in all sorts of places. It sounds a bit ordinary, don't you think?'

Horseman and Dr Pillai glanced at each other.

'What's your suggestion, Gloria?' Shiv asked.

'A name is everything, or it can be when it's the right name. Think of Save the Children, Red Cross, Habitat for Humanity, Fiji's own Homes of Hope...I could go on. They're catchy and positive. Let's look at yours: *hostel* is too specific and neutral rather than positive, while *homeless* is negative.'

'I agree when you put it like that. What about you, Doctor?'

'My goodness, I see what you mean, Ms Chung,' Dr Pillai replied.

'What you're missing is the most obvious positive words associated with this project—Joe Horseman!' Gloria looked like a magician who'd pulled off a perilous trick.

'Oh yes, excellent idea!' Shiv grinned.

Horseman frowned. 'How do you mean?'

'Really, Joe! You can't be unaware your name is famous throughout Fiji, can you? And well known in rugby-playing countries all over the world. And you're regarded so positively, with all those best-and-fairest awards. Nothing I can think of is more marketable than your name. Meri agrees.'

'I do.' Meri smiled. 'The Joe Horseman name is a real draw card.'

'It's not about me, though. It's about the kids—getting a safe roof over their heads and regular food in their bellies.' He looked at Dr Pillai, desperate for support.

'Nutritious meals build their stamina.' Dr Pillai added.

'Great copy,' Meri said as she scribbled in her notebook.

'Copy?'

'Yes, I asked Meri along to share her ideas for a publicity plan and schedule. But let's help you decide on the name of the charitable trust before we get to that.'

Horseman resisted being put on the spot. 'I need to think about that a bit more.'

Shiv gave him a sympathetic smile. 'You can take as long as you like to settle on a name. As Gloria reminded us, it's terribly important. But I've expedited the process because you want to get that roof over the boys' heads as soon as you can.'

'*Io*, I know that, Shiv.'

'So, let's benefit from our experts while we can. It's not a big deal to change our trading name from the uninspiring holding name I filled in. I think Gloria's idea has great merit. Gloria?'

Gloria beamed. '*Vinaka*, Shiv. There are several alternatives using your name, Joe. *Joe Horseman Homes, Joe Horseman Youth Foundation...*'

'I'd like the word Shiners included. That's how the idea started—with a shoe-shine boy named Tevita.'

'Great origin story,' Meri enthused as her pen flew.

'Yes, but few Fijians care about shoe-shine boys and Shiners means nothing overseas. The name has got to attract donors.'

She was right, Horseman knew, but he couldn't bring himself to cave in. Not just yet anyway.

'Ms Chung, you've made compelling arguments. But it could be a mistake to decide on the spur of the moment,' Dr Pillai said.

'Sure. I've also heard that a quick decision is a good decision.'

Shiv intervened. 'Let's come back to the name in a minute. Meri, would you like to outline your publicity ideas now?'

Meri took off her heavy-framed reading glasses and shed years. He guessed she was around thirty. Clear blue eyes that shone with enthusiasm enlivened her otherwise nondescript appearance. 'Gentlemen, I'm delighted to help this charity, and will do so as a volunteer. I've prepared a sample schedule of what needs to be done before the actual launch.'

Her fingers trembled as she passed around printed sheets. 'So, to start out you'll need a logo, letterhead, press release, photos, a website, flyers, and protocols for the use of all this material. Read through the sample schedule, and you'll see the pre-launch campaign steps. It's vital to grow public interest over a series of media exposures. Any questions?'

Shiv and Dr Pillai asked about various details, but Horseman sat stunned, then poured himself another cup of tea. He hadn't envisaged any campaigns, pre-launch, post-launch or otherwise. He'd agreed to set up the hostel as a charity for compelling legal and business reasons. Did all charities need logos and the trappings of publicity campaigns? He thought of those he knew. All had websites and other items on Meri's list, even the Sunshine Home. He looked at her tables again. It all made sense, but at a considerable cost. He gulped his lukewarm tea.

'Do you have any questions, Joe?' Shiv asked.

'*Vinaka vakalevu*, Meri. Your work has been a fast introduction to the reality of a charity. I hadn't realised it was a business, which wasn't my aim. However, I accept that the business side is a necessary means to my end. Can I see costings for these items?'

'Sure, I can prepare those.'

Gloria Chung leaned forward, her eyes bright. 'Remember that once the charity with your name is registered, supporters will donate or discount many of Meri's costed items: time, expertise and even material items like printing and stationery.'

'I can see now we need a proper business plan and budget.'

'Absolutely, you do. As I mentioned at an earlier meeting, that's a service Action for Children offers to all children's charity projects. Naturally, you can employ your own accountant if you prefer.'

'*Vinaka*, Gloria. I'm grateful.'

'One last point, gentlemen. I know you want to make a practical start. Well, you can, even without a name and without a budget. You'll see the first item of Meri's list is photos. We're having a professional photo session on Monday for our mobile pre-school project. If you could round up your Shiners and make yourselves available too, our photographer can produce a complete portfolio to use when you're ready. We've hired him for the day so—the offer's there at no cost to you.'

Horseman exchanged a look with Dr Pillai. Shiv nodded. 'That's a generous offer, Gloria. Shiners training is on Monday afternoon, so that's perfect. We accept with gratitude.'

After Gloria and Meri left, Shiv said, 'I take it you don't want to go ahead and sign the documents now?'

'I'm ready to sign, Shiv, but we should decide a name first. Gloria's quite right that we need a more appealing name. I'm just not convinced my name needs to be there,' Horseman said.

'Her arguments convinced me, Joe,' Dr Pillai said with a smile. 'And if we're going to have considerable admin costs, apart from the cost in running the hostel itself—then we'll need the money your name will bring in.'

Shiv said, 'I agree with Raj. But if you need more time...'

Frustration surged in Horseman. He couldn't stand his own indecision. On the Champion case, everyone wanted to obstruct his progress. But around this table, everyone wanted to help him. It was him who was being difficult and yes, egotistic in refusing to give his name to the project so dear to his heart. He had the ball; he could pass it or run with it and not let go.

The others waited for him.

'The Joe Horseman Trust. Shall we go for it?'

The others clapped and thumped the table. Shiv said, 'An excellent decision, I think. Rina, can you insert the new name on the form?'

'Sure, it'll take two minutes and I'll reprint the relevant pages. No problem at all.'

'Then ring Hare Krishna and get them to deliver a banquet for four on our account.'

SATURDAY

33

At ten o'clock the following morning, Horseman's case review meeting was in full flight when Superintendent Ratini walked in. All five detectives froze for a moment before getting to their feet. Ratini relished such tokens of respect due to rank but dismissed the gesture with a wave.

'Carry on. I hope you've got progress to report?'

'*Io* sir. We've discovered more evidence which DS Singh's outlining on the board. We're now trying to narrow down our suspects.'

'Aha, that's where the genuine detective work comes in! You shouldn't have a problem with DS Singh in charge of the whiteboard, eh?' Ratini's smile was more of a leer.

Horseman tamped down his growing irritation, before again recounting the alleged pranks, the positive drug tests, and the thefts of equipment from Champion.

'All three activities disrupt the filming and the contest itself, don't they? If one person's responsible for all of them, maybe their goal is to stop the show.' Ratini said.

Horseman had to admit the super could sometimes put two and two together. 'That's possible, sir. Revenge on Steve Duke for a past grievance or even a ruthless competitor?'

'But who?' Ratini demanded. 'That's what you detectives need to detect! Too much theorising and not enough action. What are you all doing this afternoon?'

'I'm going out to FIT to talk to Lui Tuvoli, who organises the Fijian interns on Champion. I know it's Saturday, but my guess is that someone from the Film and Television department will be around, even if Lui isn't.'

'He's a suspect too?' Ratini frowned.

'Not quite. Person of interest. So far, I've only his own version of what he does. DS Singh and DC Musudroka are going to
Champion to talk to our suspects about the thefts. DC Kau and
probationer Waqa will catch up with the case records.'

Ratini made the harrumphing sound that signalled he had no
particular objection to a plan. 'It's not promising, is it?' He wiped
his hands down the legs of his shorts and tramped off to his office.

***

Horseman strolled around the FIT campus at Samabula, looking
for the Film and Television department. The Institute's signposts
could certainly do with a rethink, but he enjoyed the mid-year
sunshine and freshening breeze of the trade wind. Most of all,
he enjoyed being among the lively young apprentices attending
Saturday classes after a week's hard work. He wondered whether
some of the Junior Shiners might join their ranks one day. With
the security of a safe roof over their heads, why not?

Film and Television's home was a newer building wedged between two large industrial sheds belonging to Automotive and
Engineering, respectively. Through the glass doors the place looked
deserted, but they slid open automatically. So far, so good. He
picked up a photocopied plan from the reception counter and
decided the best place to start was the television studio on the
first floor. He tapped on the door, opened it, and went in. At the
opposite end of the large room, dazzling lights illuminated a set
rigged out like a TV news studio. About seven students worked the
equipment and three were on camera. A few more hovered about.

Monitors and computer equipment cluttered the long tables lining the side walls. Just two students worked in the semi-darkness,
their dancing hands spotlighted by desk lamps. Horseman went
up to the nearest. The familiar eBay screen displayed on the old
desktop computer.

'Excuse me, I'm looking for Mr Lui Tuvoli. Would you know his
whereabouts?'

He startled the student, who lurched in his chair, all but tipping over. He stared wide-eyed as Horseman backed off a step. The boy's right hand flew to his chest, revealing an open notebook on the table.

'N-no. Sorry, don't know why I jumped like that. Lui was in earlier to set me up with this job, not sure if he's still around. His office is at the end of the corridor.'

The wavy-haired Indian kid was just a teenager. 'Are you studying Film and Television?' Horseman asked.

A smile lit up the boy's face, making him look even younger. 'Yeah, it's great.'

'If I'd had that chance, I would've grabbed it, I reckon. I'll take a photo of your news program set-up if I may. Just like the real thing!'

He raised his phone and took a few shots then bent, pretending to check them, and took another few of the notebook and eBay screen in front of him.

'Are you one of the Champion interns?'

'I wish! Only final year students got that gig. Fair enough, though. Maybe next year.'

Horseman nodded at the screen. 'Is this a course project you're working on now?'

'Kinda.' He covered the notebook with his arm.

Horseman nodded towards the screen and chuckled. 'Are you looking to buy some cheap equipment for yourself?'

It was the kid's turn to laugh. 'You're kidding! I can't even afford cheap equipment. Maybe one day, though. I'm getting an idea of prices on some items. When the department upgrades equipment, Mr Tuvoli likes to sell the old stuff if possible. He says that's like getting a big discount on the new purchase.'

'That's businesslike. What are you pricing now?'

'An old Sony monitor. Hey, aren't you Joe Horseman, the Sevens captain from a few years ago?'

The 'few years ago' stung. But, as the Portland orthopaedic surgeon told him six months before, he had to accept reality. Denying the facts wouldn't help. Melissa had said the same thing before she told him, weeping, that their long-distance romance held no future. She wouldn't be happy living in Fiji, and she couldn't expect him to move to the States. She wanted to remain friends, just like his other ex-es. Horseman didn't know if he could do that.

'That's me,' he said to the kid.

'Wow, I've seen some of your games on TV. Um, er, pleased to meet you. I'm Resh Joshi.' The kid stood up and they shook hands. 'I actually prefer soccer,' he added, looking away.

Horseman grinned. 'Good man, soccer's an awesome game. Do you play?'

'I do, in the Institute's second grade team. I'm no star.'

'You're young, you'll improve if you work at it. Persistence counts more than anything.'

'Maybe not for me. My dream is to get into sports cinematography if I can.'

'You're in the right place here, then. Don't give up and good luck!'

Horseman knocked on Lui Tuvoli's office door but there was no answer. He wasn't sorry to miss him. He wanted to think through what he had just seen and heard. If he could scrape together sufficient grounds for a search warrant for the Film and Television building, Tuvoli must be kept in the dark.

He needed to talk the search warrant over with Singh, but when he called, her phone switched him to voicemail. She must still be on the Champion set. He hoped she'd blow the case open. But in the meantime, he'd go back to the station and start on the application.

SUNDAY

34

What better place could there be on a wet Sunday morning than Arabica? It was Horseman's café of choice and fast becoming Singh's, too. When he'd first invited her there for a meeting, she hadn't liked the old warehouse interior, so bare and gloomy. The hessian sacks of beans, coffee roasting ovens and processing paraphernalia were in full view in the cavernous space. Singh preferred the cosy, colourful décor she'd grown up in. It didn't matter how bad things were, brightly decorated surroundings cheered you up. And even when life was good, surely it was better in full colour.

However, Arabica was private. With just a few widely spaced tables close to the enormous plate-glass window, Didi the proprietor catered for coffee aficionados who wanted to taste his single-source Fijian coffee products before they bought their beans or grinds. So Arabica was excellent for mulling over cases. The excellent coffee helped convert her, too.

Horseman was sitting at his favourite table in the far corner, an espresso cup by his hand, reading a file. The best boss she'd ever had, by miles. But for that fact, they could be real friends, for sure. And maybe more. If she let herself, she could fall in love with him, which would destroy her career if it came to anything. He was aware of that fact and far too honourable to do that to her. He liked her, trusted her, valued her ability as a detective. Was there anything more? She didn't know, but probably not. He did seem rather obtuse when it came to women.

He smiled his warm smile as she joined him.

'Good morning, Susie.'

'Good morning, Joe. Sorry I couldn't get back to the station yesterday. A friend's 30th party last night. A young friend!' She felt silly. What did her friend's age matter?

'Nonsense, it was Saturday night! I guess you got nothing much out of the finalists.'

'Nothing much at all. Six days off Motu Island and they're changing. More relaxed, more normal, more confident. That pressure cooker atmosphere has evaporated.'

The waiter came up. 'Latte, Susie?' She smiled and nodded.

'It's like the rugby selection trials at bootcamp. Isolation, competition, and brutal discipline. All that makes you give everything you've got.'

'Friday saw their chance of the prize restored. It also showed them they're not getting kicked out now, even if they test positive for drugs. Honestly, none of the four expressed any interest in the thefts. They all denied hearing about thefts, denied stealing themselves or suspecting anyone.'

Horseman leaned back in his chair. 'They're resuming the last challenges tomorrow. I wonder if the finalists will have the same drive? Is that million dollars enough to keep them on their toes?'

'You always say carrot and stick work best together. This lot don't believe in the stick any longer. That's my feeling,' Singh replied.

The waiter brought Singh's latte and another espresso for Horseman. 'We've got corned beef and pickle sandwiches, Joe. Proper corned beef, not tinned, that is. Didi's mum didn't feel like scones today but she's baked rock cakes instead.'

Food was what let Arabica down for Singh. Didi, the purist owner, believed coffee should be enough for anyone and refused to serve food for a long time. Nevertheless, a year ago he had given in to customer demand. But the food was basic and limited by his mother's inclinations. He still refused to install a kitchen, picking up the food from his mother each day. Singh had skipped breakfast and was hungry.

'I'm ready for an early lunch, aren't you, Joe? A sandwich and a rock cake sound good.'

Horseman ordered the same.

She'd tell him before she forgot again. 'I didn't mention that Lili and I saw Lui Tuvoli at the hospital before we visited Mili. I asked her if he'd been to see her, but she denied it. She got agitated when I asked, though.'

'Glad you mentioned that. See her again today if you can.'

Singh made a note. 'So, did you catch up with Lui Tuvoli at FIT?'

'No, better than that. I suspect he's behind the thieving racket and sells the loot on eBay.'

'Wow!'

Horseman told her about his encounter with Joshi.

'Joshi's version of what he was doing is plausible, even likely. There's hardly enough for a search warrant, really.'

'You're right, but I've filled in what I can, so we can move quickly when we get the evidence. This afternoon I'm going out to Champion to compile a list of the missing items.'

'Will there be anyone on deck today? Duke gave them the weekend off, didn't he? The idea was recharging their batteries to hit the ground running tomorrow.'

'Sure, but there's lots of workaholics in the crew. And I can't hack sitting around waiting for tomorrow.'

'Who's the workaholic here?' Singh laughed.

'Look who's pointing the finger! I bet there'll be enough people around to get a list going, even if it isn't complete. A lot of that expensive gear has serial numbers. Ratini might back a warrant application if we have details like that. We can check them against items stored at Film and Television or computer records of eBay sales. If our tech guys can access the computers there, they'll come up trumps.'

'It's worth a shot. Let's face it, we've got little else. And I'm coming with you. After lunch, that is.'

'I was hoping you'd say that. I'm having a drink with Matt Young at the Holiday Inn after we've taken the dog for a walk. Like to join us? Should be around six, but I'll call you.'

'Yes, I'd like that.'

'Here come our sandwiches now.' Horseman grinned. She'd miss this camaraderie when she was transferred.

***

Outside the city limits, Singh drove carefully past the stream of churchgoers heading home for lunch. They waved happily at the police vehicle as they walked beside the road, carrying Bibles, woven fans and umbrellas. The bright prints of *bula* shirts and dresses lightened the grey day. Singh wondered, as she often did, whether pedestrians smiled and waved because they recognised Horseman in the vehicle. When he wasn't with her, their response seemed less enthusiastic. But she couldn't be sure.

The rain eased and had stopped when they pulled up at Champion's boom gate. Simeoni was on duty. He smiled at her but went around to the passenger's window to talk to Horseman.

'*Bula*, Josefa. Did you catch the Kiwi's game against Samoa last night?'

'I did. Some impressive young players on both sides. But Folau's last try—phenomenal is the only word,' Horseman said.

'Man, exciting, eh? I don't know who you're looking for here, but a big party of Americans have gone on a diving day trip in Beqa Lagoon. Then they're having dinner at The Beachcomber, so who knows when they'll return?'

'*Vinaka*, Simi. No worries.'

Horseman looked at her. 'That might just simplify our job. Let's go.'

He was right. Not only were twenty American crew away on the diving trip, scores of local hires from around Suva had gone home for the weekend. When the detectives stopped off in the canteen, a group of lunchers beckoned them. Someone had mixed *yaqona*, kava, in a plastic bucket and was swirling the liquid then straining it through a clean tea towel. This was modern home-style *yaqona*, the only traditional element being the ground root itself and the half-coconut shell drinking vessels.

Naturally, Horseman was treated as the guest of honour and served first. He lowered his head, clapped once, accepted the bowl, and downed it amid low calls of '*Maca*', empty. When he returned it to the server, he clapped three slow, resounding claps. After that, the crew dropped all ceremony and settled down for a *yaqona*-fuelled Sunday-afternoon chat.

Eager to extract what they needed before the soporific effects of the grog kicked in, Singh said, 'I saw Mili yesterday. Isn't it great she recovered from the stonefish sting so fast? D'you know if she's back on location yet?'

The consensus was that she wasn't, but they all wanted to know about Mili and also the progress on the Ken Johnson case. After the detectives divulged what limited facts they could, Horseman told them about the suspected thefts. One or two looked surprised but most in the group nodded sagely and related incidents they'd witnessed or heard about. Even allowing for some exaggeration, Singh's impression was more Champion property was missing than she'd imagined.

Between them, the *yaqona* drinkers identified senior crew from the Production, Camera, Props, and Visual Effects departments who were around the barracks today. Singh found them on Deepika's personnel list and highlighted them in yellow while Horseman noted their places of work on the site map. Of course, the crew they were seeking could be anywhere, but the official information was a start. They made their excuses to their relaxed informants who urged them to rejoin the *yaqona* circle when they were done with their work.

'We will pray God to reveal the truth to you, *ovisa.*'

'*Vinaka vakalevu,*' Horseman replied. He shook hands all round. One middle-aged woman employed as a set dresser clung to his hand as tears ran down her cheeks, promising to pray non-stop for his success. Singh observed her skin had the dry and scaly texture of the heavy *yaqona* drinker.

'Let's hope their prayers are more effective than mine,' he grinned as they set off. 'Let's start with Don Santini, the sound recordist. I met him when I returned the microphone I found. He mentioned a small recorder also went missing but I didn't follow that up. He's got all their property on a spreadsheet, so he'll have the details. It's better to chalk up a win on our first game, don't you think, Susie?' His eyes lit up with anticipation.

Singh struggled to keep up with him, even though his gait was just slightly uneven. She was going to enjoy this afternoon.

35

Horseman found Dr Young and Tina along the dog's favourite walking route, the Suva foreshore. His heart lifted at her solid, healthy body, her thick brindled coat and her happy rush to greet him. What he loved best about her was her zest for life. She took nothing for granted, but was grateful for every meal, every walk, every human attention.

Her attitude was the legacy of her life on the streets as a diseased, starved mother of four puppies. Against his own advice, Melissa, his visiting American girlfriend, now ex-girlfriend, had rescued the filthy dog. She'd placed her in the care of a vet who'd found homes for the puppies, but no one wanted their mother. Melissa named the dog Tina, the Fijian word for mother, and with Matt's collusion, presented her to Horseman on her departure. Forced the animal on him, to be more accurate. Although Tina adored Matt and all kind humans, she knew from the moment he reluctantly took the lead from Melissa that she was Horseman's. When he was present, Tina had eyes only for him, even now he lived in a flat where pets were forbidden.

Elated to greet him, Tina soon sped back to the waterline to rummage in the shallows. Could a dog detect a stonefish? The thought panicked him. He grabbed a stick and threw it further up the beach. She left the water and chased after it.

'Matt, do dogs ever tread on stonefish?'

'Don't know, mate. There's no reason they wouldn't, especially if they're distracted.'

'I've never thought about it before. But since Mili ... maybe we should keep her away from the water.'

'Yeah, I'll look it up. Any news on the case?'

Horseman filled in his friend about his suspicion that Lui Tuvoli was behind the thefts on the location.

'He could be using the interns he supervises to pick up items they see unattended. Joshi, the boy who was on eBay yesterday, said he wasn't an intern. If that's true, Tuvoli gets other Film and Television students to flog the goods.'

'Yeah, that's odd, isn't it? The more people involved, the more risk to the scheme's security.'

'Exactly. The students cataloguing and selling may not know the items are stolen. Joshi certainly acted cagey when I looked over his shoulder, though.'

'Unless we can catch someone in the act of theft, this hypothesis of yours will be hard to test. What are you going to do?'

'I made a good start with Singh this afternoon, thanks to Duke declaring a holiday weekend. Not many crew were on deck, so we joined a *yaqona* circle in the canteen. They got quite mellow and told us which departments had suffered thefts, plus the best people to follow up with. Luckily, they're all senior crew who were working on their Sunday holiday and happy to talk with us.'

'Come on, Joe! Get to the point.'

'I'm on a roll! What I have is a list of seventeen missing items, ranging from a Japanese electric saw to a German camera lens. All top quality and saleable.'

He pulled a paper from the satchel slung over his shoulder and handed it to Dr Young, who scrutinised it with interest.

'Hell's bells! That's a lot of opportunistic theft!'

'Yep, and possibly far from complete. Some items won't have been missed yet, and there wasn't anyone from the Electrical department around. I was hoping to meet the gaffer or the best boy. But ...' Horseman grinned.

'Stop showing off, Joe. You're not in the movies yet.' They both laughed.

'You'll notice we've got brand and model number for all seventeen items, but the best evidence is the eight with serial numbers. If we locate just one of those at FIT, it'll be hard for Lui Tuvoli to explain away. If Ratini backs the search warrant application I give him tomorrow morning, we could get in there in the afternoon.'

Dr Young raised his brows as he handed the paper back. 'You've got a few *ifs* there. I hope you're right. Definitely looks suss.'

Tina sat patiently at Horseman's feet, where she'd dropped the stick. He patted her head and threw it far ahead, then they turned towards Suva Point.

'Good throw, you should switch to cricket.'

'Matt, can I sound you out about the Shiners' hostel?'

'Sure, mate.'

'You know that Raj Pillai's brother-in-law convinced us to set up a public registered charity. Well, we signed the application papers on Friday night. Now I'm having doubts about the name of the charity. It won't be a problem to change it—the papers won't go in until tomorrow at the earliest.'

'I'm glad you've bitten the bullet on the charity setup. What's the name?'

'Well, you know Action for Children have been giving us free advice. Do you know Gloria Chung?'

'No. Only that her restaurants are popular and doing well.'

'Yep, well, she's formidable. She argued that to attract donations both here and overseas, my name should be used. She also presented us with a whole lot of costs I'd never thought of to show that a lot of money is going to be needed even for a modest hostel. Everyone agreed and at the time, she persuaded me, too.'

'I think she's right. You're a babe in the woods in this venture, Joe.'

'Yes, but it's not what I wanted. I had no intention of trying to raise money overseas. Raj Pillai and I intended to provide a deposit on a building, that's all. The project's about the street boys, not about me. They're teenagers, not babies. I want them to feel they own it and use the name Shiners. Gloria says that doesn't *resonate*. I think that's the word she used.'

'I get that. But on this one I'm with the inimitable Gloria. You're embarrassed, it's so un-Fijian to put your name out there like a brand, but it's a sacrifice you should make for the success of the hostel. That's your goal, so go for it. Think of the charity name as public property, not as your personal name. What precise name did you come up with?'

'The Joe Horseman Trust.'

'Hmm, I like it. *Trust* has positive vibes. And the whole of Fiji trusts you. Go with it.'

'Okay, I need to stop dithering. We need a Board of Trustees, and I want you to be on it.'

'That's more like it. *Vinaka*, I'm honoured, mate. Let's shake on that.'

They shook.

'Gloria's got a free photography session for us at training tomorrow. Apparently initial press coverage before the charity's registered is inexplicably vital. I'll get the word out to the boys to wear their uniforms.'

'They look almost presentable in those black and tan jerseys. Can't wait to meet this dynamo, Gloria!'

'I'm not sure whether to offer her a place on the board or not. She's a bulldozer as well as a dynamo.'

'Hmm. Better be cautious. Gloria may prefer to remain an advisor. And it might be hard to get rid of a trustee. I need to read up on all this.'

'I'll get Shiv to email everything to you.'

'Right, I'll study the rules before I offer any more advice!'

'Advise away, Matt. I can ignore it if I want to.'

'Not when I'm on the Board of Trustees. Do you want to rethink that invitation?'

'No, I don't. And you can't back out now. We shook on it!'

Where the beach petered out and gave way to jumbled rocks, they turned to retrace their steps. Tina cocked her head to one side and looked up at Horseman, questioning his decision. But when he hurled the stick, she raced off as if an entire pack of rival dogs were after it too.

'Speaking of invitations, Susie said she'd like to join us at the Holiday Inn at six o'clock. I'll ring her now to make it half-past six.'

'Always a pleasure to see Susie. She didn't call in for a cuppa at Pathology after she visited Mili the other day. Stood me up, she did. But it's quarter to six now, Tina needs her dinner and we both need a wash. Hmm. You go ahead, mate, I'll get there as soon as I can, probably closer to seven. My shout—no expense spared.'

Horseman knew better than to argue. Matt felt the discrepancy in their salaries keenly and his insistence on picking up the bill now and then gave him pleasure.

36

After a Fiji Bitter or two and crisp battered fish and chips with Matt, Horseman and Susie shared a cab to Seaview Apartments. She was anxious to convert their piece of paper into a proper spreadsheet before she went to bed and Horseman failed to persuade her to leave it until the morning. But he had one more task before turning on the rugby, and it wasn't going through the case file, which he could almost recite word for word. No, it was more challenging than that. He picked up his phone.

'*Bula* Mum. It's Joe. How are you?'

'Very well, thank you, stranger. Why are you speaking in English?'

He switched to Fijian. 'I didn't realise I was, Mum. I've been speaking English most of the day, with Singh and Matt, and out at the Champion set.'

'Oh, how are Susie and Matt?'

'They're fine, Mum. They're both heavily involved in the Champion investigation, like me.'

'Please say *bula* to them from me.'

After he'd asked about the health of his sisters, brothers-in-law, nieces and nephews, and his mother's relatives back in her village, he thought it was safe to get to the point.

'Mum, I think you'll be pleased to hear that I've accepted legal advice and started the process of registering a charity to set up the Shiners' hostel.'

'Good. The idea of you doing all that as a hobby was ridiculous. And dragging poor little Dr Pillai into it with you! The man's a saint to go along with it!'

'He's a great guy and just as keen on the idea as me. But we now realise the costs will be much higher than we imagined, and we'll need an ongoing income to pay the bills. If we do things right, the charity has the potential to provide that.'

'If you do things right—yes, that's a risk, isn't it?'

'I thought you'd have more faith in me! Anyway, I called you because I'm thinking further ahead now, to when we've bought a building, made alterations and the boys are about to move in.'

'That will be an exciting day. I'll have faith in you then.'

Sister Sala Horseman, former President of the Fiji Nurses Association, had the reputation of being difficult to satisfy. Student nurses quailed before her unforgiving assessments. This quality wasn't limited to her professional role but extended to her children too.

'We'll get there if we work hard enough, Mum.'

Her approved maxim had the desired effect. 'That's true, Josefa.'

'The boys will need order and rules, as well as decent accommodation and food. They're old enough to have chores like cooking and cleaning. But on top of all this, I want them to have a firm but friendly housemother in authority. Something they've not had for years, if they ever did.'

'I've a bad feeling about what's coming, Josefa.'

'Well, I've a good feeling, Mum. I'm begging you to consider taking on this role. You'd be marvellous—just what those boys need.'

'I'm flattered, son, but are those boys just what I need at my time of life? I somehow doubt it. I like staying here in Lautoka with Eva and the grandchildren, taking off for a month or so in the village when I feel like it. I don't know that I want to come to Suva.'

'Julia, Maika and the kids would want you to come, Mum. They don't see enough of you.'

'True, true. I shouldn't always favour Eva. Spread myself around, as they say.'

'Mum, you wouldn't need to be there 24/7, every week of the year. We can work something out.' He thought desperately. 'Once you established a comfortable order in the place, you could train a deputy to take over when you wanted to spend a month in your village, or in Lautoka. After a year or so, if the deputy satisfied you, you could retire, but maybe keep in touch to make sure standards didn't drop.'

'I hope you don't think all that's easy, son! All very well in theory.'

'Just think about it Mum. Maybe you could come up with a plan for us to implement if you decided you were getting too old to take on the role yourself.'

'*Oi lei*, cheeky one! Dear me, I owe it to you to consider the idea, as you said. I'll do that and I'll talk it over with Eva and Julia. I'll consider it seriously, I promise you that. This is a good thing you're trying to do, Josefa.'

'That's not the point. These boys need help, Mum. Their need is urgent.'

Sala Horseman sighed. 'I know, son. I'll think and pray about it.'

MONDAY

37

'You want to raid the Fiji Institute of Technology! Can you possibly be serious, man?'

'*Io*, only the Film & Television Production building, sir.'

'Only! Damn and blast, Horseman, convince me this is not some fantasy.'

'Sir, Singh and I went to the Champion location yesterday and talked to the crew. They had Sunday off, so they were more chatty than usual. The spreadsheet you've got there, attached to the search warrant request, is no fantasy. It's a list detailing seventeen missing items reported to us by department managers there. Eight have serial numbers. If we found any of these at FIT, our suspicion will be justified. Lui Tuvoli is uniquely able to run such a racket, going to Champion in his role as intern liaison and now a casual purchasing officer. It would be so easy for him to collect items lifted by interns, who would be fetching and putting them away daily as part of their jobs. Tuvoli takes the stuff back to the college, where different students list them for sale on eBay.'

'Maybe, Horseman. Magistrates don't like fishing trips like yours. Don't like them at all. Why can't you confront Tuvoli and see what he has to say for himself? There could be an innocent explanation. Maybe he's got the kids finding things on eBay as part of his purchasing job.'

'That's true, and both activities may coexist, sir. What's proven is that all these items on the list belong to Champion. They're portable, saleable and they're all missing. What I witnessed on Saturday afternoon was a Film and Television student entering details from a notebook on eBay and acting cagey when I showed a friendly interest. Only a few students and staff were in the building.'

'Bloody hell, man! It's not on! You find Tuvoli and ask him politely what's going on.'

'Sir, the guy's slippery as an eel. He'll certainly have an innocent explanation. You've just supplied a good one, and I can think of others. Once he's warned, he'll make sure there's no evidence to be found if the police ever show up.'

Superintendent Ratini smiled a nasty smile. 'Don't be so sure. If there's evidence on computer or internet, our tech guys will sniff it out. Anyway, why are you so keen on pursuing alleged thefts? You're supposed to be working on the Johnson death, if I'm not mistaken.'

'*Io*, sir. It's likely Ken Johnson's death relates to the other criminal acts rife on the Champion set.'

'I suppose you've got nothing else?'

'Not much, sir.'

'Tuvoli's entitled to give his account of himself. Find him and get it! And treat him with the respect due to a citizen and educator. You never know, he may willingly show you what you want.'

Horseman bristled. Ratini treated no one with respect except his superiors. He didn't know the meaning of the word. Still, he bit his lip. The search warrant application remained on Ratini's desk. He hadn't tossed it in the bin or torn it up—yet.

'*Vinaka*, sir. I'll get going right away.'

Horseman returned to his desk. Singh was on the phone, but shot him and enquiring look. He rang to book a vehicle, but none were available from the pool. He searched his desk for taxi vouchers but couldn't find any. Singh put her phone down and smiled at him. She wore a yellow *bula* blouse patterned with white hibiscus and a navy-blue business skirt. Instead of a high ponytail, she'd cinched her hair at the nape of her neck with a tortoiseshell clasp.

'Can I help, sir?'

He slammed the drawer shut. 'No car, no taxi vouchers. I was sure I had some. Ratini's ordered me out to FIT.'

'I've got some.' She reached for her backpack, which was part-stationery cupboard and part-filing cabinet. She unzipped a small side pocket, extracted some pristine taxi vouchers, and waved them at him. 'But I haven't got much to do in the office, for a change.'

'You'd better come with me, then. Have the constables got work?'

'Yes, but only for the day.'

It was a bad sign that the team was running out of things to do. Horseman had to agree with Ratini; the Ken Johnson case had stalled.

38

As the old cab laboured up the steep road to Samabula he drank in the layers of verdant hills, softening to purple further west. The sea sparkled today in the sunshine. Having lived in grey cities overseas in his days as a rugby professional, he revelled in Fiji's beauty and never took it for granted. Many of his fellow citizens, having known nothing else, barely noticed their natural wonderland.

A helpful woman at the Film and Television reception desk told them Mr Tuvoli was teaching and would not be free for another hour.

'Best thing for you to do would be to go to the canteen. Nothing fancy but okay. It's a low building with a little lawn. Turn left and follow this road until you come to it.'

They found the place easily and took their stained plastic mugs of tea and jumbo-sized sausage rolls outside. It was pleasant in the shade of the fig tree, looking out over the eastern side of the Suva peninsular.

'I'm going to miss Suva, even though it's been less than two years. If it wasn't so expensive here, it would be my dream town.'

'A position might come up unexpectedly, you never know.'

'What? If someone dies? I couldn't be glad about that.'

'Well, I could.'

Singh laughed out loud.

'What? I'm not going to start murdering Suva detective inspectors to get you a job! But if one dies of natural causes, I can't see why we both shouldn't be glad that some good came out of it.'

'You can be very funny sometimes, Joe.'

'Why only sometimes? I thought I was often funny!'

Her noisy laugh burst out again and cheered him. They got back to Film and Television in good time and stood browsing the course brochures until Lui Tuvoli came down the stairs, a panama hat in his hand. He halted mid-stride when he saw them, as if about to turn on his heel. But he must have realised it was too late for that, so braced his shoulders, recovered his cool and went up to them, smiling and hand outstretched.

After exchanging greetings, Horseman got to the point.

'Mr Tuvoli, we're investigating a spate of thefts of film-making equipment from the Champion site over the last month. You're around the set a lot and your interns are there full time, so I wondered if you'd heard anything about that?'

Tuvoli frowned. Buying time, but he did it rather well.

'Aha, are these items lost, stolen or strayed, Inspector?' He wagged his finger in Horseman's face.

'Most of them stolen, in the opinion of the department heads. Have any of the interns mentioned it to you?'

'Um, let's go to my office. More private than standing in front of the automatic doors, eh?'

'*Vinaka*, that would be better.'

Tuvoli led them past the studio Horseman had visited on Saturday, to his office at the end of the corridor. Cabinets and shelves lined two of his office walls from floor to ceiling. Just half of one wall displayed movie posters for three versions of *Blue Lagoon* shot in Fiji. Tuvoli lifted his brows at Horseman's recognition.

He swept his hand towards them in a grand arc. 'Have you seen all three?'

'*Io*, I like the one with Jean Simmons best.'

'Good choice. But Brooke Shields in 1980 put Fiji on the map for Hollywood location managers.' He swept an arm to include a couple of visitor chairs. 'Please sit down and tell me how I can help you.'

'Have you heard any talk about equipment going missing at Champion?'

'No, but the senior crew I talk to are unlikely to mention that to me. My business there is to make sure they provide our interns with quality work experience and if needed, work out ways to improve their skills. All in collaboration with the crew, of course.'

'Have any of the interns got the sack?'

'Aha, you call a spade a spade, Inspector. Not this season, I'm pleased to report, but there have been one or two instances in previous seasons.'

'Why were they asked to leave?' Singh asked.

'*Oi lei*! You do go in for detail, don't you? Two because they were incurably slow to follow instructions. My diagnosis was they were frightened of making a mistake and not sufficiently experienced. This season I've restricted internships to final-year students. That's working out better.'

'That makes sense. Any other reasons—for dismissing interns, that is?'

'You're persistent too. That's always a good quality. One that I do my best to encourage in my own children.'

'Mr Tuvoli, has an intern got the sack for any other reason than slowness?' Horseman was already a little impatient.

'*Io*, if you must know. One lifted a very nice wide-angle lens, unfortunately just as a camera operator came to get it. Unwisely, the boy handed it back.'

This was too much. Horseman knew Tuvoli was baiting him, but he couldn't swallow his protest.

'Why do you say *unfortunately* and *unwisely*?'

'Because the student lost his place on Champion and was so ashamed, he failed his exams and left the course.'

Singh shot Horseman a warning glance. 'Have any of the current interns mentioned items missing from the set?' she asked.

'Not to me. No. But again, they're more worried about their assessments than to bother repeating rumours to me.'

'*Lui*, senior crew at Champion have identified specific items they suspect were stolen. Quite a number, actually. When I came to ask you about it on Saturday, I met a student in the studio who appeared to be entering items on eBay. He said it was a course project but was quite cagey. Of course, I wondered what was going on. Can you shed any light on what he was doing?'

Tuvoli blinked twice, his eyes shifting from Horseman to Singh as he calculated his best strategy. 'Oh, was that Joshi?'

Horseman raised his eyebrows in agreement.

'*Io*, I can easily explain. You know how funds are tight every-where, so we have to be entrepreneurial where we can. We rely on second-hand equipment, mostly hand-me-downs from the media organisations here in Fiji. Varying quality and condition. Some-times we have excess items which we sell on eBay to fund purchases. I asked Joshi to list some surplus items for sale.'

'I see. No one can argue with that sort of self-help. I suppose the Principal approves.'

'*Io*, we have his support.'

'Your students must have heard about the thefts. It did occur to us it would be easy for an intern to steal the occasional item to sell.'

'Opportunistic theft, as you say in your trade. But they'd hardly tell me about it.'

'Why not, in the throes of remorse, perhaps? Like your student last year who confessed.'

'He confessed to the camera operator, not to me. No one has confessed this year. I'm sorry, Inspector, but I can't help you.'

'*Vinaka* for your time and explanation, Mr Tuvoli. I'll leave my card. Please get in touch if you hear anything at all about this.'

As soon as they were out the front doors, Singh snorted, actually snorted. 'I knew it would go like that. I knew it! It was almost a ritual we all took part in.'

'Yep, could've written the script myself.' He chuckled. 'I suppose I *did* write my part of it, which could've been a lot better. But the outcome would've been the same. Our Lui can think on his feet, can't he?'

Singh pursed her lips in disapproval. 'He can, sorry to say. I bet he's already at the computer. Deleting all references to those items.'

'Ratini was right about one thing, though. Even if Tuvoli deletes those records, even if he closes the account, all those transactions are on eBay, and he can't delete them. Our tech guys can easily trace those.'

'True, that's a comfort. But I guess that's the end of stuff going missing from the set.'

'Singh, you sound disappointed! It'll be an interesting test, won't it? If the thefts continue, it's because Tuvoli's so arrogant he thinks dumb clucks like us can never get near him.'

Singh raised her eyebrows. 'Or, just possibly, that he was telling the truth to us and someone else is the thief.'

'No way. I'll ring the Principal and check what he knows about all this; if there's an official FIT eBay account and so on. But a search warrant's the only answer. In the meantime—'

'Yes, sir?'

'Do you know anyone in FIT admin? See if student records match up with Tuvoli's story about the dismissed Champion intern last year. We can only keep digging more little holes until eventually some might join up.'

39

Horseman was sorry the case wasn't moving fast, but at least he could get to training early for the photo shoot. A few Shiners were hanging about the Albert Park grandstand chatting. When they saw him jogging across the pitch they cheered and waved their team jerseys in the air. Great, Tevita and Pita had spread his message. He hoped the jerseys were clean enough. The black and tan symbolised the shoe-shine trade but had the added benefit of not showing the dirt, up to a point. Few boys had access to a proper laundry.

Nor to bathrooms. Trying to regard them as a stranger would, he admitted they were a scruffy lot. '*Bula*, Shiners. *Vinaka vakalevu* for coming early. The professional photographer will be here soon and the pictures he'll take of you will help raise money for your hostel. So you need to look your best. Wash your faces and hair under the taps, as well as you can. The cleanest boys can go in the front row. What's the problem, Mosese?'

'Coach, I don't follow. People will want to give us money if we look like poor and starving. Not if we wear top jerseys and have clean faces.'

The boy had a point—one born of life on the streets. God forbid they presented themselves as professional waifs to provoke pity.

'You've got a point, Mosese but, man, where's your pride? Fijian men don't skulk around like pitiful beggars! Look your best, stand up straight and walk tall. Watch how the Flying Fijians handle themselves and make them your models.'

The growing number of boys clapped, and Mosese copped a few jeers. 'Shiners, Mosese asked a fair question which showed he can think for himself. What he said has some truth, but not for healthy young men. People prefer to give their hard-earned money to help boys like you who have shown they try to help themselves. I'm going to tell the newspapers the story of how you all worked to buy your own rugby boots. Now, off to the taps.'

As they ran off with hoots and cheers, a man standing on the periphery came forward trundling a case on wheels. He had a tall, lean body and face to match under a buzz-cut that hid a receding hairline. He stretched out one hand. 'Samir Ali, I'm your photographer. I overheard your pep-talk and agree a hundred per cent. This is a real pleasure for me.'

They shook hands. 'I'm so grateful for this support, Samir. The boys will set up a trestle table for your things if you like. You're the professional here, so I won't interfere. Just tell me what you need done and when. We'll oblige.'

'Thanks. A trestle table would be good.'

Shiners appeared with wet faces and hair, shaking their heads like dogs. Some produced plastic combs, others pressed their frizzy hair into their scalps after a good shake. Those with looser curls ran their fingers through them.

Dr Pillai, Constable Lemeki from Traffic and Horseman's own constables Musudroka and Apo Kau arrived while the boys put the trestles together and Mr Ali unpacked the tools of his trade. Horseman had a quiet word with the constables—one of them must always guard the photographic equipment. How ironic and humiliating if one of the young rascals lifted a camera accessory. He wasn't certain that all of them could resist such temptation.

Although Mr Ali worked with calm efficiency, the photo shoot dragged on for Horseman. First the headshots of every boy and their trainers, then all the squad, the trainers, the team competing in the current Suva third grade and so on. The boys were beyond excited, transfixed on the camera lens and wholly obedient to Mr Ali's instructions. It was fun to watch and be a part of, but it would result in a truncated training session afterwards.

Horseman, Musudroka and Kau put the boys through an abbreviated warm-up and skills drills while Lemeki guarded the table. The photographer was checking all the shots on his laptop before packing his things away.

'If we need any retakes, it's better to get them now. No continuity problems then,' he explained.

Horseman smiled. 'Right, whatever suits you. The boys'll be delighted to pose for more photos. I've never seen them so concentrated before!'

'Kids and cameras don't always sync. Your lot make great subjects. Are you interested in getting a few action shots too, while I'm here? Whether they'll be any use for your publicity, I don't know.'

Horseman grinned and shrugged. 'Neither do I. It wouldn't hurt to have them up our sleeve, would it? Meri Street's offered to do the PR for us, but I don't expect she's thought much about it yet, not in detail. Go ahead and take what you want. *Vinaka vakalevu.*'

'Could they be playing a game? Faces are much more photogenic when they're striving to win.'

'Sure, we always finish training with a practice match. Lemeki, let's get that going now. Apo can take over guard duty.'

'I'll take shots from the sidelines. Tell them to ignore me and focus on winning. My new zoom lens should do the trick.'

The Shiners rose to the challenge, displaying vigour and determination, even skill. When Mr Ali signalled he had enough shots, Lemeki blew the whistle. The players pulled up at once, some bent double, panting, some dropped to the ground, others headed for the taps. The power of the camera amazed Horseman. Maybe he should video all their practice games for analysis, as was routine in the adult grades. He doubted the boys were ready for that yet, but he should reconsider now he'd seen the level of effort they were capable of.

Mr Ali looked up from his laptop and smiled. 'Just a quick check. We'll end up with some good action shots after processing. I'll get a memory stick to you, soon as I can.'

'*Vinaka*, I wasn't that interested in all this public relations business but now I can't wait to see the photos. Would you like to join us for our after-training meal? Simple but enjoyable. Generously provided by our team doctor, Kaviraj Pillai.'

'Thanks, I'd love to, but I've got to dash.'

'Can I help you pack up?'

'Oh, of course. I guess you need the table.'

'No hurry. We'll give the boys a break before dinner.' Mr Ali began dismantling his equipment. He inserted each component into a tailored hole in his case's foam lining.

As he unscrewed the zoom lens, he said, 'I hope my new baby's put some magic into those action shots.'

'Me, too. Where did you get it?'

'I have a wish list on eBay, and it came up! I couldn't believe that the seller was in Fiji, too.'

'Who was the seller?'

'A mystery. I got it in the post, with Fiji stamps. I wondered if it could be one of the Champion cameramen, but why would anyone want to sell this? It's pretty new.'

'*Io.* D'you mind if I check the serial number, Samir?'

Samir looked bemused. 'What's going on?'

'There's a chance this lens was stolen from the Champion set. I've got a list of missing items, which includes this model of Sony zoom lens. I really hope we can eliminate yours by checking the serial number.'

The photographer rubbed his hand over his buzzcut. 'Oh no! But we have to know, don't we?'

'I'm afraid so, Samir.'

Horseman got the list from his backpack while Samir unscrewed the cover to reveal the serial number. They matched.

Suppressing his jubilation, Horseman said, 'I'm very sorry to bring this trouble on your head, especially when you've freely given us your time and expertise.'

Mr Ali rubbed his head again and shrugged. 'Gloria paid me for the day, so you don't owe me anything, Joe. I suppose you'll take the lens now?'

'I apologise, but I must. Could you forward your communication with eBay about the transaction, please?'

'Sure. Is there any comeback from eBay for this?'

'I've never used it myself. But our tech experts will know. They'll discover the seller's account details and liaise with eBay. I'll ask them to keep you in the loop. Please get in touch at any time. Where can I reach you?'

They exchanged cards. Horseman apologised again. Mr Ali forced a weak smile and sighed, 'On the whole, I'm glad our police are on the ball. No surprise when it's Joe Horseman, I guess. I'll get the photos to you by the end of the week. The last photos taken with that bloody wonderful lens!'

TUESDAY

40

'Now, Horseman, isn't this better than going off half-cocked? Some undeniable physical evidence, eh? No one can argue with it, not even the magistrate!'

Superintendent Ratini lay the search warrant on Horseman's desk with a magician's flourish. Had he persuaded himself that it was he who had found the lens? The man's thinking was opaque.

'I'd prefer to be courteous and phone Ratu Joni about this in advance.' Before Horseman could voice his protest, Ratini added, 'But I appreciate the importance of the element of surprise, even shock, without your help, Horseman. So, I intend to lead the raid, call him when we're two or three minutes from the campus and as senior officer, present him with the warrant and remain to smooth the waters with him while the search party proceeds to the Film and Television building.'

'What if he's not in his office, sir?' Musudroka asked.

'The Principal's secretary will find his deputy and I'll present the warrant to him. Or her. Is that satisfactory to you, Detective Constable?'

Horseman mentally urged Musudroka to shut up.

'*Io*, sir.'

'You will merely give a copy of the warrant to the head of the Film and Television department, or deputy, even if that's Lui Tuvoli. Our IT experts will handle the computers, while your team, Horseman, will check all photographic equipment.'

He bristled at Ratini instructing him in the plan Horseman had written himself but took his own advice and shut up.

'*Io*, sir.'

Every police officer loved a raid. At three o'clock, after Horseman had given explicit instructions to his own team and the squad of uniforms assigned to the operation, two police vans pulled out of Suva Central and headed up the hill towards Samabula. The atmosphere inside Horseman's vehicle crackled with anticipation. The officers spoke to each other in low voices, the conversation broken by nervous chuckles.

The Principal, Ratu Joni Tuidraki, responded to Ratini's announcement with a polite but brief request to come to his office on arrival. He didn't sound shocked or even surprised, but then, that was not the chiefly way. The van dropped Ratini and one uniform at the admin building and followed the second van down the hill.

The team ran through the automatic doors. Students and staff stopped dead, open-mouthed. The department head's office was at the top of the stairs. As arranged, Singh, an IT officer and a constable ran to Tuvoli's office at the end of the corridor.

The head was out but his deputy, a middle-aged woman dressed in traditional *sulu* and tunic, drew herself up and glared when Horseman presented the search warrant. 'I'm surprised you would descend to this, Josefa Horseman,' she barked. 'You will wait while I call Ratu Joni.'

She slumped a little during her phone call. 'It seems I have no choice in this scandalous matter. I suppose I'm wasting my words, but I ask you to respect this building, and its contents, as a place of learning. If you harass my staff and students in any way, you will find you and your team the targets of an official complaint.' She braced her shoulders and raised her chin while delivering this threat. Horseman wished she was on his side.

'And deservedly so, madam. We will need keys and four escorts from your staff. The IT team will start upstairs while my team will begin downstairs with the photography equipment.'

The deputy begrudged helping them and ten minutes ticked by before she produced the keys and staff escorts. Singh's team started with the studio Horseman had visited on Saturday. He wished her luck before leading his team straight to the end of the corridor and Lui Tuvoli's office. He wasn't sorry to find Tuvoli out; it was bad enough to imagine the lecturer's gloating when they found nothing. He hoped the computers would tell a different story.

They found an efficient rhythm as the search progressed—even the staff escorts wanting to get on with the process. In each office and classroom, they searched all shelves, cupboards, and cabinets systematically, but when Horseman and Singh met at the halfway point, each discovered the other team hadn't found any items on the list from Champion.

'It makes sense, getting rid of the goods as quickly as possible. They aren't here now but it doesn't mean they never were.'

'Exactly, sir. I expected Tuvoli would keep some items for the Film and TV course, though.'

'Looks like it's purely a money-making operation, doesn't it?'

'Maybe our Lui took a few select treasures home for himself,' Singh said.

The IT team were tramping down the stairs empty-handed but for bundles of small plastic zip-wallets.

'You're not bagging the computers?' Horseman asked.

'Not anymore, new protocols now. We copy the entire contents of each computer onto a memory stick, witnessed by a staff escort who countersigns the identity label. Much better for customer relations!'

'Okay, we'll head upstairs now.'

Not one item on the list was found after an equally thorough search upstairs. Every team member would feel as exasperated as Horseman did himself. He tried to think of rooms they hadn't discovered yet. After all, most education institutions worked along the same lines.

'Have you come across a mail room, Singh?'

'No, I haven't. Saini's helpful, I'll ask her.' She approached one of the staff escorts standing apart with her colleagues.

She returned in a few moments, eyes sparkling with hope. 'It's a semi-basement cut into the slope at the back. Access via fire stairs at the end.'

A familiar voice, now angry, lifted above the level tones of a constable guarding the reception area.

'Search that mail room thoroughly, please Singh. Take my constables too. Leave no stamp or envelope unturned. I'll talk to our noisy friend here.'

'Thanks, sir!'

Tuvoli lowered his voice but not his indignation level when Horseman approached. He clutched a sports bag to his chest with both arms. 'What is this harassment? I will not permit you to search my bag. I know that's how you cops work, planting false evidence on innocent people.'

'*Bula*, Mr Tuvoli. Everything's in order, no need to worry. You weren't here when I presented a search warrant for this building to your deputy head, so I'll show it to you personally.' He took the warrant from a pocket and held it out to Tuvoli.

After scanning the first page, Tuvoli thrust it at Horseman's chest. 'This can't be valid. I'm ringing Ratu Joni right now.' He pulled out a mobile and thumbed through his contacts.

'Ratu Joni has accepted the legality of the warrant. He instructed your deputy here to cooperate with us. My superior is with him in his office now, probably having afternoon tea.'

Tuvoli's eyes widened, and his face flushed. 'When the constable's searched your bag we can go to your office for a quiet talk. I'd like to explain why the magistrate granted us a search warrant.'

For a few moments, Tuvoli clung to his sports bag and glared at Horseman, then shoved it at the constable. 'Please witness the search, Mr Tuvoli. Look, Constable Paulosi will lay the contents on the reception counter. You can assure yourself he took nothing and added nothing.'

Horseman tried to speak gently but Tuvoli clamped his jaw tight and snorted. However, he did turn his head to watch the constable place on the counter three manilla folders with papers, a library book, two film magazines, an empty lunch box, a small camera, a canvas tube, a crumpled handkerchief, and an open packet of cigarettes.

'Is that your camera?' Horseman asked.

'Of course, it is,'

'Have you got a receipt for it?'

'What? Of course, I haven't! Who keeps receipts?'

'In my experience, people who want to claim under the manufacturer's guarantee if the product is faulty. Or people who wish to claim on their insurance policy if the item is stolen. Those sorts of people.'

'Huh!' Tuvoli's snort suggested he'd never heard such a ridiculous idea.

'When and where did you buy it?'

'About two years ago, I think. Here, in Nadi airport's duty-free shop.' The man was recovering his composure now.

'Sir!' The constable held out the canvas tube. He peeled back its Velcro fastening, revealing a neat folding tripod.

'That screws onto the camera, you idiot!' Tuvoli snapped.

Horseman owed it to the constables to rebuke Tuvoli. 'No need to be rude, is there? I'll take the camera and tripod for now. Let's go to your office. You can make a statement about those two items while I tell you about our fresh evidence. Think carefully about where you might have put those receipts. Maybe at home somewhere? If you can produce them, it will save us both a lot of time.'

Tuvoli took his time writing his statement and was reading it through when Horseman's phone vibrated in his pocket. It was Singh.

'Sir, two parcels in the outward mailbag. The Customs label reads *camera accessories* on one and *sound recorder* on the other.' The elation in her voice made him smile; her words almost made him shout for joy.

'Check them and if positive, bring them up to Mr Tuvoli's office, please. I'm sure he'll have an explanation.'

41

'It's quite straightforward, as I explained.' Lui Tuvoli slowed his speech as if the detectives were inattentive toddlers. 'We're trying to help ourselves by selling Film and Television department equipment we no longer need, in order to buy what we need most. Public internet auction sites bring us the highest prices, so we use eBay. Yes, we sold these items and are sending them off to the purchasers who've paid us good money.'

Two open cardboard boxes lay on Tuvoli's desk. Singh pointed to a digital sound recorder and a wide-angle lens placed beside them.

'Did you pack these items yourself, Mr Tuvoli?'

'A student did that. I checked them and sealed the boxes. What of it?'

'Then took them to the department's mail room?'

'*Io*. Again, what of it?'

'Nothing. It's lucky for us you wanted to avoid the ridiculous cost of international postage.'

'It's legitimate department business. Why should I pay for postage myself?'

'Because we wouldn't have discovered them if you had. But you couldn't know that, I suppose,' Horseman said. 'Sergeant Singh, please explain the significance of these two items.'

Singh shot him a grateful grin before holding up the spreadsheet she'd compiled of Champion's missing equipment. 'Senior Champion crew have reported these items to us as suspected thefts.'

She pulled a highlighter from her zippered pencil case and marked two items. She found the serial numbers on the lens and recorder, and laid them before Tuvoli, pointing with the marker to numbers on the list.

'Both these items are stolen, Mr Tuvoli.' She gazed at him, her green eyes full of reproach. 'What do you have to say?'

Tuvoli peered at the serial numbers, the colour draining from his face. 'I know nothing about this outrage. To think that my students, our interns ...'

Horseman was brisk. 'I've discovered that not all items you sell go overseas. A Suva photographer showed me this lens yesterday.' He took Singh's list and highlighted the row of details. 'He's still got the packaging. It surprised him to see the Fiji stamps. So, I'll give you a lift back to the police station where you can make a statement about this thieving racket you've organised here.'

'What the—? No, that's not at all convenient. I will get independent legal advice before saying anything more.'

'Fine, that will delay us, but it's probably wise for you. Shall we say nine o'clock tomorrow morning then? Don't leave Suva in the meantime. Now, I must express my thanks to your helpful deputy head and pay my respects to Ratu Joni before we leave. *Moce mada*, see you later, Mr Tuvoli.'

***

Horseman wasn't looking forward to breaking the news to Steve Duke, who only wanted to complete the shoot and go home. But Duke would be angry if the police didn't pass on the news about his property. He took a deep breath and picked up the phone. To his surprise, Duke answered.

'Mr Duke, we've discovered sound evidence that FIT interns stole at least some of your missing equipment, then sold it online in what seems to be an operation within the Film and Television department.'

After several beats of silence, Duke exploded. 'Bloody hell! I can't believe it! Ungrateful bastards! I'd like to shoot the lot of them! I'll give them all the sack, as of now. Security will search their things and see them off the set. Right now!'

'Mr Duke, I don't know which of the interns were involved. Or how many. As items have gone missing from several departments on set, we know this isn't the work of just one thief. So far, the students' supervisor, Mr Tuvoli, denies knowing anything about this, but he's coming to the station for a formal interview tomorrow morning.'

'Lui's in on this? Good old Lui, who can find anything? Our fixer extraordinaire?'

'He's a person of interest, while we wait for forensic results.'

'I see, I see … I'd never suspect Lui. He's so likable and competent. But it's the ideal setup for a racket, now I think about it. Wow! What a bastard. A conman, really.' His voice held a hint of admiration.

'I agree, it's the ideal setup. Exactly how it happened we'll find out soon enough, with your help, Mr Duke. I certainly won't interfere with how you run your production. But it would help us if you delayed marching the interns out until my team can interview them. There are ten, aren't there? At least one will break the wall of silence when they're shown hard evidence. We can be there inside an hour. How does that sound?'

'I appreciate you've kept me in the loop all the way, Inspector. Even occasionally asked my permission! Yeah, okay, sounds reasonable. You get first crack, then one by one, they get an earful from me and collect their things.'

'There couldn't be a better reason for dismissal than stealing. But some interns may be quite innocent.'

'I reckon they all knew about it, even if some of their placements didn't offer a chance of swiping saleable items. The kid working with the scriptwriter, for instance.'

'Thanks for your cooperation, Mr Duke. We'll get going right away. See you soon.'

42

Horseman and Singh wasted no time preparing their surprise visit to Champion the same afternoon.

'Apo, see if you can get us two vehicles. I'm looking forward to making some arrests this afternoon!'

'Tani, it's your turn to man the fort. Lili and Apo need as much interview experience as they can get.'

Musudroka slumped in his chair. He hated office work. Singh knew he hankered for action in the field, but also recognised his lazy streak. Did Horseman realise he favoured Musudroka for field trips over the two newer constables? She thought he didn't and probably just picked Tani because he was a more entertaining companion.

'Right, Sergeant Singh. Five minutes to make sure this slacker knows what he needs to do because we should be back by six o'clock.'

'Yes, sir. Our raid on the Film and Television school has generated mountains of paperwork. But Tani, you'll get such a lot done in three hours!'

Musudroka put his face in his hands, then went over to Singh's desk. One thing he'd learned about his sergeant—she didn't hear any complaints about allocated tasks.

Kau magicked two LandCruisers out of the pool and forty minutes later they pulled up in the Champion car park. Steve Duke was talking to Deepika on the Personnel verandah. The director waved when he saw them walking towards their allocated interview rooms and joined them there. Why did he look so cheerful?

'Hiya, officers. I'm a lot more optimistic after this morning's shoot. We had a water-based challenge out at Motu, mainly because Mili still can't run without pain. It went swimmingly!' He grinned at his pun and the others laughed. Singh smiled politely.

'After lunch, we got a great interior elimination scene in the can, so we're on schedule. It should be fireworks tomorrow!'

'Who lost out?'

'Oh, Duane. An outstanding player. We'll miss him. Incredibly fit for a man in his mid-fifties but lacked that ruthless spark.'

'My goodness, so just Mili, Desi and Bobby left? Who's going to win?' Singh asked. If Mili was in the final three, the game must be rigged. Champion had just lost a fan.

'Oh my God, I wouldn't dare guess! But I'm here to help you after the service you gave me yesterday.'

Singh bristled at the suggestion the police search of the Film and Television school premises was a favour to the Champion director. Anyway, hadn't Duke been happy to ignore the thefts?

'Seven interns worked here today. Two weren't rostered on but one just didn't show up. Deepika will be here in a moment with a list for you. I've asked her to locate them and bring them up here if that would be a help.'

'Thanks, that would be great, Mr Duke' Horseman replied. Apo poured bottled water into the kettle and switched it on.

A moment after Duke left, Deepika rushed in with copies of a list. 'This will save you finding the names on the full staff list.'

'*Vinaka*, Deepika. Do you know any of the interns?'

'Sorry, I recognise them all, but haven't got to know them much. Mr Tuvoli liaises with their mentors and looks after anything they need.'

'I see. Well, let's start at the top of the list then. That's Tomasi for me and Lili here, and Lisa for Singh and Apo in our other office. If you can't find them, bring us anyone who's available.'

'Yes, sir. I'll find them.' She flashed a smile and disappeared.

Horseman rang Musudroka at the office. 'Tani, get out to FIT now and find three interns who aren't out here today. I'll send you their details and instructions by email in just a moment.' Singh imagined Musudroka's jubilation at his release from the office.

Apo poured tea for everyone. He and Singh carried their mugs across to the second office. They arranged the room, sat at the table, and started on their tea.

Apo frowned. 'What if Deepika can't find any of them? Maybe they heard about the FIT raid, and they've run away.'

'That's quite possible. What would that tell us?'

'That they're scared. But DI Horseman always says plenty of innocent people avoid the police. You can't conclude they're guilty because they're scared.'

'Good point. But we have grounds to suspect these interns. They're all working with different mentors, so they may not have heard.'

'I bet they've all got mobiles.'

Singh smiled. 'Apo, it's unlike you to be so negative.'

'You can't do much when people just keep saying they know nothing, Sarge.'

'True. Observe their faces and movements. Home in on their hesitations by repeating your question or suggesting an answer to them.'

'I don't think I'm much good at that, Sarge.'

'You've got more to learn, but it's just a matter of practice and repeating what you got right. It takes a few years to get good at reading people. Asking the right questions is trial and error. You need to observe—'

Deepika tapped on the open door and entered. 'Here's Lisa Viriviri, Detective Sergeant.'

Lisa Viriviri stepped into the room, a pleasant smile on her plump face. Singh saw from the list she was twenty years old and attached to the VFX department, whatever that might be. 'Apo, here's a good opening,' she whispered. 'Ask her what VFX means.'

Kau looked puzzled. 'Visual Effects, I know. I don't want to look like an ignoramus.'

'Come and sit down with us, Lisa. We're recording this afternoon's interviews.' Lisa sat down and Kau handed her a bottle of Fiji Water while Singh started the pocket recorder and stated their names and the time.

'Tell me what you do in the VFX department, Lisa,' Kau began.

'Oh, it's a wonderful chance for me, working with Adam, the compositor. I do different things. Mostly I paint out bits of rig or signs—anything that we don't want in the finished scene. Adam shows me how to combine images from different sources, but I'm not allowed to do any real ones myself.'

'It's good you're learning a lot.'

'I am. Most important is: believe nothing you see on TV or the movies. The compositor can add anything, change anything, take anything out.' She laughed.

'Have you heard about equipment going missing from the set?' Singh asked.

'I heard the police were asking about that on Monday, but that's all.'

'Has anything gone missing from VFX?'

'Adam hasn't mentioned it.'

'Have you helped yourself to anything lying around the place?' Kau asked.

'No! Of course not!' Lisa's voice became higher and louder.

'Do you know anyone who has?'

'I don't. None of my friends would steal, either.' Lisa shouted now.

'Yes, it's hard to accept, isn't it?' Kau was sympathetic.

'Still, we've found three items missing from this set that were sold on eBay by someone at your college. Our IT experts are tracing the details today. There's no doubt, Lisa.' Singh showed Lisa the list of missing items, pointing to the three highlighted rows for recovered items. 'Are any of these familiar to you?'

Lisa was no longer smiling and eager. 'No, we don't use any of this in VFX. I'm sorry.'

'Thank you, Lisa. You can go now. If you remember seeing equipment in the wrong place, or anything odd at all on the set, please call us.'

Lisa took the card Kau offered and nodded before rushing out.

'Do you think she's telling the truth, Apo?'

'*Io*, but I don't know why. She's not scared of the police.'

'I agree. We'll talk about why later. Let's finish our tea before Deepika brings us our next intern.'

Their next suspected thief looked more the part. Atish swept his greasy locks behind his ears, wiping his hands on his grubby yellow tee-shirt labelled Intern. He avoided looking at the detectives, staring down instead.

'What do you do in the Camera department, Atish?'

Atish looked out the window. 'Mostly work with Nik Seth, one of the camera operators, and sometimes with others.'

'What jobs do you do?'

'Oh, hold things, hand him things, adjust equipment, find equipment, fetch and carry, you know.'

'How useful is the job for your future, d'you think?'

Atish brightened and brought his focus in from outside to the table. 'Oh, you know, fantastic. A big production like Champion's nothing like what we do here in Fiji. Nothing like! Watch and learn, eh? Just watching and being able to help a bit—what a dream.'

'Has Nik Seth told you about some equipment disappearing around the set?'

'Oh, yeah, yeah, he mentioned that.'

'What did he say?'

'Not much. Just now and then when he can't find a lens or some other attachment. He asked me to find a couple of things, thought I maybe put them in the wrong place. But I didn't, and I couldn't find them anywhere.'

Kau persisted. 'What did Nik say then?'

'Nik says there's a thief about.'

'Do you agree, Atish?'

Atish shrugged. 'Dunno. Makes sense.'

'Does Nik suspect anyone of stealing?' Kau asked.

'He's not told me.'

'What about you?'

Atish finally looked at Kau. 'Me—a thief? No. why would I bite the hand that feeds me?'

Kau smiled in apology. 'Actually, I meant do *you* suspect anyone?'

'No, not a clue.'

'Have you seen anything on social media about the thefts?'

'No, all the interns are banned from saying anything about Champion on Facebook or anywhere else.'

'Someone at your college sold three missing items on eBay. Our IT experts are tracing the details today. These are the items we've recovered so far.' Singh placed the list in front of Atish, pointing to the highlighted rows with her pen. Atish clenched his fists, then dropped them to his lap.

'See, many of these missing items are camera accessories. Do you recognise them?' She tapped her pen on the list, insisting on his attention.

'Well, um, I know these models, but we've got more than one of each so I can't recognise them by serial numbers.' He had a point.

'Mr Duke is floored by this. He feels betrayed, too. I can understand that, can't you? He's provided you interns with work experience that you told me was fantastic. He trusted you. And you steal his tools of trade!'

Atish flushed. 'He can afford to replace them. No big deal.'

'Again, do you know who stole these things?' She tapped the list again.

'No, and it wasn't me. I just don't think it's a big deal, that's all.' He shrugged, looking into her eyes for the first time, his mouth twitching in what looked like amusement.

Singh closed the interview. If she didn't, the rage surging in her throat would explode from her mouth too. As a child, she had once picked up a cane knife on a neighbour's farm and presented it to her father with pride. He'd taken his belt off and strapped her hard on her legs and bottom. She'd never stolen again—not so much because of the pain of her punishment but because of the deep shame on her father's face and her terror that he'd rejected her forever. Once she'd returned the knife to the neighbour, he never spoke of it again.

Atish's casual attitude to theft cut her more deeply because he was Indian like her. Hadn't his family imbued him with profound respect for others and their property, whether they were rich or poor? How could he live with himself, knowing he was a low thief? Her urge to shout all this at him was hard to resist.

Kau interrupted her angry thoughts. 'I wonder if DI Horseman is doing any better than us? What will make one of them spill the beans?'

'I wanted to tell Atish that Mr Duke was going to sack them all this afternoon unless they confessed. That might work, but it's not ethical. We can't speak for Mr Duke.'

'Or he could change his mind completely. Anyway, there's only a few more days work for them here, so sacking isn't an enormous threat compared with going to prison, is it, Sarge?'

'No, you're right. No threat at all. Tuvoli's schooled them well to say nothing. We've no stick if they all do that. What we need is a nice juicy carrot.'

'Favourable consideration? Not much, is it?'

'No, but they're all so keen on their future careers ...'

Deepika was back with another intern in tow before Singh and Kau could come up with an appetising carrot.

Heneri, a gangly youth with short hair parted neatly on the side, was attached to Don Santini, head of the Sound department. He showed no signs of anxiety or fear and was friendly enough. Yet he gave the same old recital of 'didn't know, didn't hear, didn't see'. Did she dare dangle a carrot from beyond the rulebook, like Horseman sometimes did?

'Heneri, you know you'll be off the set for good if you don't help us, don't you?'

Heneri looked at her. 'Why?'

'I showed you the evidence. People at FIT have stolen Champion property and sold it online. Only the Film and TV interns work here, right? Of course, Mr Duke is angry at you.'

Heneri looked baffled. 'Not me.'

'What did Mr Tuvoli promise you to get you to steal for him?'

'Huh, I don't understand.'

'Your teacher, Mr Tuvoli, asked you to steal portable equipment and pass it on to him, for the benefit of your college.'

'No!'

'You can't argue with this evidence, Heneri. Did you pass this sound recorder on to Mr Tuvoli, or another student?' She pointed at the details of two stolen recorders on the list.

Kau interjected. 'You know you'll be kicked off the set for this, and kicked out of college too? You won't be able to graduate, so you'll never even start a career in film or TV.'

Heneri wiped sweat from his forehead. 'None of this is true!'

'It's true alright,' Kau replied.

Singh continued. 'Mr Duke told us the other day he'd like to offer a Hollywood internship to the most promising intern. Think how that would look on your resume. Any intern who told us the truth about this racket would be in the running for that prize, don't you agree, DC Kau?'

Kau thought before he spoke. 'I do. And I think Heneri's got the guts to tell the truth, Sergeant. Your parents brought you up to be honest, didn't they? What would your father's advice be?'

Heneri stared at Kau before he spoke. 'He's in prison. He always told me never to trust the cops. *Vinaka* for the reminder.' With that, he got up and walked out.

43

Back at the station, they shared their similar stories over roti and tea. Horseman laughed out loud at the tale of Heneri's interview. 'Who was it said, "never ask a question you don't know the answer to"? Seriously, you can't know the background of every stranger who walks into your interview room, can you? Lili and I didn't hit the jackpot either and we didn't have any amusing surprises like your Heneri.'

'I suppose it's funny now, but it wasn't at the time!'

Horseman took a bite of his favourite pumpkin and pea roti and chewed while he thought. 'I believed someone would confess when we showed them this evidence, too. But now I realise you couldn't get a gang of thieves that's more difficult to crack than this lot. You've got a group of students, persuaded into a criminal gang by their respected teacher. This crime is organised, but none of the thieves is a professional. Each member has a limited role, and they're loyal to each other because they know each other well in their normal lives. Nothing's stronger than peer group pressure. They rely entirely on Tuvoli for leadership, so they do as they're told. I imagine he's promised them the police can't charge any individual with stealing if they all shut up. And Tuvoli's right, dammit. There is a kind of honour among this gang of unlikely thieves. We need an eyewitness,'

Horseman drank some tea. 'I haven't heard from Musudroka yet. I'll call him again. I hope he doesn't need a rescue mission.'

Singh checked her own phone. Nothing from Tani but there was a text she'd missed from Desi Lopez asking to meet her. Did Desi want something, or had she discovered something? It wasn't really like Desi to want to help, but maybe she needed help herself.

'I've got a text from Desi, asking to meet. Are the players allowed their phones now?'

'My understanding is they're still banned, even though the finalists moved back to the main barracks and now get fed. But getting her hands on a mobile wouldn't be a problem for her.'

'No, I'll reply to this number and hope she sees the text.'

'That's all you can do. Let me try Tani again. Switching to speaker.'

'Sir, I'm just coming in by taxi. I'm bringing in Filo Nilali who wishes to speak with us.'

'Well done, DC Musudroka. We'll have an interview room ready and waiting.'

Excitement surged through Singh. This was what kept her going through the blank-faced denials in interview after interview, the prospect of a breakthrough. Would she get the same thrill in a different team, in a district where no one wanted to serve? She had little time to mull this over. Her answer was yes, she would. Here in Suva with Horseman, she was content and comfortable. Was she going soft? She'd joined up to rid the streets of criminals who exploited the honest and the weak, and the more senior her rank, the more influence she would have. Was she sure about that? Well, no, she wasn't, but her promotion recognised her hard work and why shouldn't she get better pay? Even if her future colleagues were obstructionist or lazy, she'd show them how a professional investigation was done. Just like Horseman had shown her.

Was she ready to be a detective inspector and senior investigation officer, in charge of a case? No, but she'd do it anyway, just as Horseman told her she should. She must remember this moment forever: the moment she resolved to accept whatever posting the commissioner handed to her. Still, she hoped that she wouldn't have to leave tomorrow.

44

Musudroka burst into the CID room, smiling in triumph. 'Sir, Sarge, Filo's in Interview room 2.'

'What's her story, Tani?' Horseman asked.

'She's the camera intern who didn't turn up on set today. She wasn't around the campus, either. Luckily, her family home's in Suva, so I tracked her down there. She knows about the theft racket and admits to being involved, at least marginally. She wants out, but she's scared, so she went home.'

'Well done, Tani. You've earned your seat at the interview table. Sergeant Singh, I need you and your velvet glove, too. Apo and Lili, when you're done with your notebooks and diaries, please get the running sheet up to date. We may be a while.'

'Good luck, sir!' Apo said cheerfully. His placid temperament was an asset. He never baulked at routine tasks or acted moodily like Musudroka.

'*Vinaka*! Let's hope our skillful questioning is all we need for a result.'

The three detectives settled themselves around the table where Filo sat. A constable brought a tea tray to the interview room and Singh poured everyone a cup. After Musudroka recorded the introductions, Horseman asked the first question.

'Ms Nilali, how did you learn about the systematic theft of equipment on the Champion set?'

'First from Atish. He's another camera intern. He came into the storeroom where I was tidying up and put a lens in his backpack. I asked him what he was doing, and he jumped out of his skin—he hadn't noticed me there at all. At first, he tried to deny it, but I knew what I'd seen. That's when he told me that Mr Tuvoli had a system going to get better equipment for us students. He didn't have to take any risks, just pick up smaller things when no one was around and pass them on to Mr Tuvoli or bring them back to college ourselves—whichever was safest.'

'How did you react to that?' Singh asked.

'I was shocked. I told him he was stealing but he explained that the Champion producers made millions and could afford to replace equipment. He said they didn't even care when things went missing. But the income from selling the items would make a big difference to the Film and Television school.'

'What did you do then?'

'I couldn't believe it. I did nothing until Mr Tuvoli approached me the next day.' Filo paused and reached for her tea. Her fingers trembled. She held the cup in both hands while she drank.

'Take your time, Filo. No rush.' Singh said. When Filo drained her cup, Singh poured her another and offered her milk and sugar. Filo looked at her gratefully.

'*Vinaka*, I feel better now. Where was I?'

'You just said Mr Tuvoli approached you the next day. Where were you?' Singh's voice was soft, encouraging.

'At Champion, helping Nik.'

'That's Nikhil Seth, the camera operator?'

'*Io*, I work with him a lot. He's patient and nice. Lui came and hovered during a challenge shoot in the arena. It's his job to observe us but he makes me nervous, so I make mistakes, especially after what Atish told me. Anyway, he took me aside afterwards to discuss my work. He said I was a bit clumsy and didn't anticipate Nik's needs as I should. I hadn't improved as much as he'd expected, so my internship was at risk. However, other qualities were equally important on a shoot, like cooperation, loyalty to the team. He just stood there smiling. Honest, I didn't get what he meant at first. Then he said if I could demonstrate those other qualities, he'd let me continue and advise Nik to be more patient with me.'

'What did he mean, Filo?' Musudroka asked.

'I asked him that. I suppose he could have sacked me on the spot for being so dumb.'

'You're young and innocent, Filo, not dumb at all,' Singh said. 'What happened next?'

'He told me about the fund-raising scheme, as he called it. Then he invited me to help in the scheme on condition I talk about it to no one, not even Atish or other interns in the circle, as he called it. I call it a gang. I was frightened of him then; his voice was soft but very threatening. I promised immediately. After that, he was friendly again and told me what I should do.'

'Which items did you steal, Filo?' Horseman handed her the list of missing equipment.

She raised her eyebrows. 'None, stealing is against God's commandments and the law. I won't steal. I just told Mr Tuvoli that I didn't get the chance. But I kept my promise to say nothing about the gang, until now.'

'Last Thursday you were walking on the beach with Nik Seth when Mili stepped on a stonefish. Why did you meet him there?'

Filo straightened in her chair and sipped at her tea. Her hand was steady. 'We'd worked together that day in a studio and wanted a walk in the fresh air.'

'Does Nik know about Tuvoli's gang of thieves?' Horseman asked.

'I think so. He told me that some wrongs are better ignored if you put yourself in danger trying to right them. That's rather vague, but I understood he was warning me about reporting Mr Tuvoli's scheme. I could be wrong, maybe I shouldn't have said that. I'd only found Atish stealing a few days before—I know, it was Saturday, the day before Ken's accident.'

Singh smiled. 'It sounds like you're pretty close to Nik. Do you have a romantic attachment, perhaps?'

Filo looked down into her teacup. 'No. I did like him a lot at first; it's so exciting to work with a real cinematographer. Then Atish told me Nik was married, so I dropped those silly daydreams.'

'What do you know about drugs on the set?' Horseman asked.

Filo's cup rattled when she put it back on the saucer. 'Oh, nothing really. I have heard a few rumours.'

At Horseman's nod, Musudroka asked, 'Tell us about the rumours.'

'Oh, well, just that drugs were about, and you could get them on set, despite Mr Duke's zero tolerance policy.'

'What drugs?'

'Oh, well, I heard ecstasy mentioned.'

'Has anyone offered you drugs?'

'Not directly—that's not how they do it. But when someone says drugs are around, I just assume they're offering to supply me. I don't know.'

'Was Mr Tuvoli supplying drugs?' Musudroka asked.

Filo's eyes widened. 'I never thought about that! Maybe it's possible. I don't know.'

'Part of his fund raising for the college, perhaps. Who told you drugs were on the set?'

'I can't remember. Just in passing, probably in the canteen. I don't take drugs. I feel no need to, and I haven't got the money. And especially because Mum and Dad would kill me if I did.'

Horseman wondered how effective parental threats of murder were. Maybe they'd saved a lot of children's lives. 'Why did you decide to tell us about the thefts on set?'

'I'm scared they'll scapegoat me because I haven't stolen anything. Mr Tuvoli won't trust me. Things got too much so I went home yesterday and told my parents. They're shocked about this but also sticklers for honesty. When Detective Musudroka called in this afternoon, they said God had sent him. They encouraged me to come here with him and tell the truth to the police.'

'And we're so grateful you did, Filo. Your parents will be proud of your bravery.'

Filo looked at Singh. '*Vinaka*, I'm glad I did, too. I don't feel so troubled anymore. Should I go back to Champion tomorrow, though?'

Horseman smiled. 'That's up to you, Filo. Talk with your parents. If it's any help, Mr Tuvoli won't be on the set tomorrow.'

WEDNESDAY

45

The next morning, promptly at nine o'clock, Lui Tuvoli and his solicitor Warren Stone arrived at Suva Central police station.

Horseman had encountered Warren Stone several times but hardly knew him. The Stones were a prominent part-European Suva family who owned small businesses, but Warren was the first to qualify as a lawyer. Now in his mid-forties, he was overweight and jowly, but he'd been a strong rugby winger in his youth, even playing for Fiji for a season.

This morning, Stone was playing it cool, initiating handshakes, smiling, and flattering. Did this mean he knew his client was the underdog in this game? Or was his strategy more complex? They'd soon know.

As soon as the recorder started, Stone butted in. 'Detective Inspector Horseman, my client, Mr Lui Tuvoli has prepared a Statutory Declaration about the matters you raised with him yesterday at the Fiji Institute of Technology. It may save time if I read it to you.'

'Certainly. Do you have copies for us?'

'Yes.' Stone passed copies to the detectives. Horseman scanned the page then glanced at Tuvoli, whose mouth twitched in an effort to contain his amusement.

> *I, Lui Tuvoli, senior lecturer in the Film and Television School of Fiji Institute of Technology, do solemnly declare that:*
>
> 1. *In a self-help fundraising initiative, I coordinate the sale of surplus technical equipment which is the property of the Film*

and Television School. This equipment was acquired either by purchase or donation.

2. *To achieve the best price, the equipment is often listed on Internet auction sites, such as eBay. When payment is deposited into a dedicated bank account, the items are posted to the purchaser.*

3. *Funds in the account are used to purchase new or second-hand equipment needed by the School.*

4. *I absolutely deny allegations that I engaged in any theft from the Champion film set.*

5. *I absolutely deny allegations that I knowingly received or sold items stolen from the Champion film set.*

6. *I absolutely deny allegations that I conspired with or instructed interns to steal items from the Champion film set.*

7. *I believe the above allegations have been made by the guilty parties to deflect the police investigation away from themselves.*

The document was signed by Tuvoli and witnessed by Warren Stone.

Stone looked at Horseman, satisfied with his revelations. 'I trust this statement clarifies your concerns about the alleged thefts from the Champion set.'

'*Vinaka*, Mr Stone. I agree the statement is clear and succinct. However, I have questions for Mr Tuvoli. Here's the list of items missing from the Champion location. I regret it will take some time to examine the content of the Film and Television department computers our IT experts seized yesterday. However, the internet auction site eBay has been cooperative. We have identified eleven of these missing items sold from an account owned by you over the past five weeks. Those are highlighted in pink.'

Tuvoli's mouth tightened. 'I'm the nominal account holder and signatory, in line with eBay requirements. However, the students mostly manage the trading. All part of their education. As I've declared, I know nothing about any items allegedly stolen from Champion.'

'We found two stolen items in the Film and Television mail room, packaged ready to be picked up and posted. We unwrapped them in front of you yesterday. To support your claim to ignorance of this theft and trading, we need your fingerprints.'

Stone whispered to Tuvoli, who nodded his head. 'This is a gross intrusion, but I'll cooperate. I hardly have a choice, do I?'

'*Vinaka*, Mr Tuvoli. One of the Champion interns—'

There was a knock and DC Kau put his head around the door. 'Could I speak to you, sir?' Kau looked so anxious that Horseman excused himself and got up straight away. He closed the door behind him.

'What is it, Apo?'

'Sir, Nurse Barbara rang. Desirée Lopez was found unconscious on the set. She's on her way to hospital now.'

46

Horseman suspended the interview and left Musudroka and Kau to get Tuvoli's fingerprints and take a detailed statement of his movements for the last twenty-four hours.

He tried to view Desi's collapse positively, as the hammer that might crack the case, but he couldn't. Of all the Champion players, he'd interacted with Desi the most. She was temperamental, beautiful, spiteful, intelligent, and vain. A pain in the backside for any detective, but intriguing. Alive. And he had failed her when she was in trouble. She called for help, and he assumed she was just seeking attention. How could he be so stupid to get distracted by Tuvoli's contemptible racket? He'd chosen the easier option instead of pursuing Ken Johnson's unknown killer. It was like taking his eye off the ball. An error that could be fatal.

Singh would feel just the same. Her silence as they ran up the stairs to the CID room told him that. But their feelings didn't matter. They must find out more, plan, then act.

'Singh, you ring Barbara Koroi. I'll try to get Steve Duke.'

The anxious Champion director couldn't tell him much. Desi didn't show up at eight o'clock for the last challenge of the series. Mili reported Desi hadn't been at breakfast in the canteen earlier. Duke sent a couple of production assistants to search. Within a few minutes, one of them spotted her sprawled just off the path through the trees and shrubs fringing the arena. Like Ken, Desi was unconscious but breathing. Duke ordered his own driver, Charlie, to take Desi and Barbara to Suva.

When he rang off, Horseman found Lili had brought in a tea tray, loaded with all the makings and a large packet of Paradise coconut biscuits.

'Sorry, sir. I didn't know what I should do,' she said.

Horseman smiled at her. 'You've done exactly the right thing, Lili. Please pour just three cups for now. You can open the biscuits too.'

Singh had been pacing around her desk while talking to Barbara Koroi on her mobile. She joined them at the table. A few strands of hair had broken loose from her French roll and there was a ballpoint smudge on her collar. This was as dishevelled as Singh ever got. 'Desi's just arrived, still unconscious. They'll be doing tests. You go first, sir. I need this tea right now.'

Horseman lifted his eyebrows as she slumped onto a chair. It was unlike Singh to say she needed anything, let alone be so insistent. She propped her head on her folded hands as he reported what Duke had said. Lili sipped her tea, looking at Singh with a worried frown.

When he'd finished and picked up his cup, he said, 'I'd like to hear your opinion, Detective Sergeant. Should we go out to Champion right away?'

Singh raised her head. More hair had escaped her bun and hung in front of her ears. She looked tired and vulnerable. 'I'll get myself some paracetamol. My head is throbbing.'

Lili jumped up and went to the first aid kit. 'Here are two, Sarge. Swallow them both with some tea.'

Singh glanced at Lili and straightened up.

Horseman said, 'Sergeant Singh, it's fine for our probationer to learn that detectives react emotionally, you know. We're all human. I've just been berating myself for failing Desi when she called for help. I didn't drop everything and go back out to Champion. I had my sights on Tuvoli for the thefts and just wanted to nail him. That was emotional.'

'Not really, sir. Tuvoli was the logical lead to pursue. The only lead, in fact,' Singh said.

Horseman believed the blame was all his. 'If Tuvoli hasn't left Suva since yesterday afternoon—and that's quite an *if*—he probably didn't harm Desi, and that means he didn't harm Ken. My theory that Tuvoli was a mastermind for the thefts, the drugs and Ken's murder was just wishful thinking.'

'Nonsense, it was a working hypothesis and a valid one to follow. We acknowledged Tuvoli's limited access to Motu Island made him less likely to have killed Ken in person. He could have organised it, though.'

Horseman was grateful Singh seemed determined to defend him, but he'd led her and the others down a false trail.

She continued. 'You're both kind not to mention the elephant in the room, so I will. Desi called *me* for help on *my* mobile phone. I was the only detective she contacted. I should have responded.'

Horseman couldn't let her beat herself up. 'And you did, Singh, just as soon as you discovered her message. You called the number she rang from, with no result. We should have driven back out to the set, and as senior officer, I should have made that decision. Now, let's plan for the rest of the day.'

Lili Waqa was looking from Horseman to Singh and back. 'Speak up, DC Waqa.' Horseman said.

Lili blushed. 'I'm looking at two excellent detectives. You're clever and you never give up. Desi's moody and unreliable. Don't you agree? Like the boy who cried "Wolf!" with all her accusations. You couldn't have known her message was urgent, except in hindsight.'

'Out of the mouths of babes come pearls of wisdom, isn't that right?'

Musudroka hurried in. 'Who are you calling a babe, sir? Not official language, is it? Sexist, even.'

Singh interrupted. 'Shut up, Tani, this is not the time!'

'Sorry, Sarge. Tuvoli's processed. Kau's taking his statement. What do you want me to do now?' Musudroka asked.

'Sit down, Tani and pour yourself some tea. Let's go back a few days to before we focused on Tuvoli. Mind you, he's still a suspect, but no longer top of the list. Who do we rate?' Horseman asked.

Singh said, 'The other finalists were always in our sights. All had motive and opportunity. Any could have set the tripline, too. But the drugs—that's if MDMA really was a factor in Ken's death. And then, only if Ken didn't take the pills voluntarily.'

'I agree. I wonder about Nikhil Seth, the cameraman. He accepted the fact of thefts from the set with no surprise—just shrugged them off as inevitable. I marked him as a possible accomplice for Tuvoli on set. There's also Eroni Nemo, who pops up around trouble, like when the zip-line failed and when Mili trod on a stonefish at the beach. The problem with both is motive. Means and opportunity is harder, but they could have got to Motu at night if they'd wanted to.'

'We just can't know enough about anyone on this big crew, sir. It's so easy for the killer to hide.'

'*Io*, and laugh at us.' Musudroka sounded resentful.

Horseman tried to be confident. 'We'll have the last laugh, don't worry. Here's what we'll do. Lili, you'll be on guard duty for Desi. Don't allow anyone into her room except for hospital staff with official identification. Call Singh or me if anyone else comes along, Refer any requests for information to medical staff.'

'*Io*, sir.'

'Musudroka, get us two vehicles from the pool if you can. I'd better have a word with Ratini about arresting and charging Tuvoli in connection with the stealing racket. If I get the go-ahead, I'll do that before we head out to Champion.'

The others nodded.

'DS Singh, call Duke for an update and let him know we'll be with him as soon as we can. We'll need to interview Mili, Bobby and Duane if he's still there. Nikhil and Eroni too.'

'Sure, sir.' Singh looked brighter already as she tucked her stray hair behind her ears.

Horseman shoved his chair back, then straightened his shoulders as he left to find Superintendent Ratini.

47

The south-easterly trade wind had already strengthened to a stiff breeze, whipping the sea into glittering white caps. If they had to go out to Motu Island this afternoon, the ride would be bumpy. They passed through Lami and picked up speed.

'I'm surprised Superintendent Ratini approved Tuvoli's arrest, sir,' Musudroka shouted from the back seat. Singh pressed the button to close the windows and Horseman reached over from the passenger seat to turn on the air-con.

'Our chief can be unpredictable, but he cares deeply about theft, possibly more than other crimes. He's convinced by our evidence that Tuvoli's the ringleader. and now the SOCO lab's got his fingerprints, that evidence should be irrefutable by the end of today.'

'And what if it isn't, sir?'

'What do you mean, Tani?'

'What if Tuvoli's been careful and his fingerprints don't show up anywhere?'

'Good question. The circumstantial evidence and Filo's statement are pretty conclusive, but it would be good to have additional testimony from one of the other interns.'

'Now we've arrested and charged him, one of them will surely see their game's up,' Singh said.

'I hope so. His bail conditions prevent him going to FIT or communicating with any staff or students there. Even though we can't enforce that, our media release will act as a warning or incentive to the students involved.'

'When's the release?'

'Noon—in time for the afternoon radio, the TV news, and tomorrow's papers. Now, let me check with the hospital again.'

Singh slowed down and Musudroka hung over the seat back, but Horseman didn't give them much more than monosyllables until he rang off. 'Desi's still unconscious and they're calling her state a coma now. Her symptoms resemble a drug overdose but there's nothing definite from the instant screen kit. The lab's working on her samples as top priority. I'm afraid all we can do is wait.'

Steve Duke strode forward to meet them as they pulled into the car park. Extra lines etched his lean face. 'Thanks for coming so soon. Any more news?'

'Probably not.' Horseman repeated the information Desi's doctor had given him.

'No change in the last hour, then. You'd better come to my office.'

'I want to talk to you a little later, Mr Duke. Our search officers should arrive soon, but we'd like to look at Desi's room immediately. I understand she's shared a room with Mili for the last week.'

'That's right. After Ken's death, it didn't feel right to send the contestants back out to fend for themselves, but in a way … oh, never mind.'

'After looking at Desi's room, I'd like to get your remaining staff together again. I bet more than one person has seen Desi since yesterday afternoon. The sooner we compile that information, the better for Desi.'

'Sure. I've already alerted Deepika—she'll give you a list. We have under fifty crew on deck today. As you know, we're winding down, but that means Personnel are busier than ever, paying everyone who's finishing up.'

'I understand. DS Singh will sort out the arrangements with Deepika right now. If someone can show me the way to Desi's room?'

The grey-painted barracks room that Desi and Mili had shared for the past ten days was quite spacious and probably accommodated four or more soldiers when the military was in residence. Two single beds were pushed against the end walls, as if the players wanted to be as far away from each other as possible. Unzipped sleeping bags covered the thin mattresses. A tall locker stood against the wall near the foot of each bed and a straw broom leaned against a wall. Horseman pulled aside a curtain to reveal an equally spartan bathroom smelling of wet concrete and laundry soap. There was a urinal, a toilet cubicle, a hand basin, and an open shower. A blue plastic washbag hung from a hook beside a small mirror.

Horseman wondered at the tidiness: nothing personal was on view, nothing stored under the beds or tucked beneath the thin pillows or mattresses. The two girls guarded their privacy fiercely. Each locker held an unlabelled backpack, but which one was Desi's? He checked the front pocket of one and pulled out a rolled-up blue ribbon. He unwound it to reveal a text embroidered in cream silk: *The Lord is my strength and my song; he has given me victory. Exodus 15:2.* He pictured Mili's mother giving her gifted daughter the ribbon as a talisman, perhaps to wear around her waist—it was about the right length. So the other pack must belong to Desi.

He placed the pack on the nearest bed and removed the contents of each compartment before replacing them. A few changes of light tropical pants and shorts, tops, one warm jersey and underwear, all suffering from washing in seawater, a camping set of metal eating utensils nesting in a frying pan, an all-purpose knife, a sewing kit and a handful of seeds and shells in a Ziplock bag, probably souvenirs of Motu camp. Nothing personal except for another Ziplock bag protecting a few photos, probably of her family. Well, he'd know when he met her parents later.

Horseman was bent over the photos when the door was flung open. Mili stood in the sunlight, a black silhouette.

'Oh, Inspector Horseman, what are you doing here?' Her voice was calm, puzzled rather than outraged.

'*Bula*, Mili. I'm taking a look at Desi's room. I know it's your room, too. I'm sorry to intrude but we're trying to find out what may have happened to Desi. I'm glad you've come back because I need to look through your things. '

'Alright. I suppose I don't have much choice.'

'Just take everything out of your backpack and lay it on the bed, please.'

Mili was slow to move out of the shaft of light, but when she did, Horseman could see her face was as composed as her voice. He half-expected her to protest, but she sat on her bed, opened the pack's zippers, and suddenly upended it, shaking it vigorously as her possessions fell onto the spread sleeping bag. If this was a protest, he hoped it helped her. She passed him the bag by the straps.

'Here, you'd better check. There could be anything lurking in the corners.' He shone his torch into each compartment and retrieved a neat bundle of cord, a small packet of fishing hooks and a few crumpled yellow post-it notes.

'What are these?' he asked softly.

'Oh, I think just some fans' phone numbers. Crew here, especially Fijians, hand them to me and it seems rude not to accept them, so they just end up at the bottom of my pack. Take a look if you like.' She looked up at him with a small smile.

'Thanks, we'll need to hang on to these for a bit.'

'Keep them—I don't remember whose they are any more.'

Horseman slipped the notes into an evidence bag to give the SOCOs, then spread out the items dumped from the pack onto the bed. The collection was similar to Desi's although the design of Mili's garments was more modest. Apart from the embroidery, the only decorative item was a string of shiny beads in a Ziplock bag: perhaps a necklace.

'Is this Fijian?'

'I don't think so. A fan gave it to me. Pretty, isn't it? It's a rosary but as I'm a Methodist, I wear it as costume jewellery.' In addition, Mili possessed a large black Bible with lots of coloured sticky markers, some of which had come unstuck when she emptied her pack. There was also a folder with sheet music inserted into plastic sleeves.

'You had your Bible and music with you at the Motu camp?'

'*Io*, they were allowed. They took up too much room in my pack, but I couldn't do without them.'

Horseman unrolled the embroidered text. 'Is this your work?'

'Oh no. An aunt did that. Mum insists I take it everywhere with me.' She smiled, dismissing her elders' superstition with a small wave of her hand.

'When did you last see Desi?'

'She lined up in the canteen for breakfast this morning, then ran out before she was served.'

'Did she seem alright earlier?'

'She wasn't here earlier. Maybe she got up before I did and made her bed before going out.'

'Did she often do that?'

'Never. I don't think she slept in her bed last night. Now I think about it, I didn't notice Desi in the canteen at dinnertime. I'm not saying she wasn't there at some stage, just that I didn't see her. Some Fijian guys invited me to join a *yaqona* circle after dinner. I had no choice but to accept. I was there at most for two hours, then I came back here. There was no sign of Desi.'

'Do you know where she was?'

'No, we didn't chat much. We're rivals, so of course she wouldn't confide in me.'

'Who did she hang out with in the evenings since you've been here on the set?'

'I don't really know. Sometimes she played table tennis in the rec hall. She's much more sporty than me.'

'Did you see her yesterday afternoon?'

'*Io*, we finished the shoot around half-past one, we had a quick late lunch and then we were free. I had a long nap and went down to the beach later. I saw Desi fishing with a spear in the shallows. As I said, she's very sporty and took to fishing when we camped on Motu. She's got good natural hand-eye coordination, I'll give her that. I yelled at her to look out for stonefish but I don't think she heard. That was the last time I saw her until breakfast this morning.'

'*Vinaka*, Mili, you've been very helpful.'

Shadows darkened the doorway. Ash and his assistant SOCOs knocked, entered, and hovered, kitbags in hand. 'Sergeant Jayarman will want to look through your things, Mili. You can stay while he does so if you like. He'll give you a receipt for anything he needs to take to the lab.'

Mili nodded, frowning. As Horseman left the bare barracks room, he realised Mili had not once asked about Desi's condition.

48

Singh and Musudroka burst into the interview room as soon as Horseman called out, 'Come in.' He hoped the Champion staff meeting had revealed something. Anything.

'Cracked the case, you two?' he asked.

Musudroka grinned broadly as he set down a large tray on the table. 'Sorry, sir, not quite. But by the way some staff were scribbling away in their statements, I reckon we've got some witnesses who saw Desi yesterday afternoon. The canteen gave us this lunch. Maybe we could eat while we go through what they wrote.'

'Great. Mili and Bobby were useful too. I'll put the kettle on.'

While they all helped set up lunch, Horseman filled the others in on his interview with Mili.

'No love lost between Mili and Desi, then?' Singh asked.

'No, I'm surprised how deep their rivalry goes. On Mili's side anyway.'

'I'm sure it's mutual. Thinking back to Desi's nasty comments to us about her, she always implied Mili was just the token Fijian who was meant to win.'

Musudroka's brow furrowed. 'They're so ambitious it's unreal. I don't think they have much fun on Champion, do you?'

'It's about a million dollars, not fun,' Singh replied.

'True, true. But how come they want it so bad?' Musudroka's modest level of ambition was endearing, Horseman decided.

'Mili claims the ambition comes from her parents, not herself,' Singh said. 'But that could just be a public face she puts on.'

'Bobby's more reticent, too. Out of politeness, I think.' Horseman poured boiling water on the tea leaves in the aluminium pot, stirred the brew and put the pot on the table. 'However, let's sit down and eat now. Those sandwiches look good. We've got a choice of corned beef or tuna. Dalo slices, too.'

The sandwiches were fresh and filling. After half the plate had disappeared, Singh poured the tea. 'What did Bobby have to say, sir?'

'Like Mili, he saw Desi standing in the shallows off the beach, the water up to her knees, a bag over her shoulder. He couldn't tell what she was doing.'

'Did you find Duane?'

'Yes, he's still here, booked on a flight to Los Angeles tomorrow. He saw Desi on the boatshed jetty when he was talking to Zak about borrowing a kayak. She was fishing with a rod off the end of the jetty. None of the finalists are allowed watches, but I hope some of the crew can supply accurate times. So, let's divide up the statements.'

Musudroka poured more tea while Singh divided up the statements reporting sightings of Desi the previous afternoon. She piled coloured highlighters and sticky tabs in the middle of the table. They helped themselves to more sandwiches and settled down to work.

After a period of intense highlighting and jotting, Singh said, 'Right, I'm ready to start a timeline. Let's rough it out on the whiteboard first. Tani, you can be scribe. Why don't we move the table closer to the board.'

They took half an hour to arrange all relevant witness reports on the board. Although they couldn't time most of them accurately, a rough sequence of Desi's activities emerged. She wasn't in their room before or after Mili took her afternoon nap. A couple of crew saw her heading down the track to the beach around three o'clock, carrying a bucket and fishing gear. Boatman Zak and several others saw her on the end of the jetty, fishing with her bamboo pole and line. Two people saw Eroni talking with her at some time and a third saw Desi and Eroni leaving the jetty together. This witness said the pair seemed to be arguing. Eroni peeled off at the track to the camp while Desi continued along the beach.

Later, she was fishing alone in the shallows further along, this time with her makeshift spear. One witness saw her walking up the beach with a woman in the late afternoon but couldn't give a specific time. Some late canteen diners said it was already dark when Desi came in, helped herself to the remains of the self-serve buffet, and joined them when they waved her over. She looked tired but otherwise fine. She picked at the unappetising leftovers but drained a glass of water one diner poured for her, and another after that. One witness thought she was dehydrated and urged her to drink more water before she went to bed. Desi agreed, saying she'd head for bed early.

Horseman said, 'Well, we know she didn't do that. Mili said when she woke at half past six this morning Desi's bed didn't look slept in.'

'It's possible Desi got up earlier and made her bed before going out,' Singh said.

'Sure. Mili said she's been tired and sleeping a lot since her stonefish incident,' Horseman said. 'By the way, did Eroni make a statement?'

'No, sir. He couldn't be at the meeting. He was supposed to be doing a job out at Motu Island,' Musudroka said.

'Well, I'm going to find him now and ask him a few questions. Who wants to come?' He wanted to give Singh the chance to opt out. She avoided small boats if she could, especially in choppy water.

Singh smiled as if she'd read his mind. 'I'll remove the evidence here, sir. After I've recorded it, of course.' She stepped back and took a shot of the whiteboard with her phone.

'Let's go, Tani. I've a feeling Mr Eroni Nemo can help us with our enquiries.'

49

They found Zakaraia sitting in the shade of the boathouse, enjoying a solitary smoke.

'*Io*, Dete took Eroni in the barge to Motu early this morning. We must leave the island as we found it, you know. The props team are disassembling the spirit-house and bringing back the sections to store here until next year. They'll probably get back mid-afternoon.'

'Zak, we really need to speak to Eroni as soon as we can. We know he spoke to Desi Lopez yesterday afternoon. He may be able to help us find out what happened to her.'

'Aha, you've already read my statement, I see.' Zak beamed with pride.

'*Vinaka* for that information, Zak. Do you remember anything now you maybe didn't include in your statement?'

Zak gave the question long consideration. 'No, I'm sorry. How is Desi?'

'Still unconscious when we last heard. The doctors are treating her but so far don't know what's wrong. We're waiting for news. Anything we can find out could help her.'

Zak bowed his head, perhaps in prayer. 'I can't let you borrow the speedboat if that's what you're hoping for. That would be dereliction of duty. But I can run you out to Motu myself.'

'*Vinaka vakalevu*, Zak. I'm most grateful.'

The sun broke through the clouds as they approached the island, lighting the shallow water as if from below. They helped Zak pull the speedboat up on the white sand. The crew had transformed the beach from groomed perfection to a military stockpile. Piles of ropes, poles, palm fronds, and a heap that he could only label miscellaneous junk occupied much of the area above the highwater mark.

Horseman couldn't believe all this material had come from the small makeshift camp. 'Is this all going back?'

'No. They'll store the strong, straight poles, but they'll burn the twiggy ones and thatching fronds here, along with any rubbish. They've already loaded most of the reed wall panels in the barge on the right.'

A labourer greeted the detectives cheerily and said Eroni was at the spirit-house. They found him at the top of the mound, lowering sections of the roof by ropes to his workmates waiting below. Now the temple was reduced to panels piled on top of the mound and at its foot, Horseman realised simulating its façade here, right where it stood in bygone times, had been a stroke of genius. Now it was gone, the ancient mound had lost its spirit, its ability to conjure from the past a society unrecognisable to Fijians today.

'*Bula*, Eroni, can we speak to you, please?' Horseman shouted.

Eroni, engrossed in his work, jumped but held on to his rope and waited until the section was safely on the ground.

'*Io*, Josefa Horseman. I'll come down.'

Eroni ran lightly down the uneven steps and greeted Horseman eagerly, his hand outstretched. His long frizzy hair sprang out from under his baseball cap, which also failed to contain his large ears. Horseman wondered if his suspicions of the man were wrong. After all, he'd sought out the detectives more than once and always seemed keen to help.

'This is a surprise, Inspector Horseman. Can you tell me how Desi is?'

'She's stable but the doctors still don't know what caused her collapse. I hope you can help her, Eroni.'

'I hope so. But how?'

'We've asked all the crew to tell us when they last saw Desi. We're here to ask you and your workmates that question now.'

Eroni clicked his tongue. 'I was working on Motu yesterday, too. But she was on the jetty when we got back. She was trying to fish with a pole and line. I stopped for a chat, thinking I could give her some tips.'

'And could you?'

'First, I told her she'd chosen a terrible place to fish. I've always liked Desi but she's so emotional, flying off the handle at nothing.

She showed me a small snapper she'd already caught in her bucket, as if to say she knew better. I said to throw the snapper back as it was undersize. She told me there was no point in that as the fish was already dead. I checked and she was right. I said she'd have better luck at the other end of the beach, in the shallows. She could use her spear. She was the only contestant to get the knack of the spear. Except Mili, who'd learned as a child on Taveuni.'

'Did she take your tip?'

'*Io*, she laughed and asked me to show her a good place. I was hungry and took the track back to camp, but I pointed out where I thought she should try.'

'Why did she want to go fishing?' Musudroka asked.

'She said she missed finding food on Motu. She'd been back on base for over a week, she'd finished most of the shoots and wanted to fish now she had free time. That made sense to me.' Again, that disconcerting click of his tongue against his teeth.

'Sure, me too. Do you know if she caught anything? Did you see her again?'

'I did, but not to speak to. I'm not even certain it was her. It was maybe around nine at night and I was going to bed. I switched the light off and stood at my open window looking out. Someone like Desi was walking parallel to our building, maybe twenty metres away near the trees. I'm not certain, but no one else has a shape like Desi, do they?' Eroni grinned.

'What did you do?'

'Nothing. She passed out of my sight, and I went to bed. Sorry I can't help you.'

'You've been most helpful, Eroni. *Vinaka*. We'll let you get on with your work now.' Horseman looked up at where the mock-up had stood on top of the mound. 'The spirit-house may have been fake, but it created an enchanted mood here, didn't it?'

'*Io*, sir. The place has lost its magic now,' Musudroka added.

'*Vinaka, ovisas.* Everyone in Props is proud of our spirit-house. We'll store it away carefully in our shipping container for next year.'

'Just one more thing, Mr Nemi. I've got a plan of the camp here. Could you point out your room, please?' Musudroka asked.

Eroni lifted his eyebrows in assent and Musudroka handed him the plan and a pencil. When Eroni marked his room with a cross, he said, 'All of us props guys are in this building. Desi was walking from left to right.'

'Well done, Tani,' Horseman said as they approached Eroni's workmates. Musudroka said nothing but he drew his shoulders back and walked a bit taller.

50

Zak's presence stopped the detectives from chewing over Eroni's account until they were back at the barracks. The other crew on Motu confirmed that Desi was on the jetty when their boat got back but only Eroni spoke to her or saw her later.

'When you think about it, sir, there's no conflict between what Eroni said and the other witness statements.'

'True, Tani. The witness who saw her on the beach with a woman probably saw her after Eroni left for the canteen. And if it was Desi whom Eroni saw around nine o'clock, she could have been going anywhere. His sighting also fits with Mili's story that Desi wasn't in their room when she went to bed early herself.'

'Are they all telling the truth, sir?'

'Maybe, but probably not all the truth. And crucially, what did Desi do between walking around the barracks at nine o'clock and running from the canteen at breakfast, only to collapse in the arena hedge?'

'I can't wait to tell Sarge.' The young DC was maturing, but hadn't lost his puppy-like enthusiasm, especially where Singh was involved. Horseman smiled to himself.

However, when they opened the door of their interview room, Singh wasn't alone. Steve Duke, his face glowering, was pacing about to the limited extent the room allowed. Singh looked at Horseman, her eyes wide with warning.

'Horseman, I came here to speak to you. In fact, I wanted to see you hours ago, when you first arrived this morning.'

'Yes, I'm keen to talk with you, too. But our priority today is to trace Desi's movements in order to help her doctors find out what happened to her. That's what we've been doing, and we're not finished yet. Is there news from the hospital we've missed while we've been out on Motu?'

Duke shook his head. Singh checked her phone. 'No, nothing yet, sir.'

'Call DC Waqa and check on that, will you, Tani? I know you're anxious about Desi, Mr Duke, as we all are. But is there some other reason you're here?'

'You bet, Inspector. I caught the radio news an hour ago. They reported Desi's collapse and emergency admission to hospital. Our practice is to keep Champion out of the local news. And that's not just about control of publicity. Has it ever struck you what it would be like for the families of our contestants if they hear news like this from public broadcasters? Let alone social media? No one's allowed to communicate with contestants while the competition's running, for Chrissake. And vice versa. What the hell were you thinking?'

The director's volume had risen as he spoke until he was shouting. He stopped, as if surprised at himself.

Duke was agitated so Horseman tried to be quiet and calm. 'Mr Duke, my team has been working without let-up ever since we were called in after Ken Johnson's death. We've chased all leads, promising and not so promising, and found out the Champion location has been littered with accidents, pranks, drugs, and thefts almost from the beginning. But Ken's death still raises questions we haven't answered and it's time to appeal to the wider public. Such appeals very often throw up crucial information.'

'Please sit down, Mr Duke. Let's talk about this together,' Singh said gently.

Musudroka ended his phone call. 'Lili says there's no change to Desi's condition. How about I make tea?'

Duke pulled out a plastic chair and sat, thumping his fist on the table. 'No, I don't want tea!'

Musudroka switched the kettle on and turned to the director with a friendly smile. 'That's okay, Mr Duke, but you won't mind if I go ahead, will you? Inspector Horseman and I just got back from Motu and I reckon we're ready for it!'

Duke nodded. 'I apologise, I shouldn't have been rude. But tea isn't going to fix this. Desi's parents arrive tomorrow. What on earth can I tell them?'

'Surely, you can only tell them the truth. We can only keep working to uncover more of the truth and pray Desi improves.'

'Yeah, but it's worse for me. I've met Desi's father—Len Carson's one of the best-known attorneys in the Hollywood movie industry. Well connected to producers and the big studios. He could ruin Champion if he chose.'

Horseman was dumbfounded. He glanced at Singh, who looked as confused as he felt. 'Really? Desi's told us quite a different story about her family.'

Duke smiled now. 'I bet. Which one did you get? The poor but honest Latino family? The victim of ethnic prejudice? The abused runaway? The brilliant but bullied scholarship student?'

'Your first two options. Do you agree, Singh?'

'I do. You need to tell us more, Mr Duke.'

The director shrugged. 'Desi's mother's name's Lopez and anyway, there's no rule against contestants using stage names on Champion. She's a talented little rich girl with an overactive imagination. I don't think she'd really prefer to be an oppressed victim, but who knows? Is she a fantasist? Personally, I think she's an ambitious aspiring actress practising playing different roles.'

Musudroka laid out the tea things on the table. 'Is a fantasist the same as a compulsive liar, Mr Duke?'

Duke smiled at him. 'I dunno. But they both often behave the same way. Maybe I'll have a cup of that tea after all.'

Singh turned to Duke. 'You seem to know Desi very well indeed.'

'I hadn't met her before we selected her but I do get to know the contestants, especially the finalists. I've met her dad a few times around Hollywood.'

Musudroka poured them all tea and passed around the milk and sugar.

'When did you last see Desi, Mr Duke?' Horseman asked.

The director ran a hand through his short hair, like he often did when deciding what to say. 'Well, it was probably when we finished shooting the last challenge. That was late, maybe one or one-thirty.'

'Not later in the afternoon?'

'No, I was with my editor and the cinematographer after lunch, checking the morning's footage. We were indoors for hours, eyes glued to the monitors.'

'What about later? Dinner or afterwards?'

'Nope, the canteen delivered dinner to the executive meeting in my office. We had a lot to thrash out and that was before Desi fell ill. Events have overtaken those decisions now. Everything's changed.'

'I can see that. What about after your meeting?'

Duke shook his head. 'I took a walk to clear my head before I headed off to bed. Not for too long—the breeze freshened up like it often does this time of year.'

'Did you see Desi while you were out?'

Duke shook his head again.

'I ask because another witness saw Desi around nine o'clock walking in the direction of your suite.'

'I can't account for that. Sorry, I didn't see her. If you hear from the hospital, I'd sure appreciate it if you let me know. If there's any news, they'll probably let you know first.'

'I'll do that, Mr Duke. And please get in touch with us if any further information about Desi's recent movements comes to light.'

'I will. Right now, I've got a to-do list as long as my arm to get through before I get myself to the airport to meet her parents. Thank you for the tea.'

With that, Duke got up, replaced his chair neatly under the table and strolled to the door, his hands in his pockets.

'I think the tea helped him,' Musudroka said.

'It did. You handled his anger and anxiety well. That's not easy, but it's important for a detective to stay calm as you did.' Horseman gave Musudroka a thumbs-up.

'I think Duke could know more. His reaction was a bit over the top, don't you think? I understand it's worrying that Desi's still unconscious, but ...' Singh trailed off.

'Yes, frustrating too. If only we could ask her what happened. Once we've chased up the few crew who couldn't come to the meeting this morning, we'd better head back to the station.'

practise the best answers to the challenging questions some journalists might ask. We could even record a polished interview ready-to-air for small radio stations, bloggers and internet sites that don't have the journalistic resources to make their own.'

'Really, is that needed?'

'Yes, Joe. Make it as easy as you can for the media, and they'll use it. Of course, you're famous and loved in Fiji, and in rugby worldwide. We need to build further on that base. International sport is looking to spot new stars, after all. No disrespect, Joe.'

'No, you're right, Gloria.'

'So, we need the hostel name asap. Have you decided?'

'No, not quite. I intended to put some alternatives to the Shiners at training tomorrow. They should choose, they're old enough.'

'Guided democracy, I like that, Joe. I'd appreciate a look at your short list, though. It's easier for another pair of eyes to pick up on a possible negative connotation.'

Horseman bridled at Gloria's interference but had to admit she was right. Still, he wouldn't offer her a seat on the board. He couldn't stand feeling inadequate at every meeting. 'Good idea, I'll run them past Dr Pillai and Dr Matt Young, too. Oh, maybe I didn't tell you Matt's agreed to be a Trustee?'

'No, but I'm so pleased you're making progress. I'll send you the draft tonight.'

Did he detect a slight downturn in Gloria's enthusiasm? 'Look forward to it. *Moce*, Gloria.'

His curry was cold, so he put it in the microwave again, pressed 'Reheat' and went out onto his balcony. The breeze had blown the diesel pollution out to sea, and he gulped the fresh night air. He wished an equally fresh insight would blow into his mind. His phone rang again. He hoped it was the hospital.

He sighed irritably at his mother's voice and hated himself.

'*Bula* Mum? Anything wrong?'

'No, Josefa, should there be?'

'You don't normally ring so late at night, that's all.'

'No, I don't, but I've come to a decision. I want to tell you now so I can go to bed and not start rethinking it all over again.'

'I must remember that trick. You're always more decisive than me.'

'Well ... maybe. But I find it's certainly true that if you tell someone you've made up your mind, that indecisive stress lifts right off. You're committed and you can get on with acting on what you've decided.'

'I'll remember that. What have you decided?'

'You've got a short memory, son. Oh, sorry, I guess this Champion case is tying you up in knots, eh?'

'*Io*, it's a tough one.'

'Remember you asked me if I would be housemother at your Shiners team hostel?'

'*Io*, Mum.' He held his breath.

'I'm grateful you offered me this role, Joe.' Oh no, he knew what was coming—she was letting him down gently.

'I'm going to do it, Joe. Older people need a challenge, and above all, a project where their decades of experience can help others. As you suggested, I'll commit to two years, during which I'll train a younger woman to take over. Finding the right person could be a problem, however. I recommend I'm included in a management committee, to prevent overlapping duties and ensure all staff are singing from the same songbook, so to speak.'

'Excellent idea, I agree with that. *Vinaka vakalevu*—I can't believe my luck. I thought you'd say no.'

'Really? Well, I'm off to read my Bible and go to bed. You better get cracking with that fund-raising, or I might drop dead before your boys get a roof over their heads. Then where would you be?'

His chest expanded with fresh air and renewed purpose. His curry was barely lukewarm, but he took it to the balcony and forked it into his mouth as he leaned on the railing. Just what he needed. He gazed out over the town lights to the harbour, where the red, green, and white lights of ships tracked across the black bay.

Could his dream really come to life? Thanks to the good-hearted people who surrounded him, he now believed it could. He'd cooperate with Gloria and try not to resent her efficiency. She was right, there could be no hostel without a lot of money, and soon. He'd listen to his mother, who knew all there was to know about creating a happy home for teenagers.

He went back inside, threw himself on the sofa and reached for the remote. Time for rugby. The Tonga versus Papua New Guinea international promised to be exciting. But the phone rang yet again. He turned off the sound and glanced at the caller. It was Steve Duke. Maybe he had news of Desi. He picked up.

'Any updates, Mr Duke?'

'Not about Desi, I'm afraid. I don't want to waste police time. I should've told you this already, but it's private and irrelevant to your enquiries. I want to come clean and need your assurance you'll keep my information confidential, just between you and me. Believe me, from what I've seen, Fiji media are poodles compared to our pit bulls in the States.'

Horseman tried to keep his eyes on the rugby. 'Until I hear what you've got to say, I can't make any promises, Mr Duke. But if I decide it's irrelevant, I'll keep it to myself. As to the press, they're out of bounds to the investigation team. All communication goes through our public relations office and senior officers.'

'In theory, you mean. The bastards have their ways and means. Okay ... I can account for Desi from about nine o'clock last night until five-thirty this morning. She was with me in my suite.' The director heaved a sigh of relief after his admission.

'Go on. Was this by arrangement?'

'Yeah, although I told her last time must be the last. She knew how to get her way and I went along with it. She turned up at my door the night after the finalists moved back here a week ago. Laughing at my confusion when I opened the door. How flattering to a middle-aged guy! Offering me intelligent ideas about ways to continue the show, followed by her superb body, gorgeous face, and sparkling personality. I should have resisted harder but show me the man who could say no to Desi. That night and the next she left before midnight. But last night she stayed.'

'Do you know why?'

'Now I wonder if she passed out—she went to sleep in my bed. I joined her. She got up about five and threw up a few times. After that she felt better and took a shower, then told me she was going back to her room before it got light.'

'Did either of you take any pills or drugs while you were together?'

'Not at all!'

'Did she mention what she did in the late afternoon and early evening?'

'Said she went fishing. That surprised me, but her story was she felt nostalgic for her tribe's camp on Motu, so she caught a couple of small fish, broiled them in an old pan at the beach fire pit and ate them, out of sight of anyone. Said she enjoyed being alone and fending for herself.'

'Do you believe that?'

'I dunno. She's highly capable, but whether it happened like that, I've no idea, frankly.'

'Anything else you can tell me?'

'That's it, Inspector. Look, Desi wanted to win above all else. I know she calculated that bedding me would help her do that. But of all the calculating bitches in the world, she's gotta be the most lovely, the most charming when she wants to be. I did nothing to hurt her, I promise you.' His voice cracked, and he hung up.

Horseman couldn't concentrate on the match anymore. He switched off the TV and got himself a Fiji Bitter from the fridge to aid his thinking.

THURSDAY

52

After a restless night which did nothing to banish his confusion, Horseman dragged himself out of bed and jogged through the quiet streets to Matt Young's place where Tina was waiting for him. Her eyes fixed on him, she jumped from her verandah basket and ran to the front gate, her ball in her mouth, wagging her tail off. He squatted down to greet her properly, rubbing her brindled coat as she wedged her head between his arm and thigh.

'Where's your lead, Tina?'

She dropped the ball and fetched her lead from beside her basket. Matt emerged from his front door, yawned, and waved them off. When they got to Ratu Cakobau Road, Tina strained at the lead, then sat down on the verge.

'No beach today? You want to go to the museum, do you, girl?'

The temperature dropped as they turned into the drive, shaded by enormous Pacific teak trees. In the gaps between their dark buttresses, the sunlit Thurston Gardens beckoned. 'Let's get some of those rays, Tina.'

He unclipped her lead, she ran to the fence and looked back at him, impatient. She'd once disturbed a basking mongoose here and was ever hopeful of tracking the creature down again. When he opened the gate she raced through, snuffled among some undergrowth before backing out and tearing off on another scent trail. Much like his incoherent activity on this case, he couldn't help thinking.

He leaned against the fence, face to the rising sun, and tried to relax. But the fear of a killer at the Champion camp rose in his gullet in a rush of acid. Like the mongoose, this predator was nimble, ever alert for threats. Also like the mongoose, he—or she—must have a safe burrow he could escape to in a flash.

His phone rang and he fumbled in his pocket, snatching at it impatiently. It was Apo Kau, on duty at Desi's hospital ward.

'Good morning, sir. But it's not good, I'm sorry. Desi passed away a few minutes ago. She didn't regain consciousness. The doctor said she didn't respond to treatment and her blood pressure gradually dropped until her heart failed.'

'*Vinaka*, Apo. Bad news. Finish up there now. You've been on duty all night. Go home and get some sleep.'

'*Vinaka*, sir. I'll catch a few hours, then come into the station.'

'Not until after lunch. That's an order.'

He slid his back down the fence and sat on the grass, his legs stretched out. Why was Desi's death such a knock-out blow? Wasn't it a repeat of Ken Johnson? But he hadn't known the living Ken. Whereas Desi, that flamboyant, baffling woman, was alive in his mind, shoving others aside, daring him to discover why she died.

What's more, a tripline had hurled Ken down the steps to the spirit-house, cracking his head on limestone. A tripline someone had anchored, stretched taut and tied off. Possibly Desi.

He'd believed Desi's illness was like Mili's poisoning—an accident she'd recover from. But now he must consider manslaughter and murder as well. She'd died, so couldn't confirm or deny Duke's version of Tuesday night. At least Desi was now in the care of his friend and first-rate pathologist Matt Young. Matt would explain how Desi died, but the detectives might still need to find out why.

A wet nose nudged his arm. Tina sat in his lap, reached up and licked his neck. Horseman looked into her concerned eyes, then stretched his own face away. '*Vinaka*, Tina, but no kisses on the lips! I'll take you back to Matt's. He'll be at work and that's where I've got to go, too.' Tina mouthed her slimy ball while Horseman snapped on her lead.

53

'Christ, yeah, I just heard. But thanks for calling.' Duke's voice was soft but cracking. 'Her parents touch down in three hours. Shit, I don't think I can handle this. My God, I don't. Can you help, Joe?' His plea ended in a strangled sob.

Whatever the reason for Duke's unravelling, helping him was not Horseman's job. 'I'll do whatever I can to guide the Carsons through the police process, assuming they will choose to repatriate Desi's body to the States. I helped smooth the formalities for Ken Johnson's father and he appreciated that.'

'Yes, of course. Hell, that was just six days ago but it feels like another era.'

'I know what you mean. I'm afraid I can't meet the Carsons at the airport. Where are they staying?'

'I've booked the Grand Pacific. It can't make things any worse to be comfortable, can it?'

'No. I'll get my card and a note to the hotel reception before they arrive. They'll be in shock, so please remind them they can ring me any time. Desi's postmortem will take top priority for the pathologist today. Dr Young will discover the cause of her death, you can rely on that.'

Another strangled sob. 'Will you be there?'

'At the postmortem? No, I need to talk again to the witnesses who saw Desi between Tuesday afternoon and Wednesday morning. That includes you, but I suppose you'll be with the Carsons for much of the day. Have you remembered anything else since we spoke last night? Maybe something Desi said that you didn't register at the time? Or didn't mention to me?'

'Nothing relevant. I'm sure you've heard her badmouth her rival finalists. She did some of that, but nothing specific, nothing I gave any credence to. All part of her tactics.'

'She was being tactical when you last met?'

'You betcha. Why else would she turn up at my door?' Duke's voice quavered, but to Horseman's surprise, he didn't sound bitter at all. 'We're already winding down at Champion—you know that. But now, we can't go ahead with the final face-off and selection of the winner. That's cancelled. Bobby and Mili will understand, I'm sure.'

'You haven't told them yet?'

'No chance, I only heard Desi passed away a minute or two before you called. But I'll tell them in person right away and email the staff before I leave for the airport.'

'I'm glad to hear it. I don't want to conceal your decision from Bobby and Mili when I speak with them.'

'I wouldn't ask that of you. Maybe I'll see you later today. Anyways, keep in touch if you can.'

Already his voice was stronger. Just as well, the man had an ordeal ahead. And it was time he called Singh.

***

Singh had the morning papers spread out on her desk when Horseman came into the CID room with his own bundle. 'I only saw the headlines, what's in the stories?'

'As you'd expect, shock and horror at the suggestion that a trusted educator could scheme to steal from overseas guests, especially from Champion, the source of so much foreign revenue. Of course, they all stick *alleged* in front of just about every noun.'

'Hmm. Anything stick out?'

'The *Fiji Times* editorial is in denial: "Have the police blundered?" You'd think several convictions for embezzlement of school funds by staff in the last couple of years would have got them used to the idea. Perhaps Ratu Joni's a relative of the editor. *The Sun* relishes the prospect of a scandal. "One bad apple, or are Fiji's schools rotten to the core?" So does *The Mirror*.'

'Not too bad then. The internet?'

'*Talanoa* bewails the corrupting influence of bad apples on the young.'

Musudroka hurried in and dumped his backpack on Singh's desk. '*Yadra* sir, *yadra* Sarge. I heard that. Why do they go on about bad apples? Not many Fijians have even tasted an apple, good or bad. Make more sense to talk about bad bananas, wouldn't it?'

'It would Tani. The power of a cliché, eh? But we've got bad news about Desi.'

'*Io*, Apo called me. I know. I never liked her, I admit.'

'Fine, but don't say that beyond these walls,' Singh said.

'No, Sarge. I'll put the kettle on.'

Horseman snatched up his phone as soon as it rang. 'Matt, you've found something so soon? You're a miracle worker!'

'Good morning to you, too! No, not me. It's pure coincidence that the lab came through with a positive just after Desi died. Thought I'd tell you about it. You'll get an email from them in a few minutes, anyway.'

'*Vinaka*, go ahead.'

'Looks like the poor kid was poisoned by eating pufferfish, mate. The lab found tetrodotoxin in Desi's blood sample. You were in Japan for a while, weren't you? Pufferfish is quite the delicacy there. Did you ever eat *fugu*—pufferfish?'

'My rugby hosts took me to a *fugu* restaurant once, but fortunately, that wasn't the only dish on offer. No way was I going to risk poisoning to be polite! The fugu chefs are licensed in Japan, trained to select the right fish and to prepare them safely. But there are no guarantees, and many diners suffer poisoning. Every year some people die, just to show how brave they are. Stupid, more like.'

'Yeah, the *fugu* tradition is a strange culinary custom.'

'Sorry, go on. How does tetrodotoxin work?'

'It's a neurotoxin, same kind of poison as your old friend, the banded sea krait. Remember Paradise Island?'

'How could I forget? Singh remembers them, too, don't you Singh? What a shame you can't see her shuddering! Sorry, go on.'

'Remember how Susie and Barbara treated Mili's stonefish sting with hot water? That doesn't work with tetrodotoxin—it's heat-stable and can't be destroyed by cooking, freezing, or washing. Vomiting can help, as you'd expect. But there's really no treatment other than nursing support. Blood pressure gradually drops until the heart fails.'

'She did vomit in the early hours of yesterday and complained of being tired and weak on Tuesday evening.'

'That fits. Good that you've found some witnesses.'

'Yes, several people saw her fishing on Tuesday afternoon. One or two spoke to her. She said if she caught a fish, she wanted to cook it on the beach fire-pit, reliving her first weeks on Motu.'

'Looks like she made a fatal mistake—what a tragedy.' Dr Young paused. 'However, I intend to forget that idea and examine Desi's body with a fresh mind. It's easy to miss things if you think you know the cause of death before you even begin the examination. And I'll let you get on with your detecting.'

'Thanks a million, Matt. Desi's parents arrive later this morning. Duke told me her father's a hot-shot Hollywood lawyer. Duke's quaking in his boots.'

'Poor souls. This is the worst day of their lives. If they want to see Desi, you can tell them this afternoon after two o'clock. I'll be here. I never know what to say to parents who've lost a child, but I'll do my best.'

***

Horseman sipped his tea after relaying Steve Duke's admission and the pathologist's latest news.

'I can understand Desi's fishing now. Suppose she intended to get a pufferfish to poison Mili or Bobby? There's plenty of them about,' Musudroka said.

'*Io*, plenty of people who eat them in Fiji get sick, too. Occasionally someone dies. I must say, your theory didn't occur to me, but it's possible.'

'She would hardly have eaten the fish by herself, though,' Singh said. 'Not when food was available in the canteen.'

Musudroka's excitement ramped up. 'Right, Sarge. She cooked it for someone who joined her on the beach. Maybe Desi didn't know what parts were poisonous and by chance, her intended victim didn't eat the bad bits.'

'Or we could switch that around. Maybe Desi was the intended victim and ignorant the pufferfish was toxic. But her companion knew and made sure she ate the lethal parts,' Horseman said.

Singh frowned. 'Maybe that companion is not at all well. I'll check with Barbara Koroi if anyone's come to her with the right symptoms.'

Horseman looked at his phone. 'I've got emails from the lab and from Matt. Print them out for me, please Tani. Matt's attachment will tell us all we need to know about the symptoms of puffer fish poisoning. When's Lili coming in, DS Singh?'

'After lunch, sir. She was at the hospital until midnight.'

'That's fine. Let her and Apo know we're off to Champion as soon as we can get our skates on.'

'Who's on our list, sir?'

'Eroni, Bobby, Mili, the witnesses who saw Desi on the beach on Tuesday.' He studied his phone. 'And any patients who consulted the nurse yesterday about nausea, vomiting, abdominal pain, numbness, or dizziness. Anyone you'd like to add?'

'I'll think about it on the road, sir.'

Musudroka piped up. 'What about Mr Duke, sir? After what he's told you—'

'I've already had a conversation with him this morning. Now he's on his way to the airport to meet Desi's parents, so he won't be back at the set for hours. But anyway, Duke's only goal is to produce a successful Champion series. Injury or death of the players endangers that. Now he's told me the series is dead. That will be quite a blow to his reputation and career. I can't think of a single reason why he would harm any of his contestants.'

'Maybe he's in love with Desi, sir.'

He reminded himself how young Musudroka was. 'True, people commit crimes for love. But I doubt love was what Desi Lopez and Steve Duke shared.'

Musudroka looked bewildered. 'Crime? Do you think Desi's death could be murder, sir?'

'Too soon to say. We keep our minds open, Tani. Collect our vehicle from the pool and deliver this envelope to reception at the Grand

Pacific Hotel, with instructions to deliver it to Mr and Mrs Carson when they register. Then pick us up outside the station on your way to the Champion set.'

54

'Let's hope that Bobby and Mili will open up now they know Duke's cancelled shooting the final episode,' Singh said as the LandCruiser bowled along.

'Why would they?' Musudroka asked.

'Their ambition to be crowned Champion might have got in the way of honesty, don't you think? Let's be positive,' Singh replied.

When they knocked on the door of the Personnel office, the ever-efficient Deepika opened the door, her usual smile replaced by a small frown. 'Good morning, officers. We're all devastated here today. None of us imagined that poor Desi would die, did we? Such a beautiful girl! How did she die?'

'We're waiting for her postmortem report. It's very sad. Hard to accept, too,' Horseman replied.

'It is. For all of us.' After a few solemn moments, her cheeriness returned. 'Thanks for the text, Sergeant Singh. I've located all the people you need to speak with. I'll send Eroni Nemi along first because he's wanted at Motu Island today to finish cleaning up there.'

'I'm grateful, Deepika. The order of interviews doesn't matter. We want to cause as little disruption here as possible.'

***

Eroni's knock was tentative, and his manner subdued when he greeted the detectives. Still, he looked confident enough as he sat at the interview table and uncapped the bottle of water that Musudroka offered him.

Horseman began. 'Do you agree with Mr Duke's decision to cancel the show's final episode, Mr Nemi?'

'It's not my concern, sir. I'm glad I don't have to decide such matters. He probably had little choice after two contestants died. We have to pay respect to the dead. On the other hand, it may seem unfair to the two survivors who have worked so hard to win. But you can ask them that—take no notice of me.'

'I want you to think back to Tuesday afternoon, when you returned from Motu Island and saw Desi fishing from the jetty. You advised her to try fishing with her spear further along the beach, correct?'

'*Io*, sir. She said she'd try.'

'Tell us what you did next.'

'We walked along at the water's edge. She said she missed Motu and wanted to catch a few fish again and cook them over the barbecue fire. She even had her camping pan set with her in her canvas bag. I pointed out what I thought was a good spot.'

'Were you worried about dangers like stonefish?' Musudroka asked.

'No, she was wearing plastic water sandals. When I got to the path back to the barracks, I wished her good luck and came back here.'

'Did you return to the beach later?'

'No, not at all.'

'Did you see Desi again that afternoon or night?'

'No, never again. On Wednesday morning they rushed her to hospital. I'm sorry she's dead, sir.'

'Have you heard how she died, Mr Nemi?' Musudroka asked.

'I heard it could be pufferfish poison. Is that right?'

As soon as he was out the door, Musudroka groaned. 'How did they know about the poison?'

'The coconut wireless is my guess.'

'It's going to be just like last time we were here, I know it.'

'Stay hopeful, Tani, and get the next witness.'

***

Bobby O'Leary was next. His face was very pale between his freckles.

'How do you feel about Mr Duke's decision to cancel the show's last episode, Mr O'Leary?'

Bobby rubbed his face with a trembling hand. 'I for one couldn't continue, even though the so-called final face-off whips up lots of contrived suspense. But what Steve had planned for us, I don't know of course.'

'Do you mean they rig the outcome?' Singh asked, unable to keep her disapproval from her voice.

'No, I mean I don't know.'

'Why couldn't you continue?' Horseman asked.

Bobby's eyebrows shot up. He looked from one detective to another, suddenly animated. 'Two finalists dead, and one near miss with Mili? What started off so beautifully—this series—is now a disaster and has to be ended. I mean, I'm not superstitious, but this is more than bad luck, surely. Some here are saying Champion is cursed.'

'Really?' Horseman said, but he knew those rumours would be flying free.

'Yeah. I mean, I'll comply with my contract, but the sooner I get outa here, the better I'll feel. I don't wanna be next to die!'

'I understand, the events of the last ten days have been a series of terrible shocks. But please think back to Tuesday afternoon. Did you see Desi after the film shoot finished?'

'Yeah, standing in the sea, but she wasn't very close. I couldn't tell what she was doing. I'm not sure of the time. I had a rest then went for a walk. That's when I saw her.'

'I think people cause bad luck, not curses, Bobby. I've asked you before whether you suspect anyone of responsibility for the so-called pranks that have undermined the contestants' confidence. Have you any suspicions now?'

'No, but I suppose we can eliminate Ken and Desi, at least.'

'Why?' Singh asked.

'Well, because they're dead of course.'

'Do you think their deaths weren't accidental, then?' Horseman asked.

'I don't know for sure, but if they weren't accidents, it makes sense that the prankster escalated his activities and killed them.'

'It's possible. I can see you've thought a lot about this. Do you suspect anyone?' Singh asked.

'How can I? These are the people I've lived among and got to know over six weeks! I don't have enough imagination, I guess. But murder must be a logical possibility.'

***

The next witness was Eleni, a Fijian woman Singh and Musudroka had talked to on Wednesday. She was so delighted to meet Horseman, he had to ease his hand from her firm grasp after a full minute. Maybe she was someone who took Desi's death in her sturdy, middle-aged stride.

'Eleni, is this the statement you wrote for Sergeant Singh yesterday?' He passed the single sheet to her.

Eleni glanced at the paper and beamed. '*Io*, that's mine.'

'Can you tell me more about your sighting of Desirée Lopez, please?'

'Just as I said to Sergeant Singh yesterday.' Eleni smiled at Singh. 'But I'm happy to repeat it to you, Josefa Horseman. As you know, I work a broken shift in the canteen and on Tuesday I had a long break between clearing up after lunch and prepping for dinner. I wandered down to the beach to enjoy the fresh air and had a yarn with Zakaraia, the boatman, who's a cousin of mine. You know, he got me my job here, for which I'm grateful. But he had work to do, so I sat on the verandah for a while, watching the comings and goings. It's so relaxing watching the hustle and bustle, isn't it?'

Horseman almost regretted instructing Eleni to give more detail, but he smiled to encourage her. 'True, true, Eleni. You've hit on an insight there. Did you see Desi on the jetty?'

'No, I didn't. Time was getting on, so I headed back to the canteen, but something made me keep on walking westward to the more desert-ed end of the beach. Maybe the sun from the west warming my skin. Anyway, I recognised Desi ahead of me, a bag over her shoulder and a bucket in her hand. So tall and that lovely wavy hair, I was certain it was her. Desi was so graceful, I watched her for a minute. What's the expression—poetry in motion? That was Desi. Then another woman strolled up to her and they spoke for a bit. Then they walked together away from the beach.'

'Did you recognise the woman?'

'No, she had a *sulu* tied around her waist and a loose top with long sleeves and a sports cap. Her hair was either short or tucked up in her cap, I couldn't tell. Maybe Fijian but I can't be sure because they were some distance away.'

'Did the other woman come along the path to the barracks?'

'No, we all were well to the west of the end of the path. She seemed to come from the scrub beyond the highwater mark. Then I suddenly realised I might be late for the dinner shift and hurried back.'

Singh passed a plan of the Champion location and a pencil to Eleni. 'Can you show me where Desi met the other woman, please?'

Eleni examined the map with care, then pointed to a spot.

'Here, quite close to the firepit? Please mark the place with a cross, if you're sure.'

'*Io*, I'm pretty sure. But I can't be precise, you understand. I couldn't see the firepit, barbecue, whatever you want to call it—it's in a hollow behind the highwater mark for protection from the wind. But I know it's somewhere around there.' Eleni drew a neat cross and looked from Singh to Horseman, anxious that the detectives understood her testimony had limits. Her scrupulous honesty tugged at Horseman's heart.

'Are you positive the person Desi met was a woman, Eleni? A *sulu*, loose top, cap—couldn't it have been a man?' Horseman said.

'Oh no, she was a woman. Not as tall as Desi, and curvy. I can tell a woman from a man, even these days and even from a distance! I'll swear whoever I saw with Desi was a woman.'

***

Musudroka hovered around Mili protectively as he ushered her in. He pulled her chair out for her and uncapped the bottle of water he placed within her reach. Horseman understood why when he saw Mili's red eyes, hunched body and trembling hands. He nodded to Singh.

'Mili, how do you feel about Mr Duke's decision to cancel the show's final episode?' Singh asked.

Mili sniffed. 'I can't believe it. Desi was so strong, so how could she die from a stomach upset?' She straightened in her chair a little. 'Still, Mr Duke could devise a workaround and film it, even if the executives decided down the track to shelve this series for a while, out of respect for the dead. Couldn't he?' This finalist was clearly upset, but by what?

'You told us yesterday you saw Desi fishing alone off the beach on Tuesday afternoon,' Singh continued.

'Yes, that's true. But I didn't tell you the whole truth and I want to tell you now.' She looked up, her brown eyes brimming with tears. The detectives waited.

'Later I was coming back from my walk and saw Desi heading up the sand towards the scrub, carrying her fishing gear. I could smell smoke then saw a wisp rise from where the firepit's located. The next thing was—a man appeared from behind the sand ridge, and she joined him. Oh my goodness ... I feel like a traitor! It was Eroni.' Tears flowed down her cheeks. Singh pushed the box of tissues across the table while Musudroka handed Mili her water.

Horseman nodded at Musudroka who followed him out the door. 'Please call Zakaraia and ask him where Eroni is now. I want him back here, no matter what job he's in the middle of. We'll take him to the station—get him out of his comfort zone and let him stew for a bit.'

55

When they returned to Suva Central with a compliant Eroni in the back seat with Singh, both probationers were already in the office, busily writing up their notes. Musudroka booked Eroni into Interview Room 2 and posted a uniform constable outside the door.

'*Bula*, Apo, *bula*, Lili. I wasn't expecting you until after lunch. You've both done well, Musudroka too, so lunch is on me. Let's go to the Flea Market takeaway stalls and I'll buy you your choice.' While this level of generosity wasn't sustainable, an occasional tangible reward motivated the young DCs. And he didn't want them to refuse his invitation because they had no money to pay their way, even at the Flea Market.

Armed with rotis, hamburgers and chips, they crossed the road and ate their lunch in the tiny park near the seawall. The noise of the traffic lumbering along Stinson Parade prevented conversation but the breeze off the water blew the diesel fumes away from them. The detectives munched in quiet companionship, their faces turned to the implacable sea, then strolled back to the station where Eroni was waiting for them. Horseman asked Lili to take notes.

'Has Mr Nemi had something to eat?' Horseman asked the constable on guard duty.

'*Io*, sir. Some bananas and bread. He's got a cup of tea now. Would you like one?'

'*Vinaka* but no. How about you, Lili?'

Lili declined too and they entered the room. Eroni smiled at them both, looking more puzzled than frightened. He repeated his previous statement, that he'd left Desi to go back to the barracks after pointing out a promising fishing spot to her. He wouldn't budge, even when

Horseman told him a witness had seen him further up the beach talking to Desi when she'd left off fishing.

'Who is this witness, sir? Why would you believe him rather than me?'

Horseman avoided naming witnesses to a suspect. After all, without physical evidence, a contradiction didn't mean much and might rebound badly on the witness. But sometimes when he was desperate, the tactic could be worth a try. Like now. Eroni was Mili's devoted fan, so hardly a threat to her.

'Mili told us she saw you. We can't think of a reason why she would lie.'

For a few seconds, Eroni stared, his eyes round, his mouth open. Then his face crumpled and his whole body seemed to shrink. Horseman nudged the half-full cup of tea closer to him and he picked it up with a trembling hand.

'Time to tell us the whole truth.'

Eroni clicked his tongue. '*Io*, sir, I will. I did return to the beach later, to see if Desi had any luck.'

'Did she know you were coming back?'

'No, sir. I just thought I'd check if she was still there. She was happy because she caught another fish. She wanted me to help her make a fire in the pit and cook it there. She said she could manage it by herself, she'd brought her pan and knife, but she could do with some help, and she'd like some company.'

'Man, a pufferfish! You know perfectly well they're poisonous!'

'*Io*, but I know how to fillet them to make them safe. I was careful. Desi got a small fire going while I cleaned and carved the fish. She cooked it in her little pan and said it was delicious.'

'Did you eat any?'

'No, it was small, and Desi was hungry. I don't like pufferfish much.'

'Why didn't you tell us this morning? You already knew she died of pufferfish poison.'

'But I cleaned the fish properly. I meant her no harm.' Eroni rubbed his eyes.

'Mr Nemi, I'm arresting you for obstructing a police enquiry. You'll be held here while we prepare charges relating to recklessly endangering the life of Desirée Lopez. You can pray that the Superintendent doesn't upgrade that to manslaughter. Detective Constable Waqa will explain your rights to you and take your new statement. This time, leave nothing out.'

Horseman called Apo Kau down to assist Lili. He had to get out. He couldn't look at Eroni Nemi any longer. Of course, the man wouldn't give up the full truth. What a charade this was, a damned waste of time. Nemi would admit not one iota more than the police evidence forced him to. And that evidence was pretty thin. Horseman would question him again later in the afternoon, this time with Singh's support.

While he climbed the stairs to the office, his chest felt squeezed by a broad belt tightening notch by notch. He grasped the rail, bent over and exhaled through his mouth. Nice and slow, counting from one to five. Then in through his nose, deep and slow, counting from one to five again. Melissa, his physical therapist had taught him this when he'd last had a panic attack two years ago in Oregon. She reckoned his terror of failure caused the attack, not physical stress. Who knew? But he was grateful for her technique and much more besides. Now was not the time to indulge in regret for what was over. He gradually controlled his rasping breaths and walked to his desk.

Singh looked up with a smile that changed to a frown. 'What's the matter, sir? You don't look right.'

'I'm fine. I'll get myself a glass of water.'

Musudroka brought a jug of water from the kitchen and filled the glass on Horseman's desk. 'We didn't have any drinks with our lunch, sir. Drink up! You'll be right in no time.'

'I'm boiling the kettle, sir,' yelled Singh. 'Won't be long!'

As he drank, his eyes filled at the kindness of his colleagues. This excessive emotion wasn't like him and not to his liking at all. He wanted his usual pragmatic self back and soon. He went to the men's toilet and splashed water on his face, mopping it with paper towel. He looked pale, his skin drooping. Dehydration, alright. He lifted his eyebrows, turned up his mouth and returned to his desk to drink some more. Singh brought the tea tray, set out the cups and produced a packet of Paradise coconut biscuits.

She put on a bright smile, but her eyes were full of concern. 'We'll have our tea here for a change and you can tell us about Eroni.'

After recounting Eroni's interview, Horseman raised the matter that troubled him. 'Susie, what penetrated Eroni's defences was when I told him it was Mili who'd seen him with Desi on the beach. He was flabbergasted at first, then he just caved in. And when Mili admitted she'd seen them both, she got weepy and said she felt like a traitor. Remember?'

'Yes, I do. Desi's death was a shock. Everyone expected she'd get better.'

'Shock could explain it. There seemed to be no love lost between the two girls, so we can rule out grief. But Eroni and Mili must have a closer connection. Aren't they both from Taveuni? Mili denied they were relatives, but you never know. Musudroka, check that out, will you?'

'I'll do my best, sir. You know, even if they aren't related, just dobbing in another Fijian might make her feel bad.'

'Saying you've seen one person talking to another is hardly *dobbing*, Tani.'

'Well, Mili knows he's a big fan of hers. And she does care about her fans. That might explain her feelings. She had scraps of paper with phone numbers in her backpack. She said fans working on the set gave them to her and she believed she should accept them out of loyalty.'

'Good point. That reminds me, has Ash been in touch about the SOCO search yesterday? He's got those phone numbers.'

'Nothing yet,' Singh said. 'They've got a mountain of stuff to process from the raid on the Film and Television school.'

'True, but most of that would be with IT, wouldn't it? Please check with Ash, Tani.'

'*Io*, sir.'

'And even more important, make sure you and Apo get to training on time this afternoon, no matter what you're doing. Sergeant Singh and I need to talk to Eroni again, so I could be late.'

Musudroka's eyes lit up. 'Don't worry, sir. We'll be on time!'

Horeseman rang Duke to say Eroni Nemi was in police custody. He knew Nemi's arrest would not top Duke's current concerns, but he was surprised by the director's unruffled reaction. When Horseman asked if Champion would supply a lawyer for Nemi, he replied that the props carpenter could rely on a solicitor provided by the Fiji justice system.

'Your public lawyers are competent enough, aren't they, Inspector?'

'Yes, they are. No problem. May I ask about Desi's parents?'

Duke's tone softened. 'Christ knows, that's the toughest job I've ever had to do in my life. I hope it is anyways. They arrived, anxious but hopeful and I had to kill their hopes stone dead. They wanted to see Desi immediately. I must say Dr Young treated them with great respect and sympathy. Something more, too—a genuine friendliness. I guess he's had a lot of experience, but I'd say he handled everything perfectly. He told them about the pufferfish poison and said he'd call them after the autopsy. His openness meant a lot to the Carsons. I took them back to the Grand Pacific to rest this afternoon. They appreciated your note and would like to see you tomorrow mid-morning. They'll call you when they feel up to it.'

'Any time. That sounds like you did your job well. And it's over now.'

'I'm sure glad of that. Any progress your end, please keep me informed, Inspector.'

56

Horseman got no further with Eroni Nemi during a frustrating repeat of the suspect's performance earlier that day. Unfairly, Horseman was hoping Singh would work miracles for him, but none happened. Eroni largely ignored Singh and directed all his replies to Horseman. Far from being unsettled by his long wait in the interview room, Eroni had gained in composure and confidence. So when Horseman jogged up to the Albert Park sideline, the vigorous combat of the Shiners' practice game lifted his heart.

Mosese intercepted the ball and charged at full speed, weaving and pushing challengers aside until, noting a threat from his right, he passed it to Simi on his left. Simi stumbled but held on for a straight run to the touch line, for the last ten metres dragging in his wake a failed tackler who wouldn't give up. All went quiet for Pita's conversion kick which sailed high between the posts.

Shouted insults, cheers and ritual handshakes ended the game. The boys noticed Horseman on the sideline and cheered him too. Some players flopped on the ground, but most stampeded to the taps, ducking their heads underneath the spout so they could drink and sluice their faces simultaneously.

Horseman spotted Matt Young talking with Dr Pillai and Constable Lemeki. Clearly, the pathologist took his appointment to the board of the Joe Horseman Trust seriously.

This afternoon, Dr Pillai had supplied boiled *dalo*, breadfruit and sausages. Dr Pillai's neighbour had donated a hessian sugar sack of oranges.

'Each boy can take four oranges away with him,' Dr Pillai explained.

'What you do is more than feeding them, Raj. They're learning what it means to be reliable, too.'

'I'm grateful for a chance to help, Joe. After all, being able to rely on a meal twice a week isn't much for a child, is it? That's going to change when they get their hostel.'

'Let's see if they'll agree on a name for it. Gloria wants it finalised for the publicity.' Horseman's voice cracked. What was wrong with him today? Dr Pillai showed no sign he'd noticed. Matt Young strolled over to join them. 'You've got some talent here, Joe. I'm sorry I haven't looked in for a good while.'

'No problem. Can I ask about Desi?'

'Yeah, what a crying shame. Perfectly healthy young woman. No violence or injury that I could find. Tissue samples have gone to the lab with a top priority order. Subject to more toxicology tests, it looks like heart failure caused by tetrodotoxin poisoning. Her parents are in pieces, as you'd expect.'

'Yes. They want to see me tomorrow morning. I've got a job to do here now but I'm not sure I can cope.'

'What name do you like best, Joe?' Dr Pillai asked.

'I'm thinking Junior Shiners House or Home of the Junior Shiners or Shiners House. Overall, I prefer House to Home which has children's orphanage connotations for me. And I think Junior should be in there because if they do go on to play as an adult team, I don't want Tevita thinking he can live there all his life! Just joking, I think stressing the youth of the tenants will encourage donors. Hostel is too impersonal. So yeah, it seems I favour my first option.'

He'd intended to address the boys together, but now couldn't handle it. They were sitting in groups on the grass, yarning, eating, and laughing. He approached one group, sat down, and talked with them about their hostel. Dr Pillai, Dr Young and Constable Lemeki followed, each chatting to a different group and moving on. Horseman had feared chaos but found this casual approach relaxing.

When all the boys had voiced their thoughts, the adults conferred and this time, Horseman found his normal voice. 'Boys, it seems most of you like Junior Shiners House, so that's what the name will be!' The usual hoots and cheers greeted the news. Then Tevita stood up and they all quieted.

'*Vinaka vakalevu*, Joe, Dr Pillai, Constable Lemeki, and the new doctor. Junior Shiners House is a good name. Boys understand that you have to buy a house and that costs a lot of money. We are all businessmen. We can help, too. We been saving money to give you. We know not enough but we hope you will be happy.'

He pulled a filthy drawstring bag from around his neck. 'Two hundred and thirty-seven dollars and twenty-one cents!'

Tevita punched the air and handed over the bag of cash to Horseman, grinning in triumph while his teammates roared in self-congratulation.

Horseman now knew the secret Tevita had refused to divulge; the reason he'd been working at the entrance of Jubilee Arcade in his precious free time. He rubbed his eyes again.

FRIDAY

57

Horseman telephoned Dr Young the next morning from the station. 'I'm about to leave for my meeting with Desi's parents. Anything new yet?'

'Sorry, mate. With luck, the lab might have some results by the end of the day, but probably not all of them. I've certified death from tetrodotoxin poisoning, with the usual proviso about outstanding lab test results on tissue samples.'

'Are you suggesting accidental death?'

'That's your job, mate. As Desi's body bears no evidence of violence, the poisoning could well have been accidental. But equally, it could have been a malicious and deceptive act by someone else. Does the guy you're holding fit that frame?'

'I think so. A small matter of lack of conclusive evidence, though. So far.'

'There'll need to be an inquest after all the test results are in, and I can finalise my report. But there's no need for Mr and Mrs Carson to attend—they weren't witnesses. We can release her body today if they want to take her home.'

'I'll tell them that.'

'Your Shiners came good yesterday, didn't they? Raising all that cash? They're a credit to you, Joe.'

'I was gobsmacked. But I shouldn't have been. Remember when I couldn't get Khan's Sports Emporium to sponsor rugby shoes for the squad? After a couple of months, every last one of them had managed to get a pair—mostly from the second-hand warehouses.'

'You hope! I bet some boys nicked theirs from front porches at night.'

'This time, you're the one without any critical evidence, Dr Young. Gotta go now. *Moce mada.*'

Singh accepted Horseman's invitation to go with him to the Grand Pacific Hotel. They walked along bustling Victoria Parade, past shops and restaurants and offices old and new. The waterfront hotel, which had once routinely hosted royalty, diplomats, writers and film stars, was already abandoned when Horseman first came to Suva as a new student at the University of the South Pacific. He found its derelict grandeur sad, a relic of old times forever vanished.

His economics lecturer had explained the site was a symptom of Fiji's declining prosperity due to political instability frightening off investors. But after twenty years crumbling behind a rusty security fence, the old wreck had reopened in time to celebrate its centenary. Few of Suva's population would ever enter its doors, but the sparkling white colonial architecture cheered them up.

A welcoming receptionist escorted them to a small reading room furnished with mahogany bookshelves, a desk against a wall and four comfortable armchairs. Perfect—it was private without intruding on the Carson's personal suite. The detectives introduced themselves and expressed their condolences. Desi's height, athletic build and wide mouth came from her father, while Catalina had given Desi her lustrous black hair, dark eyes, and perfect complexion. If she'd lived, Desi may have also become a bit overweight in middle age like her mother.

Both parents were composed but red-eyed and haggard. Horseman explained the options permitted by Fiji law for the disposal of Desi's body, although he avoided the word disposal. Len and Catalina had already decided they would bring her home to California so her relatives and friends could farewell her. A waiter served coffee and delicate amaretti biscuits, which relaxed them all just a little. Singh then gently guided them through the official forms and well before an hour was up, they had filled them out.

'I assume Mr Duke will book your flights, Mr Carson?'

'Yeah, Desirée's contract included a generous insurance policy, but I consider it's more appropriate if I liaise with Steve about all that.'

'Of course, I apologise for intruding.'

'Not at all, not at all. I don't underestimate the trouble you've taken to make this tragedy easier for us to cope with. We're both grateful, aren't we, Cat?'

Len Carson spoke just above a whisper, but his wife could only nod with a sad little smile. The waiter returned and poured more coffee for them all. Singh offered the biscuits to Mrs Carson, and she took one. A good sign.

After a minute's silence, Mr Carson pressed his hands to his face, then placed them on his knees firmly. 'Steve tells me you spoke to Desi several times during your investigation into Ken Johnson's death.'

'Yes, that's true. Your daughter was an important witness. Another finalist found Ken unconscious after falling onto rocks, but Desi had the presence of mind to call the location nurse on their emergency radio and then try to revive Ken. As you know, Ken didn't survive but Desi gave him the best chance anyone could.'

Singh smiled her approval, a soft light in her eyes.

'Oh, I didn't know that. Thank you,' Catalina whispered.

Mr Carson leaned forward, his eyes intent. 'Did your questions ever rub her up the wrong way? Did you see her temper?'

How to respond to this? Desi wasn't the only family member to like provoking a reaction. Under the circumstances, he must take the question seriously. 'Bad temper? Not really. But I'll be open, Mr Carson. Desirée's attitude did change from one interview to another and even from one question to another. Sometimes frankly hostile to us, to contestants or crew, and sometimes cooperative, contributing her observations in a thoughtful way.' He hesitated.

Singh filled the gap. 'We were with her enough to recognise how intelligent she was.'

Mr Carson focused on Horseman. 'Did she ever hit on you? You're her type.'

Horseman stared at Mr Carson. *Like dad, like daughter* came to mind. 'Never. Desi's foremost quality that we saw was the strength of her ambition. Wouldn't you say, DS Singh?'

Susie nodded firmly. 'Absolutely. She seemed intensely focused on winning Champion.'

Mrs Carson nodded while tears rolled down each cheek.

'Dr Young explained about the pufferfish poison. I've heard about it in Japan, naturally. How did she come to eat that? Was it voluntary? Did she know what she was eating?'

'We've arrested a man working at Champion who says Desirée caught a pufferfish in the shallow water off the beach and asked him to help her cook it. He recognised the fish but doesn't know if Desi did. He claims he knew how to clean and fillet it safely. Only Desi ate it.'

Mrs Carson's tears flowed faster, and she gulped back a sob.

'What's the charge?'

'My superintendent is considering that today. Definitely obstructing a police enquiry, and possibly recklessly endangering Desirée's life.'

'Hmm, I'm in contracts, so not my field. But why wouldn't you go for manslaughter?'

'We don't have enough evidence now, but that's certainly a prospect.'

'Perhaps you can help us, Mr Carson. Would Desi have recognised a pufferfish?'

'I can't say. I wouldn't—I've never taken to fishing. I don't think Desi did either. Do you know, Cat?'

'If she did, I never knew about it. Maybe she did a bit of fishing at summer camps, but that would've been at freshwater lakes. Who knows what she did at Stanford?'

Even Horseman knew Stanford was a top-tier university. He exchanged a glance with Singh who lifted her eyebrows ever so slightly. So much for the poor little victim Desi from the wrong side of the tracks.

'Do you suspect this guy you're holding of malicious intent?'

'We have no evidence of that, sir.'

'But you suspect him, anyway?'

'We're keeping our minds open, Mr Carson, and vigorously pursuing all leads. Can you help us? You know your daughter.'

Desi's father looked at Horseman as if considering whether to say what was on his mind.

'Desi always knew how to make people angry, even when she was a small child. She did that to both of us, didn't she, Cat?'

Mrs Carson reached out to grasp her husband's arm and nodded. 'It's true,' she whispered.

'And to others, too. Home, school, anywhere. Nice as pie one minute, nasty goading the next. To be plain, Inspector Horseman, I wouldn't be surprised if she provoked someone so bad that he wanted her gone for good.'

Mrs Carson's sharp intake of breath was her loudest utterance since Horseman had met her.

'We'd be glad if you would join us for lunch here,' Mr Carson said.

'Many thanks, but we need to press on,' Horseman said.

'Understood. Godspeed, then, detectives.'

When they reached Victoria Parade, Horseman said, 'Man, Len Carson was a surprise! How many dads criticise their newly dead daughters?'

'Don't know, I guess it's taboo, but some would. I respect his honesty, actually. My reading was he really feared Desi's habitual behaviour could put her in danger and he wanted us to know about it. I thought he was trying to help.'

'What if he wasn't honest, though?'

They strolled along in the direction of their police station, pondering. Singh said, 'We can't know one way or the other, but his idea is definitely a lead, and it could apply to Eroni, couldn't it? I mean, his appearance is odd. What if Desi's teasing and ridicule became a torment and he seized his chance when she showed him the pufferfish?'

'Her goading would provide him with a motive, for sure. Don't know if I buy it, though. Tell you what, Republic of Cappuccino's just opposite. I could kill a couple of panini. Let's jaywalk, Singh!'

They dodged between the crawling vehicles with ease and entered the noisy cafe. 'No one will hear us in here. Let's work out a new approach with Eroni this afternoon.'

58

Prompting Eroni to narrate the precise chronology of his doings on Tuesday afternoon didn't trip him up at all. He stuck to his most recent official statement about his actions, observations, and the order in which they happened.

It was time to lay their cards on the table.

'Mr Nemi, you wanted Mili to win Champion, didn't you?'

He smiled. '*Io*, don't you, sir? The whole population of Fiji wants her to win!'

Singh said, 'Yes, me too. But your desire for her to win was stronger than most, I'm sure. She told us once what a loyal fan you were.'

Eroni's dark brown skin flushed darker. He looked down. 'Did she? Yes, I'm a big fan. She's a superb singer. Her songs bring tears to the eyes. I like to sing myself, you know, but haven't gone further than my church choir.'

'Well, your choir training has made you a very good judge of singers, hasn't it?' Horseman added.

'*Io*, sir. Mili should have won The Voice, in my opinion. She was the best. Probably the Americans would never want a Fijian to win.'

'Mili's a US citizen, isn't she?'

'Maybe, but they would still be prejudiced against her.'

'Could you use your position on the crew here to help her in the Champion contest?'

'Not really, but I tried my best. I only saw her briefly when the contestants came to the arena for the challenges. Sometimes we had a few words, often just waved. When the challenges were on Motu and I had to set up the props in advance, we would have a brief chat. She was always friendly and polite.'

'Did she ever ask a favour of you?' Singh asked.

'No, what sort of favour?'

'Oh, let me think—perhaps lend her a tool, or take a message to someone in the barracks? Anything, really. I understand the contestants had a lot of restrictions.'

'That's true, but that's an important part of the game.'

'But to have a fan on the crew—she must have been tempted to ask you for help.'

'I don't know. I was friendly, that's all.'

'Friendly enough to lend her a tool which would give her an advantage over the others?'

'I didn't do that.'

'I think Mili wanted to win the game too. Didn't she ask you to play pranks on the front runners, to make them nervous and perform badly? That was clever of her.'

'No, how could I do that? Anyway, she certainly didn't ask me. And she's not ambitious enough, actually. She told me it was her parents who always put pressure on her. Winning isn't so important to her. But she loves to sing for an audience.'

'Tell the truth, Eroni. Did Mili ask you to put the giant millipede in Desi's sleeping bag?'

'No!'

'What about the rotten octopus? What about the bucket over the toilet door? What about the zipline?'

'No, no no!'

'Because the pranks worked didn't they? They did make the players lose focus and Mili, who isn't athletic, made her way to the finals.'

'You forget that she was a prank victim too.'

'Ah yes, the bucket of seawater. You forget that if you play a prank on yourself, it's not very scary, is it? Not if your pal and fan sets it up for you. Isn't that so?'

Eroni recovered his composure and shrugged. 'I don't know. Maybe.'

'Definitely, Eroni. Especially when that fan is your cousin.'

'Cousin?' Eroni dropped his head and smoothed his shoulder length crinkly hair.

'*Io*, Eroni. You told us you weren't even a clansman to Mili. But she told me you're her cousin.'

'Very distant cousin, maybe.'

'Come on, Eroni. All Fijians know who they're related to.'

'My family moved off Taveuni, I told you. Then her parents moved to the States and we didn't see each other for years. It's all complicated. I'm older than her, too.'

'No more games, Eroni. Here's what we believe, straight up. You're Mili's devoted fan and relative and determined that she win Champion, just like every Fijian. You start off with pranks that aren't so dangerous, but you can see Ken Johnson's a much stronger player than Mili, so you decide to engineer a fall. With a bit of luck, he'll break an ankle or a leg and be out of the game. We know you didn't mean to kill him. You just wanted to help Mili.'

Eroni clicked his tongue in distaste. 'No, I didn't. How could I?'

'Easily. You only had to borrow a kayak from the boatshed and paddle to Motu on a cloudy night. Setting up a booby trap on the steps to the spirit-house would be simple for you. Then paddle back.'

'I guess I could have done that. But sir, I did not. Please believe me.'

'When the finalists moved to the barracks after Ken died, you could spend more time with Mili, couldn't you? After all, you were walking together on the beach when she trod on that stonefish, weren't you?'

'That was lucky because you ran off for help, which saved her from serious harm. Thanks to Sergeant Singh here.'

'*Io, vinaka*, Sergeant,' Eroni mumbled, wary.

'But Desi was different from Mili, eh? She liked to tease you, even insult you, isn't that right?'

'Not really. No more than anyone else. She was moody, that's all.'

'I think she poked fun of you, Eroni. She said really nasty things to Mili and you, too. And she was a threat to Mili. Desi did much better than Mili in the challenges, didn't she? She was faster and stronger, better coordination—that's what Mili told me about her. How could Mili defeat Desi, never mind Bobby?'

'Champion's not just about the challenges, you know.'

'Correct. It's about plotting and scheming to bring others down. Who do you think is better at that: Mili or Desi?'

Eroni said nothing.

'I'd say Desi, myself. And Bobby's no schemer at all, is he? So, when Desi asked you to help cook her pufferfish, it was a golden opportunity, wasn't it?'

'Why? How?'

'You know how lethal the poison is—even if Desi didn't die, she was bound to get very sick and be out of the game. It was your chance to eliminate Mili's strongest rival.'

'I prepared the fish properly!'

'Desi still died. At best, you let her eat a dangerous fish which you refused to eat yourself, believing Desi's death would help your idol win Champion. I understand that was tempting, Eroni.'

Singh lowered her voice. 'That makes perfect sense to me, too. That's what happened, isn't it?'

'No,' Eroni whispered.

'Then tell us what really happened, Eroni,' Singh said gently.

'No, I've already told you. I'm not going to say any more.' He slumped in his chair, looking sad and defeated. His chin dropped to his chest, his eyes closed.

Hell! So much for their oh-so-clever interview strategy. Eroni knew they couldn't prove their plausible theory, so why should he say any more?

59

Horseman and Singh emerged from the corridor into the crowded general office. Eight members of the public fronted the counter and others formed an orderly queue channelled by police tape. Some noticed Horseman, smiled and nudged their neighbours.

'We had to try, sir,' Singh said in a determinedly cheery tone.

'We did. I still like our hypothesis: Eroni's an obsessed fan who'll do anything to help Mili win. He's responsible for some, if not all the pranks. I don't think he'd be involved with drugs—I think Tuvoli did that as well as the thefts. But his statement about Desi lines up with what the witnesses saw. She presented him with the chance to eliminate her and he seized it.'

'A plausible theory in dire need of evidence, sir.'

Horseman pulled out his mobile and saw a string of texts and emails clamouring for his attention. 'You'll have some of these too. Let's go up to the office and check through them. With luck, the lab might have come through with some evidence for us. What? No need to look so sceptical, Singh.'

One of the texts was indeed from the SOCO lab. Horseman called Ash straight away.

'Dare I hope, Ash?'

'Always, sir. The results I've got for you will be more useful for the good old *purposes of elimination* however. Both girls' prints are all over their room, as we would expect. First, the notes from Mili's bag. No good fingerprints but we've rung all the phone numbers to save you time. All except one is genuine. They all belong to Champion crew, mostly Fijians who confirmed they'd passed Mili their numbers. I'll email a list if you want to investigate them further.'

'*Vinaka*, please send the list. Anything else?'

'Moving on to Desirée Lopez. All the good prints on her things are her own. We've got a good half-palm print from the toilet rim and traces of vomit. No surprise there, given tetrodotoxin poisoning. Do you need DNA on that?'

'No, we have a witness to her vomiting. I don't think you got back to me about the grit in Ken Johnson's wound.'

'Didn't I, sir? Sorry. I'll hunt out the analysis, but I remember the result. Our environmental samples matched the samples from Ken's wound precisely.'

'Good, that loose end's tied off, finally.'

'All for now, boss. Have the IT nerds been in touch?'

'Let me check...yeah, I've got an email here. *Vinaka*, Ash.'

Horseman forwarded the email to the team and printed it out. 'Great news! Conclusive evidence linking the Film and Television's IP address and eBay account with some of the items stolen from Champion. Their attempts to bury the traces were pretty crude, according to our geeks. There are also incriminating email messages between Tuvoli and some of the students—nothing direct, but oblique references which in context and with other evidence, are highly suggestive of a conspiracy led by Tuvoli. Let his solicitor refute the irrefutable, eh?'

Musudroka and Kau hooted and punched the air.

'So, we're just left with two suspicious deaths to clear up,' Singh said.

'Just! There's no message from the pathology lab but I'll ring Matt Young anyway.' When the pathologist's phone switched to voicemail, Horseman sighed.

'Hoping won't get us anywhere,' he said to the team. 'Any practical ideas are worth hearing.'

Apo Kau stretched both arms above his head and rotated his shoulders before he spoke. 'Sir, I've been thinking about the canteen worker, Eleni—we spoke to her yesterday. She saw someone with Desi on the beach near the fireplace, too. But she insisted it was a woman.'

'*Io*. Her impression contradicted Mili, who positively identified Eroni Nemi. I believe Eroni's short stature and slim build made Eleni mistake him for a woman.'

Kau frowned in concentration for a few moments. 'What was Eroni wearing? Eleni and Mili couldn't give us precise times for their sightings.'

'Do you mean that Eroni and the woman Eleni saw are two different people?'

'Possibly, sir. The woman may have seen Desirée well before Eroni appeared on the beach, or the other way around.'

'Good thinking, Apo. I'll need to check whether we asked Eroni what he was wearing. Do you remember, Sergeant Singh?'

'No, sir. I'll check. If Eroni wasn't wearing a *sulu* and loose shirt, the two sightings were of different people at different times.'

'Good. Tani and Apo, I want each of you to listen to one of Eroni's last two interviews. Sergeant Singh and I will go through our notes. If there's no mention of Eroni's clothes that afternoon, we'll ask him.'

The detectives settled to their tasks, relieved to focus on something specific instead of feeling frustrated by their lack of critical evidence. However, before any of them had finished, Horseman's phone rang.

'Hey, Horseman, it's Steve Duke. Something really nice has happened here on location for a change. As you know, we're winding up. In fact, most of our remaining crew are finishing up today, with just a skeleton team remaining until next Wednesday, when we'll lock the last shipping container and barracks door. Well, the Fijian crew leaders asked me if they could host a kava ceremony after work to farewell us Americans. I know you don't call your brew *kava*, do you?'

'No, it's *yaqona* in Fijian but it's the same plant. Nobody minds if you call it kava.'

'I agreed, of course. They want to hold it today, as many of them won't be back again this year. It will be the real traditional ritual, not like the casual grog sessions they get up to amongst themselves. As the Fijians held a formal ceremony to welcome us here, I guess it's fitting and might give us all some closure, I hope.'

'I hope so too, Mr Duke. Fijians have a strong sense of occasion, so I'm not surprised your crew took this on.' Their gesture warmed his heart. In times of disaster, Fijians turned to ceremony for comfort and a touch of healing.

'They've invited very few outsiders: just a representative of the landowners and their pastor. However, the guys are very keen for you and all your officers to come if you can.'

'*Vinaka vakalevu*. You understand it's difficult here today. However, I'm grateful for the invitation and I will certainly attend with at least some of my team. What time, Mr Duke?'

'I appreciate you making the effort, Inspector. The ceremony starts at five o'clock. I understand Fiji time applies, though.'

'We'll do our best to be on time and we'll pick up a gift of *yaqona* for the hosts. I'm sure you know the etiquette for guests?'

'Oh hell, I forgot. I remembered someone arranged that for us at our welcome ceremony.'

'We'll be passing the market, so I can bring a bundle of roots for you to present, if that's easier for you. The roots are more formal than a bag of grounds.'

'Yes, please, that would be a real favour.'

Horseman relayed their changed plans, which the team approved. Lili would stay in the office to monitor communications and complete checking for details on what Eroni was wearing when he met Desi that fateful Tuesday afternoon. To save time looking for parking, Musudroka would run down to the market now and buy the two biggest bundles of *yaqona*, wrapped in newspaper as tradition demanded.

'We may be guests but don't forget we're all still on duty, detectives. Only one cup of *yaqona*!'

60

Horseman had never before entered the spirit-house interior set. Steve Duke and his assistant director, Dave, ushered the police past a storage bay and through a narrow arch. They chuckled at their guests' wide-eyed surprise.

'This is where the tribal council scenes are shot, with the votes, the eliminations and all that. Did our props builders do well, Inspector?'

The set must be five times bigger than the mock-up facade on Motu Island. Bathed in a warm light, the reed-lined walls glowed golden, the steep round rafters soared into darkness. Where did they find craftsmen to bind the timber joints in such intricate patterns of black, red and cream sinnet cord? Or was he gazing with wonder at an illusion? He resisted the urge to reach up and scratch the nearest sinnet binding. He was a guest, after all, and should mind his manners.

'Very well indeed, Mr Duke. May I ask if this is all real?'

'Ah, we must guard our movie-world secrets, detectives. But from your faces, I'd say it works for you Fijians. And if it works for you, the American audience will be spellbound.'

Horseman handed Duke a bundle of *yaqona* roots, wrapped in newspaper like a bunch of flowers and tied with pink ribbon.

'Hey, thanks a lot, I appreciate this.'

A dozen or more Fijians bustled on a low dais which occupied a third of the room. An oversized patterned tapa cloth draped the wall behind the dais. Two men moved apart, and Horseman saw they were filling a ceremonial carved *tanoa*, the serving bowl for *yaqona*, from a blue plastic bucket. He feared he was exposing another illusion.

He turned to Duke. 'Maybe we've come a bit early. It seems they're not quite ready for us yet.'

'That's Fiji time for you. Okay, let's wait outside with the others, then.'

More people joined the guests gathered outside and Horseman greeted those he'd met: finalist Bobby O'Leary, photographer Nikhil Seth, sound recordist Don Santori, props master Jack Owens, personnel clerk Deepika, and a few others. All the Fijians would be inside helping, except for Eroni Nemi, of course. He was surprised how many people he didn't recognise. After about ten minutes of quiet chat, Duke returned, and the crowd hushed. With the director were Desi's parents, looking exhausted but also interested in the place where their daughter had lived the last weeks of her life. Duke introduced them to a few people who expressed their sympathy while looking uncomfortable. The Carsons shook hands gravely, saying very little.

Then Mr Carson noticed Horseman and strolled across. 'Hello, Inspector. It's a relief to see someone I've met before.'

Horseman held out his hand and they shook. 'You look quite different, if I may say so. The male hotel staff wear skirts, but I didn't expect to see you in one. I spotted some men in skirts walking along the road as we drove past, though. Forgive my rudeness, you look smart.'

'Thank you. We call the garment a *sulu* and it's worn by both sexes. Men's formal *sulus* have a waistband and pockets and we prefer them for occasions like this to show our hosts respect. My two young colleagues have smartened themselves up, too.' He waved an arm towards Kau and Musudroka.

'What interests me is that this morning you wore a casual shirt, long pants and shoes, but now you're in a smart dress shirt and tie with a skirt and bare feet in sandals.' Mr Carson smiled.

Horseman spread his hands. 'Fashions vary, don't they? We Pacific Islanders are proud of our *sulu*.'

'As you should be—dare to be different, huh? That looks like a college tie.'

'Fiji Rugby Union, sir.'

'Really? Forgive me, I'm not myself today.'

'Not at all, Mr Carson. It's a good sign that you can take a lively interest in our customs on such a day.'

A young man dressed in a grass skirt, his upper body shiny with coconut oil, appeared at the studio entrance.

'It looks like they're ready for us now,' Duke said as he and Catalina Carson joined Horseman and Mr Carson.

The usher directed the guests to leave their shoes in the storage bay and Nete, the boatman's assistant, showed the guests where to sit. Layers of pandanus mats covered the entire floor, perfuming the set with sunny straw. Nete placed Horseman with Duke and the Carsons in the front row, Singh and the constables further back among the rest of the Champion crew. Horseman's right knee behaved itself and he lowered himself to sit cross-legged with only a little discomfort.

The hefty carved *tanoa* sat on the mat below the dais.

The quiet chatter built up again as the Fijian crew filed onto the dais and sat in two rows. Horseman spotted Mili and Eleni, the canteen cook, who insisted she saw Desi meet a woman on the beach. Then Zakaraia the boatman came in and sat at the front of the dais, above the *tanoa*, followed by an older man, no doubt the pastor.

Was Zak a local chief? He glanced at Duke.

'Zak's the headman of a nearby village. The chief's currently away,' Duke said, looking pleased to be passing on local knowledge to the police. Horseman now understood Zak's easy authority as boatman.

Then six women came forward, each carrying a garland of flowers and leaves. They solemnly tied garlands around the necks of Zak the headman, the pastor, Steve Duke, Mr and Mrs Carson, and to his surprise, Horseman. He breathed in the sweet scent of gardenia and frangipani. Glancing at Duke, he knelt to lay his present of *yaqona* beside the *tanoa*. Duke followed suit and Zak clapped three times.

The pastor spoke. 'Our chief accepts your most generous offering with humble thanks. May God protect you on your journey home.'

Zak welcomed the foreign guests in Fijian, heaping them with effusive praise, thanking them for employing his chief's people and expressing deep sorrow that two young people had met with fatal accidents on his clan's land. Fortunately for his guests, he switched to English after a few minutes.

'We are most grateful to welcome Mr and Mrs Carson, parents of our beloved Champion contestant, Desirée Lopez. We pray they will forgive us for not keeping their daughter safe on our land.' He bowed his head and brought his hands together in three resounding hollow-palmed claps, echoed by those behind him. Mr Carson leaned towards Horseman and whispered, 'What should I do?'

Horseman whispered back. 'Just one clap.'

Mr Carson clapped once, and all the Fijians smiled and nodded.

Now was the time the *yaqona* mixing should begin, but instead, Mili walked forward and stepped off the platform. She sat on its edge, so her head was lower than Zak's head. She looked old-fashioned but striking in a long red *sulu* and matching tunic, no doubt borrowed from an older woman. She'd wrapped her red beads in rows around her wrist. Was she going to address the Carsons?

As the first soft notes of Fiji's farewell song, 'Isa Lei', filled the room, Horseman wondered why she'd been runner-up in The Voice. How could anyone better the beauty of her voice and interpretation? Her pace was slow, and as her volume gradually strengthened, her clear, pure tones kindled yearning, love, and pain in his heart. How could anyone be immune to Mili's song? Glancing around, he saw Catalina Carson wiping tears from her cheeks while Zak allowed his to flow freely. Silence followed her final extended note.

Moments passed before one guest began the applause which rose to a crescendo. Meanwhile, Nete and his helper carried a length of bamboo and a sinnet bag to the half-full *tanoa*. Muscles rippled beneath their gleaming skin as one poured water from the bamboo tube and the other swirled the sinnet bag through the *tanoa*, wringing it with both hands then swirling again and again until the mixture was right. Nete, moving with military precision, scooped up a cup of the greyish brew and knelt before the chief. He bowed his head to the mat, and proffered the cup, his arms outstretched above his head. Zak clapped three times, took the cup and downed it amid approving shouts of '*maca*, empty!'

Zak invited guests to take photos or videos. The solemnity lifted as Mili and a few others joined the boys to serve *yaqona* to each guest, then to the Fijian hosts. Horseman felt the familiar tingling of his lips and tongue after he downed his cup. This brew was pretty strong. Zak and the pastor got to their feet and stepped down from the dais to greet the Carsons. Those guests who were stiff and cramped could now get up or lean against a wall with both legs stretched in front of them.

When the servers were well into the second round, guests and hosts alike were more relaxed, breaking into small groups to indulge in quiet chat. *Yaqona* did that. The detectives mingled in an unobtrusive manner, exchanging pleasantries with those who approached them.

The Fijian hosts lifted the cover from a table laden with finger food and soon all the hosts were either serving *yaqona*, mixing more in the *tanoa*, or circulating with trays of delicacies. Horseman welcomed the food; it would protect first-time *yaqona* drinkers from inebriation and falling into a stupor. Even the Carsons looked less haggard and more relaxed as they talked with Barbara Koroi. Indeed, a *yaqona*-induced sense of content invaded his own mind after he downed his third cup. No one could bring back the dead. Life continues. If only he could prove what had happened to Ken and Desi.

A gasp and strangled moan behind him made him turn. Steve Duke bent double, his arms wrapped around his belly. He fell to the mat, writhing. Horseman and Barbara Koroi hastened to help while others recoiled in shock. Singh and the constables came to Horseman's side, waiting for orders.

'Is Mr Duke allergic to anything?' Barbara yelled.

'I don't think so,' Dave called out, rushing forward.

'I know he's had *yaqona* many times, so it couldn't be that,' Barbara said. She felt Duke's brow and his pulse. 'Are you allergic to anything, Steve?' He shook his head but couldn't speak.

'I think they made a strong brew tonight, though,' Horseman said.

'No matter how strong, *yaqona* wouldn't cause this kind of pain. It would knock him out first.'

Duke rocked and clutched his belly, his face contorted with pain. Someone came up with a glass of water, another with a first aid box.

'I'll give him an emetic if I can get it into him. His pain's so bad he's clenching his jaw and it's gone into spasm. Can you hold him still while I try?' Barbara spoke softly to Horseman. She grabbed a bottle from the box and tipped some of its contents into the half-filled glass Singh held. Horseman sat on the ground, hauling the flailing Duke between his legs, hugging his body from behind. This stilled Duke a little, but Horseman could feel the man's muscles and tendons tensed to breaking point. Singh stirred the glass and handed it to Barbara, who tried to get some liquid into Duke's rigid mouth. More ran down his chin than went in.

'Apo, Tani, find out what he's eaten,' Horseman ordered.

'That's my first thought—poisoning,' Barbara continued. 'However, whatever he's taken may be coincidental. Many problems can cause severe abdominal pain: colitis, appendicitis, inflammatory bowel disease, renal colic—the list goes on. Even diverticulitis. We must rush him to hospital! A CAT-scan and blood tests will narrow down the list.'

The nurse ground up some Panadol tablets, mixed them with a few drops of water and spooned it into Duke's mouth. He swallowed some and spat the rest, moaning piteously all the while.

'Not what he needs, but any slight relief is better than none. I'll force in some anti-cramp pills too if he can take some.'

'Dave, is Charlie here? If not, please get a car to the entrance to take Mr Duke to hospital in Suva? Susie, please find someone to drive the Carsons back to the hotel. They're in no state to witness such distress.'

Musudroka appeared. 'I've got a list of everything Mr Duke ate, sir. As far as the servers can remember, that is.'

'Good, give that to Nurse Koroi and you can go to the hospital with them and phone me with every single thing that happens there, no matter how small.'

Mili ran up and stared at Duke. 'What's wrong?' she asked Barbara, clasping her hands across her red tunic.

'He's in acute pain but we don't know the cause yet. We're rushing him to hospital right away.'

He stared at the last piece of the puzzle, or rather, the empty space where it fitted. In a flash, the solution came to him. His favoured theory was inside out, mirror image or just plain wrong. If his lightning strike of insight was right, the picture made sense now.

'Mili, *Vinaka vakalevu* for singing for us. I've never heard "Isa Lei" sung so beautifully. I hope you haven't lost that bracelet you wore when you sang,' Horseman said.

Mili's face softened. 'Oh no, I've got it safe, *vinaka*. It was loose and got caught on a nail, so I took it off.'

Barbara looked up from Duke, whose spasmodic jerks were increasing, despite Horseman's restraining arms. 'Your rosary pea bracelet, Mili? You must be careful with that, you know.'

'*Vinaka*, Barbara. *Io*, you've explained. And I am careful, I promise you.'

Dave, Simeoni, and Zak came in to lift Duke to the waiting vehicle. Horseman hauled himself up and jiggled his stiff joints.

'Mili, I need to see your bracelet. Sergeant Singh will go with you to get it.'

Mili frowned. 'But why? I can't see any reason why you need it.'

'Just for elimination.'

Singh touched Mili's hand lightly. 'You're a fabulous singer, Mili. You made all of us cry. Let's go and find that bracelet now.'

As they walked away, Horseman whispered, 'Before you go, Barbara. Did you know Mili's bracelet was toxic?'

'*Io*, it's made of rosary pea seeds, from one of the world's deadliest plants. Intact, they're harmless. But if the glossy skin breaks, the seeds become lethal. But Joe, you don't think ... Mili wouldn't harm anyone!'

'We're going to check. What's the toxin called?'

'Abrin. It's quite similar to ricin.'

'Does the rosary pea grow around here?'

'I've never seen it. It's in Fiji but I believe it's native to India. Look, Joe—'

'*Vinaka*, Barbara, please go and look after Mr Duke. It might help the hospital doctor to mention there's a chance he ingested abrin from a rosary pea seed. Good luck!'

Barbara's eyes widened in dismay, then she nodded and hurried out.

61

Horseman had never felt such despair as on this case. The prankster had been taunting and misleading them all along. Two people had died and now, heaven forbid, a third death could be imminent. He had solved nothing except a corrupt stealing racket organised from within an elite Fijian college. A racket that distracted him from his main investigation, would wreck the college's reputation and smear the character of its innocent principal, Ratu Joni Tuidraki. He wished he'd never stumbled on that sordid red herring.

He'd saved no one from danger—no one. But now he was certain the prankster and killer were the same clever, ruthless individual. He still couldn't accept that individual was Mili, but rationally, it must be her. Certainly not her ardent fan, Eroni, who was still languishing in the station lockup while the Champion director thrashed on the floor, groaning. But he needed to talk through his reasoning with Singh, the only colleague he could confide in. He relied on her intelligence, common sense, and something more—maybe her trust. A minute ago, she'd tuned in to his intention, having no idea why he wanted the bracelet, and coaxed Mili to go with her. That was trust. But she was ignorant of the pretty seed's poison, too. That was danger.

Singh and Mili had been gone for maybe thirty seconds, but they should be back. He assumed Mili had put the beads she'd worn for her performance in a bag she'd brought to the studio. But the women weren't in the spirit-house studio, so he checked the storerooms and ancillary areas behind the panels of golden reeds. He couldn't see Kau either. But Kau answered his phone when Horseman called.

'Where are you Apo?'

'Outside the studio entrance. It wasn't easy to get Mr Duke into the LandCruiser, but they got off a minute ago. Tani's driving.'

'Have you seen Sergeant Singh or Mili?'

'No, but I was helping Nurse Barbara and Mr Duke. I could easily have missed them.'

'They may be in Mili's room. I'll go there. Watch out for them and keep in radio contact.'

Horseman ran along the car park and cut across the grass to the barracks hut where Desi and Mili had stayed for the last two weeks. The door was closed but a light glowed through a lowered blind. He stood beside the open louvres. Singh's voice was clear.

'—so pretty. The high gloss on the seeds and the scarlet and black. What a shame it broke.'

'Yes, it broke once before. I mended it but it didn't last. See, a few seeds have come off.' Mili's higher voice sounded strained.

'Well, you've saved them in the bag. It wouldn't be hard to find someone competent to repair it. Just go down to the Suva craft market after you leave here. Let's look. Hmm, two seeds got crushed, but the repairer could adjust the spacing so you'd never miss them.'

'Would you like a drink of water, Sergeant?'

'No thanks, let's go back to the studio.'

'*Yaqona* makes me so thirsty, I always need water afterwards. And I only drank one cup tonight!'

'It was a strong mix, I agree. What were those boys thinking?'

'Well, I need a drink,' Mili repeated.

Horseman moved to the door.

Mili continued. 'And here's one for you. You must be dry after that brew.'

Horseman flung the door open. The two women sat on Mili's bed, faces upturned, mouths open in shock. Singh had a ziplock bag in one hand. Mili had a cup half-raised to her mouth. Her other hand held out a cup to Singh.

In two strides he reached the bed and grabbed both cups, set them on the bedside table and handed Singh an evidence bag. 'The broken seeds in the bracelet are poisonous. Put it in here, Sergeant. Did you touch it?'

Singh's face cleared of confusion. 'No, just the bag.'

'Did you lace that water, Mili?'

Mili just stared. But her shock was wearing off quickly. Now her mouth twitched with amusement.

'I'm sure your laboratories will be able to tell you, Inspector Horseman.' He realised she was now showing her nature for the first time: the prankster, the trickster.

'Mili, have you handled any crushed seeds?'

She lifted her eyebrows. Not to agree, but to tease.

He pulled a pair of search gloves from his pocket. 'Please put these on.'

She took her time complying, still looking partly amused, partly challenging.

'Mili Kepa, you are under arrest for using poison with intent to endanger the life of Steven Duke. Sergeant Singh, please caution the prisoner, then choose a change of suitable clothes for her in custody.'

He radioed Kau. 'We have Mili under arrest. If you can find Zak, thank him for his hospitality and apologise for leaving suddenly. Tell him Mili is safe with us. Bring the car up to Mili's door. We'll wait inside until you come. I don't want gawking in the car park. Over.'

'Got it, sir. Out.'

'Mili, let's wait until we get to the station to hear your story.'

62

Mili walked into the Suva Central station, still clad in the traditional *sulu* and fitted tunic popular with Fijian women twice her age and more. She brought the reception area to a standstill. With chiefly poise, she inclined her head ever so slightly towards the officers who stared as she followed DC Kau down the corridor to Interview Room 3. Ash was already waiting to swab her hands and take away her costume. Singh stayed with her while she changed.

'Organise a guard and tea and biscuits for her, Apo. Then join us upstairs.'

Horseman could do with tea himself. Lili Waqa realised this at a glance when she looked up from her filing.

'Would you like tea, sir?'

'*Io*, Lili, that's exactly what we both need. What's been happening here?'

'Pretty quiet, sir. I've printed out the lab reports from the SOCOs and Pathology. They're on your desk. How about you?'

'My head's spinning because I had to give up my favourite theory and that's traumatic for me. After Mr Duke collapsed in front of us, I realised our prankster and our killer was Mili. We've brought her in, together with physical evidence, I believe. Sergeant Singh has been very brave, as you would expect—'

Singh overheard him as she walked in. 'Sir, what nonsense! I had no idea I was in danger!'

'You're always cool under fire. Don't you agree, DC Waqa?'

'*Io*, sir.' Lili looked at Singh with admiration.

'Kau's coming up in a minute. Make the tea, please Lili, then we'll talk about what happened.'

***

'How are you feeling now, Mili?' Horseman asked as they entered the interview room.

'Quite strange, Inspector. I've been thinking.' Her back was straight, her clasped hands rested lightly on the scarred wooden table. The modest, vulnerable persona they'd seen for the last two weeks was gone. But was this confident, poised woman the real Mili?

'Good, we'd like to ask you some questions now.'

Mili waved a regal hand. 'Go ahead.'

Mili nodded. Singh set up the recorder and began the interview.

'I understand you refused to have a legal representative here with you.'

'That's correct. I don't need a lawyer.'

'Well, you can change your mind and ask for one at any time. Let's start with this evening's events, Mili. Did you help with the preparations for the farewell ceremony?'

'Only a little. They were happy I agreed to sing "Isa Lei", so they wanted me to rest and prepare for my performance.'

'Did you crush some rosary pea seeds in advance?' Singh asked.

'Yes, it's safer to use gloves. I put the grounds in a tiny plastic tube I returned to my pocket after I'd shaken it into Steve's cup. I couldn't rely on my first plan: to break one or two open with my fingernails while the bracelet was on my wrist, then let the bracelet droop into Steve's cup as I picked it up. Although I ended up doing that to make extra certain, and it was plain sailing.'

Now the key question. Singh leaned forward a little. 'Did you intend to kill Steve?'

Mili paused for five seconds. 'Not really. I wanted him to suffer.'

'Why, Mili?'

'He brought me here as a token native. He would never have let me win.'

'How do you know that?' Horseman asked.

'Desirée Lopez told me.'

'And you believed her?'

'Not entirely, I guess. But the idea rang true.'

'Perhaps that was just her strategy to undermine your confidence.' Singh suggested.

Mili shrugged. 'Well, it succeeded. Steve was nice to me, but when I tried to get into his bed to improve my chances, he turned me down. I was so humiliated I vowed to pay him back. But I never thought he'd shut down the show without crowning a Champion. That was his lowest blow.'

'Tell me about the pranks,' Horseman said.

'Aha. You tell me, Inspector and I'll say if you're correct.' Mili's lifted eyebrows and teasing tone were back.

'You intended the pranks to disable or demoralise players you regarded as threats. Eroni Nemi knew or suspected you were behind them, so he staged one in the arena to deflect suspicion from the players.'

Mili wagged her head from side to side, evaluating. 'Fair enough. I certainly didn't imagine Ken would die. I'm sorry about that. I wanted him out of contention, but a broken ankle would have been enough.'

Horseman's mind rebelled against the mounting evidence that Fiji's beloved songbird was so cold-blooded, maybe even a psychopath. He glanced at Singh.

Singh leaned towards Mili, smiling. 'I'm curious about how you managed the drugs, Mili. I mean, Mr Duke enforces his policy of zero-tolerance, doesn't he?'

Mili leaned away and shrugged. 'As far as that's possible. I'll give Steve credit: he's sincere about that. But I had no real trouble getting them. I kept quiet until most of the players were voted out. I was very discreet, but the word flew and nearly all the players came begging. Ecstasy helps when you're so tired and hungry, like we were after the first week. I hoped they'd think twice about voting their supplier off the game and I was right.'

'Did Lui Tuvoli supply you?' Horseman asked.

'What gave you that idea?' Mili asked, surprised. 'If you already know, I may as well confirm the fact. Wow, a rugby hulk with brains! I underestimated you.'

Singh came in again. 'Your stonefish poisoning intrigues me. How did you engineer that? Was it Eroni Nemi's idea?'

'No, you're wrong there. Eroni is a dear clansman and totally loyal fan—always on my side. But clever, he is not, except in a practical way. The idea was mine. You were calling me in for questions so often, I needed to deflect you! Eroni found the stonefish and brought it to the water's edge in a bucket. I said a prayer, then put my foot on its spines for an instant.'

Singh looked horrified. 'That was courageous. You took a risk, you know.'

Mili smiled, basking in the praise. 'I know. But Eroni raced off to get you. I was certain you and Nurse Barbara would know the correct first aid. The pain was worth it because you did cross me off your suspects list.'

'Temporarily.' Horseman protested abruptly. He pictured Eroni's genuine terror. How did she persuade him to endanger her life?

Singh permitted herself a tiny frown, which was code for him to shut up. 'I must say I don't understand Desirée. I hope you can help me,' Singh said.

'Spoiled little rich kid, Sergeant. And a fantasist. Toxic ambition, too. That's my reading, anyway.' Her smile was complacent.

Singh reached out and patted Mili's hand in appeasement. 'Actually, I meant I don't understand your elaborate method of killing her. Why did you bring a puffer fish into it?'

Mili looked relieved. 'Oh, I didn't, not at all. I simply took the opportunity she handed me on a plate. Or in a bucket really. She'd caught two fish and invited me to help her cook and eat them. She didn't know one of them was poisonous. It was pure chance we met on the beach that afternoon. An uncle once showed me how to clean and slice pufferfish. I tried to do that properly.'

'How did Eroni know you told us you saw him with Desi on the beach?'

'He didn't, but he's so devoted he will always lie to protect me.'

'Did you eat the pufferfish yourself?'

'No, I wasn't hungry, and there was a chance I'd get sick, no matter how careful I'd been. And there was only a mouthful on the tiny snapper, so we tossed that to a heron nearby.'

'Let's leave it there for tonight, Mili. I don't want to tire you. I appreciate your cooperation, but we'll need to talk some more in the morning. Sergeant Singh will stay with you while I get a woman constable to take you to the custody section and look after you.'

'But you haven't charged me!'

'You're under arrest on suspicion of endangering the life of Steve Duke by poison, so we can detain you for forty-eight hours for questioning. My superior officer will decide on the precise charges. I would pray hard for Mr Duke's recovery, if I were you, Mili.'

EPILOGUE

Ten days later, the entire CID staff gathered on the detectives' floor, waiting for Detective Chief Superintendent Tauvaga to arrive. The big man walked in right on time, smiled at his juniors, and quelled the hubbub simply by raising his hands.

'*Bula vinaka*, officers. I congratulate Detective Inspector Susila Singh on her appointment to Labasa CID, headquarters for Vanua Levu Command. All of you, her Suva colleagues, will miss her dedication, efficiency, and knowledge. I will miss her, too. However, I won't wish her success, because her own qualities guarantee she will succeed in all her professional endeavours. Nevertheless, I wish her happiness in Labasa.'

Everyone applauded warmly, then fell on the buffet lunch Ratini had ordered for this occasion. Horseman watched Singh making the rounds of her colleagues until the chief super caught his eye.

'Joe, you deserve to know that these Champion prosecutions are getting messy.' Tauvaga said.

Horseman bridled. 'Really, sir? They struck me as watertight.'

'Yes and no. The evidence against Lui Tuvoli for drug supply, conspiracy to steal, receiving stolen goods and ancillary charges is strong, thanks to the cooperation of a few FIT interns. Tuvoli's solicitor would prefer to avoid a trial, but his client so far refuses to accept reality and plead guilty. The scoundrel wants immunity from prosecution! That's not on!'

'I'm glad to hear that, sir. And the latest on Mili?'

'Messy. As you know, the media storm following the arrest of Fiji's beloved songbird for manslaughter sparked crazy accusations of racism by the Champion executives. Her solicitor claims her confession to you is invalid and has arranged a psychiatric examination for Mili.'

'Hell!'

'She's still on bail at her parents' home on Taveuni. Thank the Lord it's off the beaten track. However, given any Fijian jury will be prejudiced in Mili's favour, the prosecutor advises downgrading the manslaughter charge to reckless endangerment of life for both Ken and Desirée. He argues a jury is more likely to convict her on that charge.'

'Hmm, I'm not surprised. What are the chances they'll declare her unfit to stand trial?'

Tauvaga spread his hands in the air. 'I don't want to bet on that one. Wait and watch, Joe.'

After a final round of benevolent handshakes, the chief super left, an obsequious Ratini at his side.

Horseman found Singh at the ravaged buffet table, looking forlorn. 'What's the difference between a plague of mice and detectives, sir?'

'None, by the look of this table. And Susie, no more *sirs*! How about a quiet coffee?'

'Always, Joe.' But she changed her mind when they crossed the road and Hare Krishna's was right before her. 'You know, I suddenly want an ice-cream, quite badly.'

Singh stuck to her favourite ginger-and-nutmeg while Horseman opted for mango-and-passionfruit. Ice cream would melt instantly on the street, so they sat side-by-side at the window counter. Between licks, Horseman told her what Tauvaga had said about the Champion cases.

'It's lucky for Mili that Steve Duke recovered, then.' She sounded outraged.

'Yep. But I can't see a jury, even a jury of fans, going for *not guilty* on three charges of reckless endangerment of life.'

'I hope you're right.'

'You know, Champion is set up to encourage the crimes we've seen. I mean, a million-dollar prize, super-charged competition in a stressful environment, fatigue and hunger—some contestants won't cope well. Add in the system of shifting alliances, secrecy, betrayal of stronger rivals—that will weaken any honest player's grasp of reality.'

'It's not cricket, Joe!'

'Ha, no! Nor rugby. If your opponent has the ball, you bring him to the ground if you can. What Champion calls tactics and strategy involves the worst human failings of deceit, pretence, and exploiting others for your advantage. It corrupts the players in order to provide entertainment. The audience then views what used to be regarded as bad behaviour as desirable and clever.' Noticing Singh's frown, he smiled. 'Am I going too far, Susie?'

'Maybe, but you're entitled to your point of view. I find the show entertaining. Without Mili, all could have gone well.' She brightened. 'I got a call from Kiti, the estate agent. She's found a tenant for the rest of my lease on my flat. You know, if I can save more in Labasa, I'd like to buy that flat. Kiti thinks the owner would consider an offer.'

'Wonderful, that will bring you back to Suva!'

'Who knows? It may be simply a shrewd investment.' Her eyes were laughing.

'When's your flight?'

'Tomorrow afternoon. That will give me a full day and two nights to get settled into my temporary digs before I report on Monday morning.'

'Sleepy Labasa won't know what's hit them.'

'Don't be rude! When you come to visit, I'll take you to my sister's farm for the best goat curry in the world.'

'I'd hate to miss that! I've got a car booked tomorrow. Can I drive you to the airport?'

'We'll both be charged with corruption next! Thank you, Joe, but airport send-offs aren't my thing.' She gazed out the window.

He understood. 'Well, onto Arabica for your last decent coffee for a while?'

'Absolutely. But who knows what hidden coffee treasure awaits me in Labasa?' She tightened her trembling lips, but her shaky voice gave her away. Turning away from him, she bent over her backpack, fumbling with a strap. Pretending not to notice the dark teardrop splodges on the purple canvas, Horseman went to the counter and paid the bill. When he held the door open, she smiled up at him and stepped out to the steamy street, her head high.

Glossary and Guide to Fijian Pronunciation

bula – hello
moce – goodbye or goodnight
moce mada – see you later
io – yes
oi lei – wow! /oh no!
ovisa – police officer
ratu - chief
vakalevu – very much
vinaka – thank you
yaqona – kava (the plant, its roots, ground powder and drink)

Acronyms
DI – detective inspector
DS – detective sergeant
DC – detective constable
DCS – detective chief superintendent
SOCO – scene of crime officer

Spelling
The Fijian alphabet is based on English but it is phonetic, so each sound is always represented by only one letter, unlike English.

Vowels

a as in father
e as in let
i as in Fiji
o as in or
u as in flu

Consonants

Most consonants are pronounced roughly as in English,
with the following important exceptions.
b = *mb* as in member eg. bula = mbu-la
d = *nd* as in tender eg. dina = ndi-na
g = *ng* as in singer eg. liga = ling-a
q = *ng* as in stronger eg. yaqona = yang-gona
c = *th* as in father eg. maca = ma-tha

Welcome gift for Fiji Fan Club members

I hope you enjoyed this book. Like other *Fiji Islands Mysteries* readers, you may have also enjoyed discovering Fiji. My years in these beautiful islands inspired me to write this series.

When I published *Death on Paradise Island*, I began a blog which has evolved to include Fijian food, customs, history, sport—whatever occurs to me. I was so delighted with readers' responses, I compiled the best into an illustrated e-book with hot links to cool music and videos, too. *Finding Fiji* is a short, subjective collection that enriches readers' enjoyment of my novels.

Finding Fiji is exclusive to Fiji Fan Club members, so I invite you to join us today. Each month, I'll send you some news about my books and Fiji. I'll also share the latest crime fiction promos. As a welcome gift, I'll present you with *Finding Fiji and* my prequel novella, *Death of a Hero: How it all began.*

Join the Fiji Fan Club here: bmallsopp.com

Enjoy this book? You can make a big difference.

As an indie author, I don't have the financial muscle of a major world publisher behind me. However, I do have loyal readers who loved my first book and took the trouble to post reviews online. These reviews brought my book to the attention of other readers.

I would be most grateful if you could spend a few minutes posting a short review on Amazon, BookBub, Goodreads or your favourite book review site. Just a line or two will encourage potential readers to try a new author.

If you enjoyed this book, please consider recommending the *Fiji Islands Mysteries* to your community library or book club.

About the author

B.M. Allsopp writes the *Fiji Islands Mysteries* series. She lived in the South Pacific islands for fourteen years, including four in Fiji, where she worked at the University of the South Pacific in Suva. An avid crime fiction fan, she aims to share her love of Fiji with fellow mystery readers. She now lives in Sydney with her husband and tabby cat. You're always welcome at her online home: www.bmallsopp.com

Fiji Islands Mysteries

DEATH OF A HERO: HOW IT ALL BEGAN:
Fiji Islands Mysteries Prequel
Meet young Joe Horseman. How much will he risk to save his dead hero's honour?
When Horseman finds his rugby captain's corpse in the changing shed, he vows to help investigate. But the police refuse to pass him the ball.

DEATH ON PARADISE ISLAND
Fiji Islands Mysteries 1
An island paradise. A grisly murder. Can a detective put his rugby days behind him to tackle a killer case?
DI Joe Horseman knows he'll have to up his game when guests at an island resort witness a young maid's corpse wash ashore.

DEATH BY TRADITION
Fiji Islands Mysteries 2
Must DI Joe Horseman sacrifice his chance at love to catch a killer?
Horseman can't wait for his American girlfriend, to join him in Fiji. So he sets a deadline to crack a murder case in the remote highlands, But dangers loom through the mountain mist.

DEATH BEYOND THE LIMIT
Fiji Islands Mysteries 3
Can a landlubber detective combat evil on the high seas?
DI Joe Horseman stares into the eyes of a severed head fished out of a shark's gut. Did the tiger shark kill Jona or was he already dead when it clamped its teeth around his neck?

DEATH SENTENCE

FIJI ISLANDS MYSTERIES 4

A notorious convict is freed. The public wants him dead.

When Dev Reddy is released, the Fiji media whip up an outcry in Suva. As protest threatens to escalate to riot, DI Joe Horseman fears Reddy's parole may be a sentence of death.

DEATH OFF CAMERA

FIJI ISLANDS MYSTERIES 5

A TV reality hit. Players dying to win.

Champion, the TV game show sensation, is shooting a new series in Fiji. When a young finalist dies, DI Joe Horseman must unpick Champion's tangle of ambition, fantasy and greed to stop a killer.

More details and buy links at: bmallsopp.com/books

Acknowledgements

I could never have begun the *Fiji Islands Mysteries* without the help of Mr Waisea Vakamocea, retired senior officer of the Fiji Police Force, who answered my many questions. Fiction demands simplified and accelerated police procedures, so I am entirely responsible for any errors and shortcuts.

Despite my viewing of several TV reality series for research purposes, I knew nothing about film production until I met John Blick of Shadow Play Films. John and his colleagues Greg and Julian generously opened my eyes to some realities of filming on location, including thefts of equipment. Again, any mistakes in this area are mine.

For editorial advice, I was lucky to find Troy Lambert, who is both a successful mystery author and editor. Troy's professional evaluation of my manuscript was most helpful. As for the volunteer advance readers of Horseman's Cavalry who pointed out many errors and told me how much they enjoyed the story, I can't thank them enough.

Finally, I thank Peter Williamson for his advice through reading draft after draft, his enthusiasm for my writing and constant support.

Made in the USA
Las Vegas, NV
10 December 2023